THE
NEW
ONE

ALSO BY EVIE GREEN

We Hear Voices

THE NEW ONE

EVIE GREEN

BERKLEY
NEW YORK

BERKLEY
An imprint of Penguin Random House LLC
penguinrandomhouse.com

Copyright © 2023 by Emily Barr
Readers Guide copyright © 2023 by Emily Barr

Library of Congress Cataloging-in-Publication Data
Names: Green, Evie, author.
Title: The new one / Evie Green.
Description: First Edition. | New York : Berkley, 2023.
Identifiers: LCCN 2022037536 (print) | LCCN 2022037537 (ebook) |
ISBN 9780593439234 (trade paperback) | ISBN 9780593439241 (ebook)
Subjects: LCGFT: Novels.
Classification: LCC PR6102.A77 N49 2023 (print) | LCC PR6102.A77 (ebook) |
DDC 823/.92--dc23/eng/20220812
LC record available at https://lccn.loc.gov/2022037536
LC ebook record available at https://lccn.loc.gov/2022037537

First Edition: March 2023

Printed in the United States of America
1st Printing

Book design by Daniel Brount

For Lottie, my real teenage daughter

PROLOGUE

I LISTEN FOR A LONG TIME BEFORE ANY OF THE WORDS make sense. When they do, I can grab only a word here or there. *Soleil. Le weekend.*

I try to hold on to the other words but I can't reach them. Everything comes and goes. I am floating.

......

After a while I realize I am not floating. I have a body.

I am in a body.

I am a body.

My eyes are closed, and after a long time I think that since I am back in my body, I might try to open them. After some more time, I try. It doesn't work.

......

I know there is noise, but I can't make sense of it. My sense of smell seems as if someone switched it on, and it is unbearable. The smells crowd into my head and I want them to go away. It smells like medicine, clean things, chemicals. Not home.

■ ■ ■ ■ ■

Things hurt. People do things to me. They poke me and move me, and sometimes it hurts and sometimes I don't feel anything. I sense light outside my eyelids. It goes away and comes back. It gets darker and then lighter. I drift back to my dark place, and I come up again.

■ ■ ■ ■ ■

One day the sounds start to form shapes and I find that I know a word. I know that it is the word for the person I need, the person who will pull me out of here.

■ ■ ■ ■ ■

I try to make my mouth say it: "Mum."

1

SHE HAD BEEN DAYDREAMING. THE WATER HAD EVAPORATED and the cauliflower was sticking to the bottom of the pan and the potatoes were burning, because she'd forgotten all of it. It was salvageable, but she didn't want it.

"Oh, shut up," she told it nonsensically, and turned off the gas ring. Everything annoyed her.

She tried to focus on the television. It was a reality show, one that usually distracted her just enough. Tonight, though, it wasn't working.

Scarlett wasn't missing. She was *out*. If she hadn't overdone the cover story by throwing in Leanne, it wouldn't have been worrying yet. It was still all right.

She messaged her. **Please just send a text.** Nothing happened. She messaged again and called her phone and she didn't answer.

She turned the TV off and messaged Ed, hating the fact that she was admitting defeat again. He replied at ten forty-five.

Fuck's sake honey! Again?!????
Yeah, I'll find her.

At least he replied to her when it was about Scarlett. Since he worked late nights and she worked early mornings, they hardly saw each other. That was why they were still together.

She looked at the photo on the wall. They had been happy once.

It was a picture of the three of them taken when Scarlett was about four. They had been on the beach at Perranporth, standing in front of the Atlantic Ocean, the beach wide and sandy around them. Their hair was blowing around and they were laughing. Scarlett stood between them, holding their hands.

They had been happy because Scarlett had been a dreamy child. They had been happy because their relationship was newer, and they weren't ground down by life. Scarlett had been an adorable little girl, always asking questions about everything. They had kept her supplied with books from the library, had tried to find the answers she needed, had done everything they could to help her have a better life than they did.

She had learned to read before she went to school, and together they had all learned a bit of French from an app. Her parents agreed (as all parents probably did) that their daughter was exceptionally bright and brilliant, and as the years went by, they encouraged her to do her homework, to be top of the class, to excel at everything and keep her options wide open.

She was exactly average-sized for her age, which seemed like a good thing: she could never be teased for being too big or too small. She had curly dark hair and intense brown eyes, and she would climb into bed with them at night, cuddling up and whispering, "I love you so much, Mummy." She used to ask for a baby brother. Her favorite color was blue. She wanted to see snow. She wanted to have snowball fights, to climb mountains, to see the pyramids. She wanted to do everything.

She had been the best child ever. And then, a few weeks before she turned thirteen, Scarlett had changed.

- - - - -

She stood at the window *again* and waited *again,* still calling Scarlett every couple of minutes. She left voice mails, using a deliberately calm tone. She made a big effort and managed not to shout. It was raining harder now, a heavy rain that bounced off the roof. Maud, who lived in a camper van at the edge of the field, came past in her wellies to let her dog pee, saw her at the window and stopped. This was good: Maud was older than she was, and her best friend. Maud always calmed her down.

"Is it that girl again?" Maud said, and everything felt better.

Breathe in. Breathe out. Nod. It will be all right. It had always been all right. Scarlett came home. She had come home every day, every night. She shouted about the fact that they lived in a caravan, complained about how embarrassing it all was, how shabby they were, but she came back all the same. They had become a shouty family. They all yelled at one another every day, and she had no idea how to stop.

"It is." She looked at the rain. "Come in."

She didn't like the dog, Shabba, but she knew he was important to Maud: he had been her constant companion since her wife had died. He was big and aggressive, but she let him in anyway and he shook the rain off his coat all over everything in the living area. She pretended not to care, though she knew the van would smell of wet dog for days now. She didn't think Maud noticed that smell anymore.

"She said she was with a friend," she said. "Leanne. But I

called the mother to check, and she's not. She was lying *again*."
She felt the rage growing, and made an effort to push it down.
Sometimes she felt like a volcano, the fury bubbling up inside
until it erupted all over everything. "She fell out with Leanne
ages ago. Basically, Leanne hates Scarlett. Leanne's in bed asleep
because it's a school night. Leanne's mother thinks I'm the worst
parent ever, correctly, and Ed's looking for her on his way back
from work."

Maud grimaced and took off the woolen hat she was wearing.
She had cut her hair very short a while ago, and it suited her face.
She was about seventy and intensely active. She opened her arms
for a hug; she smelled of wood fire and wet dog, but that didn't
matter. They held each other tightly.

"She'll turn up," Maud said. "Ed will find her. He always
does. You know that. Want me to wait with you, hon?"

"Would you? I was going to eat because I remembered I didn't
have lunch, but I was making an omelet and some potato wedges
and then they burned, and I've got a cauliflower that fell off the
tractor, but it's stuck to the pan. Are you hungry?"

Maud smiled. "You make it sound so tempting. No, thanks. I
didn't forget to eat. Never do. I don't know how you keep doing
that. Let's rescue your dinner, and when that girl gets back she
can have something too, once you've finished shouting. And Ed
can eat too."

"He'll be fine," she muttered. "He eats at work."

She let Maud get going on the crap food, sitting down and then
standing up again when Shabba put his drooly face in her lap.

"Oh, God, Maud," she said. "What am I going to do? I don't
know where she goes. I don't know who she's with. She's fourteen! When I ask who she's with, she yells at me. She says she
has a boyfriend but then she says she's messing with me, and I
hope she is but I'm terrified that she's not. I mean, it would be

OK to have a boyfriend, but not a secret one. Not a secret one who keeps her out late at night and makes her hate us. I think I hear her on the phone to him sometimes. She doesn't even try at schoolwork—she's closing off all her options, wasting her brain. And I don't feel that I'm my own person anymore. I'm just a shit mother and that's my whole identity. I can't throw her out, and she knows it, so we end up living by her rules. We just fight all the time."

Maud had heard this before, many times over. "I know, sweetheart," she said. "I know. And she always comes back. Ed always finds her. And she'll grow up. We've all caused our mothers to tear their hair out." Their eyes met. "Though she is extreme. I admit that. But you know what? That girl of yours will be sitting right here in a couple of years, holding her head in her hands and apologizing. That's a promise. She's still bright. She'll still make something of herself. And if there's any justice in the world, she'll have her own wayward daughter one day."

She closed her eyes. "A couple of years?"

"Less!"

"I hope you're right."

She was seeing the scenes in her head. They were vivid, and they flashed up, unwanted and real. Scarlett dead on a road. Drunk in the gutter. Attacked, abducted, choking on vomit. She shook her head and tried to dislodge them. How had it come to this? She remembered her own childhood: she hadn't been a terrible daughter; she definitely hadn't been like Scarlett. From this distance she saw her childhood with her beekeeping parents as idyllic. She had worked in their little shop, helped with the bees, sold the honey. She had more or less followed the rules. Where had she gone wrong?

Soon the cauliflower was revived, and Maud was whisking eggs with a fork. Against the odds, the food smelled good. The dog had his paws up on her sofa and his head under the curtain so he could stare out at the chickens. Every now and then he gave a little growl.

She was grateful to Maud and didn't quite know how to say it. She wasn't sure that she'd be able to eat anything, but she was going to try.

"Here you go, sweetheart," said Maud. "Eat. I'll keep the rest warm."

· · · · ·

She was staring at a piece of omelet when the door opened and slammed shut. Scarlett was in front of her, tossing her hair, her face smeared with makeup.

She felt the rage rising. Then it erupted.

"Where the hell have you been?" she yelled. "Why won't you ever come home? Why did you lie about Leanne? Why—"

Maud put a hand on her arm, and she knew she needed to control herself.

"I fucking hate you!" That was her daughter. "I hope you die!"

She had always been certain that no child of hers would swear. Ground rules. Unacceptable. She had said the things you say before your child actually does it, and they're stronger than you and you don't want them to run away, so you have no idea how to stop it.

Everyone heard them shouting all over the campsite; they were notorious. She hated being this family. She took a deep breath, and another, thought of the people listening and tried to calm down.

"Why won't you let us help you?" she said, trying to use a different voice, and then she stopped. It wouldn't help. Nothing ever helped.

"Go to your room," said Ed, his voice tight.

Scarlett's room was right there: they had no privacy from one another and that was part of the problem.

The dog turned and growled and Scarlett screamed, "Shut that fucking animal up!"

Scarlett was wild. She was drunk. Quite possibly, she was more than drunk. Her hair was all over the place, her dress ripped, and she had lipstick smeared around her mouth.

"I really, *really* fucking hate you!" she shouted. "Both of you. You're pathetic! I wish I had rich parents! I wish we lived in a house! I wish I was a fucking orphan. You know, at the children's home they get actual bedrooms."

"And we wish we had a proper daughter," said Ed. He was a big man, red-faced and bearded, with the uncompromising manner of the chef. He generally said what came into his mind, the way they did in the kitchen. "Or no daughter at all. Just fuck off!"

"I did! And you came and found me! Do you realize how embarrassing it is to have my dad turning up and making me go home? God, I hate you."

"Don't speak to your father like that!"

She knew she and Ed had to stick together. She also knew, for sure, that the moment Scarlett came through this, they would split up. Their family was flames and ash. It was ruined.

"Cheers," said Ed. "Hey, Maud." He sighed. "Sorry. I suppose you'd have heard it across the site anyway. Everyone knows our business. Hello, Shabba. Hey, honey." He gave her a quick kiss on the lips.

"Why does *she* always have to be here?" said Scarlett, glaring at Maud, and she disappeared around the partition into her tiny bedroom, where she stamped her feet lots of times like a toddler, making the whole structure shake.

Maud put an arm around each of their shoulders.

"I'm sorry you're going through this, my loves," she said quietly. "Makes me less sad that I never had one. One day she'll turn that passion around and use it for something good."

"I will not!"

"She'll grow up," said Maud. "And she'll be asleep soon."

"Not going to sleep!"

"Shall I put the TV on?" Maud clicked it back onto the reality channel, which was showing strangers getting married, and cut Ed a slice of omelet, which he plainly didn't want. They sat down to pretend to eat.

Maud was staying because otherwise the three of them would tear one another apart. They were in a terrible place and there was, as far as she could see, no way out.

2

SHE YAWNED AND LOOKED AT THE CLOCK. IT WAS TEN PAST three and Ed was shaking her shoulder. The van was silent and so was the world outside, apart from the rain, which was still bouncing off the metal roof.

"Wake up."

"What?" she said. She sat up, her senses on full alert.

"Sorry," he whispered. "I've been wired. Can't sleep. I heard Scarlett on the phone. She was upset. She didn't want to see whoever it was, and then she said they couldn't come to the caravan and she'd come and meet them at the end of the road."

She reached for a sweater. "Now?"

"She can't go out in the middle of the night."

"No."

"I'll stop her in her doorway. Can you double-lock the door and take the keys out? With you inside, I mean. Keep her in the van. If she doesn't go out, whoever it is will come here and we can finally sort this out."

"She'll smash the window."

"I'll stop her," he said again. "I'll grab her."

"And hold her until morning? She'll bite you."

"She's a kid. We have to keep her safe. What else can we do? Could we drug her? No. Have you got anything better?"

She tried to think of something. "I wish I did."

She pulled on her pajama trousers and thick socks and tip-toed out into the living area. The caravan door was bolted shut. She locked it with its key too and put it in her pocket.

Scarlett crept out of her room, wearing jeans and a sweater, her hair tied back, her makeup done. Ed grabbed her.

She heard the scuffle, the shouting, the swearing, and tried to ignore it. She sat in the little alcove by the table, curled up, trying to block it all out, not wanting to join the fight.

Scarlett had been brilliant at walking and talking and asking questions, but terrible at sleeping. When she was a baby, they had ended up bringing her into their bed and sleeping with her on top of the bedding, between them, wrapped in her own little blanket made from an old one of theirs. They'd lived in a house back then, a little rented one, and it had been cozy and, with hindsight, luxurious. Scarlett would sleep for a few hours at a time, fists clenched on either side of her head, before waking with little hiccuping mews that built into wails. When she kept them awake all night, they used to joke about what kind of teen-ager she would be, but they'd had no idea.

She had been the most beautiful baby, with soft black hair, huge eyes, long eyelashes, rosebud lips. And when she finally learned to sleep through the night in her own bed, they had congratulated themselves. They had always known they wouldn't have a second child; like everyone else, they couldn't afford it. She was their only one, and no matter how little she slept, they adored her.

If you'd told her, back on that first morning when she woke amazed to have slept right through the night, the morning when she had rushed in a panic to check that Scarlett was still alive, that one day she would be curled into a ball in the early hours of a Friday morning because her fourteen-year-old daughter was trying to leave the house to meet someone at three in the morning, she wouldn't have believed it. Not her daughter! That was the kind of thing that happened to other parents.

Bad parents.

She took the key out of her pocket and held it tightly in her hand.

She leaned her head against the wall and closed her eyes.

▪ ▪ ▪ ▪ ▪

She was dozy, half believing that she was carrying baby Scarlett in her arms, and so she didn't react fast enough when teen Scarlett yanked her fingers back and took the key. She was gone in a blur.

"Come back!" Ed was shouting.

She must have bitten him or kicked him off. Then they were both gone. She pulled on her boots and set off after them, leaving the door repeatedly slamming in the wind. Her hand hurt but she didn't care. Scarlett was running toward the road, jumping through mud and puddles. The rain was stopping and the sky was clearing and she could see the dim figures of her daughter sprinting across the grass and her husband running after her in the moonlight. The grass was wet. A dog barked somewhere in the distance. The stars above were infinite.

She got to the road and stopped. At the end of the drive that led to their site, there was a big road with no pavements. In one direction it led to the A30, the main road that led out of Cornwall and east toward Devon and the rest of the world. In the other direction it went to the center of the town. The road curved around, so she didn't know which way they had gone. It was dark and quiet, so she stood still, pathetic and cold in her pajamas and wellies, listening to owls and foxes and waiting.

She heard a car in the distance and ran toward it, around the corner toward the city. Her feet slammed the tarmac as she sprinted. She saw them. She saw the lights approaching. She ran as fast as she could, and she saw Scarlett and she saw the car and she ran faster, faster, faster because she could see what was going to happen and knew that she could change it.

She ran faster than she had ever run in her life because she needed to save her daughter.

The car didn't slow down. It slowed, but not enough.

3

THE CHAIR WAS PLASTIC. SHE WAS SLUMPED OVER AND HER
neck ached. She yawned, tried to stretch. Someone's hand was
on her shoulder.

Where was she?

It was daylight, though she couldn't see a window because
there were closed curtains on three sides and a blank wall on the
fourth. She was entirely disoriented. There was a bed in front of
her. She was sitting in a chair, in a building. It was a hospital.
The person in the bed was . . .

She gasped and sat forward. Everything came back. Scarlett
was in hospital, and there were tubes and wires and machines.
Her hair was held back by a green plastic cap, and there was a
tube going into her nose, another into her hand, and lots of
other things that she couldn't process. Underneath it all, it was
Scarlett.

"Tamsyn," said Ed. "Wake up, darling. It's me, Ed."

She jolted into full alertness. He was behind her, and it was his hand. He had said *Tamsyn*. That was her name. He was Ed. He was her husband. What mattered, though, was Scarlett. She focused and stretched and it started to come back, though it was foggy.

"I'm sorry to wake you, but the doctor's coming round. Do you remember what happened? Scarlett's accident? She was hit by a car that didn't stop. We were both there. You collapsed from the stress and they've given you some medication, so you probably feel weird. But you're OK, and Scarlett's where she needs to be to recover."

Machines were flashing, and her daughter was right there in bed, unconscious, hooked up to everything that was keeping her alive. Scarlett was alive. Tamsyn leaned forward to stare into her face.

"Oh, shit," she said, and ran her fingers through her hair.

Ed touched her hair too. On the other side of the curtain, someone coughed, and then there was a shuffling of feet.

She looked around, then back at Scarlett. She sat forward, staring at her daughter. Scarlett's face was still. She didn't react to anything. She didn't look peaceful; she was absent.

Tamsyn listened to the voices of the doctors and didn't quite want them to come to the cubicle, because she knew that whatever they were going to say would be bad. She couldn't bear to hear it. She checked her own body, but she wasn't injured, and as far as she could see, neither was Ed. It was just Scarlett. Oh, God. They had wanted Scarlett to stop going out, to stop being awful, to stop shouting at them, and now she had stopped.

The curtains parted and a woman came in. She was wearing a nurse's uniform and had glossy dark hair and a kind face.

"Hello, Tamsyn," she said. "The doctor's just on his way."

And then the doctor was there. A man.

. . . . .

"I'm afraid your daughter is in a very serious condition," he said.

She wanted to say *I know that* but managed not to. She just nodded.

"The upshot is," said the man, who was bald but with bushy eyebrows, "that she does have a chance of regaining consciousness and all we can do for the moment is wait. I'm optimistic, but it's not like it is in the movies, I'm afraid. If she does wake up, there's a real chance of lasting damage."

"When will we know?" said Ed.

She looked at him: he looked terrible. She touched her own face, knowing that she must have been the same. Ravaged by horror. Older. Different. A new person.

The man closed his eyes briefly, then opened them and smiled with his mouth but not his eyes. "I'm afraid I can't give you much of a timescale. We'll take it a day at a time. Essentially, the sooner she wakes up, the more positive the signs for recovery."

There were two women with him. He turned to the younger one. She didn't look much older than Scarlett, and Tamsyn was furious with her for being healthy and upright, for having a functioning brain. She was jealous of her mother for having a bright and sensible daughter who was a high achiever and healthy too.

"My name's Poppy," she said, her voice nervous. "I work in hospital admin. The finance office has told us that your insurance covers Scarlett for eight weeks of treatment, so with any luck she'll be fine by then."

"What happens if she's not?" said Ed.

"We'll talk about that if the time approaches," said Poppy. "There are various options. For now let's just work on getting her better."

"Well, yes," said Ed. "Of course. But just so we know. Would the insurance company come along and switch off these machines when our money runs out?"

"Ed!" said Tamsyn.

The other woman, the nurse with glossy hair, stepped in.

"There are always options," she said. "I'm Maya. I'm a nurse here, and I'm going to be doing everything I can to give Scarlett the best possible chance of getting better."

Tamsyn looked at Maya, who gave her a warm smile. She felt the tears finally coming. Ed put an arm around her shoulder and pulled her close to him. Everyone looked at them. Everyone was so tense. Nothing happened. After a while Ed said he had to go to work. He left and she stayed.

She sat there. She waited. Days passed, and then weeks.

4

ONE OF THEM, USUALLY TAMSYN, WAS AT THE HOSPITAL ALL the time. They had less money because she didn't go to work anymore (how could she be anywhere other than here with Scarlett?), but as they didn't have to feed Scarlett's teenage appetite or pay for her electricity or water, it didn't seem to make much difference financially, and Tamsyn didn't worry about money for a moment. Winter was turning to spring, and she didn't want to go home at all. She was stretched like an elastic band, watching Scarlett and waiting. She and Ed hardly saw each other, because she was always at the hospital and he was at work or at home sleeping, and on the occasional night when she went home to sleep, he would sit with Scarlett. They agreed that their daughter would never be left on the ward on her own, and she never was.

They saw each other in passing. He would take hold of her and look into her face, and she would look back, and they didn't even need to say anything.

There were three other beds in Scarlett's ward, and although the curtains were always closed so Tamsyn never saw them, she couldn't avoid the fact that the people in those beds kept dying.

Tamsyn tried hard not to think about the fact that it was Scarlett's turn. *It doesn't work like that,* she told herself. *It doesn't.*

She waited instead for Scarlett to wake up, but it went on and on not happening. She didn't wake up and she didn't die. She stayed in the place in between.

Every now and then, Maya would take Tamsyn into a side room and give her a cup of tea and say, "How are you doing? Are you feeling all right in yourself?" and she was touched but batted the questions away because she didn't matter. Only Scarlett mattered. She did like Maya, though. She was the only one Tamsyn was happy to see. She felt comfortable with her, felt she actually cared. Her accent was unusual in Cornwall: when Tamsyn asked, she said she was Swiss-Lebanese but had grown up in Canada. Tamsyn wondered, but didn't ask, how she'd ended up in Truro.

"I'm fine," she would tell her. "It's not about me."

Maya would nod and say things like "You have to look after yourself too, you know," but Tamsyn ignored that, and she ignored Poppy from the finance office, who smiled and tried to stop to chat every time she came round.

They were horribly close to the eight-week insurance cutoff when Maya popped her head inside the curtains and said, "Hey, Tamsyn! I've got someone here to chat to you. Is that OK?"

They both looked at Scarlett, who was the same as ever. Her face was gray, and she was lying still, supported by tubes, as she always was. Tamsyn could barely remember now what Scarlett had been like before. She knew her daughter had been difficult, wayward, rude and all those other things, but that seemed like an odd dream. Scarlett had been wildly alive, but all that life had been a precursor to this. This stopping of everything. She was technically alive, but there was no life in her anymore. She hadn't shifted on the Glasgow Coma Scale. Everything was done by machines. The air around her was medical and desperate. Being at her bedside was boring, tense, terrifying. Nothing ever happened but you knew the world could change entirely, for good or for bad, at any moment.

. . . . .

She wondered whether Ed felt as guilty as she did. Both of them had wished for Scarlett to be different, to stop doing the things she did, and now she was different and she had stopped.

Tamsyn didn't want to see anyone for a chat in case they were here to talk about the future. The insurance. The unthinkable. She would sit here every single day until the end of time rather than face that.

A man walked through the curtains.

"Tamsyn," said Maya, "don't worry. It's not what you think. This is Luca Holgate."

Luca Holgate was a white man with overstyled hair, maybe about forty and wearing an expensive suit. He didn't look like a doctor but he had authority. Maya stood next to her, put a hand on her shoulder for support. Maya was here so often that Tamsyn had no idea how she managed to look after any other patients.

"Mrs. Trelawney," said Luca Holgate, holding out a hand for her to shake.

She frowned. She didn't want to shake his hand. She wished Ed was there to deal with him. Tamsyn's world had shrunk right down so she could deal only with talking to Scarlett, which she did ceaselessly in a quiet voice so she didn't disturb the other patients and their visitors. She couldn't believe she had been so angry for so long; she was never going to shout ever again.

Scarlett's medical cover was due to end in nine days. She needed a miracle, not a smarmy man in a suit.

"Really, Tamsyn," said Maya, "don't worry. Luca would like to discuss something with you. An opportunity."

Maya stood behind her and massaged her shoulders, and Tamsyn leaned into her. That made her feel strong enough to turn her face to the man and try to make it smile.

"Oh, yes?" she said.

"I know you don't like to leave Scarlett alone," said Maya. "Would it be OK for me to sit with her? Then you and Luca can talk in private."

Tamsyn frowned. "I want you to come too. Please come."

Maya and Luca looked at each other. After a while, Maya nodded.

"I'll find someone to stay with Scarlett," she said, and she went off and made a phone call.

Poppy from the finance office arrived with files of paperwork under her arm, smiled at them all and sat down.

"Not a problem," she said. "Happy to help."

Tamsyn thought that was weird, but she stayed at Maya's side. Maya was gorgeous, warm and glamorous, and Tamsyn trusted her above everyone else in this hospital.

"We won't be far away," said Luca.

He spoke perfect English with a slight accent from somewhere like Scandinavia. Austria. She didn't know. She didn't know anything.

"I asked the staff up here to find us a space, and they've given us this room."

She followed him into one of those rooms with a TV and sofa and piles of tatty magazines, turning to check that Maya was still with them. The room was used by people who were waiting for their relatives to get better or to die. She and Ed never came into these rooms because they were always with Scarlett.

The sofa was squashier than she had expected, and she sank down, her knees higher than her hips. She felt disadvantaged, particularly when Luca sat on a proper chair, much higher than her, so she stood up and sat on a proper chair too. That was better. Maya took the squashy sofa.

"Right," said Luca, taking a folder out of his shoulder bag and putting it on the table. "First of all, Mrs. Trelawney, I wanted to extend my deepest sympathies to you and your husband about your daughter's accident. It's a horrific thing to happen. Every parent's worst nightmare."

Tamsyn tried to agree but found she couldn't speak. She managed a tiny nod, a jerk of the head.

"I know she hasn't responded in the way everyone hoped she might so far, and again, I'm deeply sorry."

She managed to say, "Thanks." He was looking at her hard as if he were assessing her, but she didn't know why.

"I can see you're fearing the worst from this conversation, but you don't need to. I've traveled here from Switzerland because Scarlett meets a particular set of criteria, and I would like to offer her a place on a trial we're running."

"A drugs trial?"

Her heart started beating faster, harder. Was this it? Salvation? Scarlett was going to get better with a magical new drug. A part of Tamsyn had been hoping for this all along, and she hadn't even realized it until now. She remembered an old film about a drug that woke people up. Would it be like that? Was Luca Holgate, in fact, the miracle?

"Not exactly, though she will be getting the very best medical care." He took a deep breath and looked away for a moment, then turned back to her with a smile. "This hospital is doing brilliant work in difficult conditions but they can't do as much as we would do for your daughter. I work for a company called VitaNova, which means *new life*. My job is to find people around the world in the same situation as Scarlett and to, in a way, re-build them. Maya actually works with me. She's been on a sec-ondment over here."

She looked at Maya, who was smiling her encouragement. "Rebuild?"

He looked more confident. "Yes. What I can't do, unfortu-nately, is wake Scarlett and take her back to the girl she was before her accident, though I can offer you all the very best chance of that happening. However, what I'm offering might be the next best thing. You know about AI and consciousness? The astonishing advances that have been made recently, particularly with regard to memory?"

Tamsyn shrugged. She lived in a world in which astonishing advances in AI were irrelevant, but yes, she was vaguely aware that it was a thing.

"Sure," she said.

"We're at a point where humans and AI can decide to evolve together, or they can take separate paths. Our position is that we believe that we need to do it together. It is absolutely crucial for the future of the human race. That's what our research is about: creating a human-AI interface. Does that make sense?"

She nodded, even though she didn't really have a clue what he was talking about.

"Great. So I'm offering to pull together everything that made Scarlett into the person she was—*is*—and to put it into a new body, which will be grown from her own tissue. The body won't just be like Scarlett. It will *be* Scarlett. She will be indistinguish-able from her old self. Depending on what you consider makes a person into herself, she will be Scarlett—or, if you prefer, Scarlett two-point-oh. A reanimation. It's the way forward for all of you."

Tamsyn couldn't speak. Luca let the silence grow. She could feel him studying her reaction.

"AI?" she said in the end. She forced herself to look into his eyes, then snapped her gaze away. She looked at the carpet, coming away from the floor where it met the wall. "Like a robot?"

"No. I don't mean a robot. I do, arguably, mean a cyborg." His voice was calm.

Tamsyn supposed this was his job, trying to sell this stuff to people. Like hell was she going to let him give them a *cyborg* as some kind of consolation. The idea made her stomach churn. Just because they were poor, that didn't mean a man in an expensive suit could foist an experimental robot on them. Cyborg. It wasn't fair. She wanted a drugs trial! A miraculous one!

Maya leaned forward and touched her arm. "Tamsyn," she said, "I know I've been nursing lately, but like Luca said, I'm a part of his project. I work with him. I've been observing Scarlett, making sure we'd be able to work well together. And the good news is, she's perfect. And so are you. And Ed. We can bring her back for you."

"How does that sound?" Luca said.

Tamsyn felt his eyes on her, and she was aware of her old clothes, frayed and shabby at the edges. At least these jeans didn't have a hole in the knee. She knew her hair was unwashed, her skin was shit and there were bones jutting out, not in a sexy way but because she didn't have enough to eat. Some people were affected the other way by a lack of money and opportunity, and Tamsyn had been bigger once, but after they moved to the trailer park, she had swung the other way.

These weeks of sitting at Scarlett's bedside and eating hospital toast and food from the neighbors had actually been good for her; she was aware that her hair and skin had improved, and she'd put on a bit of weight. That said far too much, she thought, about her old life.

"When you say the . . . the cyborg thing would be '*grown from her own tissue,'*" she said, knowing that she was slow to take this in, "you mean a clone."

"We prefer to call it a second self," Luca said, his voice smooth. "But as you may know, the laws are slightly different in Switzerland from the way they are in much of the rest of the world. We can look for potential beneficiaries of our scheme only in certain countries and only among people in Scarlett's situation. It's classed as a radical medical treatment for people with no other options. That's part of our legal terms. And traveling long haul isn't ideal for a patient in this condition." He gestured in the vague direction of Scarlett's ward. "Which means that, as the European Union countries aren't amenable to what we're doing, we are looking particularly in the UK. Maya's observations confirm that Scarlett is an ideal candidate." He gave Tamsyn a searching look. "This is life changing for you," he said, and she felt herself flinch, because if ever there was a life that needed changing, hers was it.

Luca was slick and well nourished. He probably took vitamins every day. His clothes cost more money than Tamsyn had ever held in her hands. He was offering her something he thought was amazing. Life changing.

"So it's part . . . second self and part AI?" She sensed it was better to use his words than to say *clone* and *robot*.

"Yes!" He was pleased with her. "Hybrid technology. It's a trial, and it very much wouldn't involve giving up on your daughter. Quite the opposite. If you sign up for this, we would ask you, your husband and Scarlett to travel to our clinic. She will be given top-notch care for the entire trial from Dr. Singh, our specialist, who is at the top of her field, and you and Ed will be given everything you need to start a new life in Switzerland. You won't need to move back here unless you want to."

She noticed that he switched from *would* to *will* during that speech.

"Where's your clinic?"

"Geneva. Have you ever visited?"

Tamsyn managed to shake her head without laughing or crying. Of course she hadn't visited Geneva.

Maya saw that and stepped in. "It's a beautiful part of the world, Tamsyn," she said. "We'll get you a comfortable place to live and you'll have everything you need. You won't need to work. If Ed would like to, we'll find him a job, but that'll be up to him. He's a chef, right? Finding work would be very straightforward. And Tamsyn—here's the best part: Scarlett will have round-the-clock care at a state-of-the-art clinic with Dr. Singh, as Luca said. She's an incredible doctor. The best. Scarlett will have a private room in a discreet, dedicated facility. We will guarantee her the best possible chance of waking up and recovering, and to be honest, having spent time with her, I think there is a chance of a recovery of some sort." She paused. "We won't set any time limit."

For a moment Tamsyn let herself imagine it. She imagined living in a comfortable apartment in Geneva. It didn't work because she didn't know what to picture. A lake? Mountains? Cows with bells round their necks? Chocolate? Cuckoo clocks? She knew nothing about what Switzerland was actually like.

"But what," she said, "about the robot clone?" She screwed her eyes shut in self-reproach. She had said the wrong word twice.

"She's not a robot or a clone." Luca's voice was sharp, and Maya gave him a look.

"Sorry! I was trying too hard to get it right and that made me get it wrong. The . . . hybrid?"

"Yes, or the reanimation."

"Where does it—she, I mean—where does she live?"

"That's what this is all about," said Luca. "She lives with you as your daughter. It works best if you think of her as Scarlett's twin. For instance, she won't be called Scarlett. She'll have a different name. That seems to make it easier."

"And what happens when Scarlett wakes up?"

He sighed. "The best possible outcome. Leave that side of things to us. When Scarlett regains consciousness, and before she's ready to come home, we have a few courses of action open to us, and you and Ed will be in the driving seat. If you want the reanimation to leave, then it'll be no problem at all. She'll tell you she's going on a trip, and she'll pack a bag and come straight back to our clinic. Scarlett won't need to meet her second self. Unless . . ." He stopped. "Well, it's up to you. The reanimation will do what you want her to do."

Tamsyn shook her head. She couldn't begin to take this in.

Maya touched her arm again. "We've given you a lot to think about. Why don't you go and discuss it with Ed? You don't have to say anything right now."

"In fact," said Luca, "why don't the two of you go out for some food tonight and talk it over? We can make a reservation, and the bill will come straight to us. I'll ask Poppy to sort it out and let you know. Talk it over. We would love to welcome you all on board. Love to."

"We really would," said Maya. "I've become very attached to you and Scarlett, Tamsyn, and I think this is a great opportunity for you. I'll sit with Scarlett tonight. If anything changes with her, I'll call you straightaway."

"Why us?" she said as they both stood up.

"We spend a lot of time looking for the right people," Luca said. "And I think you, Ed and Scarlett are exactly the right people."

5

THE RESTAURANT WAS IN A SMART HOTEL. SHE WASN'T dressed properly, but she didn't care. Her black trousers weren't as shabby as they used to be after a day in the fields, and she didn't feel conspicuous. No one turned to stare at her. Nobody muttered. No one took any notice of her at all, and she wouldn't have cared if they had.

She and Ed sat opposite each other by candlelight, and they drank wine and ate things she had barely heard of. Langoustines. Artichokes. Mango. She knew that Ed was familiar with this stuff, but she certainly wasn't. It tasted weird but she liked it.

"The fact is," said Ed, topping up her glass with the most amazing wine, "that of course we have to do it, and this Luca Holgate character knows that perfectly well. We all know it. There is no dilemma at all."

She felt the tension drain away. "We do, don't we?" She hadn't wanted to face it, but as soon as she did, she felt something light up inside her. "The hospital will switch her off in just over a week if we don't. We have no choice at all. No decision to make. Just a weird sort of lifeline that we have to take. Whatever happens, it's the only option."

"Exactly. Who's going to say, 'No, thank you. We'd rather stay here living our shit lives and watch our daughter die'? No one. That's who."

"Not me."

They looked at each other, and there were tears in their eyes. Tamsyn had hardly let herself cry at all, but once she started, it seemed she couldn't stop. Tears ran down her cheeks and dripped off her chin. They had come so close to losing everything, and now there was hope. There was a lifeline that came with weird conditions attached. She didn't want to move to Geneva—Truro was her home and she had never lived anywhere else—but she would do it in a heartbeat.

"So what do you think about the . . . What are we meant to say?" Ed said, half smiling.

"Replacement," she said, sniffing.

A waiter was next to her, offering a new napkin, and she turned to smile her thanks, then turned back to Ed. Did the waiter think they were breaking up? He probably did.

"No. Not replacement. *Reanimation.* I'll take it as the condition for keeping Scarlett alive. Of course I will. I can't even imagine it, but I'll live with it, since it seems we have to."

"I think it'll be fine. I mean, maybe it really will be like Scarlett?" He looked at her and his eyes filled with tears. He looked away and visibly regained control of himself. "Maybe it won't. Maybe it'll be a bit like her. Like her sister would have been if she'd had one. Like he said, it's going to be a part of her. I mean, cloning? I thought human cloning was *so* banned, but they seem to have found a loophole. So bring it on. Whatever it is, we'll suck it up. It's going to be the price we pay for getting the real Scarlett the treatment she needs."

"I guess the reanimation isn't going to be out with unsuitable people all night, is it?"

"I'm imagining it'll be programmed to be polite."

"If it really does look like her," Tamsyn said, "then we can probably come to think of it as being like having a photo of her around the place, but in three-D. A temporary three-D printout."

Ed managed a weak smile. "Made from body parts."

Tamsyn shuddered, but they came to terms with it very quickly in the end.

6

IT HAPPENED FASTER THAN EITHER OF THEM HAD EXPECTED.
They called Luca from the restaurant to accept his offer, as he
must have known they would. The next morning Tamsyn sat by
Scarlett's bed, drinking coffee and changing her mind. It was the
cloning thing: it both repelled her and brought her back again.
She hated it—what could be more monstrous than a human
clone? A person, not born but made? A Frankenstein's monster?
A human-robot hybrid? And then she looked at Scarlett, inert
and absent, kept alive only by machinery, and she thought that if
she was happy to have her daughter kept alive by technology, why
shouldn't she accept the next step and allow technology to bring
her back? She was one of the only people in history, surely, to be
given the opportunity of having her daughter regrown. It was
impossible, and yet it seemed to be real.

Another patient on the ward had died in the night: he was a
man in his thirties who'd been there for a few weeks. Tamsyn
had no idea what had happened to put him there because she
never really spoke to the other families. Since Scarlett had been
there, everyone else had died at least twice. She thought that the

other three beds had collectively hosted seven people. Scarlett was already lucky.

She looked at her daughter and tried to will her back to life. You can be as moody as you like, she told her telepathically. She took Scarlett's hand. Please, darling. Come back before we have to do this. You don't have to tell me where the clothes came from. We can draw a line under everything. Every little bit of it. Maybe we can find a way to get a house.

There wasn't so much as a flicker. She'd stopped expecting it.

When a smiling young woman turned up next to her and said, "Hi, Tamsyn! How are you doing?" it took her a while to realize that it was Maya. Maya was dressed in a dusky pink dress and a cream raincoat. She looked as if she'd taken a wrong turn somewhere in New York. Tamsyn wondered what she had actually made of Truro over the past two months.

"You look different," she managed to say.

"Yes. Now that the decision's made, I'm in a different mode. Don't worry, though! I'm still here for you, every step of the way. Could I have your house keys?"

"My keys?"

"Yes," said Maya. "I'm helping organize your move, and as well as securing your apartment in Geneva, that involves shipping out everything you want to take with you from your home here. As much, or as little, as you'd like. We just need to have a look around to work out what level of removal you're going to need."

"We don't really have anything," Tamsyn said. "You know it's not a house? It's a static caravan. I don't want to take anything. Give it all to Maud. She lives in the purple van at the end of the row. Can you ask her to take the chickens?" She handed over her keys and made excuses for the state of the place.

"Don't you worry about that," said Maya, "not for one second."

Tamsyn was going through the caravan in her mind. She had

spent so little time there lately that she could barely remember what was in it.

"I want the photo on the wall," she said. "That's it. The only thing. The photo of the three of us. And Scarlett's clothes. And mine and Ed's too, I guess."

"Of course! I'll be along later with details of your new apartment. We're finalizing the lease today but if we get this one— Oh, my God, it's absolutely beautiful, Tamsyn! You will adore it. Luca was so excited when you called last night. He's told everyone to make sure we get you the best there is. Seriously, you're not going to *know* yourselves. We're all so delighted."

They both looked at Scarlett. Tamsyn wondered whether Maya too was thinking about the other Scarlett. The new one.

She was.

"If we do secure this apartment," Maya said carefully, "there are four bedrooms. So, you know, the reanimation will have her own room, and Scarlett's room will be right there waiting for her when she wakes up. Plus you'll have a spare room you can use as a home office or gym. Whatever you like. It's a different world, I can tell you."

Tamsyn managed a little smile. "I can't begin to imagine."

"You're not going to know what's hit you," Maya said, and then gave Scarlett a shocked look, clearly regretting her choice of words.

It hung there for a moment, and they gave each other tiny smiles and Maya muttered an apology and walked away.

Tamsyn couldn't picture a beautiful new apartment in a city that slick, stylish people like Maya *adored*. With a private room and proper care for Scarlett. It felt impossible, like stepping into a movie. She texted Ed to say, **I'm going to stop second-guessing myself. I'm going to embrace every bit of this. I don't** care if we have to live with a robot clone. We just need the best care for our girl.

Too right, he replied at once. **Yes. The only thing we can do is go with it.**

∎∎∎∎∎

Two rushed days after that, they were on an airplane, waiting to take off. They had traveled into London by train and then straight out of it on the Heathrow Express, so all Tamsyn had seen of the city was Paddington Station, which had a high glass ceiling and lots of people, and shops that sold food and greetings cards.

Saying good-bye to Scarlett had torn her to pieces. It went against every instinct she had, and it was only the fact that if she stopped this process Scarlett's insurance would run out that made her go through with it. However, unless this was all some elaborate trick (*And it could be,* she thought. *It really could.*), then Scarlett was being prepared for a medical flight to Geneva, while this commercial plane was going to carry Tamsyn and Ed through the air, which felt impossible, though everyone around them looked as if they flew everywhere all the time. Tomorrow, they would be with Scarlett again. She clung to that.

∎∎∎∎∎

The plane was not what she had expected. She could stretch her legs out without touching the back of the seat in front. She put a soft blanket over her lap just because she could.

"I had no idea air travel was like this," she said to Ed.

"I think it's because we're in business class," he told her, and looked round at a curtain behind them. "Through there, it's much more cramped, apparently."

She tipped the seat back and then snapped it upright again,

smiling over at the steward who had already been around to introduce himself. Everything smelled new and clean and, to Tamsyn's nose, aggressively perfumed, but she supposed that was because she was used to living in a world that smelled like cauliflower and mud and three people in a confined space, with a shower block that was a long walk away and had minimal water pressure.

She squeezed Ed's hand. He looked even less comfortable than she felt, though he was remarkably gorgeous in a new jacket and shirt. She looked down at her new jeans and white shirt. She felt different. It was weird, being in this in-between space: neither in the life they knew, nor the life to come.

He squeezed her hand back. His hand was big and warm, and she felt the comfort in his touch.

The plane started to move. She held his hand tightly. This was all for Scarlett. That was what mattered.

She stared out the window at the drizzly airport. The buildings were ugly and there was scraggly grass around the place, but all the same: this was Heathrow Airport and she had never expected to see it, let alone to be leaving it in business class. They went faster and faster, and she was suddenly scared. The process was familiar from the TV, but she wanted to scream. She closed her eyes and waited, but nothing happened, and when she opened them and looked out the window, they were up in the air, the airport buildings and the houses around it, the roads and rivers and fields, all becoming smaller and smaller below them.

She and Ed looked at each other. They were still holding hands. That hadn't happened, she thought, for a long time.

"We're in the air," he whispered, as awestruck as she was.

The steward came back with two glasses of champagne on a tray, and she took one and clinked it against Ed's.

"To Scarlett," she said.

"To Scarlett's recovery," he said, "and to you, Tamsyn. To you."

When they landed in Geneva it was dark. They went out through the airport, showing their passports and saying they were there as tourists, as instructed by Maya. "We'll get visas sorted once you're settled," she'd told them. "But you're allowed in for ninety days, no questions asked, so we'll take it from there." The passport inspector couldn't have been less interested, and that was, Tamsyn realized, because no matter how she felt, they looked as if they belonged.

"When does Scarlett arrive?" she said as they waited for their bags to come round on a conveyor belt.

Ed looked at a clock on the white wall. "Later," he said. "And they're taking her straight to the clinic. Don't worry. She's in the best hands now."

She knew that her daughter was being taken to a hospital none of them could imagine, that if she woke up there—*when* she woke up there—Scarlett would have no idea where she was. Tamsyn imagined explaining that she was in Switzerland having the best treatment the world could offer. She smiled as she pictured Scarlett's easy acceptance of that. Finally, her real life would be, through the worst and most circuitous of routes, catching up with the life she would have chosen. She would wake up living in a luxurious apartment in Switzerland, with the very best medical care at her fingertips.

And with a robot clone. Tamsyn sent the thought away. There was no need to think about it for the moment.

7

TAMSYN KNEW BY THE SMELL THAT SHE WASN'T AT HOME
before she remembered any of the rest of it. This place smelled
like flowers. The sheets were brand-new and felt amazing against
her skin. She opened her eyes: the ceiling was much too far away.

She looked across and saw that Ed too was farther away than
he would have been at home, because they were in a massive
bed—though he was also closer than usual because they hadn't
shared a bed for months. He was asleep on his side, facing her,
and she took the time to stare at his face. He was forty-five, and
his face was weathered by stress and wind, and had the un-
healthy, blotchy pallor of the chef. His beard was tidier than it
usually was, and it melted her heart when she remembered him
carefully trimming it before they left so he could look as smart
as possible for their new life.

There was a clock on her bedside table. It was half past seven
and she wanted to look at everything, because their arrival last
night had been a blur. She got up quietly and decided that, to
avoid waking him, she'd shower in one of the four (four!) bathrooms that weren't attached to this room.

This flat really did have five bathrooms and four bedrooms. All of that for (currently) two people. The whole place was massive, on the top floor of a grand old building, and apparently there was a roof terrace with a view, though the concierge hadn't shown it to them last night because they had been overwhelmed by everything.

She made herself smell different, showering with all the scented products that were in the guest bathroom. There was a silk kimono thing in there too, so she put that on and went to look for coffee and the view.

It was too much. She was used to living in a metal box with a shared bathroom. That was home. It was friendly. She could touch every boundary of her real home by taking a few steps. She understood it.

This, she didn't get at all. The apartment was perhaps fifteen times the size of their caravan in Truro, maybe more than that. The floors were polished wooden parquet with rugs in exactly the right places: it was like living in the kind of world she used to watch on television, to the point where she really thought she had somehow stepped through a screen into a Netflix drama. Nothing could be real. She walked slowly around, feeling the warm wood beneath her bare feet. She discovered two identical bedrooms, both done up for teenage girls with four-poster beds with gauzy hangings. One had a pink-and-white duvet cover and pink-and-white rugs and everything else. The other was blue and white. Scarlett had never had much time for pink, and so Tamsyn walked into the blue one. Scarlett's room.

"Darling," she whispered, "you're going to love your bedroom."

She could see blue sky and a city view from the window. She sat on the bed, which was softer than she had expected, and put a hand gently on the pillow. Scarlett's pillow. They wouldn't have put it there, would they? Not if they didn't expect her to sleep here. She opened the wardrobe and saw that it was filled with new clothes. They were beautiful, classy clothes, the kind of things a princess might wear. The few clothes that had come from home looked trashy next to them. She decided to find a charity shop and get rid of them.

She closed the door to the pink room and decided not to open it until she had to.

She walked on and emerged in a huge, fully equipped kitchen that was separated by folding doors (currently open) from a living room with floor-to-ceiling windows. Beyond that was the roof terrace. Maya had told her there was a terrace, but she'd imagined a little balcony. This, however, was another room: it was as big as their bedroom, with pots of geraniums and jasmine, a wooden table and chairs, terra-cotta tiles on the ground that stretched to a white wall at the end. The wall was high enough to keep them safe but low enough to look over. The sky was blue, the sun shining.

She wanted to do something kind for Ed and decided to make him coffee and then breakfast. He liked coffee, and they hadn't eaten much last night. She found a machine with a set of instructions next to it. After ten minutes of trying to work it out, she was holding the nicest coffee she had ever had. A moment after that, she was outside on the terrace, leaning on the bright white wall with the sun shining on her head, shivering slightly as she looked out across an incredible, unlikely city.

It stretched ahead of her, building after building, street after street. She could see a lake in the distance, with a huge fountain that sprayed water high into the air. Behind that, against a pale blue sky, there was a misty ridge of mountains. The air was clear and crystalline, and that was because this was Switzerland.

The air was warmer because, although Scarlett's accident had happened in winter, now it was spring.

Scarlett was out there somewhere, in her clinic, and at ten o'clock a car was going to pick them up to take them to see her. Tamsyn wouldn't quite believe in any of this until that happened: she couldn't shake the feeling that she had signed a lot of paperwork without reading it (Ed had read it) and allowed a bunch of persuasive strangers to put her on an airplane while they kidnapped her sick daughter. Until she set eyes on Scarlett, she wouldn't relax. What kind of luxury trap was this?

She gazed out, letting the sun dry her hair, wondering whether one of the buildings she was looking at housed her daughter. Was she looking at Scarlett? She worked hard on not panicking, making a point of *not* entertaining the thought that she might not have survived the journey or that this might have been some kind of trick or heist. Maybe the police would arrive and arrest them for something. The whole thing could be an elaborate setup.

Either she or Ed had been at Scarlett's bedside for every moment since the accident until Luca Holgate had come along, and now they didn't even know where in this entire city she was.

However, if Luca hadn't come along, Scarlett's life support would have been switched off this week. And she had survived the journey. Of course she had. Someone would have told them if she hadn't.

Ed was behind her, putting his arms around her. She leaned back onto him. Everything, including the dynamic between them, felt different. They hadn't had sex for ages. Now, as long as Scarlett had indeed made the journey safely and this hospital turned out to be real, Tamsyn thought perhaps they might be able to think about it.

"Hey," he said.

"Yeah."

Given that she didn't want to launch into a conversation

about kidnapping or fake hospitals, or indeed sex, there wasn't much else to say. They both surveyed their new world.

"Want me to make you a coffee?" she said in the end. "I worked out how to do it."

◼ ◼ ◼ ◼ ◼

The clinic wasn't a *hospital* at all. It was a white building on the other side of the city, a small place with a discreet sign reading VITANOVA beside the door and a few marble steps leading up to the entrance. Inside, quiet piano music played from invisible speakers, and a reception desk had the words VITANOVA: BE YOUR BEST SELF above it. They stood in a hallway that had flowers on tables, a black door that was closed and a wide staircase. Everyone they saw wore a white coat, and everybody knew who Tamsyn and Ed were. They greeted them in English and they all said, "How are you finding Geneva?" and "We're so pleased to have Scarlett with us," and things like that, and Tamsyn gradually felt herself relaxing.

Scarlett had survived the journey. Of course she had. Everyone said she was settled in her room, and they were delighted with the way the transfer had gone.

Maya took them up the stairs to the second floor, where she registered them with the facial recognition software that meant all the doors would open as they approached.

"This means," she said, adjusting some settings, "that you can come in anytime you like. Day or night, you can visit your daughter. You don't need to do anything other than turn your face to the camera as you walk."

She led them along a corridor and stopped at the last room before a heavy door that blocked the passage. SCARLETT TRE-LAWNEY was engraved on a brass plaque on Scarlett's door. They had actually done that for her. Tamsyn loved it: she thought she would take a picture of it when no one else was around so she would always remember it, even after Scarlett woke up.

Maya stood back. "After you," she said.

Tamsyn looked at Ed and they both walked into the room. There was a woman in there wearing a white coat, her black hair in a bun. She smiled and stepped forward to greet them.

"I'm Dr. Singh," she said. "I'm Scarlett's doctor."

Tamsyn felt comfortable with her at once. She remembered what it had been like in Truro, with the different doctors, all of them brilliant but all overstretched, coming round, reading Scarlett's chart, checking her and dashing off to the next patient. It had often been a different doctor every day. Dr. Singh was chic and reassuring and seemed to be the only doctor who would work with their daughter.

Scarlett's private room was incredible. It was more the way Tamsyn imagined a hotel room to be than a hospital room. Everything in here was clean and pretty. The floor was covered in white tiles, and the walls were a pale blue, like the sky on a spring day. Scarlett lay in a single bed with a pale blue blanket over her. The machinery that was keeping her alive was more subtle here, sleeker, but it was the same stuff as before. There were still tubes. Everything was monitored.

And there was Scarlett: she was still there, still hanging on. Tamsyn left Ed talking to Dr. Singh and ran over to sit beside her daughter and take her hand.

"Darling," she said. "Hello, my darling. It's Mum and Dad. We're here. We've missed you while you were traveling, but here we all are. In Switzerland."

When she looked up, Dr. Singh was looking at her with a little smile.

"Yes," she said, "I can see you know how to do this. Keep talking. There's every chance she can hear you."

Tamsyn looked up at the doctor and smiled. She carried on talking. "We're in Geneva. You traveled here on a special medical plane. Dad and I flew on a normal one, and here we all are with Dr. Singh, who you'll know by now. You won't believe what it's like when you wake up. You have a private room, and everything here is white and blue because Maya asked me your favorite color and I said blue. I hope that's all right. Your window has a view all the way to the mountains. It's absolutely gorgeous."

Ed sat on the other side. "And our new apartment is something quite incredible. Honestly, Scarlett. You're going to love it. It's everything you ever wanted. I'll tell you what: it's strange even sleeping in a building again, but I guess you're more used to that than I am by this point." His voice cracked.

They chatted away unselfconsciously, because they were used to it. Dr. Singh and Ed went out of the room to talk, but they didn't say Tamsyn had to go with them, so she stayed where she was and carried on telling Scarlett everything. She told her about the plane, the taxi to the apartment, the coffee machine, the roof terrace. She told her about everything in the apartment except for the pink room. They stayed for two hours and then, although they had never done this back in Cornwall, they prepared to leave the building together. Scarlett had round-the-clock care, and they needed to start to understand their strange new world.

▪▪▪▪▪

Maya and Luca sat them down on a patterned sofa before they left. They were in a room that smelled of an expensive scent, and they drank mint tea.

"I just wanted to run through the timings," said Luca, sipping his tea. He looked at home there in a way he hadn't in Truro. "Now that we have Scarlett, we're going absolutely full steam

ahead with the reanimation project. It will take at least a month.
Meanwhile you don't need to worry about anything. You're on the
system, authorized to visit anytime you like, twenty-four-seven.
Occasionally you may arrive and find she's not in her room, and
that's not a cause for alarm. We will need to move her from time
to time, both for her own stimulation treatments and for our reanimation work."

"Sure," said Ed.

Tamsyn's position on the reanimation was hardening. It had
been relatively easy to ignore it during the flurry of uprooting
their lives and heading into the unknown, and now that she was
here, she knew she had to continue that way. She would deal
with it when she absolutely had to and not a moment before. It
was one thing too many.

"Do you want me to go through the stages of the reanimation
process?" said Luca.

Tamsyn said, "No!" with all the force she had.

Ed took her hand. "I'd be interested," he said, "but Tamsyn's
going to deal with it a bit later in the process. That's OK, isn't it?"

"Of course it is!" said Maya. "It's completely fine. I'm sure I'd
do the same in your position."

In the end, Tamsyn kissed Ed good-bye and left him there to
talk it through.

▪ ▪ ▪ ▪ ▪

"You can use the map on your phone," said Maya. "Your address
is programmed in, as home, so you can easily find your way back.
If you want a ride anywhere at any point, just send me a message
and I'll get a car to you. Always keep your phone charged and on
you. The city is safe and you'll be fine. You can pay for anything
with your phone." She showed Tamsyn how. "You don't need
cash, but have some anyway, just in case." Maya gave her a purse

containing notes, coins, a little map of the city, a card for public transport and a map of the trams.

Tamsyn had to work to overcome her unease. The world was harsh, and things like this didn't happen. Everything was too easy. This new life was too luxurious. It was, she felt, too good to be true. She had to remind herself about the downsides. Scarlett and the robot. Those were heavy downsides. They would outweigh anything. All the same, Tamsyn was sure things were happening under the surface. She knew Ed and she weren't being told everything. She didn't entirely trust Luca Holgate.

She exited the building as quickly as she could. She had no idea why he wanted to engage with the cloning thing before he had to, but she was glad he did. He could listen to all that, and it meant she wouldn't have to.

. . . . .

Tamsyn had never known anything like this place. She had gone from Cornwall's lingering drizzle to Geneva's perfect spring. Even though she felt like an alien trying to blend in on a new planet, when she caught a glimpse of herself in a shopwindow, she was surprised to see someone who looked as if she was at home. She was wearing black jeans and a floral peasant blouse (which was, she supposed, ironic), because they were the first things she'd seen when she looked in her walk-in wardrobe this morning, and her hair was scraped back and tied in a ponytail because she needed to get it cut. Now she would be able to. Her shoes were ankle boots with a small heel, but she soon got used to walking in them. She was wearing a cream raincoat with a belt, but she hadn't done it up because it was too warm. The woman in the reflection blended with her surroundings. She didn't stand out at all.

Tamsyn looked normal. She had leaped from being a peasant

working in fields and living (though she had never applied the word to herself before) in poverty, to a woman who strolled around Geneva looking normal, a woman who wandered down to the shore of the lake and stared at the thing that wasn't so much a fountain as a violent jet of water that shot up much higher into the sky than seemed possible.

One day she would walk around these streets with Scarlett. They would stand by the lake and watch the jet and smell the water in the air and feel the sunshine and maybe sit in a café and drink hot chocolate, because Scarlett had loved hot chocolate.

She didn't think about the details. She made an effort not to remember that when Scarlett woke up, this new life would start to end. Wouldn't it? Surely Scarlett's getting better would be the finishing point, even though she had a bedroom in the apartment. Tamsyn certainly didn't think about the other girl, the interloper who was going to be with them in about a month.

A month was ages. It would be fine.

8

ED'S ALARM WENT OFF FOR HIS FIRST DAY AT WORK. IT WAS
the same sound as the one she used to use at home. It would go
off in the early hours when it was still dark, and she'd jump up,
dress and creep out to go to a job cleaning or picking fruit or
vegetables.

She rolled over in bed and reached in the dark for her husband, and he reached for her. They both slept naked, which they
hadn't done for fifteen years or so. She pushed her body up
against his. He pulled her in close and whispered in her ear, "I
set the alarm a bit early." His voice being so close to her ear made
the hairs stand up on her arms, made her whole body shiver.

▪▪▪▪▪

They had been in Geneva for five days, and Tamsyn felt she had,
unexpectedly, fallen in love with Ed all over again. Their relationship was new. She couldn't keep her hands off him, and he
couldn't keep his hands, or right now his fingers, off her. They
were obsessed with each other, taking all the comfort they could
from each other's bodies. She knew this new life was so weird

that no one could understand what she was going through but Ed, and it was the same for him. Life had flung them together and they were clinging to each other.

She loved that part of it. When Ed was holding her like that, when he was touching her, when he was inside her, she could put everything else aside. She was energized. It gave her all the strength she needed.

Afterward, Ed rushed around getting ready. She pulled on her kimono and made him a coffee and a poached egg for breakfast. She liked looking after him. He looked after her too.

The apartment was starting to feel like home.

"Can I come to your café?" she said as he started shoveling in his food.

"Of course you can!" He hesitated. "Tell you what. If I can find out in advance when I get a break, I'll text you. Then I can actually see you. I'd hate to know you were there and not be able to get out of the kitchen."

"Thank you."

They were so careful of each other's feelings now. It was an entirely different relationship. He kissed her on the lips and held her tight before he left. Then he was gone, and she was alone.

She wasn't allowed to visit Scarlett until after one because they were doing some treatments with her and she wouldn't be available.

Tamsyn shuddered at that. She didn't want to think about the treatments because she knew what it meant.

She pushed it away and imagined Ed arriving at work. They'd visited the café a couple of days ago. It was next to the lake. The water was still and flat, a different element from the salt water of the Atlantic at home. At home it splashed and roared and tossed boats around and threw spray at the road. The water in Geneva stayed where it was meant to be. The shores of the lake were tidy and beautiful, the lake still, reflecting the sky, the distant mountains. The café had been charming and friendly. Ed would be happy there, she was sure.

She winced as her head pulsed with a sharp pain.

Something is wrong.

The thought burst through, and she tried to push it away. Of course something was wrong. Scarlett was in a coma.

It's Ed.

It was not Ed. Ed was exactly where everything was right. She knew they'd been in a rocky place at home, but now they weren't. Now they were somewhere wonderful, getting through this together.

She went to the bathroom to find a painkiller. She probably wasn't drinking enough water.

■ ■ ■ ■ ■

The apartment was empty. Even though there were tiny cameras in every room (Maya had pointed them out), they weren't turned on yet because they were there to monitor . . . Tamsyn couldn't finish the thought. But she knew that no one was watching her at that moment.

She and Ed each had a laptop as part of their new surroundings. In their old lives, they had managed with secondhand phones and the weak signal that the site Wi-Fi offered. Tamsyn hadn't even known how to work her laptop at first. She was fine with it now. It was, as Maya had said, intuitive.

Ed hadn't taken his to work: of course he hadn't. It was beside the bed.

She hoped their new relationship wasn't too good to be true. She sat on the bed. They'd been here only a few days: there wouldn't even be anything on Ed's laptop, would there? So there would be no harm in looking.

It wanted his fingerprint to unlock it, but she clicked the button to use a password instead. She had watched him set it but he hadn't told her what it was, and she didn't know how many attempts the laptop would give her.

It would definitely contain the word *Scarlett*. Would it be her full name, Scarlett Sophie Trelawney? No. *ScarlettSophie* didn't work either. She tried variations on their daughter's name, walking away for fifteen minutes after every two attempts to make it look less like she was hacking. She worked out that the password had to be fifteen characters long because after fifteen characters it gave the option of pressing ENTER. After an hour and a quarter, she put Scarlett's first name and her own middle name and Scarlett's age, and *ScarlettHoney14* unlocked it.

He'd left the web page open on local Geneva news, and Tamsyn barely glanced at it. There was some financial stuff, a thing about a cyberattack, a thing about a fire with no casualties. News was less dramatic here than it was at home. She opened his e-mail. Nothing. She looked in the Sent folder.

And there it was. One single e-mail, and it was to Jimmy, his brother. Ed and Jimmy had never been close, and Jimmy hadn't even come to visit when Scarlett had had her accident. However, he clearly knew things Tamsyn didn't.

She read the e-mail.

Hey Jim,

We're here. It's trippy. Attaching a couple of pics of the apartment because I don't have the words. This is legitimately where we live.

It's going well with Tamsyn. Really well actually. I do feel weird. Guilty, but trying to get over it. Looking forward. Tamsyn and I are a team and I'm embracing this. She has no idea and is settling into the new life brilliantly.

Scarlett's care is ace. Her own room, a doctor who only has a couple of patients, lovely nursing staff. Everything we wanted, the reason we're here.

Keep in touch, Jim. Thanks for being there even though we don't always agree, right?

E

She felt sick.

Guilty, but trying to get over it.

She has no idea.

She slammed the laptop closed, then opened it again to make sure she was leaving it as she'd found it, with local news on the screen.

That instinct, the voice in her head, had been right. Here it was, written in words in front of her. He felt guilty, and she had no idea why.

He'd always worked late. There had been moments when she'd thought he might have been up to something, but she hadn't entertained the thoughts because she hadn't wanted to.

She knew he'd kept an overnight bag, packed, under their bed. She'd rationalized it away: there had always been more immediate things to worry about. The bag almost felt like a comfort after a while because he never took it anywhere, however difficult Scarlett became, however much Tamsyn herself lashed out. He was always poised, ready to leave, but he never did.

She ran over the e-mail in her head again and tried to convince herself it was nothing. That he was feeling guilty because of the way he used to shout at Scarlett. Tamsyn had that guilt all right. It had to be that, and even if it wasn't, it didn't matter anymore.

She put the laptop quickly away when someone knocked on the door. Anyone outside would have pressed the buzzer, and she would look at them on the screen before letting them in. This time, however, the knock came from right outside the front door. It was a real knock, knuckles on wood.

She closed the laptop and moved through the apartment.

"Hello?" she said quietly beside the door.

"Hi!" said a woman's voice so close that Tamsyn took a step back. "Sorry to disturb you. I'm Aurelie. I live downstairs. I just thought I'd call by and say hello! Don't worry, though. You don't have to let me in."

Her voice sounded happy, and she spoke lightly accented English.

Tamsyn opened the door at once. Aurelie from downstairs was, she thought, a bit older than she was, perhaps in her early fifties. She had long black hair and olive skin, and she was wearing a bright orange dress and sandals with jewels on them. She was carrying a bottle of champagne, and there were two stiff paper bags on the ground next to her, from designer shops. Tamsyn didn't know much about shops, but she knew those particular ones were expensive.

"Welcome to the building!" Aurelie said. "It's nice to have people up here again." She handed Tamsyn the champagne and picked up the bags and brought them in. "The booze is from me. These were just outside your door. A present from someone, but nothing to do with me, I'm afraid."

Tamsyn felt herself smiling. "Come in," she said. She looked at the bottle in her hand. "Shall we have a glass of this?"

She looked into the bags. One had a silky dress in it, the other a shoebox. She put them in her bedroom to look at later. They would be from Maya, who often left Ed and Tamsyn gifts.

Aurelie asked polite questions about the family. Tamsyn managed to sidestep the questions of how many children she had and where they were, and asked everything she could think of about Aurelie's life instead, and the conversation flowed away from the difficult things.

The champagne made her dizzy. And just like that, she had a friend.

Two hours later when Aurelie left, Tamsyn went back to the computer to look at the e-mail again. Even though nobody had been anywhere near the laptop the whole time, the message had disappeared.

She was sure she had seen it. She could remember what it said. And yet it wasn't there. It wasn't in the deleted folder. It had gone. She should have taken a photograph of it, but she hadn't.

The only person who had been in the apartment was Aurelie, and she hadn't been anywhere near the bedroom. It had been there, and now it wasn't. Tamsyn shook her head and decided she would put the e-mail from her mind. She wouldn't think about it again.

She tried on her new dress and shoes instead, and marveled at the glamorous woman in the mirror, turning from side to side, picturing herself on a red carpet.

Thank you so much for the gifts, she wrote to Maya. **They're amazing. I don't feel like myself at all.**

You're welcome! Maya replied. **And get used to it. This is who you are now.**

9

One month later

SHE HADN'T WANTED THIS DAY TO ARRIVE, BUT HERE IT WAS. Yesterday Ed had taken her hand and looked into her eyes and told her that she had to face it. It was time. The reanimation was ready, and they had to live with it because that was the whole deal.

It wasn't going to be just the two of them anymore. She and Ed were still grabbing each other at every opportunity, still talking to each other late into the night, staring at each other with wonder and love (and she was sure he was as sincere as she was: he wouldn't have been able to fake it). But now they were going to have someone else living with them. A cyborg disguised as their daughter.

People had been to the apartment to check the electronics because everything was going to be monitored remotely. She had gone into the pink bedroom for long enough to see that it was still there and fully equipped, and had backed out crying. So many things had arrived over the past couple of days: new clothes and shoes, gadgets and jewelry. Everything a teenage girl could possibly want or need. It was almost too much.

They were going to the clinic to pick up a daughter, but it was the wrong one. It wasn't a daughter at all. It was a monster.

Not a monster. A *reanimation*.

A monster, though.

Ed was holding the elevator door for her. The car was downstairs. Her heart was pounding. He put an arm around her shoulders and she leaned into him as the lift doors closed.

"Oh, my God," she said. "I don't think I can."

"Hey," said Ed. He kissed the top of her head. "It's not going to be easy, but, darling—we have to. They know what they're doing. Try to look at it like this: they've made something that comes from Scarlett. Whatever she's like—your three-D printout or an actual girl—she is part of Scarlett. But yeah, I'm shitting myself. It doesn't get easier, however much you rationalize it."

He opened the car door and she got in.

"Hello there!"

"Maya!" Tamsyn said, looking at the driver. "Oh. I didn't know you were picking us up. How are you? Are you here so I don't run away?"

Maya looked over her shoulder and raised her eyebrows. "Did you not read the e-mails? I'm fine. Thanks. You two are looking amazing, might I say. Quite the *Genevois*."

"Thanks."

"Sorry," said Ed, getting in next to Tamsyn. "You know that Tam doesn't read any of it. I've stayed on top of it all, though. Good to see you. Thanks for coming to collect us. It's nice to have a familiar face. You, I mean. Not . . . Yeah."

"I'm so excited," Maya said, indicating and pulling out. "Honestly, please don't worry. I've seen her and she's remarkable. One of the biggest successes this project has ever had. There's nothing for you to worry about. I know it's easy for me to say that, but please believe me. You don't need to be dreading this. You'll look back and wonder why you did."

Tamsyn tuned out. It was indeed easy for Maya to say that kind of thing.

There was no traffic on the route to the clinic. For once, Tamsyn wished there was. She wanted this to be so slow that they never actually got there. She asked Maya to put the radio on, because she was desperate for some outside-world distraction. Maya put on a radio station playing Europop. Maya started humming along. She was, Tamsyn thought, in an extremely good mood.

The news came on, and even the headlines about distant war and climate catastrophe soothed Tamsyn because it was the way her world had always been. She understood it well enough in French, which surprised her: she had started going to French conversation classes and was picking it up just fine. It clicked in her brain: she had known some French long ago and it was rushing back. At the end of the bulletin was a story about a series of fires in Geneva, and Tamsyn was interested because Geneva still seemed to her like a place in which nothing as elemental as that could ever happen. She opened her mouth to ask Maya, but Maya, looking at her in the rearview mirror, spoke first.

"Even Switzerland's not totally law-abiding," she said. "In fact you'd be surprised at some of the things that go on. Anyway, look. We're here."

█ █ █ █ █

They let Tamsyn visit the real Scarlett first. She had been there every day and knew what to do, from the hand sanitizing to looking at the camera in the right way so the door would open without her slowing her pace. She did it mechanically, and soon she was in Scarlett's blue room, holding her hand and looking at her perfect face.

She wasn't sure if she was imagining it, but she felt that Scarlett was closer to the surface these days. Her face sometimes flickered. Tamsyn knew she wasn't allowed to talk to Scarlett about the reanimation, because she could be listening to and understanding everything and it would shock her too much.

"Darling," she said, "I love you so much. I love *you*. You're my baby. My girl. My baby girl. Get better soon. We have lots of plans. Dad's job's going well, and I'm quite good at French. We're not going back, darling. We live in Geneva now. That old life is done and we're never going to live in a caravan again. We have a new life and you're going to love it." She hoped all that was true.

She stayed so long, telling Scarlett about International School and learning French, that Maya had to come to collect her.

Maya was bouncing as she walked, grinning and humming.

"It's time," she said, pushing her hair behind her ear. "Honestly, Tamsyn. I've just been with her, and I know you don't believe this yet but you're going to love her. Absolutely adore her. You do remember that she won't know exactly what she is? She'll think she's had an accident and woken up."

Tamsyn nodded, looking at the sunlight on the white wall. *This,* she thought, *might be the worst part of it.* The cyborg was going to think she was actually Scarlett, and Tamsyn wasn't allowed to tell her she wasn't. It bubbled inside her, toxic and horrible.

"She's not properly conscious yet," Maya was saying. "We're going to bring her to consciousness just before she meets you."

Tamsyn knew that this raised a thousand questions but she pushed them down. She didn't care.

. . . . .

Maya sat her next to Ed in the room where they'd had that mint tea a month ago, when Tamsyn had run off rather than listen to the details. She'd had a good month ignoring it all, visiting Scarlett, kissing Ed, learning French and yoga and meeting up with Aurelie, but she hadn't been able to make it go away.

She thought about the fact that the cyborg wasn't conscious yet. Neither was Scarlett. Maybe the new one would wake up as a rogue robot and they'd have to get rid of it. It could still go wrong. It still might not happen. She might get another month while they made a better one. Then another and another.

Tamsyn's heart pounded and she could feel blood racing around every vein. The blue chair in Scarlett's room folded out into a bed. She could just live here with her and Dr. Singh and never see the thing at all, not even once.

She started to stand up. Ed pulled her back down.

As well as Maya and Luca, the wonderful Dr. Singh was there, plus a collection of familiar faces and a man Tamsyn didn't think she had met before. That man seemed to be in charge. He had longish thick hair that was so black it was almost blue. He introduced himself as Johann. She instinctively disliked him.

"Tamsyn and Ed, thank you so much for being here," Johann said from the vantage point of sitting on the table and thus being higher than everyone else. "Thank you for trusting us with your wonderful daughter. We've worked intensely on this for the past month and we're extremely excited about the result. As you know, we've been working on the hybrid project for several years now, and I have to say I think Scarlett is our triumph."

"Hybrid?" Tamsyn looked at Maya. She'd forgotten that it was called a hybrid, like a car.

"Tamsyn's struggled to focus on the detail," Maya said to Johann, "which is understandable." She turned back to Tamsyn. "You remember. The reanimation project uses a hybrid of AI and human duplication. So while Scarlett's been here, we've used her DNA to—well, essentially to furnish the body of the reanimation, but the brain is augmented with artificial intelligence." She threw a look to Johann and Luca.

"Right," said Johann. "Should I go over the rest of the basics?" Maya nodded, so he continued. "We'll be monitoring her intensely, Tamsyn. Any problems, look into any of the cameras and ask for help and someone will be right there. And you must make sure that she doesn't, under any circumstances, go into France. The French border is very close to Geneva, and it's easy to cross it. For legal reasons, your new daughter absolutely cannot do that. She is programmed not to want to go there, but she might do it by mistake and you have to stop her. Understood?"

Tamsyn sighed and gave a little nod. It had never occurred to her that they could leave the city. Why would they when Scarlett was here? As far as she was concerned, it would be pretty easy not to go to France.

"She's programmed to complete and protect the family. And remember not to tell her about Scarlett until she works it out herself. That's crucial for her sense of self. Finally, she needs a name now. We'd normally expect to do it before this moment, but as you said, Ed, it's Tamsyn's decision really and she hasn't been in a place to consider it."

Ed put a hand on Tamsyn's thigh. It was the only comforting thing in her world, and she turned to him.

"What do you think?" he said, his voice gentle. "What shall we call her?"

Tamsyn shook her head. She couldn't do this.

"What have you been calling her?" Ed said. "While you worked on her?"

"Crimson," said Maya, and then flushed. "Project Crimson. Sorry. Was I not meant to . . ."

"That's fine," said Tamsyn. "We can call it Crimson."

"No, we can't," said Ed. "Tam. No one's called that. She needs a real name. Let's call her Sophie, Scarlett's middle name. Sophie."

Tamsyn shrugged. "If this is Sophie, then it's not Scarlett's middle name anymore."

Ed nodded. The medical people looked at one another, and Johann left the room.

While he was gone, the atmosphere was electric. Tamsyn could feel the charged electrons zipping around the place. Johann took longer than she had expected, and she thought that perhaps something had gone wrong. Maybe the robot didn't want to meet her either and had run away or broken itself. But then there were footsteps outside in the corridor.

Tamsyn looked up.

10

"AND . . . YOU'RE HERE. HELLO, SOPHIE."

I open my eyes.

Everything flows into me.

I'm in a room that smells of clean things and machines. I'm standing up. That's weird. How can I wake standing up? It's a small room with three computers and some chairs. I sit on one.

The walls are dark blue and the windows are high, so I can't see what's outside. Everything appears like the sun rising. How did I get here?

"Where am I?" I look at the man. Longish slick hair, fifty-one years old. Should I be scared of him? How do I know he's fifty-one? I look down at myself. Jeans, a sweatshirt, blue Converse trainers. These aren't my usual clothes but I like them.

As I think about it, things come into focus. I live in a place with mud and rain, flowers and the ocean. What am I doing here?

My name is Scarlett Sophie, but he said *Sophie*.

"You had an accident, Sophie," says the man, looking at me with greedy eyes. "Don't worry. We've rebuilt you. I'm Johann.

You're better now, and your parents are here. Tamsyn and Ed. So let's go and see them, shall we? Then we can explain it all to you."

My parents. Tamsyn and Ed.

Pictures come into my mind. I need to see them. They didn't like me. But I think they loved me. They are the people I need.

I wasn't a good daughter. Now the only thing I want is to be the best daughter in the world. I feel my face smiling. I feel my eyes wanting to cry.

I follow him out of the room. I know that I had an accident, but I seem to be good at walking. Nothing hurts. Whatever they did to fix me has worked.

"They're just up here," he says. "Let's see how you get on with the stairs."

I don't like him. I take the stairs two, then three at a time, just to show him. I wait at the top, and he puts a hand on my arm, laughing. I pull away.

"Good girl," he says. "They're going to be so happy to see you, Sophie. It's just in here." He stands back. "After you."

11

IT WASN'T A SIMULATION OF SCARLETT OR A *REANIMATION* or a robot or a clone or a monster. It was Scarlett. This was Tamsyn's daughter, upright, healthy, smiling an uncertain smile at them. She had Scarlett's wild hair, though it was styled in an expensive way that had never happened before, just brushing her shoulders. She wore skinny jeans and a sweatshirt, like Scarlett on a casual day, and blue trainers that Scarlett would have loved.

It was everything Tamsyn had been dreaming of, because this was Scarlett walking toward them, looking happy and relieved. She felt all her wishes coming true in real time. If she hadn't just been sitting beside the real, unconscious Scarlett, she would never have believed that this wasn't her, miraculously recovered.

That girl walked into the room with Scarlett's walk. She gave Tamsyn and Ed a smile that they hadn't seen since a year before the accident. It was a wide smile that showed her perfect teeth. Her teeth were better than they used to be because they had been fixed by Swiss doctors. *Made* by Swiss doctors.

Tamsyn couldn't stop staring. Ed, however, walked right up

to her and hugged her tight. Tamsyn looked at her husband burying his face in Scarlett's hair.

This was everything she had needed all along. They had made Scarlett better and there she was, and Ed was getting the first hug. Tamsyn stood up and took a few steps. Her vision was a bit blurry, and she blinked the tears away.

Ed stepped back and held an arm out to her, and she walked into the hug with one arm around her husband and the other hanging on as tightly as she possibly could to her incredible re-animated daughter. She was supposed to call her Sophie, but in fact, this was Scarlett. Every single part of her was Scarlett. She even smelled like Scarlett.

Scarlett was back.

And Scarlett was unresponsive in her bed. She was in two places at once.

▪ ▪ ▪ ▪ ▪

In the end they had to step away from one another and engage again with everyone else in the room, though when Tamsyn looked, she saw they were all looking on with expressions of tearful delight and (in Johann's case) smug self-congratulation. No one wanted them to hurry up and get on with anything.

Now that this was actually Scarlett, they needed to get her home. Tamsyn wanted to show her the apartment, her four-poster bed, her view across this city. She needed to show her Geneva, the lake, the mountains. Everything.

She was a mother again. She was going to do it properly this time.

"Wow," said Maya when Tamsyn smiled at her. "That was the most incredible thing I've ever seen."

"Beyond our dreams," said Johann. "Sophie, how are you feeling?"

Everyone looked at Scarlett. Sophie. Tamsyn reminded herself that they had to call her Sophie now. That was OK. It was her middle name after all. She was glad Ed had overruled her when she'd said Crimson. People often decided to be called by their middle names.

Sophie didn't speak for a while and a slow dread swept through Tamsyn. Maybe she wouldn't be able to talk at all. Perhaps she would have a robot voice. She might say something that made no sense, something that brought the whole thing crashing down.

"I'm feeling great," said Sophie. "What happened to me? How did you fix it?"

It was almost Scarlett's voice, but with a slight accent. Tamsyn thought the accent sounded a bit American, but then she realized it was the accent Johann had. It was the voice of someone who spoke fluent English, but not as their first language, and who had learned it from someone American.

It wasn't Scarlett's voice.

Johann read her expression.

"She's picked up the accents of the team who have been talking to her over the past few weeks," he said. "Before she was conscious, she was functioning but on an immediate level. Like a baby, in a way: interacting but without being aware of it or remembering. Consciousness is different, and we always leave that until everything else is in place. Sophie and I have been interacting intensely, though she won't remember it, and so she's taken on traces of my accent. Don't worry. It'll take her about a week of living with you, and then she'll be speaking like an English girl."

He turned to Sophie, who was looking characteristically annoyed at being sidelined.

"Sorry," he said. "You were in a road accident. We used the latest technology to fix you. And look! You're perfect."

She stretched her legs, touched her face, looked around.

"The latest technology involves me talking without being conscious?"

Johann nodded.

"Right. Weird. So where even are we?" She looked at the room, her eyes bright.

Tamsyn watched her gaze go to the window. The view was urban, without mountains or lake, but it was visibly not Cornwall.

"Switzerland," said Ed.

"Geneva," said Tamsyn.

"What? No way!" Sophie laughed. "I thought it must be London. Seriously? *Switzerland*? Is this a hospital?"

"It's a private clinic, darling," said Ed. "But we can take you home. To our new apartment. If you'd like that?"

"Yeah," said Sophie. "Sure. Of course I would. But first I want to know what's happened. Like, what day is it? How did I get here? What have you done to me, because I feel amazing? Not like someone who's had a road accident. Like someone incredible. Wow."

Johann and Maya explained to Sophie about the AI in her brain, and Tamsyn watched her nodding, taking it all in. They didn't mention the cloning part or Scarlett. Ed stood next to her and put an arm around her shoulders and together they watched their daughter making sense of her new world. Tamsyn was overwhelmed by love.

■ ■ ■ ■ ■

As Sophie learned about her brain interface, Dr. Singh took Tamsyn out into the corridor, and then into another room. She closed the door and turned to face her. Though she'd looked happy enough, Dr. Singh had been the only one who wasn't jubilant. The others looked as though they would be high-fiving like people in the control room when a mission landed on the moon the moment they were alone.

Tamsyn loved Dr. Singh. She loved her serious manner, her quiet reassurance. She was in her forties, and the exact same height as Tamsyn, and she always wore a lovely floral perfume. They looked directly into each other's eyes. She trusted Dr. Singh with Scarlett's care.

"Before you go," said Dr. Singh, "and apologies if this comes across as patronizing in any way, because I don't mean it to be— it's important that you bear in mind that, while Sophie is an incredible achievement, she is not actually Scarlett. You saw Scarlett earlier this morning, and she's still there. Her GCS is improving, and while that doesn't offer any guarantees, it means something. The girl grilling Johann and Maya in there *isn't* your daughter in the same way Scarlett is. I know Sophie couldn't exist without Scarlett, and I know that she's remarkable, and having overseen Scarlett's care for five weeks, I'm also emotional at the sight of someone who appears to be her up and about and walking and talking. But it is important that you remember that Scarlett is here in her bed while Sophie was produced by technology."

Tamsyn nodded. She knew Dr. Singh was right, that it was going to be difficult to remember that fact. She also knew that if the original Scarlett woke up, Sophie might leave. However, she couldn't focus on any of that right now. She looked at the door, desperate to get back to the miracle girl.

"Yes," she said, "you're right. I will remember."

Dr. Singh looked as if she wanted to say something else. She started and then hesitated.

"What?" said Tamsyn. She was desperate to get back to life as a family of three. "It's OK. You can say it."

"Just . . . don't forget to come and visit Scarlett. You know that there's a chance she can hear you. It's important for her recovery that she hears your voice on a regular basis."

"Of course," said Tamsyn.

"Until you saw Sophie, you were against the idea of her," Dr. Singh said, and Tamsyn bristled. She didn't need to be reminded of that. "You joined this project for practical reasons, for Scarlett's care. All that's changed is that the reanimation is better than you expected it to be. Her. Better than you expected *her* to be. It's always a surprise," she added. "The results they're getting these days are remarkable."

"I won't forget Scarlett," said Tamsyn. "I mean, she's my daughter. Of course I won't!"

The doctor raised her hands. "Apologies. I'm sorry. Just— well, just know that we continue to do everything we can to care for Scarlett. And that we are here for both your daughters and your entire family. I hope that Sophie brings you happiness. I'll let you get back to her."

■ ■ ■ ■ ■

They went home in the car, Ed in the front but turning around to look at Sophie the whole time, and Tamsyn next to her, holding her hand. Her hand was warm. It felt like Scarlett's hand. Tamsyn wished she had read all the information because she wasn't sure if Sophie's hand was made from human flesh or not.

It had to be, didn't it? That was what cloning meant. Did it matter, though? If you asked her what her own hand was made from, she'd only be able to say things like *atoms* and *maybe carbon?* and *humans are mostly water.* Sophie's hand was atoms too and maybe carbon and water. That was fine. They were the same. It was all Tamsyn needed.

She watched Sophie looking out the window.

"Geneva," Sophie said under her breath. "Trippy."

"It's an amazing city," said Tamsyn. "I can't wait to show you everything. Look—that's the lake over there. You see the water? That's the fountain. It's massive. It's called the Jet d'Eau. Jet of water."

They both stared at the huge water jet that shot high into the sky from the city all day long.

Sophie nodded. "Yes," she said. "I can see why."

Tamsyn didn't care about fountains; she just wanted to look at Sophie. Sophie turned to her and they stared into each other's eyes and smiled at the same moment.

This, she thought. *This should be the thing that made Sophie not-Scarlett.* A replica of her daughter wouldn't have had Scarlett behind the eyes, but this one did. It wasn't the difficult Scarlett either. It wasn't the one who hated her parents. It wasn't the Scarlett who had run away from home in the middle of the night and been hit with a thud and a screech by a car that drove away.

Tamsyn gasped and tried to hide it. She hadn't allowed herself to think back to that night for a long time, because it led to such depths that if she let herself sink, she'd never have come back up. She had found that if she pushed it out of her mind whenever it attempted to come in, she could get by, and she hadn't even tried to remember the moment of the accident itself. She could remember running out of the caravan and then being at the hospital. She would never allow herself to go back to the things in between.

It had been the worst night of her life and it always would be, but it was in the past. It had not, in fact, led to irreversible disaster because, in the strangest of ways, she had her daughter back and a new life. It had taken them down a new path.

The Scarlett in Sophie's eyes was young Scarlett, little Scarlett. This was the serious girl—the bright one, the bookish one, the one who loved her parents—grown up. It was the Scarlett in the old photo. She had come through her difficult stage, and there she was, on the other side. The accident had pulled her through the moodiness and she was perfect in every way. Although Tamsyn knew she wasn't the real Scarlett, she also felt she *was* the real Scarlett in a more profound way than anything else, and that made the fact that she was in a new body irrelevant.

Tamsyn kept pointing things out as they drove back to the apartment, and then they were getting out of the car and the spring air was on her face, with the smell of the roses that were growing on a first-floor balcony. She felt the weight of Ed's arm on her shoulder and turned.

"Wow," he said. "You literally look like a different person."

"I feel like one," she said, and she realized it was true. "I really do. I've got everything."

"Me too," he said. "I knew what we were supposed to expect, but all the same, I never dared imagine this."

Sophie was looking from Tamsyn to Ed and back again.

"Am I brilliant?" she said. "Am I doing better than you thought? Did you think I might not be able to walk?"

"Yes. All of that, I guess," said Ed, and Sophie nodded, pleased.

"Do we live in here?" She looked up. It was an old apartment block, red and white brick, with wrought iron balconies and flowers in window boxes. There was a black cat on a balcony about halfway up. Black cats used to mean good luck, Tamsyn was sure, and she thanked it for its presence.

"Yes," said Ed, "this is us. We're on the top floor. It's a long way from where we used to live, right?"

Sophie didn't answer.

"Do you remember the caravan?" Tamsyn asked.

"Yeah," she said. "Of course. There were two nice women in a purple van."

"Maud and Ally," said Tamsyn. "Yes! They looked after you quite often when you were younger. Ally died about a year ago, but Maud's still there." She tried to remember when she'd last heard from Maud. "I think she is, anyway."

"Ally died? That's sad." Sophie screwed her face up. "I remember school. My friend Leanne? I remember reading books. I think my memories are from a few years ago. I don't think I have anything recent. It's all a bit foggy."

Tamsyn and Ed exchanged a look. Scarlett's difficult year had been cut out and thrown away.

They went up in the lift, the three of them standing close together. Just before the doors opened on the top floor, Tamsyn put her arm around Sophie's shoulder and pulled her close. She buried her face in her daughter's hair and inhaled. She was the luckiest woman in the history of the world, the only one who had lost her child and then been given her back.

12

TAMSYN HAD BECOME USED TO THEIR LUXURY APARTMENT. She realized how monstrous that was when she saw it through the eyes of a girl who remembered growing up in poverty.

"I know you said it was going to be nice but . . . is this seriously our home? All this? Just us and no one else?"

"It is," said Ed. "It's incredible, isn't it?"

They stood in the hall and looked at the polished parquet, the huge windows, the magic luxury of it all. It had been a haven for Tamsyn and Ed for the past five weeks, and now it was a family home.

"And it's because of me?" said Sophie. "The people at the clinic gave us this home because of my accident?"

"Yes," he said, "we live here because of you. And we're going to be very happy here now we've got you with us."

She looked into the corners. "Those are the cameras, right, so they can see how I get on with my fabulous new brain?" She blinked a few times. "This is weird. The whole thing is weird. But hey, I can live with it. I mean, it's not forever, right? The cameras, I mean."

"That's right," said Ed. "The cameras aren't forever. But we're not going back to Cornwall. That part's forever. Whatever it takes, we'll find a way to stay here."

"This apartment?"

He smiled. "They'll probably downsize us at some point."

Sophie turned to Tamsyn. "Can I see my room?"

Maybe, Tamsyn thought, Sophie should have had the blue room, which she had locked. It was the nicer of the two, not just because it wasn't pink but because its view was greener and prettier. Sophie would probably prefer the blue sheets. In a way it all belonged to her anyway.

Tamsyn remembered Dr. Singh telling her not to forget Scarlett in the clinic, and stopped herself just in time.

"You're in here," she said, and she pushed the door of the pink room and ushered Sophie in. Tamsyn had no idea whether the drawers and wardrobe were stocked with the same clothes as the ones in the other room, but she thought they probably were.

"Oh, my goodness," said Sophie. "Look at it!"

She ran to the window and looked out. She crouched and ran her fingertips over the soft carpet. She sat on the bed and bounced a bit, then lay back and looked up at the gauzy drapes.

"Isn't it wonderful?" Tamsyn hesitated. "Are you tired?"

"No," said Sophie. "I'm not tired at all. But I wouldn't mind a bit of time in here just to get used to it all. It's a lot to take in. I mean, I just woke up in a new world. It feels like a dream. Like I haven't actually woken up at all." She looked around. "All this stuff! Where did it come from?"

"They deliver gifts all the time. Honestly, it's surreal. So I'll leave you to it. I guess it's lunchtime. I'll make some lunch and we can answer all your questions. Do you . . . do you feel like eating the same sort of food as before . . . ?"

What a stupid question! She knew all the information about this was in the documents that she had refused to read.

Sophie turned and smiled at her. "Of course," she said. "I'd love some lunch actually. Thanks. Anything at all."

"Do you mind," Tamsyn said, "if I give you another hug?"

"Of course I don't mind," said Sophie. "You're my mother. You can hug me all you want. Actually, it's your job. So you'd better do it lots."

▪ ▪ ▪ ▪ ▪

Sophie was the best thing in the world, the most amazing thing that had ever happened, and it was important that she knew that.

Tamsyn was only a little bit disquieted. She pictured Scarlett, in her bed at the clinic, gray complexioned and incapable of anything. Then she would think of Sophie, bright and alive, hanging out in her room. It didn't feel possible that there were two versions of the same girl.

Tamsyn made a salad and set the table on the terrace with a baguette, butter, several types of cheese, sparkling water and a bottle of rosé for herself and Ed because this was surely a thing that was worth celebrating with a drink. Ed was pacing around the flat and she intercepted him the next time he came past.

"Ed?" she said.

She looked up into his face and saw that he still loved her. She loved him even more than before.

"Darling." He kissed her, then stepped back, grinning.

"Did you imagine her being like this? So completely—" She couldn't think of the word so just let it hang.

"I hoped for it," he said. "I knew they *said* she would be wonderful, but you can't know, can you, until you see it? I get the impression that they never know quite how something's going to work until it's in front of them. It's a big tech company working with all kinds of shady partners right on the edge of what's legal. Talking themselves up is part of what they do. I did know that she wasn't going to be the *I am a robot* thing you were imagining. Or the three-D printout or any of that."

"Where's the information?" Tamsyn said.

"You have to log in on the iPad," he said. "I'll get it up for you. Have a read and I'll come and get you when Sophie's ready for lunch."

- - - - -

Tamsyn lay on the bed on her stomach, propped up on her elbows, feet in the air, and started to read. The moment she started, she couldn't believe she hadn't looked at this before. She had ignored it all at every turn, knowing that Ed had her back. Why, though? Why had she been so horrified by the idea of knowing anything about Sophie?

Engaging with the information had felt like a betrayal of Scarlett. If she had actually read it, however, she would have known that Sophie absolutely was a reanimation of Scarlett. She *was* Scarlett. A DNA test would confirm it. Unlike identical twins, they even had the same fingerprints. Tamsyn was gripped by every word.

Sophie's body had been grown quickly from Scarlett's tissue, so she was made from Scarlett. Her brain was a human-AI interface, so she was technically a cyborg, but that didn't feel sinister because the human part was one hundred percent Scarlett. It felt brilliant, amazing, the beginning of a new era for the human race. The Singularity.

The interface was why they had said the word *hybrid* so many times. Scarlett's brain didn't do much at the moment, but Sophie's brain did everything in a way that regular human brains couldn't. She had Scarlett's original brain, more or less, but with help.

She had superpowers.

The reanimation will speak English and French fluently, she read, and she wondered why they had left it at that. Why not let Sophie speak Spanish and Japanese and German and Russian too? Why not every language?

Because that wouldn't have been Scarlett. Scarlett spoke English and she spoke schoolgirl French. This version of her lived in a French-speaking area of Switzerland and so her life would be easier if her French was fluent. Tamsyn wondered whether they would be able to add, say, Japanese if Sophie wanted to go and live in Japan one day.

She felt how far the horizons of her world had expanded.

She will have Scarlett's memories, but after our consultations with Mr. Trelawney, we are aiming to cut the memories off at around the age of twelve. Her personality will be made from a mixture of the organic personality that comes from Scarlett's brain combined with programming. She will be eager to please, eager to learn, friendly, intelligent and loving, with a predisposition to eating for pleasure and health and to exercising regularly and good hygiene. She will be devoted to her family.

Tamsyn refused to allow her mind to travel to the way Scarlett had been in the year before the accident, when none of those attributes had applied. She was also sure not to think about the vanishing e-mail she was almost certain she had read.

Ed's laptop was nearby. She could look again.

None of that mattered now. She had to look forward, not back.

·····

She was briefly horrified to discover, deep in the information about how the team monitored Sophie's progress, the phrase "and through the cameras implanted on the retinas."

They were looking out through Sophie's eyes! That made her feel weird, for herself and for Sophie, who had no privacy at all. She felt a surge of protectiveness for this girl who hadn't consented to any of this, who had, as far as she knew, had an accident and been rebuilt. Didn't she have to agree to cameras in her eyes? No, because she was fourteen. Tamsyn and Ed had consented for her. Ed had done it.

Tamsyn didn't feel any less love for Sophie now that she knew her sunny disposition was implanted electronically. That was hardly Sophie's fault. If anything it made her love Sophie more. Tamsyn stared at the iPad with tears in her eyes. Poor gorgeous Sophie.

The door opened, and Ed poked his head around it.

"Fancy some lunch, then, darling?" he said. "She's ready."

13

TAMSYN, ED AND SOPHIE WERE WALKING THROUGH A PARK beside the lake in the center of the city. It was a sunny day and there were a few wispy clouds in the sky. Sophie kept stopping and looking around. She looked at the water, the clean pathway, the woman walking past with a dog in a pram, the boats on the water. They had just walked past a clock made of flowers. A young man in tartan trousers smiled as he walked past them. An old man was talking in a furious whisper on his phone.

"I don't think it's real," she said, stopping. "I can't get my head around the fact that this is where I am. Am I lying in a hospital bed? Is this something I'm creating to entertain myself? I mean, one thing I know about myself is that I live in a caravan. And I'm sorry, but no medical trial would do this."

Tamsyn put an arm around her. Sophie didn't flinch. She didn't pull away. She leaned in and rested her head on Tamsyn and Tamsyn held her as tightly as she could, her fingertips on Sophie's bare shoulder. Scarlett hadn't allowed her to do anything like that for ages.

"It's real," she told her daughter quietly. "Geneva. Our home.

We used to live in a caravan and now we live here. It's actually happening." She paused. "Or if it's not, then we're hallucinating it together. And this is some big technology they're trialing. It's in their interests to treat us well."

Sophie was breathing heavily. "Why, though?" she said. "Why would they do that? Why would they put in all this tech just to make me better? Lots of people have accidents. It happens all the time. Why me?"

"It was your type of injury," said Ed quickly. "We were lucky in a horrible way. They were looking for people like you. We came here. They repaired your brain and your body. It worked. We've had to give up our privacy for a while, but look what we've got in return."

"I should be dead." Sophie looked round. "And I'm not. I'm here. Powered by tech. What happened in my accident?"

This had come up several times. Tamsyn and Ed had agreed on their answer, so Tamsyn stepped in.

"You were walking on the side of the road, doing nothing wrong, and a car hit you and drove off."

Sophie nodded and they kept walking. The sun was warm but not too hot. The water sparkled. The gardens were perfectly tended. They walked in silence.

"I mean, who makes a clock out of flowers?" Sophie said.

She caught Tamsyn's eye and they both laughed. Sophie was wearing a vest top and a pair of shorts, and she looked healthy. Alive. Full of vitality. Tamsyn never wanted to look at anything else.

"People with civic pride, I guess," said Ed. "And people who can afford to keep it all working."

"Geneva's on the French border," Sophie said. "That makes me feel weird. I want to be here, not France."

Ed smiled at Tamsyn. "That's absolutely fine by us."

Tamsyn had never been this happy. Even though Scarlett was still sick, she had her daughter back. It was magical.

"Drink?" said Ed, and they walked through the park until they came to a café on the water's edge.

Sophie looked dubious.

"It's going to be expensive, though," she said. "I mean, right on the lake."

"See that one over there?" Ed pointed across the water. "That's the Venezia, where I work. It's expensive there too but it's fine. It doesn't matter anymore, Soph. It really doesn't. We have enough money. They tried out their treatment on you, and it worked, and we get a new life because of it. They're happy to throw money at us because you're their success story, and they're going to make that money back tenfold."

Sophie shook her head. "This is so trippy."

"It's our life now," said Tamsyn. "I promise."

"What don't I know?"

Tamsyn couldn't answer. Ed, seeing that, stepped in.

"Nothing. This is it."

A huge grin spread across Sophie's face, and she took both her parents' hands and led them over to the café, where she ordered their drinks in perfect French.

14

SOPHIE MADE THEIR LIVES COMPLETE, BUT THREE WEEKS later, she started school. This was, as far as Tamsyn was concerned, a terrifying thing that had happened too fast.

She sat on the terrace with Maya. The sun was strong, and she was wearing a straw hat to keep it out of her eyes.

"Can't you implant everything she needs to know into her brain?" she asked. "I mean, why put her through this? All her trouble started when she was away from us the first time round. It was people she met at school. The wrong crowd. You have no idea how quickly that can spiral. I can't have that happening again. She'd be safer if she was with me. We could do home education. She can teach herself everything, and she probably knows more than we do anyway."

"Tamsyn," Maya said.

She touched the other woman's arm in that gentle way she did, which actually meant she was being steely. Tamsyn angled her hat to shade more of her face because she didn't want Maya looking at her.

"She needs to go to school. It's part of the process. It's not necessarily about education, though she needs to learn critical thinking and other skills. It's about socialization. Remember, no one at her school is going to know that she's a hybrid. She'll be a regular new girl, and we will be watching closely from a number of different perspectives to see how she fits in. This is important."

That brought Tamsyn up short. "How will you be watching?" She gestured to her own eyes. "Through Sophie, I know, but how do you get *a number of perspectives* from that?"

"We have cameras around the school," Maya said casually. "The school principal and a couple of other people there are on board with us, and the project has made a generous donation to thank them for their participation. So we've been able to put unobtrusive cameras around the building. And as you say, we have Sophie's own feed."

Tamsyn didn't like to think about Sophie's *feed*. She was able to get on with family life only by pretending it wasn't there.

"Also," said Maya, "she *wants* to go to school, Tamsyn, so can you let yourself be led by that if nothing else? Her integration into family life with you and Ed has been a spectacular success. Seeing how you bonded with her was a key part of the project, and your first meeting with her was the most amazing thing I've ever seen. Now she needs friends. She *wants* friends, Tamsyn. She has to have them if she's going to grow up in today's world. It won't be like it was before, I promise."

Tamsyn leaned back in her chair. The sun was warmer than it had ever been in Cornwall. She knew Maya was right. Sophie needed to go to school. It wasn't school as an educational institution that had caused Scarlett's problems. It was the people she'd met there, and then, beyond that, the people she had met through them. A few older siblings, some friends of friends, and then she was gone. Actually Tamsyn and Ed had never quite known who had triggered Scarlett's troubles.

"I'll just miss her," she said. "And I'll worry about her. Could she maybe go to a girls' school?"

"She could not," said Maya. "As you know, she's going to a wonderful coed International School. She'll be taught in French and English and she'll be fine, I promise you. It's going to be an incredible opportunity."

"Will she be with the children of the superrich?"

Maya considered this seriously. "Not the *super*rich. The very rich and the rich, I'd say."

"So what's she going to say when other people's parents are oligarchs or bankers or whatever? What's her story? I bet the school fees are more than Ed and I have earned in our entire lives."

"Yeah, they are," said Maya. "But she doesn't need a story. Honestly. You wouldn't believe how much kids at a place like that will just take it for granted that if she's there, she's one of them. If anyone asks, maybe she can say that rather than a stay-at-home mother, you're a reclusive writer or something?"

Tamsyn nodded. "We could do that. Does she need uni-forms?"

"Not in the conventional sense. But she will need to fit in, so we've ordered a selection of new clothes to be delivered that will work for her socially. You know. We want her to wear the right fashions. All of that."

Tamsyn walked over to the edge of the terrace, tipped her hat back and leaned on the wall to look at the mountains on the horizon. This was all so strange. She genuinely felt that Sophie was her daughter, but at the same time, she was still visiting Scarlett. The guilt would have consumed her were it not for that thing Luca had said about thinking of the girls as twins. If she could hold on to that, reinvent herself as a mother of two, then she could do it. She had twin daughters. One was very ill in hospital, and the other was . . . Sophie. Unusual for twins, of course, was that neither girl knew the other existed. Sophie hadn't asked about Scarlett. Tamsyn and Ed didn't mention her. They just slipped away to visit, one at a time, in secret. Sophie had asked about the locked bedroom just once, and Tamsyn had told her it was a part of the apartment they didn't use, then changed the subject.

She looked around at the buildings nearby and wondered for a moment about all the other lives going on around her. Were any of their neighbors involved in anything this complicated? She started back when she saw a figure in a window below her, across the street, who seemed to be looking at her through binoculars.

She pulled back from the wall, out of sight. When she looked back, though, there was no one there. She shook her head and went to sit down, out of sight of random people who were probably actually bird-watchers or plane watchers.

She looked back over her shoulder. The sun was warm on her cheek. "If . . . When Scarlett wakes up, will she go to the same school?"

"No," said Maya straightaway. "The bilingual approach wouldn't work for her. She will go to the British school, I guess. An English-medium one anyway."

Tamsyn looked out again, very much appreciating Maya's use of *she will* instead of *she would*. Maya had done that better than she had. The city gleamed below her. There was no sign of anyone watching her. She decided not to mention it.

Their old van in Cornwall was fading from her mind. She didn't know when, or whether, they would ever go back. She e-mailed Maud from time to time, but Maud never wrote back. Ed's brother, Jimmy, wrote to her now rather than to Ed, and she replied carefully, reading her messages over several times before she sent them.

At first she had thought of that vanishing e-mail every day and had wanted to demand answers. She'd needed to know why Ed had been feeling guilty and what it was she had *no idea* about, but she knew Jim would report to Ed if she asked, and so she didn't.

Instead, she told Jimmy their news, doing her best to convey the fact that they had been catapulted to a completely different world, but she didn't say much anymore. It felt too stark. It was scary how quickly she had acclimatized to a world in which she had new clothes, a huge apartment with a view, a cleaning service that came twice a week and twin daughters. She had her friend Aurelie and her French and yoga classes. It seemed cruel to keep relaying her news back to a place where the people had been forgotten, where they scraped by from day to day.

Jimmy knew only that Scarlett had a place on a medical trial. He didn't know about Sophie at all, and so when, after Sophie had been with them for a few weeks, Tamsyn sent a photo of herself and Ed with Sophie, she had just written, **Look how well things are going**, and left it at that. Jim responded, typically for him, with a row of happy emojis and nothing else.

▪ ▪ ▪ ▪ ▪

"There you are! Mum, I was looking for you!"

"Oh, darling," said Tamsyn, and she walked over to Sophie and hugged her, because she could, and because Sophie looked as if she needed it.

Sophie hugged her back and pulled up another chair on the terrace. The chairs were heavy, wooden, with thick cushions. Tamsyn sat back down.

"Maya and I were talking about school. How are you feeling?"

Sophie started to answer, stopped and then started again. Her voice was more hesitant than Tamsyn had heard it before.

"Oh, Mum, you know what? This is where I want to say, 'Stop stressing! I'm fine. I can't wait to go!' But actually . . ."

She took a few deep breaths, then stood up and walked over to the edge of the terrace and looked away from them, out across the city. Tamsyn hoped no one was watching her.

"I guess," Sophie said back over her shoulder, "in theory I'm excited about learning and friends, but, you know—it's been a while since I can remember talking to anyone my own age, and school . . . It's going to be a building full of them. I seem to have forgotten everything I ever learned and—"

Tamsyn saw that Sophie was struggling. She walked across the terrace, the tiles warm under her bare feet, and stood beside her daughter, putting an arm around her shoulders and pulling her in close. They looked at Geneva together. *Geneva.* It felt impossible to be there with Sophie. She checked. All the nearby windows were blank or shuttered.

"It really is going to be OK," she said, stroking Sophie's hair. "But I know it doesn't feel that way. You had your accident and woke up in a different country, and now we're throwing you into a new environment again. I know it's hard. I also know you're going to ace it. Truly, darling. You're brilliant. Plus it's only for a few hours and then you get to come home, and I'll always be here. Always."

Sophie leaned into her and Tamsyn felt her daughter's breathing calming.

"Oh, Mum," Sophie said quietly, "you know how to make things better."

This was all she had ever wanted. Her child was worried, and she, Tamsyn, had made her feel better. She hugged Sophie as tightly as she could, feeling like a proper mother.

"You'll have friends," she said. "And I promise you're going to find the work absolutely fine, so don't stress about that for a second." She turned round. "Right, Maya?"

Maya came and stood on Tamsyn's other side. "Your mother's right," she said. "Seriously, Sophie, you have literally no worries on that front. You're going to find schoolwork easy, because of the reconstruction work that you've had. You're not the first kid with reconstruction and augmentation to go to school. You won't even be the only one at *your* school."

"I'm not alone?" said Sophie.

Tamsyn noticed that over the past few weeks Sophie's voice had changed. She didn't have a Cornish accent but she sounded more British than American. Tamsyn had felt herself losing her accent too. They were all meeting somewhere in the middle.

"You know I'm going to be checking everyone out now," Sophie said. "I'm sure I'll find them."

"Let me know if you do," said Maya. "That would be great data."

▪ ▪ ▪ ▪ ▪

On the first day Sophie dressed for school in jeans, a T-shirt and a sweatshirt. She didn't look smart enough to Tamsyn, but everyone assured them this would turn out to be the correct attire, and several different versions of it had been delivered over the past few days, along with a few more formal outfits and a weird pink party dress that Sophie had handed back to Maya with a headshake. She had a slouchy backpack and a fabulous selection of stationery.

Tamsyn stood on the pavement, the May sunshine warm on her head, and hugged her daughter as tightly as she could, savoring her smell, her reality, her perfection. She hated the idea of Sophie being away from her. She was terrified that there would be another accident, that she would lose her daughter all over again.

"You've got this, darling," she said, and the way that Sophie listened to her filled her heart. "You're amazing and everyone will see that. I love you. Have a wonderful time. I'll see you when you get home, and I want to hear all about every single moment of your day."

"Love you too, Mum! And thank you. Don't worry." Her voice wobbled. "I'm sure I'll be fine."

The car drove off, and Tamsyn was bereft.

* * * * *

All the same, she knew what she had to do.

15

I DON'T WANT TO GO TO SCHOOL, BUT HERE I AM, SITTING IN
the back of a chauffeur-driven car, heading there.

"Can we go somewhere else?" I say to the driver.

He looks briefly over his shoulder. *"Desolé, mademoiselle,"* he
says, and I realize I spoke French to him, and that he's speaking
it back. He grins. I grin back.

"It was worth a try."

......

We're driving beside the lake. I know it'll be OK, and maybe
having school filling my brain is a good thing, because it pushes
out the other stuff.

I need to be a good daughter. That's why I'm here. They
brought me back because my parents needed their child. I have
to complete the family as their only child. I know that in the
same way that I know that the sun is shining and that my name
is Sophie and that I'm on the way to school.

There's something wrong, though, inside this family. They

think I don't notice them going to the clinic without me. They think I haven't started to piece things together.

And more than that, there's something wrong with this trial. It's too perfect and way too blingy for a medical trial, even an AI one. It feels wrong. Mum and Dad are too trusting. There's a lot for me to work out here.

I'm almost enjoying being nervous about school, because I'm pretty sure it'll be OK now that I have my new powers. I don't remember much of the year before my accident, but I remember enough. I remember that things changed, and I know who did it.

J.

I stare at the lake. The lake and the mountains are so pretty. School.

■ ■ ■ ■ ■

I hope I'm wearing the right clothes. I know Maya says I am, but in spite of what she thinks, she doesn't know everything. Mum thought I should be dressed more formally, and that's because they have school uniforms in Cornwall. At my old school everyone wore a shirt and tie and blazer, like miniature office workers. Here, they promise I'll be OK in jeans and a sweatshirt, but I've packed a skirt and a blouse at the bottom of my backpack just in case. I'll ask to visit the toilet and do a quick change if I have to. It's a chiffon skirt, so it won't crease, and I folded the blouse carefully.

Why did they deliver a horrible pink dress? It had a sticking-out skirt like a child's party dress. I guess they were testing me to see what I really wanted. I hope the other girls aren't dressed like that.

The clicking of an indicator echoes through my skull. It means we're here. I want to tell him to switch it off and keep driving.

"Voilà!" says the driver.

The school has a dropping-off circle, and we're in a queue of cars moving very slowly. I see a boy getting out of the car in front of us. He's wearing jeans and a black T-shirt and his hair is all over the place. A girl gets out of the car in front of his: she's in jeans too and a bright white shirt. A man in his twenties, some kind of cool teacher, gives me a wave as he passes. The boy from the car in front sees me and waits.

"À cet après midi!" I say to the driver in my most cheerful voice, and I step out of the car.

"Hi," says the boy. "Are you new? I'm Noah."

16

TAMSYN SET OFF ON FOOT TOWARD THE LAKE. ED WAS working at the Venezia café five days a week now, and she and Sophie had visited for coffee regularly. Sophie, like Scarlett, loved hot chocolate, but unlike Scarlett she was cultivating an interest in coffee too because she thought it would be more sophisticated. Ed's new workplace made a spectacular hot chocolate with marshmallows and Chantilly cream, so Sophie's preferred order was one of those with an espresso on the side.

They would sit outside in the sun and talk about nothing in particular, and Tamsyn had felt the part of her that had withered away growing back. She had felt herself to be a crap mother with an out-of-control child trapped in an inescapable hell. When she talked to Sophie and knew that she was soothing her and making her feel better, she felt like a good mother again. The hell had been escapable after all, and they had done it.

They had done it at a cost. She shivered at the thought.

Right now both of her precious daughters were away from her. One was at school, and the other was lying exactly where she always was. Sometimes Tamsyn thought Scarlett seemed closer to being alert, but at other times she thought she was seeing what she wanted to see, because actually Scarlett was always the same. She might be the same forever, and Tamsyn wasn't sure what would happen then. Would they keep her like that, suspended between life and death, until Sophie was grown-up and independent, or until Tamsyn and Ed died, or until Scarlett herself was an old woman? She had no idea at what point Dr. Singh, or her successor, would give up on Scarlett.

Of course, Tamsyn longed for her daughter to wake up. It was slipping away, though, as a thing that felt real, because a part of Scarlett had already woken up and was right now making new friends and finding her way around her new school.

- - - - -

She sat at a metal table outside, feeling the heat rising from the pavement. A woman at the next table, a woman in her forties like Tamsyn, gave her a quick smile and went back to her book. A young man with green hair looked up from his laptop and seemed about to say something, but before he could, a waitress came to take her order. The waitress was a young woman with her hair in a sharp bob, and since Tamsyn hadn't met her before, she said, in her careful French, *"Est-ce que vous pouvez dire à Ed que sa femme est ici?"* Could you tell Ed his wife is here? That request would have been met with a volley of obscenities at any other place he'd worked, but at this relaxed café, they seemed to like family visits.

The young woman grinned. *"Bien sûr!"* she said, and then when Tamsyn's coffee arrived, it was delivered by Ed, with a custard tart on the side.

"So?" he said as he put it down. He sat beside her. "How was it?"

He was wearing his work uniform: a red-and-white-striped

T-shirt and white trousers, with a white apron over the top. Tamsyn looked at him and thought how much she loved him. Everyone else seemed to get divorced, but she and Ed had weathered everything life had flung at them and they were stronger than ever.

"It went well. She was brave. I know she was scared but she got into the car and left. She's amazing."

"And so are you." He looked at her. "And by the way, you look beautiful. That's a lovely dress."

She smoothed it down, pleased. She was wearing a floaty summer dress in green and yellow, with a denim jacket. She was happy with the ensemble: it was a million miles away from anything she'd ever worn at home, where her clothes had been functional, generally found in a charity shop or passed on by someone from a neighboring van.

The charity shops at home had sometimes stocked clothes like this after someone rich and stylish had had a benevolent clear out, but it would never have occurred to Tamsyn to pick them up, to imagine wearing them. Everything was different here. Her hair had been cut and colored twice, so she supposed that would carry on, every month or so, for as long as they lived here. She didn't have gray hairs anymore, even though she had quite liked them at home. She wore a little bit of makeup, which was also something of a first, over the past twenty years at least. Maya had directed her to Internet tutorials when she didn't know how to put it on, and she was getting better.

She was, in fact, transformed, though she hadn't noticed a particular moment when it had happened. At first she had been grateful for anything anyone suggested she should do with her time because it took her mind off her dread of Sophie's arrival, mad though that seemed in retrospect. Then French class and yoga and her beauty regime had become habit, and now she could feel herself starting to take it all for granted.

She and Ed were having a lot of sex, and it was as if they'd just met. She couldn't keep her hands off him. It was wonderful. She felt new and alive. If it wasn't for the fact that Scarlett was unresponsive, she would have been properly happy. It had never really occurred to her before that she could be someone who might have a happy life.

She had just about convinced herself that she'd imagined the vanishing e-mail. She hardly thought about it, and she didn't want to ask because she didn't want to know the answer. She was too happy. There was no need. She blanked it out.

She picked up the coffee and took a sip.

"Gorgeous," she said.

The custard tart was looking at her, but she was saving it. Ever since Luca had paid for them to go to dinner back in Truro, food had been one of her huge joys. She was going to love eating this. She was putting on weight but she liked it. She liked her new, softer body. She leaned over and kissed Ed on the lips. He kissed her back. Why had they not always kissed all the time? She loved it. He made her feel like a giddy teenager.

"So," said Ed, when they pulled apart, "tenterhooks until four, yeah?"

She smiled and picked up her coffee. "Oh, God. I hope she's OK. There are so many things to worry about. The other kids. The fact that it's the first time I've spent a day away from her. But you know Sophie. She'll take it in her stride."

Ed put an arm around her shoulder and she leaned into him. "Bet you don't know what to do with yourself."

"I'm going to visit Scarlett," she said. "And then I guess I'll just wait by the front door until Sophie comes home."

"Of course." He inhaled a jagged breath. "Give Scarlett a kiss from her old dad. I'd better get back to work." As he was starting to walk away, he turned back. "Oh, how did Lena do? The waitress? She's new."

They both looked over at Lena, who was in her twenties, skinny and stylish. Tamsyn looked back at him.

"She did great," Tamsyn said.

She felt uneasy but told herself it was nothing. She didn't think about the e-mail. Lena was "new," so it couldn't have involved her.

Ed nodded and went inside. Tamsyn sat in the sunshine and smiled at people who walked past and sipped her coffee and ate her custard tart slowly, savoring every crumb. She looked at the sunshine on the surface of the lake and at the people walking around, living their easy lives.

Whatever had happened with Ed, they were back on track again now and she trusted him.

All those people weren't living easy lives. It just looked as if they were. Look at her: she looked like a middle-aged woman who didn't have to work, filling the day while her teenager was at school, sitting in the sunshine and looking at reflected mountains. Nobody who looked at her would see a woman who, a few months ago, had worked in the cauliflower fields in a corner of Europe that the world had forgotten. Nobody would imagine that the daughter who was at school represented a secretive project at the cutting edge of medical technology or that her original daughter lay in a coma—always, always unresponsive, never so much as twitching—in a private room in an unremarkable-looking building across town.

The green-haired man stood up to leave. He paused at her table.

"Have a good day," he said. He looked as if he wanted to say something else, but stopped himself.

"Thanks," she said. "You too."

She stood up and asked Lena for the bill.

"There is no need," she said in English. "Ed already paid."

Thanks for the coffee, she messaged him as she walked away.
Love you 🖤.

· · · · ·

As Tamsyn stood in the doorway, she looked into Scarlett's room and thought how much she owed to machines right now. They kept Scarlett alive, and other machinery—machinery she would never understand—was implanted in Sophie and had made her real. Technology was incredible. She half knew now what the Singularity was and that Sophie was a part of it, part of the merging of humans with AI. She knew about transhumanism, and she could just about understand that Sophie was a transhuman and a cyborg, but since Sophie was also her daughter, she couldn't be remotely scared of any of it. If Sophie was part of the Singularity, then as far as Tamsyn was concerned, it couldn't come soon enough.

She sat at Scarlett's bedside and took her hand. She was still Scarlett, but Tamsyn couldn't help but compare her with Sophie. Her hair had grown back since they'd shaved it to do whatever they had done to access her brain to create Sophie, but instead of seeing it as Scarlett's short hair, Tamsyn realized she was seeing it as *shorter than Sophie's*. Her skin was duller than Sophie's. Her eyes were more closed, her breathing more artificial, her stature more horizontal.

"Hello, my darling," she said, overcome with remorse. "We miss you so much. I hope you can wake up and come and live with us in our new home. Your bedroom is waiting. It's a lovely room. You have a four-poster bed and a view across the city. Your duvet and things are blue. You like blue, don't you? I hope you still do. You can see the lake. Do you remember?" She told her this stuff every time, and she hoped that in some way, some of it was going in. "Please wake up. Please get better. We have a wonderful new life here, and you have the best people looking after you. I know you must love Dr. Singh."

She stopped and looked at Scarlett. People in comas weren't the way they were in movies or on television. Scarlett didn't look as if she was dreaming. She didn't look as if she might be hearing and understanding. There were tubes everywhere. She smelled weird. Tamsyn knew that Scarlett might be able to hear, because Dr. Singh always reminded her about it, so she carried on talking, but she also knew that there was a strong chance that Scarlett would never hear anything again.

"I called in at Dad's work on the way here," she said. "I had a coffee and a custard tart. I can't wait to take you there. It's called La Venezia. That means *Venice* in Italian. The custard tart was perfect. The pastry was all flaky. Full of butter. We can go there when you're better. We can sit outside the café in the sunshine. It's close to the lake. You'll love it. Dad's really happy there and it's only open during the day, so although he has an early start making the bread and all that, he never has to work at night. It's not like before. Not at all. Nothing is like before."

She wondered what would happen if she told Scarlett about Sophie. It was strictly forbidden, but all the same, Scarlett was unconscious. She wouldn't hear.

"It would potentially be very distressing," Dr. Singh had said. "Hearing is often the last sense to go and the first to return. She could well be hearing things from time to time or indeed all the time. And for her to piece together the fact that a version of her exists in your life now, without a careful explanation of what this involves, could upset her."

That *could*, Tamsyn had thought, was a classic piece of steely understatement from Dr. Singh.

She battled to remember that Scarlett wasn't Sophie, but more and more she felt that Scarlett was lying here as the source material, and science had animated her spirit as a high-tech sort of resurrection, a material ghost, and that Scarlett and Sophie were two parts of the same organism. Of course they were: they were the same girl.

But the source girl couldn't know that. It wasn't a fact that would hasten her recovery.

"The sun's shining today," she said, looking at the window. "This city is so pretty in the sun."

17

THIS CITY IS SO PRETTY IN THE SUN.

> This
> city
> is
> so
> pretty
>
> in
>
> the
>
> sun

It's like waking up, but it's not waking up. I'm in a dark place, a cave, a tiny space that is just for me. I'm sitting cross-legged in the corner. There's no light but there are words.

This city is so pretty in the sun.

Nothing else. Just strings of words.

> This city
> so pretty
> sun.

I try to grip that, to hold on to the words as they float past me. Is this a city? Is it pretty? In the sun?

> Pretty?
> In?
> The?
> Sun?

I half know the words. I feel myself slipping under again. Just before I go, more words come into my cave.

The pastry was all flaky. Full of butter.

I don't know what those words mean.

. . . . .

Good-bye, darling.

I'll be back soon.

I love you.

> This city
> is so pretty
> in the sun.

18

AT SEVEN MINUTES PAST FOUR, THE BUZZER WENT. AS TAMsyn had been standing next to it and could see Sophie's face filling the screen, she pressed the button before the buzzing had even stopped and ran out of the apartment to wait by the elevator.

She heard the smooth purr of its machinery. She paced around the white-tiled hallway, over to the window, back to the elevator. She pressed the button to call it, pressed it again and again and again as if that might make it accelerate and deliver Sophie sooner. This was the way she had felt ten years ago when a serious little Scarlett had started school at the age of four, though then, of course, Tamsyn had been standing outside a Cornish school in the rain rather than waiting beside the elevator in a luxury apartment. There was something about sending your child into a world that couldn't and wouldn't accommodate *you* that made it an immense loss, a rite of passage. Sophie was going to spend her days in a world that had a place for Tamsyn's child but not for her, and that made her sad, even though it shouldn't have because it was exactly what life was about.

She wanted to know everything that had happened to Sophie

today from the moment she had got into that car at eight o'clock. Everything.

The doors opened, and there she was. Tamsyn looked at her: she was smiling and her face looked genuinely happy. Sophie stepped into her embrace and allowed Tamsyn to hug her for as long as she wanted. She held her tight, felt her breathing.

"So?" Tamsyn said as they walked into the apartment.

Sophie grinned. "It was great," she said. "I liked it. You and Maya were right that the work was easy. I could remember things that I didn't know I knew. It feels weird in my head when that happens. I feel different when I know something with my brain from the way I do when I know something with my . . . I don't know. Augmented brain? Does that make sense?"

"It does," said Tamsyn, though she couldn't begin to imagine what Sophie felt like. It was too much to think about, and so she shoved it in the part of her own brain where she put things that were too much, and closed the door. "How about the people?" she said, hoping for safer ground.

"Great!" Sophie tossed her hair back and smiled. "Amazing. They were so friendly to me! It was strange being with so many people my own age. You know? It was kind of a whole new world. Although I remember being at my old school, this one was so different that I felt every single thing about it was new."

"You're sure they were nice to you?" What Tamsyn wanted to ask was, Did they offer you cigarettes? Did they try to get you to skip lessons? Did they drink? Take drugs? She managed not to say any of it.

Sophie laughed. "Of course they were nice, Mum! It's an international school, and people come and go all the time. It's not a weird thing having a new person turning up. I mostly spent the day with a couple of girls, Gemma and Amina. Gemma was new recently too, and they both said they knew what it felt like and they just showed me everything and they were super lovely. I was fine with the work. The building was amazing. It's like a chalet by the lake, and it's easy to find your way around. Don't worry, Mum! I'm going to be completely fine. I promise I am. I mean, it's strange being in a new place and having so much to take in, and the day did go on forever, and I mainly just wanted to get home to you, but I liked it. I'll go again!"

"Perfect," said Tamsyn. "I remember that feeling, when you start something new and your first day just goes on and on. So which lessons did you like best?"

She put the kettle on. Scarlett had always got on best with subjects like English and history, and worst with sciences. Tamsyn had no idea whether that had crossed over to Sophie.

"Probably physics. My brain did that thing where I almost felt it clicking into place. The weirdest thing." She laughed. "I've never felt more AI! But it did mean I felt like I knew it all already, and so when I felt brave enough, I asked some questions, and the teacher was a bit surprised."

Tamsyn smiled at the image.

"You did something that everyone would have found incredibly difficult, and I'm proud of you. How was the French?"

Sophie paused to think about it. "I think it was fine," she said. "Yes. It must have been."

Tamsyn felt her heart bursting with pride and happiness, so she walked over to Sophie and hugged her again.

"Can we go and visit Dad?"

"Of course we can! Let's go and meet him from work, and if you like, we can go for an early dinner or something."

Tamsyn paused to appreciate the fact that she had said that sentence so casually. She, who had so recently tried to fashion dinner from a stolen cauliflower, who used to forget to eat at all half the time.

Sophie went to put her school things away (it took an effort not to remember Scarlett kicking her bag into a corner as soon as she came into the caravan), and Tamsyn felt the tension draining away. Sophie wasn't going to get into trouble at school. She wasn't going to go out at night with strangers or fall under the spell of a mystery person, a destructive influence. She wasn't going to yell. Not only that, but she had no idea that she'd ever been the kind of girl to do any of those things. And of course, she hadn't. This was Sophie. She both was and wasn't Scarlett.

"Some of the others go to a thing called BJJ," said Sophie as they walked through the clean streets down toward the lake. "It sounds cool. Brazilian jujitsu. Martial arts but amazing for fitness too."

The sun was lower in the sky and their shadows were long.

"Would you like to try it?"

Tamsyn looked at her shadow and her daughter's beside it, both of them stretched and tall and thin. They were almost the same height now.

"Yeah," Sophie said. "I might give it a go if that's OK. I mean, if the doctors say so and if you do too. I saw what they can do and it looked awesome. I'd love to be able to do that. And self-defense is always good, right?"

Tamsyn felt a moment of pure happiness. She told herself that Scarlett would want them to be happy, but in fact she had no idea what Scarlett would want. The Scarlett of the past year hadn't cared about her parents' happiness and would have been furious about Sophie's existence.

Tamsyn loved the idea of Sophie doing a martial art.

"Absolutely," she said. "You should definitely do it! What else are they into?"

Sophie smiled. "For some reason, they love old horror movies. Do we have a DVD player?"

"I don't think so. Can't you just stream them?"

"No. It's about the retro tech. Like vinyl. The same kind of thing. If we could get one, I could borrow the DVDs to catch up."

Scarlett would have wanted to join the trend for retro horror, even if she was as new to it as Sophie was. That was why Tamsyn was happy: Scarlett was beside her, wearing a pair of shorts and a white linen shirt over a vest top, with sunglasses on her head and strappy sandals on her feet, talking about Brazilian jujitsu and DVD players. It was impossible to feel the absence of someone who was beside her, skipping along and chatting about her plans.

* * * * *

They met Ed outside the Venezia (Tamsyn had a quick look for Lena, but she wasn't around) and walked into the old town. The early-evening air was warm and gorgeous, and even the pollution, such as it was, felt hot and summery. The pavements were clean. The people they passed were chic and well-dressed, and although they didn't smile or say hello, they didn't look at the three of them as if they were two peasants and a cyborg either. The cars here were shiny and new, almost all of them electric and silent. The buildings were well-kept, with geraniums in window boxes, shiny front doors and clean windows. Tamsyn could hardly remember the stress and mud of home anymore. Had she really worked picking daffodils, cauliflowers, cabbages? Cleaning offices before dawn? She knew she had, even though her new life had smoothed away the calluses and rough skin. She needed to remember that old life, because her new one was intoxicating and it would be easy to assume that this was just the way things were. No wonder rich people cared only about staying rich.

"This one's meant to be nice for a drink."

Ed indicated a bar on a wide pavement with outside tables

made from wrought iron and a striped canopy above the doorway. It was like Paris in the sixties, Tamsyn thought, though she
was hazy about that sort of thing. They took a table in the golden
sunshine and ordered drinks. She had a glass of white wine—she
had developed a taste for it as soon as she'd tasted her first sau-
vignon blanc in that restaurant back in Truro—and Ed was
drinking cold lager. Sophie, like a dream teenager, asked for a
lemonade.

"Well," Tamsyn said, "just look at us!"

And she let the happiness flow through her. She stopped
fighting it. She was, under the circumstances, living the perfect
life. Everything that had been wrong was right. It was, she
thought, OK for her to enjoy it.

She looked at Ed. "You know what?" she said. "I'm happy."

He nodded, understanding at once. "Me too," he said.

"Me three," said Sophie straightaway. "Dad, Mum calmed me
down before school in that magic way she has, but I was still
scared. I mean, whatever Maya said about the other students, I
was pretty sure that no one else had really had a huge accident
and damaged their brain, been patched up with AI and all that.
I thought I would feel different and weird next to everyone else,
and I didn't know if I would be able to talk to them, but I didn't
feel weird and I could talk. I felt like I belonged. And the people
felt like they could become my friends."

She smiled at Tamsyn, a huge smile that made her eyes crin-
kle, her cheeks change shape. Tamsyn remembered that smile
from when Scarlett was young. It had always filled her with joy.

Later they found a fondue restaurant with red-and-white-
checked tablecloths and candles on the tables. Sophie talked a
bit more about school, and Ed and Tamsyn both listened rapt.

"The building is kind of old and modern at the same time,"
Sophie said. "I really love the light. It makes you want to get

things done, you know? You can see the lake through most of the windows."

Tamsyn and Ed exchanged glances. This was almost too perfect.

It was starting to get dark outside, and a waitress came round to light the candles on the tables. The adults were drinking wine, and Sophie had switched to sparkling water. Tamsyn held up her glass.

"Cheers to you, Sophie," she said. "We're unbelievably proud of you."

"We are," said Ed.

Sophie shrugged and looked a bit embarrassed. "It was fun," she said. "So I don't feel I need any congratulations. But—"

Something crossed her face and she leaned forward, lowering her voice even though no one else was within earshot. There was classical music playing in the background, which would have stopped anyone listening unless they were standing right beside them.

"Mum," she said quietly. Her voice was serious. "Dad. There's only one other thing that's been worrying me. It's just one thing. Now that I don't have to worry so much about school, it's the biggest thing. Can I ask you? Promise you won't be upset?"

19

TAMSYN PUT DOWN HER GLASS.

"Of course," she said. "Seriously, you can ask us anything. That's what we're here for: to help you. To be here for you." She said it calmly, but her heart was racing. Was this where it started to crumble? She had no idea what was coming, but she didn't like it.

"OK." Sophie put down her fondue fork.

Tamsyn liked the way they came with different-colored spots on the end so you didn't get them mixed up. Sophie had picked the red one. Tamsyn wondered whether that was because it was scarlet. It was both strange and perfect to her that Sophie had Scarlett's early memories.

"Fire away," said Ed, looking at Sophie in a way that told Tamsyn that he wasn't seriously worried about what was coming.

"OK. So . . . this is going to sound mad but— Well, it's about me, really. I remember living in Cornwall. I remember what it was like when I was little, and I know I had an accident, though I know there are things I don't remember. So—what *are* the things I don't know? I know I was rebuilt in the clinic and that I have an AI interface, and that's how I can speak French and understand physics and all that. I know that, and I can even feel it happening, but there are things that just don't make sense." She took a shuddering breath in.

"Soph—what are they?" said Ed, his voice gentle.

"OK. First, why do you still go to the VitaNova clinic without me? You try not to let me see it but I know you do. I've heard you talking about it when you don't know I'm listening. So what's at the clinic now that I'm home? Do you really just go to talk about me to the team? Why don't I go too? And also, why is there another bedroom exactly like mine at home? Yeah, it's locked, but it's not exactly hard to open. When I put it together, it makes me think that . . ." She stopped talking, shook her head, then took another deep breath. "I think there might be two of me," she said quickly.

Tamsyn looked over to Ed but saw, to her surprise, that he was looking at Sophie with a grin on his face, as if this was a good thing. She looked back at Sophie and saw again how difficult it had been for her to ask these questions.

"Darling," she said. "OK."

She looked at Ed again, wanting him to take the lead. He knew the rules better than she did.

He leaned toward Sophie and said, "Sophie. Darling girl. Does the name Scarlett mean anything to you?"

"Yes! It does!" she said, raising her voice slightly. "Yes, and that's another thing I don't understand. I know Scarlett is a part of my name. In my memories people call me Scarlett. Scarlett Sophie. I thought it was a nickname or something. Scarlet Sophie means *red Sophie*. I like red things." She picked up the fondue fork and showed them the red dot as proof. "Scarlet is the adjective, and Sophie is the noun. So Sophie's my name. I get that. But now I'm just called Sophie. Right? I'm not Scarlett anymore."

"Right," said Ed, but then he stopped.

Tamsyn saw that he wasn't grinning anymore. The enormity of the moment had caught up with him. She tried to find a way of saying the right things herself.

She knew that working this out was an important part of Sophie's development. She knew that when Sophie started asking questions, they were supposed to answer them. She hadn't expected it to happen so soon.

She took a deep breath and did her best.

"OK." She reached for Sophie's hand and squeezed it. "Well, first of all, we both adore you and you coming back to us is a miracle. A real miracle. OK? You're the best thing that has ever happened and I hope you know that." She looked to Ed for backup.

"You so are," he said, and he took Sophie's other hand. He felt for Tamsyn's knee under the table and squeezed it.

Sophie nodded. "Yes. You both make me feel that all the time."

"And everything you think about how you came back to us is true." Tamsyn was choosing her words carefully, wishing Ed would do it instead. "There's just one part you don't know. One thing about how they made you into the amazing young woman you are."

"They reanimated my tissue and augmented my brain with AI. Making me into a hybrid. There's more than that?" Sophie gave a tight smile. "Because that's quite a lot."

"Did they ever use the word—"

Tamsyn stopped, swallowed. This was a hard one to say but she was going to have to do it. As soon as she said the word, Sophie would know. Sophie knew anyway. She just didn't want to believe it.

Tamsyn closed her eyes as she said: "It's a word they hate, so actually they would never use it, but did they say anything like *human duplication*? Anything that means the same kind of thing as . . . cloning?"

"Cloning?" Sophie said it loudly, and the waitress looked over briefly. She lowered her voice. "No. They didn't. Oh, my God. What do you mean? You can't clone humans. It's illegal."

Tamsyn needed the experts. She could call Maya, she thought. She would. She'd do it as soon as she could. Her phone was right there on the table. She looked at Ed, who nodded at her to continue.

"It's not illegal in all circumstances," she said quietly, parroting the things she had read in the file. "There are certain provisions under Swiss law. There are tight regulations around using cloning techniques to reanimate someone after the kind of accident you had. That's why we're here in Switzerland. Because it's illegal in most countries. In Britain, it's legal in theory but it doesn't happen, because there isn't the infrastructure. But that's why they can recruit over there. Because they're not bound by European law, which bans it." She needed help. She looked at Ed and he nodded again, so she carried on. "Your original body wasn't responding to treatment. So they used that . . . technology to take a part of that body and regrow everything you needed, as you just said. And then used the AI to augment everything, again like you said. And here you are: our miracle daughter."

She watched Sophie's mind working. Part brain, part machine. Tamsyn saw her understand.

"My original body is still there in the clinic," she said, her voice small. "It's still alive."

"Yes. That's why you're Sophie, darling. Scarlett's in the hospital, and Sophie is right here. Scarlett hasn't been doing well. Sophie has. Scarlett is being kept alive by technology. And you were reanimated by technology. We owe technology everything."

Sophie's voice rose. "I don't understand. Why would they rebuild me but leave part of me hanging on like that? Once they had *me,* why do they need to keep the other part? Are they going to make another one?" She touched her face, held up her hands and looked at them. She put a finger on each temple. "Cloning," she whispered. "Right. That's weird. This is a very freaking weird thing to find out about yourself. Very. Freaking. Freaking. Weird. I mean, it makes everything make sense but still . . . cloning." She paused. "I can't swear! I'm trying to swear but I can't say the words. I've never tried before. Not since I've been here."

Tamsyn's eyes met Ed's. Scarlett had sworn at them all the time, had said *fucking* every other word as a reflex. She felt, in an illogical way, that now that Sophie knew about Scarlett, the two of them were starting to merge. Was this where her perfect daughter shifted and changed and started to hate her, like the other one had? Clearly Sophie had been programmed not to swear, but up to now she hadn't even tried. Now she had.

"Johann and the team said this was something you had to come to yourself," said Tamsyn. "Otherwise we would have made sure you knew straightaway. She doesn't know about you either. I mean, even if she can hear, no one talks about any of this in her room."

"It's still alive." She was talking to herself more than to them. "I'm alive twice. I exist in two places. But we're separate. I'm separate from myself." She looked at Tamsyn and then at Ed. "What happens if the other one gets better? Oh! The bedroom. Right. It comes to live with us. We share everything."

At last, Ed spoke. "For one thing, Scarlett is a human. She's *she*, not *it*. And if she recovers, we'll have two daughters. Twins. Identical twins are clones after all. That's literally what they are. And that's who you two would be. Do you remember how you always wanted a sibling when you were small?"

Sophie looked thoughtful. She started to speak and then stopped. She swallowed, took a sip of water, reached across and picked up Ed's beer and took a big swig and then knocked back the rest of Tamsyn's wine and composed herself.

"I wanted a brother," she said, and Tamsyn remembered that she was right. Scarlett had always asked for a baby brother. "But yeah, it makes sense. I want to go to the clinic and see her right now. I have the right to do that. She's my other self. She's me."

Tamsyn took her hand. "Darling, I know. She is. I'd love to take you. But they've told us not to do that. It would be too strange for you. It would be a weird experience for anyone, and you're only fourteen."

"Nearly fifteen."

"Yes! It's going to be your birthday in a few weeks!" She was so relieved that the conversation had reached a patch of safe ground, even if only in passing, that she seized it. "We should have a party. What would you like to do? We'll make it amazing. We've never been able to afford to have a real party before, have we? This time we can do something special. You can invite whoever you want from school, and we'll do anything." She cast around for ideas. "A trip on the lake? To the mountains? A restaurant, the cinema. Whatever people do. Whatever you want." She knew she was being over-the-top, too grateful for this new subject.

"Yes," said Sophie. "Thank you. That would be lovely. But it's her birthday too, and so my best present would be going to visit myself. To celebrate our birthday."

Tamsyn just nodded. She didn't know what to say to that. Tamsyn would, of course, visit Scarlett on her fifteenth birthday, but they wouldn't let Sophie go with her. Scarlett was closely guarded, and Tamsyn didn't get to make the rules.

Ed leaned forward.

"Soph, you should perhaps have two birthdays," he said. "Like the royal family. One official one—that would be June seventeenth— and one that is the day when you, Sophie Trelawney, actually came into being, which would be a few weeks ago."

Tamsyn frowned, but Sophie nodded. She looked supremely unbothered by this.

"You're right," she said. "I'll have two. My birthday and my rebirthday. I suppose I'll need to ask Johann and the team exactly when that was. I mean, I guess I could pinpoint when I became aware of myself and my surroundings, because that was the day I met you two, but that's not the same. We don't celebrate the day babies become aware of themselves, do we? We celebrate the day they start to exist. So I'd like to do that. Have a day that's just mine."

Tamsyn wondered how a fourteen-year-old could have been talking in such a calm, adult way. She put her uncertainties aside and agreed with Sophie that this was indeed an excellent idea. They started to talk about going to the mountains for the upcoming birthday, and conversation became easier, but as soon as Sophie got up to go to the loo, Tamsyn looked at Ed and it came flooding back.

"Oh, my God," she said. "Do we need to call Maya?"

"You handled it brilliantly. Sorry I didn't join in. I . . . Well, I found it a bit much. Everything kind of hit me. It was like an out-of-body thing. Like here I am with my darling wife and daughter, and my daughter's worked out about her other self in a coma, and she's done it so quickly and brilliantly, and one moment I was fine and then it paralyzed me. Sorry. I just had to leave it to you."

Tamsyn put her hand on his knee and rubbed it. "Did I really do all right? I was just hoping for the best."

Ed shifted his chair closer to hers, and she leaned on him. He put an arm around her shoulders and kissed the top of her head.

"She worked it out," he said. "They said she would, and then she did. It changes everything, doesn't it? We handle it however we want. We're her parents, right? It's up to us. You told her the truth in as gentle a way as you could, and she's accepted it. I'd say it couldn't have gone any better. I knew you'd do it better than me, and you did."

"Oh, for fuck's sake," she said, blinking back tears, wiping the underneath of her eye with a finger to try to avoid smudging her makeup. She saw that Ed was blinking hard too. "So do I ask Maya if Sophie can visit the clinic?"

"We need to tell them that she asked, and they'll say no. They'll say no because of Scarlett, but they'll be pleased she wants to. This isn't meant to be something to worry about. It's something to celebrate, even though it feels more complicated. She's clever. That second-birthday thing I said? That was something they suggested to make her feel special. And she liked it. Brilliant."

The worries faded a little. Tamsyn caught the waitress's eye and signaled for another little carafe of wine.

"She *is* brilliant," she said with a smile. She picked up her fork again and stuck a piece of bread on the end and dipped it into the cheese, which was still just liquid enough to be scooped up. By the time Sophie came back, Tamsyn was eating and drinking and feeling cautiously balanced again.

"Excuse me?" Sophie said to the waitress when they were

finishing up. She held out her phone. "Could you take a photo of us? A family picture?"

She said it in French, but Tamsyn understood. It was easy to understand French when you were living here, it turned out.

They both leaned in toward her, and the waitress took a series of pictures of the three of them, happy and smiling. They were a family. A family minus one twin.

20

SMILE FOR THE CAMERA. HOLD THE SMILE. PRETEND PRE-
tend pretend.

Have they noticed I'm faking it? I look at my mother. I'm
pretty sure she's so pleased that I know the huge secret, the massive great fact they hadn't thought to tell me, that she's pretending that now everything's fine and we can all be happy. She's
going with it and hoping it's true.

I look at my dad. It's hard to tell with him.

I went to the loo because I had to get myself under control. I
didn't want them to see me angry. I didn't want to make a scene,
because I have to be a good daughter.

I have to protect the family.

The family has three people in it.

I also needed to give them a moment to talk about me. They
needed to reassure each other that they've handled it well. I
know they did. I could see it on their faces.

"So I guess I'll keep going to school and just wait for her to get
better," I say. "I'm actually interested to learn all I can, in the science lessons in particular. The whole atmosphere is so different."

Actually, from what I can remember, the atmosphere isn't so far from my old school. Both are buildings full of teenagers. Both had a disruptive contingent, a borderline-druggy group, a collection of alpha girls. The only difference is that the geeks are cooler here, and there are more of them.

Us. I'm one of them now. There are more of *us*. I can remember how I used to love books and reading but now I'm obsessed with science. It's a weird thing, knowing that I'm desperate to find out more about all that because of the way I've been rebuilt.

Built. I haven't been rebuilt. I've been built.

My family has three people in it. Ed, Tamsyn and Sophie. We have no place for a Scarlett. I have to be a good daughter and protect the family, and that means making sure Scarlett never comes back to spoil things.

And I now have a lot more questions about VitaNova. A lot. What they're doing isn't possible, and I need to find out what, or who, is behind it.

21

TAMSYN WAS WAITING ON THE TERRACE IN THE HEAT OF THE morning, looking back at the door to the apartment. As soon as Sophie appeared, she stood up.

"Happy birthday, darling!"

Sophie smiled and spun around on the spot, ending in a dramatic pose that made Tamsyn laugh.

"Thank you, Mother!" she said, walking over to her.

Sophie was, Tamsyn thought, trying out new mannerisms from school. She'd taken up BJJ and loved it, and was constantly practicing her moves. She was changing, stretching out into the world and becoming her own person. She had taken her rebuilt body and was using it to do everything it could possibly do, knowing that her other self could do nothing.

"I can't believe you're fifteen," Tamsyn said. "I mean, I know you don't remember your fourteenth birthday, but believe me, it was different. We were all different. Our home was—" She stopped. There was no point.

"I remember the van, Mum," said Sophie.

She accepted Tamsyn's hug and returned it. She smelled

lovely, like body spray and expensive toiletries. Her hair reached all the way down her back, and her perfect skin had the youthful glow of a cosmetics ad. Next birthday she would be sixteen: that was almost an adult. She was beautiful, gorgeous and perfect.

"Are you OK to go to school today?" asked Tamsyn. "It's your birthday. I'd call in sick for you if you wanted."

Sophie looked at her sharply. "Could I visit Scarlett with you if I didn't go?"

"Sorry, sweetie. You know what they say about that. Hearing is the first sense to come back. It would be too much for her to find out that way."

"But if I just stood there and looked at her, she wouldn't know I was there."

"Not today."

"One day, though?"

"One day."

Sophie was insistent about wanting to see her twin. They had been through it with the team, and everyone agreed that Sophie could stand quietly and look at Scarlett at some fuzzy point in the future. Tamsyn was pretty sure they didn't intend it to happen unless Scarlett fully woke up and had to be told the truth, which, in spite of Dr. Singh's constant positivity, seemed increasingly unlikely.

"Then I'll go to school. I want to see my friends, and I have a physics test."

Tamsyn laughed. "Can't miss your birthday physics test."

Ed stepped out into the sun and held out his arms. Tamsyn watched Sophie run into them. He picked her up and spun her around, then kissed the top of her head when he put her down. The sky was deep blue above their heads, the huge window behind them reflecting city and mountains.

"Happy birthday, you wonderful girl," he said.

Tamsyn knew that Ed saw the situation in a more straightforward way than she did, and she wished she could be like him. To him, Sophie was Scarlett 2.0, and he didn't need to be sad about the Scarlett in the clinic in the same way he used to because she was in his arms right now, fizzing with excitement and joy. He had made the leap, and however hard she tried, Tamsyn couldn't do the last part of it. She couldn't blend her daughters, not quite. They were separate, and that meant that there was another version of Sophie, unconscious and unreachable, also turning fifteen.

Also, she knew that Sophie was pleased Scarlett had had the accident. She had to be, because otherwise she wouldn't exist. That was a difficult thing for anyone to get to grips with. It made Tamsyn's world feel complicated, difficult.

She would visit this afternoon. For now, no matter what else there was, she was happy because she had been a mother for fifteen years and that felt significant, and the fact that Sophie's wasn't the body Tamsyn had pushed out into the world barely mattered at all.

She walked across the balcony, its tiles hot under her bare feet, and squeezed her way into their hug. They held one another tight.

"Bugger," said Ed. "I have to get to work. Just quickly open this, OK?"

He handed Sophie a small package.

"It's from us," said Tamsyn unnecessarily. "There are more things, but we can do them later when we're all back home. And there's a massive pile of stuff from VitaNova."

"Thank you, parents!" said Sophie, and she ripped off the blue-and-white wrapping paper and uncovered a long, slim box. "Oh, my God," she said, opening it, but already knowing what it was. "I can't believe you went back and got it!"

She took out a necklace that she'd admired in the window of a jeweler's a couple of weeks ago. It was a silver chain with two interlinked stars on it, both covered with tiny diamonds, and Tamsyn knew why she wanted it. Sophie held up her hair and gave the necklace to Tamsyn. Tamsyn fastened it at the back of her perfect neck, and Sophie twirled round. She ran inside and over to a mirror, then ran back.

"It's absolutely perfect. I love it. Thank you, thank you!"

It was remarkable, Tamsyn thought, what a constantly re-plenished bank account could do. Sophie barely looked at the presents from VitaNova.

"I'll open them later," she said. "Why do they give us stuff all the time, though? Why do they think we'd want constant gifts? It makes things meaningless."

Tamsyn shrugged. If these were their problems now, she was fine with it.

"Have a brilliant day," said Ed, and he bustled off to work, promising to come back with the best birthday cake either of them had ever seen.

Then Sophie's car arrived, and she was off too, in a flurry of hair and perfume and happiness, and Tamsyn was alone with a pile of unwanted presents.

She was alone most days, and she had grown to savor it, though recently, and particularly today, she found that when no one else was with her, one truth would push its way into her head and take over her whole being.

That fact was the thing no one ever mentioned: Scarlett wasn't going to get better, and that meant that, sooner or later, they would have to give up on her and settle into life as a family of three forever. Tamsyn had no idea how long the clinic would keep her life support going. It was the question that came back over and over again. Would Scarlett turn sixteen, twenty, forty, sixty in the same bed, being turned over and washed by nurses, outsourcing all the business of being alive to technology? She might be in there, desperate for it to end. Or she might not be there at all.

What was the point in keeping Scarlett half alive when she already existed brilliantly in the world? Wasn't it, Tamsyn wondered, time to start seeing Sophie as the same person, to stop hanging on to the husk?

It was all questions. There were no answers.

The moment Tamsyn was alone, it came flooding in, and she was pleased that, because she'd known this would happen, she had lined up a busy day for herself. She was going to a café with Aurelie at half past nine, and had a French class at midday, then yoga at two. She planned to go to visit Scarlett twice: between coffee and French, and then again between yoga and half past five, when Sophie would be home. She was late on Fridays because she went to chess club. She was bringing Amina and Gemma home for burgers and a sleepover, which was apparently the correct thing to do.

She showered and dressed in a red agnès b. dress and gold sandals. God, clothes were amazing. She knew she looked good: she had put on enough weight to look healthy, and she didn't care that her hips were rounder and her stomach was convex now, because she loved food, and now that it was available, she most certainly wasn't going to diet. And her skin was so much better.

She put on a little foundation to smooth things out, a bit of eyeliner and mascara, and lip gloss. Her hair was well cut and colored, shoulder length and layered. Being rich was incredible.

She felt like a different person now that she lived this different life. She had been angry and frustrated all the time back at home, and now, in spite of everything, she was always calm. She had been waiting for Ed to leave before, but now they were happy again. Much happier than they'd ever been.

Aurelie knocked at the door. She was wearing bright blue today, and she was carrying a huge present wrapped in blue paper with yellow ribbon, and a smaller one wrapped the same way.

"Has she gone?"

Tamsyn nodded.

"Well, give her this from me. What a fabulous day to be turning fifteen." Aurelie put the big one on the table and handed Tamsyn the smaller parcel. "And this one's for Scarlett."

"Thank you! Thank you so much."

Aurelie hadn't met Scarlett, and Tamsyn was touched that she had thought of her. The moment Sophie had found out about Scarlett, Tamsyn had told Aurelie about her other daughter, Sophie's twin, very sick in a clinic. It was lovely of her to be so thoughtful.

"Sophie was pretty happy. And she'll be so pleased that you got her a present."

"Are you going to the hospital?"

"Straight after our coffee."

"Then let's get you caffeinated. Still OK to go out?"

Tamsyn looked around the apartment. She knew she was starting to take it for granted, because she wanted to go somewhere new.

"Yes, please," she said. "We could try that Spanish place?"

As Tamsyn packed up the things she needed in the leather satchel she used as a handbag and added the little present to the one she had wrapped herself, Aurelie said, "I always remember the kids being born, when it's their birthdays. I guess you had a section, right?" and she nodded noncommittally because people had C-sections with twins. Her real birth story had no place in her new life. Every time Scarlett's birthday came round, though, it pulled her back: the impossibility of getting a human who was ready to breathe and live in the world out of her body. The labor hadn't been dramatic compared to other people's stories: Scarlett had been born naturally over the course of twenty-four hours. All the same, the pain was something that had stayed with Tamsyn no matter what people said. She remembered sweating and swearing, all dignity gone, knowing that she couldn't do this but that she had no choice. There hadn't been an anesthetist available, so she'd had no epidural. It had been the most primal thing: the emergence of a brand-new human into the world accompanied by Tamsyn's roars of pain. For a fraction of a second, Scarlett had been the youngest person in the entire world.

She had come out fighting, wriggling and then screaming. She had been ready to deal with everything that came her way, and now she wasn't.

·····

They took the lift down to the street and set off toward the café. Aurelie chatted to her, getting it exactly right, because Tamsyn knew that she was going to have to work hard to keep everything together today, and she didn't have the strength to think of things to talk about. The child she had pushed out of her body fifteen years ago was unresponsive in hospital and had been that way for months. While Ed saw Sophie as the exact child who had emerged fifteen years earlier, Tamsyn supposed she saw her as an offshoot. Scarlett was a river, and she had branched off in two directions. She was a path with a fork in it, the branch of a tree, a geranium that had grown two flowers.

Tamsyn didn't want to see it that way. She wanted to be like Ed; it would be so much easier.

The café was new and shiny, with a marble floor and metallic fittings. It was a bit clinical, but she had churros for breakfast and that was perfect.

. . . . .

Scarlett was the same as ever except that someone had tied a helium balloon to the end of her bed. It was pink and it read JOYEUX ANNIVERSAIRE in jaunty letters. It bobbed in her white-and-blue room, looking tragic. The contrast with Sophie dancing around the place, dashing off to school to do physics and see her friends and play chess and come home for burgers and movies was too much. Tamsyn tried again to think of Sophie as Scarlett's avatar, but it didn't work. They were separate people, and Scarlett was not living through Sophie, however much Tamsyn wished she were.

Scarlett was lying still, as she always did, surrounded by the machines. Here was the dark underside of the sparkling dancing girl who had dashed off to school.

Tamsyn sat on the chair beside the bed. She could remember how it had become normal to doze in a chair, night after night, back in Cornwall. Jerking awake every half hour or so to check on Scarlett. The idea of Scarlett left alone had been horrific back then. It had been a primal thing: Tamsyn couldn't allow her baby to be scared and unprotected. Whatever she was going through, they were going through it with her.

How quickly that had changed in Switzerland.

She touched Scarlett's shoulder.

"Happy birthday, darling!" she said. She kissed her daughter's forehead. "Fifteen years old! When you're better we'll have a lovely party." She sat back in her chair and looked at Scarlett, as unresponsive now as she had been since the accident. "Oh, Scarlett," she whispered, "I don't think you're going to get better, darling."

She gasped. She hadn't intended to say it out loud. Not voicing that thought had been a talisman. She was sure everyone thought it, but the words couldn't be spoken. She remembered how many times Dr. Singh had said that hearing was the last thing to go and the first to come back, and she screwed her eyes closed and decided that Scarlett couldn't have heard, and that if she just carried on talking, saying positive things, then it would be as if it had never happened.

"I mean, I can't wait for you to get better," she said. "That's what I meant. You know I told you about our neighbor Aurelie? She used to live in Norway. It's so international here. Her daughter lives in Oslo and her son's in Paris. Isn't that exciting? She's on her own, so we go to cafés together and she's been so lovely to me. She's really helped me settle in. She got you a present. I'll open it for you if you like. Shall I? Yes, I will. Here we go. It's a little teddy bear. I'll put it next to you. I'm sure that'll be OK. . . ."

Tamsyn was used to this. Chattering to Scarlett about anything that came into her mind, while ruthlessly excising all traces of Sophie from her stories, came naturally now.

"Anyway," she said after talking nonstop for half an hour, "I need to go to my French class. I'll come back after it, OK? I love you. Happy birthday, darling. I got you some new pajamas. I'll ask the nurses to put them on you later. I've left them on the chair."

She was halfway to the door when it happened.

Scarlett spoke.

22

HAPPY BIRTHDAY.

Happy
birthday
darling.

They reach me down in my cave, and they are words I know. They change my safe place because they are attached to things from before. They bring a balloon into my cave and make the light a little brighter.

Happy means you feel good. *Birthday* means you have presents. The words fill the cave.

There's a balloon and a cake and a present suddenly there on the ground beside me. I look at it all. Happy birthday. These are the things it means.

And then the balloon and cake and present lose their colors. They turn gray and fade away. They fade because the other words come. New words—gray words, bad words—crowd in and push it all away. The new words stop everything, because the new words go like this:

I don't think you're going to get better.

i don't think
you are
going
to get
better.

She is Mum. And she is saying

i don't think you are going to get better
darling

I see the words hanging in front of me and I try to make them go away.

Yes, I am

Yes, I am

I am going to get better. I have been getting better down here. Sometimes I hear things. I'm fixing myself.

I know you are Mum.

I saw pictures of the happy-birthday things.

I am going to get better.

Yes, I am

Yes, I am

Yes, I am

Yes

I

am.

You are wrong. I am going to get better. Because I am here.

• • • • •

I don't listen to the rest of her words because I know that I have to make the bad words go away. I can send the words from my cave to the place where she is. They are three little words. I can do it. I imagine the things I have to do to send those words from my cave into her world.

I try and try and try.

When it finally works, they don't come out in the way I wanted. But they come out. The words go from here like a balloon, all the way up and up and up and up to there.

Yes, I am.

They go from me into the world, and I am back. They pull me with them, and I leave the cave and fly into the other world. Here I have a mouth and that means I can speak.

• • • • •

"Yes, I am."

I say it out loud, and everything changes.

23

TAMSYN STARED AT SCARLETT. SHE DIDN'T DARE TO BLINK.
Had that happened? Had Scarlett whispered?

She had heard it. Scarlett had said, *Yes, I am.* It was hoarse
and strange but it had been a version of her voice. Tamsyn would
have known that voice anywhere, at any time, however disguised
it was, however quiet.

She pressed the emergency button. She opened the door and
shouted, "Help! Help me! I need Dr. Singh."

She came back to Scarlett's bedside and picked up her hand
and stared into her face. Shame broke over her. A tsunami of
horror.

Yes, I am. She hadn't imagined those words. *Yes, I am* was
Scarlett's response to the thing Tamsyn had said, and the thing
Tamsyn had said was: *I don't think you're going to get better.* She
had said a lot of other things since then, but she knew what
Scarlett meant.

She held the edge of the bed and gasped. There was no air.
They said the atmosphere was purified, but under the smells of

lemon and yuzu, it smelled like bleach and chlorine and bad things. She wanted to choke on it.

Scarlett had heard those words. Her words—the first time Tamsyn had vocalized the fact that she thought her daughter was never getting better—had been the thing that pulled Scarlett back. Scarlett had heard her saying it and had, in true Scarlett fashion, come back to life to contradict her. Tamsyn felt the horror seep into every atom of her being. Her daughter had heard her giving up. Was there a paradox there? Had it taken Tamsyn giving up to bring Scarlett back?

Were they back to the old dynamic whereby Tamsyn would say something annoying and Scarlett would argue?

She looked at her daughter. Scarlett and Sophie were different, because Sophie was healthy and active, entirely alive, and Scarlett had been unconscious and absent while the world changed around her. Scarlett had a tube going into her nose. She had a cannula. She was constantly monitored. She had shown no signs of being present before now. She hadn't responded to anything. Her hair was much shorter than Sophie's because the clinic staff cut it regularly after it started to grow back. It was easier for everyone, and cleaner, if it was short. Her skin didn't glow like Sophie's. Sophie glowed from inside, and Scarlett was an opaque gray.

She was a sick version of her healthy twin. It was hard not to feel sometimes that Sophie had stolen the spark, the life force.

"Darling," said Tamsyn, taking her daughter's unresponsive hand, "come back. You can do it. Come back to us. Please, darling. Come back."

Her daughter had been going to die, and now she wasn't. Tamsyn had told Scarlett she wasn't going to get better, and Scarlett had come back to argue. The room filled with people. They all wanted to know what had happened, and when Tamsyn opened her mouth to tell them what had happened, she found that a lie came out.

She lied to everyone, and this time Scarlett didn't say anything.

24

YES, I AM.

Those are the words that bring me back into the world. I say them and I hear things starting to happen but it's too much and I fall back beneath the surface. I go farther down. I sink deeper and deeper and deeper, all the way back to the place I know is safe. Everything is dark and comfortable and I think I'll stay here for a long time.

I have lived here for a long time already. It's a place I know. I'm at home.

It's a comfortable place. It's lit by one candle today, and I blow that out because I'm too tired. I lie back on the ground, which is velvet today, and let nothing happen at all.

No one will find me here. I can stay as long as I want. There are some words. I ignore the *HAPPY BIRTHDAY* ones. *This city is so pretty in the sun* sits over to one side. *The pastry was all flaky, full of butter* is behind it. That one is just a collection of words. The city and the sun are things I almost know, so that one is my favorite. Then there is the word that came to me by itself: *Mum. Mum* means comfort and safety. This place here: this place is Mum.

I don't like the thing she said.

I actually have no idea what this place is. I haven't got a word that means *me*. I don't know what I am or where or who or why or other things. But I sink down. I'm all right here. I'll go back when I have to.

Then the HAPPY BIRTHDAY edges in front of the other words, and there are pictures around it. I don't want to see them. The HAPPY BIRTHDAY has a cake next to it and I know what that is, and I don't want to know what it is. I need to stay here where I'm safe.

I look around and I try to close my eyes, but I don't need eyes for this. This one is huge, and it's lit up brightly in pink. I hate pink. It is right behind me, and it says YES, I AM. It's shining like the sun.

The sun? Is it pretty in the sun?

I don't like it. It means change. I turn my back on it, but then it's in front of me too. *Yes, I am.* It's everywhere I look. Happy birthday. Yes, I am. Happy birthday. Yes, I am. Happy birthday. Yes, I am. Happy birthday. Yes, I am.

■ ■ ■ ■ ■

The light comes in and I feel myself rising again. I try to cling to the safe place but it's not dark anymore, and the candle goes out again, and the city is so pretty in the sun and the pastry was all flaky full of butter and happy birthday yes I am.

The words are helium balloons. They are pulling me up, out of my safe place. They're pulling me into a new one, where the light hurts and I'm not safe and I don't understand and I'm scared.

"Oh, darling," says a voice. "Darling, come back. You can do it. Come back to us. Please, darling. Come back."

I try to take those words back down with me. I want to put

come back to us in the dark place and look at it for a long time. I know those are words that have meaning. I want to look at them until I feel the meaning.

It's your birthday.

I am the *you.*

It's *my* birthday.

▪ ▪ ▪ ▪ ▪

"Darling," she says, "it's Mum."

Mum.

It's Mum. But it can't be Mum.

25

THE CLINIC STAFF HAD CHECKED SCARLETT OVER AND DR.
Singh had left her other patient to come to Scarlett's room, but
nothing was actually different. It was written down and recorded,
and Tamsyn kept having to repeat her lie. She'd said that Scarlett's *Yes, I am* was a response to Tamsyn's saying: *You're going to
get better, aren't you?* She thought she would probably tell that to
Ed too, because she couldn't bear to repeat the words she had
really said, to allow it to become the official narrative, recorded
and repeated whenever they talked about Scarlett.

Tamsyn looked at her daughter and waited for her to say
something more, but it didn't happen. She didn't just wake up.
Her eyes were still closed and she was the same as she had always been. Tamsyn talked and talked but Scarlett didn't respond.

In the end it was half past four, and Sophie was going to be
home from school with her friends, so Tamsyn knew she had to
go. She took a taxi back to the apartment, trying to see their new
life through Scarlett's eyes. She had talked about Scarlett waking
up and coming back but she hadn't really expected it to happen.
It had been something she said, a lucky charm. Now she tried to

picture the reality. She looked at herself, in her nice dress and sandals, with her expensive haircut, and wondered at how different she must be from the mother Scarlett remembered. She spoke French. Apart from everything to do with Scarlett, she was happy now. She had been unhappy before. That was the biggest difference: money could buy happiness, because it stopped you worrying about the day-to-day things and allowed you to walk by the lake and look at the sunshine.

Also, she and Ed had been in a bad, dark place in Cornwall, and now they were in love again. Would Scarlett notice that? Would it make her happier too?

As she watched the clean city go past, with its cafés and chocolate shops, its lake and its birds, she couldn't stop thinking about Scarlett coming back into their lives properly. How would Scarlett react to Sophie? How would Sophie adapt to Scarlett? They had never been a family of four: how did it work when there were as many children as adults, and when one of the adults was at work most of the time?

Above all, though—above everything else—was the fact that Tamsyn was, on a very deep level, scared of Scarlett. Mothering was easy with Sophie, and Scarlett used to make it feel impossible. Tamsyn was used to having a compliant, happy, engaged daughter now. She didn't know how she would manage when the difficult one was back.

But she would manage. Scarlett, like Sophie, might have no memories after the age of twelve. She had been difficult for only a year. The accident would have stopped all that. She would be reset. It was going to be fine.

⬛ ⬛ ⬛ ⬛ ⬛

Ed was waiting at home. Tamsyn told him about Scarlett (the lying version) and he cried for half an hour in her arms, then called Dr. Singh and cried down the phone too. He arranged to go to the clinic after Sophie's party so that when Scarlett woke up again someone would be there. They couldn't do what they used to do in Truro and have one of them at her bedside all the time, but they could get as close to that as possible. Tamsyn had mentally rearranged her life: she was going to stop French and yoga and spend all the time Sophie was at school sitting with Scarlett, talking to her, doing everything she could to pull her back. Ed would go after work every day for a few hours, and both of them would spend nights there sometimes too.

Their lives, which had been balanced, were changing. Tamsyn felt Scarlett, the silent satellite member of the family, pulling them into her orbit. She had gone from being the absent, half-secret one to the biggest, most volatile presence just by whispering three words.

Sophie was due home, and Ed was standing on the balcony and looking out in the direction of the clinic. Tamsyn walked up behind him and put her arms around his waist.

"Hey," he said without turning round.

She rested her cheek on his back. "Hey," she said. "You OK?"

"Yeah. Momentous, right? I'm quite . . . Well, I guess I'm in the process of pulling myself together for Soph. That's the aim anyway."

"I can't believe it. On her birthday."

"She didn't say anything else?"

"No. But she will. I mean, she probably will. Oh, God, Ed, if we hadn't come here, they would have switched her off. Switched her off! She was in there all along, and now she's spoken."

He turned round and took Tamsyn in his arms.

"They gave us a lifeline and we took it. That was our job. It's working. We just need to take it one day at a time. Right now we need to switch to being Sophie's parents and make sure she has an amazing birthday, right?"

Tamsyn nodded.

"So let's do it. For both of them."

"Sophie probably doesn't need to know?"

"Not when she has her friends here."

There wasn't actually much to do. There was already a huge banner in the living room: it read HAPPY BIRTHDAY, SOPHIE! JOYEUX ANNIVERSAIRE, SOPHIE! There were balloons around the place and a well-stocked fridge. Ed had managed to bring a birthday cake home in spite of the messages Tamsyn had sent while he was decorating it. They would order the burgers once the girls had decided what they wanted. Everything was ready.

The buzzer sounded. Tamsyn had often told Sophie she could have a set of keys, but she didn't want them.

"I like knowing that my mother will let me in when I get home," she said. "It's more friendly. There's just something safe and reassuring about it."

"So do we tell her tomorrow?" said Tamsyn when Sophie and her friends were on their way up.

"Maybe we do," said Ed. "But yeah, for now we have to make everything about her party."

· · · · ·

Sophie, Gemma and Amina burst into the apartment in a whirl of laughter and smiles and excitement and perfume, and Tamsyn couldn't stop smiling as she looked at them. At the same time, she mentally added Scarlett into the mix. *That would work,* she thought. *Two of Sophie, plus two others.* Though the girls would need separate friendship groups. These were Sophie's friends. Scarlett would find her own, and her friends would be different.

They might be less straightforward. Tamsyn remembered Scarlett before, and shivered.

"Hello, girls!" she said, forcing herself back into the present. "How was school?"

"Hello, Mrs. Trelawney," said Amina with impeccable manners. "It was good. Thanks. I mean, it's Friday and it's Sophie's birthday! Gemma and I sat in the sun while Sophie played chess. She's so weird! Thank you so much for having us here tonight. Your apartment is amazing."

"Thank you for coming," Tamsyn said. "And truly, thank you both for being such good friends to Sophie. I know you were both welcoming to her from her very first day, and it means a lot to us."

Amina was tall, with black hair in an artfully messy bun. Gemma was small and blond and American. She gave Tamsyn a bright white smile.

"We love Sophie," she said. "And I love birthdays, so this couldn't be any more perfect. And Amina's right: your home is beautiful."

They all said a few more polite things, and then Sophie shepherded the girls into her room before coming back and hugging Tamsyn.

"Thank you so much, Mum," she said. "This is just right."

■ ■ ■ ■ ■

Tamsyn didn't have anything to do. She didn't know what she had expected: the girls were hardly going to want to play party games. They stayed in Sophie's room, watching those old movies on the DVD player Tamsyn had ordered for her, and Tamsyn heard squeals from time to time and gales of laughter, screams.

She and Ed exchanged glances. The contrast between the two girls was hard to compute, but at least she had him. He understood. They had been through every moment of this together.

"Hey," he said. "This is how it's meant to be, right?"

"I know."

"Scarlett spoke. That's immense. I know it brings all kinds of things with it, but it's a massive step toward the thing we want most of all, right? We can be a family of four."

"But . . ." She stopped. "Do you remember back in Cornwall? We asked what would happen when Scarlett woke up, and they said Sophie would say she was going on a trip, and she'd pack a bag and leave. And at the time we thought it was the thing we wanted. But it's not. We can't have Sophie leaving, Ed. We can't. I can't lose her." She realized she was crying. A burst of laughter came from the direction of Sophie's room, and then she was sobbing into his chest. "We can't let Sophie go. Where would she go? I love her too much. I need her to stay."

"Hey!" He stroked her hair and she relaxed a bit. "Stop it, honey. Stop crying, darling. It won't happen. That's why we've been talking ever since about becoming a family of four. Luca said Sophie leaving was *one of* the options; at the time it was the one we needed to hear. Remember, we thought Sophie was going to be . . ." He stopped, because they both knew it would be wrong to say any of those words. "And we accepted the project as a lifeline for Scarlett. What Luca actually said was that if Scarlett woke up, it was going to be up to us. The team doesn't want Sophie to take herself away forever. Why would they? They love her being here. Johann says she's the most successful reanimation they've ever had. We all want the same thing. Twin daughters. But you know that. We talk about it all the time. That's why Scarlett has a bedroom."

Tamsyn sniffed and nodded.

"I know," she said. "But until today it felt like a dream. Like a fantasy. Sorry." She patted Ed's chest. "I've covered your lovely T-shirt in mascara."

"Gives me an excuse to change. I'm not used to having a wardrobe full of things I actually want to wear."

"We really get to do this? I mean, I know we do, but it suddenly feels like it could actually happen."

"We really get to do this. Forever."

New worries rushed in. "What if the girls don't get on?"

"Stop it!" He pulled her back into a hug and spoke into her hair. "Tamsyn, honey. It doesn't matter. They're fifteen. It's going to take Scarlett a long time to get out of that clinic, realistically, and we can't have any idea what kind of damage she's sustained. They're only a few years off being adults. I think they'll get on—I think they'll realize that they owe their existence to each other. Even if they didn't get on at all, they'd have to live in the same household for only a few years."

"I don't want them to only live in the same household for a few years!" Tamsyn said, crying again. "I want them both forever!"

"Oh, sorry! Well, you get them both as your daughters forever, right? And I'm afraid you're stuck with me, no matter what. We've been through everything. We'll get through this next bit."

They ordered burgers from a hugely expensive American place in town. All three girls ordered vegan lab meat, and Tamsyn, who had never eaten meat because of the economics of it and didn't fancy fake meat either, went for a mushroom burger. Only Ed chose a burger made from dead animal, and he refused to apologize. Tamsyn added a salad and a selection of potato and sweet potato fries to the order, and all the fizzy drinks the girls wanted, and Ed opened a bottle of champagne and poured it for everyone while they waited for the delivery to arrive.

They all toasted Sophie, and Tamsyn made eye contact with Ed and knew that they were both adding Scarlett. She was surprised when Sophie put her glass down after one sip and said: "I'd like to make another toast actually, because it's not just *my* birthday." She picked up her glass. "To my twin sister, Scarlett, in hospital. I hope she'll be here with us all for our sixteenth birthday."

Amina and Gemma weren't surprised to hear about Scarlett, and Tamsyn wondered what Sophie had said about her. She knew that she wouldn't have told them she was a clone, so she followed her lead and said, "Yes. To Scarlett. To both our beautiful daughters."

Everyone looked serious, and Gemma said, "I can't even imagine how hard it must be to have her in the hospital like that. I think you're all amazing for carrying on like you do."

Tamsyn found she couldn't answer. Ed stepped in.

"It's difficult," he said. "But Sophie keeps us going. And we're hopeful that Scarlett's condition will improve, so, like Sophie says, maybe she *will* be here for their next birthday."

■ ■ ■ ■ ■

The cake was huge and brightly colored, with a big letter S on it and a circle of candles around the edge. There were sugar roses and tiny meringues, and Tamsyn tried to imagine her former self looking at it, but their old life in Cornwall was starting to feel unreal. Geneva was real life, and Cornwall felt like a weird dream. It couldn't really have happened. How could anyone go from that to this? Nobody got to do a thing like that. The world was set up in a way that meant it didn't happen.

She put it from her mind and cut big slices of cake for everyone, and an extra slice for Scarlett.

26

SHE'S WAKING UP.

They think I don't know but I've heard them talking. She spoke to Mum on my birthday. The next day Mum unlocked the other bedroom and went in for a long time. She locked it again when she came out, but I took the key from her bedroom and went in myself when she was out on the terrace.

It was horrible. I'd been in before, but this time I was imagining the original version of me moving in there soon, and I had to work really hard not to cry. It was like my room, but a little bit nicer. The colors were better. The view was prettier. Everything in the room was almost exactly the same.

They gave me the second-best room.

Also known as the worst.

I know that the real girl is waking up and they won't need me anymore. I'm not a real girl: I read through all the information on their special iPad and discovered, among other things, that there are cameras implanted on my retinas. Scientists watch the world through my eyes. They see what I'm seeing. It makes me so furious that when I found out, I took a piece of paper and wrote

FUCK OFF on it and looked at it for a long time. I might not be able to say it but I can still write it.

I can't get my head round any of this, and if Scarlett wakes up properly, one of the options is to send me away.

Hello? Send me away? I think not. I'm here now and I'm not going to let her push me out. If this needs to be a war, then that's what we'll have.

My job is to make my family happy. My family has three people in it. Me, Mum and Dad. She doesn't belong here; if she has to wake up, she should go to Cornwall.

Eight days after my fifteenth birthday, I wait until they're both asleep, and then I pick up Dad's set of keys and leave the apartment. I'm wearing running clothes, and I just run until I get there. The city is safe and the clinic is only a few miles away. I'm there in no time, running over the bridge, along residential streets, from one patch of streetlamp light to the next. I'm so brilliantly made that I'm hardly out of breath.

The place is well guarded, so I know I don't have much time. I hope my face and fingerprints are still logged with their system.

They are. I just walk in. The security guard barely looks up.

I have no idea where to find her, so I take the stairs and walk around until finally I find a corridor with high windows on one side and identical doors on the other, and one of them, the last one before a big metal door that blocks the route, has a plaque saying SCARLETT TRELAWNEY on it, and I open the door and go straight in.

There's only one camera. I see it at once. It's focused on the bed and the chair beside it. There's nothing capturing the rest of the room.

I stand a meter or so from the bed. Her skin is terrible. She smells quite bad, and there are tubes and machines everywhere.

It feels weird. This is my source material, my discarded husk, and I need to get rid of her. I like things the way they are and I'm not going to be second-best.

"My darling sister." I say it loudly: this room is probably bugged. "Poor, sweet Scarlett."

Is that too much? There's no point being subtle about it, I guess.

I glance at the machines and look quickly away. All I have to do is switch off the life support. It's easy, and I'll have to do it in the most controlled, slow way I can, keeping the cameras in my eyes focused on Scarlett in her bed. I check the machines; they are plugged into the wall down at the floor.

I walk over to her and look down.

"My sister." I touch the skin on her arm. It's warmer than I expected. It'll be cold soon enough.

"Scarlett," I say.

I'll need to take four steps to my left, then crouch down and reach over with my left hand without looking that way again. I should be able to pull out all four in about twenty seconds and then I'll leave. They'll know I've been here, but when she's dead again, it'll be too late. They won't rush to the room if I just say a few nice things and leave.

"They won't even let me look at you," I say. "I don't know why. I can't sleep for imagining you, so I had to sneak out so we could meet. I just had to and I'm glad I did. It's so wonderful to see you. Everything's going to be fine. You'll see."

I take the four steps, continuing my monologue, and crouch down. I'm reaching out when the door handle moves.

Someone is coming in.

I stand up.

"Sophie?"

I turn. Dr. Singh is standing there.

"What? I just wanted to come and see my sister."

She looks at me. I hold her gaze and wait it out. I win.

"Are you sure?"

"What are you saying?" Deny and act affronted. That's all I can do. My heart is pounding. I was so psyched up for that.

"Sophie!" says Johann. He's filling the doorway. "You came to see her! Interesting."

I shrug. Fully thwarted this time. I turn my focus to him.

"I just wanted to see her, Johann. I was so curious. I couldn't stand it that everyone can visit apart from me when I *am* her."

"You have a point," says Johann, giving me a huge predatory smile. "I—"

Dr. Singh steps forward.

"Johann. I'm sorry, but I can't have this. Sophie can't be in here. Full stop. And I'm not sure her motivation was as clear-cut as she's saying."

Dr. Singh doesn't like me. I've always known it and now I understand why. She's obsessed with Scarlett. I'm nothing to her apart from now: right now I'm a danger to her precious comatose baby.

I make a confused face. "Well, my *motivation* was to see my sister, Dr. Singh. What else would it be? Though she's not really my sister, is she? My self. I was visiting myself. I've asked and asked and asked but no one will let me, so I had to find my own way."

She ushers us both out of the room, closes the door and turns on me.

"Whatever you say, Sophie. The fact remains: I can't have my patient being upset by something that she can't understand. She's not ready to know about you. We know she can hear, and I can't have you telling her you're her sister. It's too much. You're going to need to be more patient."

Johann looks between us, and he chooses me.

"I understand, Sophie," he says. "I know it's frustrating but we're going to have to follow the good doctor's rules. I'll take you home."

He half hugs me. He smells of sweat and expensive cologne. I give him my biggest smile.

"Can you turn my eye cameras off?" I say since he seems receptive. "It's such an invasion. You watch me from the outside all the time anyway. I hate it."

He nods. "Understood. We'll think about it. I'll talk to the team."

We agree that my parents don't need to know about my trip because it would only worry them. As we walk away, I turn to look back at Dr. Singh. She gives me a look, and for a second, I am certain she knows exactly what I was about to do.

27

ONCE SCARLETT STARTED GETTING BETTER, IT HAPPENED quickly. She started with muttered sounds and occasional words, and then she opened her eyes. She looked at Tamsyn. She looked at the window. She didn't say much, but she took it all in, a strange expression on her face. She couldn't have a conversation, but Tamsyn and Ed saw her looking at them, coming back into the world.

"Mum," she said after two weeks. Her voice was croaky, but it was still her voice.

"That's right, darling," Tamsyn said. "I'm Mum."

In July she started talking in phrases, then sentences, then asking questions, and by August she was taking hesitant steps and strengthening her muscles with hours of physio every day.

Twice, she looked at Tamsyn and said, "There was another girl."

Tamsyn asked about the other girl, but she couldn't say more than that. It was unsettling.

Whenever Tamsyn came into the clinic, Dr. Singh seemed to be with Scarlett. Often she was just sitting in Tamsyn's chair by the bed, talking. Sometimes there would be a couple of physios in there too, helping her to move and stretch. Scarlett never seemed to be alone anymore.

. . . . .

"This is really the most wonderful thing," said Dr. Singh as Tamsyn arrived one August morning. "She is the most determined patient I think I've ever had, and she's shaping up for a full recovery. Aren't you, Scarlett? You want to get up and about. She knows where we are. Is that right, Scarlett?"

Scarlett nodded. "Geneva," she said. "Switzerland. Geneva, Switzerland. We live in Switzerland so I can get better."

Her voice was still hoarse, which Dr. Singh had explained was because she had spent so much time on a ventilator. She'd had a tube down her throat breathing for her, and it had damaged her vocal cords. But it would get better in time probably. "And if it doesn't, you'll just have a lovely husky voice."

"Yes, we do! Geneva, Switzerland!" Tamsyn grinned and went to sit on the other side of her bed. "That's amazing! I can't wait for you to come home. Our life is so different. You remember when we lived in Cornwall? You lived all your life there until now. Then you had an accident and we were lucky enough to be offered medical treatment here. So here you are with the best doctors you could possibly have." They went over these things all the time, because it was good for Scarlett to have it reinforced.

Tamsyn had to tell Scarlett about Sophie now, and she was starting to see that a part of Scarlett already knew. She talked about *the other girl* from time to time: someone must have hinted at Sophie's existence in spite of all the precautions.

The time had arrived, however, to tell her properly. Sophie was doing a holiday course in coding, which meant she was out of the house all day every day this week, but next week she would be at home.

And next week they wanted Scarlett to go home too. She had to know. No one could postpone it any longer.

Even though Scarlett had been in the clinic for months, Tamsyn wasn't sure anyone was ready for this change: she felt Johann and his team were rushing it because they were greedy for data. Dr. Singh was trying her best to slow it down. She had fought Johann hard over the timing and lost; now she said she was going to visit every day, and the physios would come over daily too.

"I know that it's important for her to start to see what day-to-day life in Geneva will look like," Dr. Singh had said. "To see something beyond these walls. You have that roof terrace, right? That will be just the place for her. Sitting on the balcony, looking out at the city. As she likes to say"—Dr. Singh smiled—"this city looks so pretty in the sun."

For some reason, that was a phrase Scarlett used all the time. Tamsyn smiled at it too.

"I know that it's good that she'll get to experience that and to feel the sun on her skin, and just start to get used to life again. But we need everything else to be as calm as possible, because, of course, she's going to have to deal with the fact that she suddenly has a twin sister. And I hope she's going to be OK with that. I'm going to need you and Ed to supervise them constantly, Tamsyn. Don't leave them alone together. It's too much."

Meanwhile Luca, Maya and Johann were working with Sophie. Unlike Dr. Singh, they were excited at the prospect of seeing the twins learning to live with each other.

"I don't mean to be callous," Johann had said the other day, "but it's unusual for a patient like Scarlett to wake up. We're delighted that she's on course to make a reasonably full recovery. We've carried out this procedure twenty-four times, and Scarlett's the only one who's come back to us. So we are very excited indeed to see what's going to happen next. Our priority is making sure Sophie is ready for it. Be assured we have both girls' well-being as an absolute priority."

*****

Sophie had, of course, worked out what was going on, and she had spent the time since her birthday asking to visit her twin. Tamsyn had been afraid she might just turn up at the clinic, but she hadn't, and now she didn't need to.

Ed and Tamsyn had divided things up, so Ed spent almost every night at the clinic while Tamsyn spent night after night alone in their huge marital bed in their massive bedroom. She would stretch out and come nowhere near the edges, missing Ed desperately.

*****

Now Tamsyn took Scarlett's hand. It was time to tell her that she was right about the other girl. She had rehearsed the words. So-phie's team was listening, but only Tamsyn and Dr. Singh were in the room.

The knowledge that she had an invisible audience was unset-tling. She knew they were monitored constantly in most areas of the apartment, but she had managed to stop thinking about it when she was at home.

She took a deep breath and reminded herself to follow the script. The script would lead her through, and then there would be no more secrets.

"Scarlett," she said, "there's something you need to know, dar-ling. Are you OK to listen carefully? We didn't tell you before because you needed to get stronger first. And actually I think you kind of know this already."

Scarlett turned her head and fixed Tamsyn with a look. Real Scarlett was there behind her eyes. Whether or not her body ended up working as it had before, this was Scarlett. Tamsyn was still a bit scared of her. A part of her expected Scarlett to swear in her face. She was always partly braced for Scarlett to tell her to fuck off.

"What?" Like most of Scarlett's words, it came out as a whisper.

"Right." Tamsyn felt Dr. Singh's eyes on her but kept her gaze on Scarlett. "Don't worry. It's nothing terrible; it's just something we haven't been able to tell you before about our life here." She inhaled, exhaled, inhaled again. "You've mentioned another girl a few times. I don't know when you heard about her, but it's true. There *is* another girl, or rather—the same girl." She took a deep breath. "When you had the accident, you were very ill in hospital in Truro. As you know, we did have health insurance, but we didn't have enough for them to keep treating you for a long time. That time was coming to an end, and you weren't getting better."

Scarlett nodded.

"So we were invited to come here and join a medical trial, and they gave us the most wonderful place to live and I seem to have learned French pretty well, and Dad has a job, and look at how brilliantly you're doing!"

"I know all that."

"So, darling, we've never told you exactly what the medical trial is, and now you need to know. This is a trial that involves some really cutting-edge medical techniques." This was it. She looked into her daughter's eyes and recited the words she had practiced so many times. "While you've been slowly fixing yourself, they took some of your tissue and worked with it to reanimate it and to grow it. They used your brain and an AI system—a computer system—to re-create you. Basically, while you've been here, they made a reanimated version of you, Scarlett. A second self." She paused, but Scarlett didn't react. "And it worked. You always wanted a brother or sister, darling, and now you have one. A sister. A twin. She's the other girl."

It sounded impossible, but every word had been true. She waited.

"Say it again," Scarlett said. "All of it."

So Tamsyn did. She recited the script again, exactly the same.

"This isn't real," Scarlett said. "Is it a dream? They made a new version of me with my body and computers. You're calling it a twin. I'm an only child. I don't think this is real." She shifted in her bed, moving away from her mother. She looked at Dr. Singh. "Is it real?" she said to her. "Is Tamsyn real?"

"Yes," said Dr. Singh, "your mother is real, and so is everything she said. I'm sorry, darling. I know it's difficult, but I've seen it all happening. I've met your reanimation. It's OK. She's like you, Scarlett. Try not to worry. We can talk about it as much as you want."

"It *is* real, darling," Tamsyn said. "You have a sister. She's called Sophie. We're calling you twins because that's what you are. You didn't come about in the way that identical twins usually do, but you're the same as you would have been if an egg had divided back in the womb. I think Sophie will be a good friend to you. She's excited about meeting you. A sister and a friend. She's lovely."

Scarlett shook her head and lay back on the pillow and stared at the ceiling. For the rest of the visit, she didn't make eye contact with Tamsyn or say anything. After a while she closed her eyes and either fell asleep or pretended to.

•••••

When Sophie came home from coding camp, she was excited.

"Did you tell her?" she said. "What did she say? Can I visit?"

She danced around, trying out some jujitsu moves, then dropping down into a split. It was hard to keep up with Sophie, who was so relentlessly alive. She was growing up too: even in the short time that she'd been with them, she had changed. She looked older, more sure of herself. In some lights she could be eighteen. It was, Tamsyn thought, her confidence. She knew so much, could do so much, and she was bursting with potential.

Sophie was a personification of everything Scarlett had lost. Sophie was spinning around the flat while Scarlett couldn't stand up on her own.

"You have to remember, darling," she said, "that Scarlett's going to take a while to process this. She's still healing, and it's a big thing to take in. Remember how you felt at the restaurant that night? She'll be happy when she's got her head round it."

"It's a lot. When can I see her?"

"Slow down, sweetie! It's hard to have a conversation when you're a blur. I don't know. Remember, she processes things differently from you. It might take a while."

Sophie stopped moving and jutted her bottom lip like a child's sulk. "I'm impatient!"

"I'm pleased you're excited," said Tamsyn, though she was beginning to feel a tiny bit of suspicion.

She'd never felt that Sophie had the capacity to be anything other than entirely straightforward, but this didn't feel genuine. It reminded her weirdly of the night of Scarlett's accident when she had said she was staying at Leanne's house. She had pushed it too far, to the point where Tamsyn hadn't been able to believe her even though life would have been simpler if she could have. And now Sophie was doing the same thing. She was being too agreeable, too excited. A part of her was trying to tell Tamsyn something was wrong.

She walked over to Sophie and put an arm around her. "It's OK," she said. "Honestly, I know this is scary, and it's scary for her too, but remember, we're in this together. None of us expected it to happen so soon. Johann said they've done this twenty-four times and the source person has never woken up before. So that's twenty-three other people like you who *haven't* had to confront this situation. And you're the youngest, and you do. It's going to be so positive. It truly is. I mean, I can see it because for me it's everything in the world, the idea of having both my daughters at home. I totally believe that having a sister will turn out to be a wonderful thing for both of you."

"Can I meet the other twenty-three?"

That wasn't what Tamsyn had expected. She was relieved.

"Well, let's ask Johann. It would be good, wouldn't it? I'm sure we could arrange it. For you to meet one of them at least."

Sophie walked toward the corner of the room and looked up at the tiny camera. "Hey," she said, "Johann, please can I meet the others like me? And while I'm here, can you *please* take the cameras out of my eyes now? You said you'd look at it ages ago. I'm a human too, and it's so intrusive. I'm pretty sure you can't actually do that to someone. I mean, call me a cyborg or whatever, but I have a human brain and I think I have some rights here."

She turned away, emotional.

"Yes," said Tamsyn. She looked up at the corner too. "I agree with her," she said loudly. "Give her a bit of privacy. Please. The rest of us don't have cameras in our eyes, and surely you've seen enough."

"Exactly!" Sophie's voice was tight. "It's shoot. It's not fair. They tell me I'm a human like everyone else but better, but then they don't even let me look at something without them watching."

Tamsyn nodded. "You're right. You have a right to privacy."

"Thank you. And, Mum? Stop worrying about me and Scarlett. We get a sibling at last. I'm sure we'll understand each other in the way twins do. She's the original one, and I'm the new one, and we're going to be a team. I promise. It's an adjustment, but it's going to be fine."

"You're the two most amazing girls who ever lived. Sophie, never forget that Dad and I adore you forever. You, Sophie—you gave me my life back. It's the most incredible thing that's ever happened. Never, ever forget it. You must never feel anything other than utterly wonderful, special and magical."

Sophie looked at Tamsyn for a long time, then hugged her tightly.

28

AS SOON AS THE NURSE ENTERS IN THE MORNING, I START talking.

"I feel weak. My body hurts. I need to stay a few more days."

She smiles. "I'll fetch Dr. Singh. Can you sit up?"

I wriggle into a sitting position, and the nurse Amalia (she is my favorite) helps me get comfortable. My body doesn't actually hurt any more than usual. I know Amalia knows that and I know Dr. Singh will know it too. My broken legs were healed long ago while I slept, and my physical problems are more about learning to use my muscles again than anything else, apart from getting my stupid brain back into gear. Muscles and brain: those are the things I'm working on, and I can do those things at home.

Home. Whatever that means. I try to imagine the place everyone says is *a lovely apartment, so luxurious and different from the caravan.* But I can't. Sometimes it's a palace in my head, and sometimes it's just a couple of rooms, which would be luxurious after the caravan. I've looked at photos on phones, but I can't translate the squares of pixels into anything real.

This little world, the world of this hospital room, is all the home I need. Someone else has taken my place in the family. I don't belong there anymore. I belong here.

At first I was excited to see the city that was so pretty in the sun, and to go back into the family. All the bad things (the things I can't look at when they come into my head, the things I send away) are still in Cornwall, and now we're here and Mum and Dad look happy. It was a dream come true until the other girl came in. I thought she might have been a dream, but then Mum told me about Sophie.

I was in a coma, and while I was asleep, they replaced me.

. . . . .

When Dr. Singh comes in, I'm drinking a mango-and-orange smoothie. Drinking still feels weird, and I haven't managed to eat anything scratchy yet.

"How's my favorite patient?" she says, and I smile because that's our little joke.

She told me that she has three other patients in the clinic but I'm the only one who's awake. I'm the only one who's getting better. I'm the only one who talks back when she talks to me, and so of course I'm her favorite.

"Bad," I say. "Don't make me go. Please. Can I stay?"

"You're in luck," she says, and sits down.

I love every single thing about Dr. Singh. I love her white coat and the trousers and T-shirt she wears underneath it. I love her long hair, always tightly tied back. Once I asked how long it was and she undid it and it went all the way down her back as far as her bum. She's a bit younger than Mum, I think. Now that Mum has Sophie, I think I would like Dr. Singh to be my mum.

"I don't have to go?"

"If it was up to me, Scarlett, you'd be here for weeks yet. I think it's too soon. I know it's strange to live in a clinic, but—" I see her starting to say something, and then stopping. "Well, my personal opinion is that it's the best place for you right now. But on the other hand, you do need fresh air, and this place has no garden, balcony, whatever. Anyway, I've largely been overruled, but I did get you another night."

"I get to stay here tonight?"

"And you and Sophie will have a chance to meet properly before you're flung into living together twenty-four-seven."

It's not ideal but it'll do for now. Maybe I can postpone it one day at a time. I agree to everything and then wait for her. Wait for me.

I wonder why she said *properly*?

I remember the impression of someone else in the room, in the dark, the singsong words. The other girl. Dr. Singh was there. She knows.

▪ ▪ ▪ ▪ ▪

Dad comes in a couple of hours later. I look at him without really listening while he says all the usual things. His beard is shorter and neater than it used to be, and his skin looks better. He's not angry with me anymore: he used to hate me. I reach out, just because I can, because we don't have to fight anymore. He grips my hand with his.

I can tell that he's building up to something, and in the end, I can't bear it.

"Is she here?"

He stops. He gives me a little smile.

"Yes," he said. "Point taken. 'Get on with it, old man'—right?"

I nod and he steps back and looks through the door to a place I can't see.

"Sophie," he says, "come in, darling. Sophie, meet Scarlett. Scarlett, meet Sophie."

I close my eyes and try to sink back down, because I can still do that sometimes if I need to. Then I remind myself to be brave because I can't actually escape, and I pull myself back up and force my eyes open and look at the door.

I hear my own voice—my old voice, the one that didn't get torn to pieces by tubes—saying, "Oh, my God! Scarlett!"

There are feet on the floor running toward me, and then she takes my hand. There I am, me but not me. She's smiling, and after a couple of seconds, I manage to smile back.

She is the other girl. I thought it was a dream, but it was real. I know it as soon as I hear her voice. She fills the room in the same way. She said nice things to me, but Dr. Singh came in and was annoyed with her. Dr. Singh doesn't trust her.

And that's why Dr. Singh is trying, one day at a time, to keep me here.

Sophie is me but healthy. The sister I didn't have, the impossible new twin. I think of the stories from those programs Mum used to watch: twins separated at birth. That's how I feel: I'm back with the person I never imagined but who makes sense now that I see her.

She's looking at me with a smile on her face and distrust in her eyes.

"How about this?" she says quietly. "Oh, my God. There are two of us. Let's get you better and we can swap places and trick people and all those things twins do."

"No one would ever think I was you," I whisper. "But yeah, if we could, I'd like that."

I look into her eyes. My eyes are light brown flecked with gold. They are actually really pretty.

"Don't worry," she says. "You have a lovely bedroom. Mine is across the hallway from yours. They're the same but different. Mirror twins like us. You're not going to believe where we live. It feels normal now, but it's massive and beautiful, on the top floor of the building, and we can see all the way across the city."

I want to say, *This city is so pretty in the sun,* the mantra that helped me on my journey back, but I manage not to.

"I can't imagine it," I say instead. "I mean, I really can't. Mum and Dad, somewhere so— All I remember is living in the van."

"Yeah. And you've been stuck in this room for months, you poor thing. So at home, even when you're feeling a bit . . . shaky, you can sit out on the terrace. It's huge, and we have these wooden lounger things with cushions on them. So you can relax outside, get a bit of sun. You like books, right? They've put so many books in your room. So you can just lie there and read in the sun and get your strength back. It'll be like solar power."

"That sounds cool," I say. "Thank you. Tell me what it's like. What's school like?"

As she answers, talking about her friends, the school on the shore of the lake, the car that takes her there every day, I just watch her. She is me. She isn't a copy or a version of me. She is my other self. My heart is pounding and pounding.

She is my other self, and she hates me. She doesn't say it, but I can feel it.

Everyone hated me at school too. I push it away.

Her skin is clear and glowing. Her hair is long like Dr. Singh's, except it's a bit curly. I touch the back of my neck. My hair came off when I was ill, and it's still short. Sophie is wearing a short blue dress with pink roses on it, and she has clumpy shoes on. It looks good. There's a pink rose hair clip in her hair.

I realize that I was pretty before the accident. I didn't know it because my life was so fucked up. Everyone at school looked at me and laughed, and I had to be the person they said I was.

I see myself in the mirror sometimes. I try not to, but I've seen enough. Her hair shines and bounces, while mine hangs limp. She is stylishly dressed, while I'm always in the pajamas Mum brought in on my birthday or a white hospital nightshirt thing. I have the teddy a neighbor gave me tucked next to me, and I realize how babyish it is and push it under the sheet.

I know Sophie must be happy that she's the brilliant one and I'm the sick one. She is looking at me as she talks, and I feel all kinds of feelings. They swirl around, disappearing before I can tell what they are.

"And after school I sometimes go to visit Dad at the café," she's saying.

"What's Dad's café like?" Mum told me about the flaky pastry full of butter, but I want her to keep talking.

Instead of answering, she says: "I thought I was you. It took me ages to work out that I wasn't."

It's a punch to the stomach. She must have been confused, maybe furious, to find that I was still alive.

"How did you find out?"

She shrugs. "I knew Mum and Dad were coming here every day, and at first I thought they were just coming to see the team to talk about me, but then I realized they weren't because they never took me with them, and also Johann comes to visit every week and they never acted as if they'd seen him between visits. I had to work out what they were doing here, and I got there in the end."

"You're clever."

She shrugs. "I'm a cyborg!"

"How does that feel?"

"I don't know." She grins. "Quite cool, I guess."

I whisper so quietly that I'm not sure she can hear. "You came to see me in the night. Dr. Singh made you leave."

She doesn't answer; she just takes my hand and puts something in it. She closes my fingers around it and tells me with her eyes to keep it secret.

Dad steps forward. "That was the best thing I've ever seen," he says, putting an arm around Sophie. "You see? We're all going to get along just fine. Can I take a photo of you two?"

She sits close to me and we both smile.

I think I have a piece of paper in my hand, folded up small. I tuck it out of sight with the teddy. The room fills with people.

Sophie talked about someone called Johann, and now he's here. I haven't seen him before. He has slicked-back hair and a big sharky smile. There's Maya, who I think I've met. She has tears in her eyes when she looks at me. A man called Luca keeps staring and says he met me at the hospital in Cornwall and he can't believe what a miracle it is. Maya says she worked as my nurse in Truro. It washes over me: I don't care enough to make the effort to focus. My head is full of Sophie.

Sophie is talking for both of us. I just watch her and listen.

"Don't worry about us," she says. "We're going to be great. I had no idea I was missing her, but here she is and it feels perfect. I can't wait until she's up and about."

"Sophie," says Dr. Singh, pushing her way through to my bedside, "Scarlett won't be able to dash around town with you for a while. Getting this far has taken months. It's going to take the best part of a year before she can live in any way like you do. And she'll mainly need you to leave her to get on with it. Do you understand what I'm saying? I need you to leave her to heal."

"Yeah," says Sophie, "sure. But she'll get there. I can help her with French if she wants."

I watch Dr. Singh. She doesn't trust Sophie. She looks back at me, sees that I want to ask something and leans down.

"Why does she speak French?" I whisper. "And not me?"

"It's her AI," she says, and pats my shoulder.

Of course. I should have known that.

"We can talk about that later. Maybe Maya can sit with you and explain it all."

I nod. I'll be stuck at home with no friends, and Sophie will be sashaying around being popular. Dr. Singh told her to stay away from me but I feel like everyone else wants us to be together all the time. No one else sees it: just Dr. Singh. Dr. Singh won't be there.

I'm so, so tired. I close my eyes. The soft black place is pulling me down and I let it. I melt away from here and back into my safe place.

I understand everything there. I know what there is and where it is. There's velvet and there's a candle, and I have my little collection of words and birthday things. No one can come here apart from me. The last thing I hear is Dr. Singh's voice saying: "Out, everyone! Take this outside right now. Look at her."

· · · · ·

When I wake up, there are two physios in the room, waiting. Sophie has gone. I stretch my muscles and do my exercises as well as I can, motivated by the thought of my new Geneva life, because maybe it will be all right. I imagine myself saying *This is my sister, Sophie.* If I want to have friends, to keep up with her, I have to get myself better.

I swing my legs off the edge of the bed and stand up. I'm quite good at this now, even though it's shaky, and by my old standards, I'm crap. I walk across the room, holding the rail they always bring in, then turn around and walk back. That wouldn't be much for Sophie but it's massive for me. I'm going to catch up.

I lift things and stretch things and concentrate on doing it as well as I can. Unless anything changes, I'm going home tomorrow, to the apartment with the roof terrace. I'll go to school one distant day when I'm ready. I have to learn to be part of a family of four.

Mum, Dad, Scarlett and Sophie.

I nearly died and I'm coming back. They didn't expect me to get better, but here I am.

They replaced me because they thought I was going to die.

She doesn't want to be a twin. She wants to be the only one.

The only person who cares about me more than Sophie is trying to keep us apart.

. . . . .

When my old life in Cornwall comes back into my mind, the letter J is at its forefront. I push it away. I close my eyes and drift down as far as I can go. I'm halfway there when I remember that Sophie gave me a note, and that pulls me back. I find it under the duvet and hold it in my fist. She's me; I should be able to predict what this note will say.

It's probably a threat. But she wouldn't write that down. So it's probably not. It's probably a nice note, and it's probably insincere. I know she came into my room, and my feeling is that she was trying to harm me, though I think that only because of the look in Dr. Singh's eyes. Maybe Sophie just wanted to talk.

My fingers shake as I open the note, and the first thing I notice is that we have almost, but not quite, the same handwriting.

I look at it and I see straightaway that it's nicer than I expected. It's a lovely letter, and it has an apology hidden in it. I read it, relieved, and I fall down, into the safe place, and sleep for a long time.

29

TAMSYN WAS LYING ON THE SUN LOUNGER, HOPING THAT everything was going to be all right. She hadn't felt able to go to the hospital to watch the girls meeting: she didn't have the strength for it.

"It'll be fine," Ed had said. "I've got two weeks off, so let me be the driving force. OK? Go and think about something else for a while."

She lay here now in the sun and hoped that the rays were imparting some kind of magical strength. Some kind of ability to say the right thing, to look after two children with different needs at the same time.

She thought about pulling the dead flowers off the geraniums but couldn't move. She closed her eyes and felt the heat on her eyelids. She was covered in sun cream, but even so she knew she shouldn't be out there like this, in the full glare of the sun in the middle of an August day.

She must have drifted off because she was woken by Sophie saying: "Mum! Oh, no, she's asleep. Sorry."

Tamsyn sat up and looked round. The shade from the wall

had almost reached her. Her phone, on the ground beside her, showed that Sophie and Ed had both tried to call.

"Hey!" she called, and Sophie came back. She was glowing, and a wave of relief broke over Tamsyn. "How did it go?" she said.

"Oh, Mum, it was brilliant. I can't tell you. I'm going to help her get better. Honestly, you don't need to worry at all. Poor Scarlett! We're the same but different. I feel bad that I can speak French, and I've still got our real voice, and I can do martial arts and dance and all those things. And she's still getting used to walking. So I'm going to help her." She looked around the roof terrace. "We can get her walking around here maybe, in the fresh air. I was telling her about the sun loungers, how when she's tired she can just lie out here and read a book. Truly, as soon as I saw her, I just felt like 'Oh, hello. It's you! We're in this together.'"

Tamsyn swung her legs around and stood up. "Seriously?" she said. "You promise?"

"Seriously. Promise."

"Then that's the best thing I've ever heard."

Tamsyn felt the tension melting away. Dr. Singh had been right: the girls needed to meet before living together. Now Sophie seemed happy, and as far as Tamsyn could tell, it was real.

Ed stepped out too. "She's right," he said, touching both their shoulders. "It couldn't have gone better. It was one of those things that's worse when you're waiting for it than it is when it happens. Honestly, Tam, you should have seen them together. It was . . ."

He stopped and blinked several times, overcome with emotion.

Sophie took his phone and opened it with her thumbprint, which she had added to both of their phones weeks ago.

"Look," she said, after she found a picture and held it out to Tamsyn.

She took the phone and stared at it. There they were, her two daughters. Sophie had her arm around Scarlett, who was sitting up. Sophie was perched on the very edge of the bed and was grinning at her sister. Scarlett's illness was more apparent than ever beside her twin. She looked hesitant but happy.

"Oh, my God," said Tamsyn. "This is the most incredible picture. Your first meeting. Can you send it to me?"

"We already did," said Ed. "It'll be on your phone."

She found it. There it was: the most precious picture she had ever had. She made it into her lock-screen image at once.

"So," she said, "it's going to be OK for Scarlett to come home tomorrow?"

"It's going to be the best thing ever," said Sophie, and as far as Tamsyn could tell, she meant it.

· · · · ·

Tamsyn had a shower to wake herself properly and went to make sure Scarlett's room was completely ready. It was a beautiful room, and even though she wanted to do extra-nice things to it, she had already filled the drawers with comfortable clothes for lounging and recuperating in. There were already fresh flowers. Everything was clean and shiny. She walked over to the gauzy four-poster and pulled back a corner of the duvet to make it look extra inviting.

When Sophie went back to school next month, Tamsyn would devote her days to Scarlett's rehabilitation. She could see it stretching out in front of her. It was everything she had wanted since the accident. Her baby recovering.

She wondered how many other people had teams of physios and doctors visiting them at home all the time. How had this happened? Was it too good to be true?

No. They were a part of the trial, and this trial seemed to be working for everyone. There was no downside, no payback. Science was advancing. Everyone was winning. They had to be.

＊＊＊＊＊

The next day Tamsyn wanted to go to the clinic to bring Scarlett home, but somehow it had been decided that Ed would do it. She couldn't remember who had said it, but she knew that she was staying home with Sophie while Ed set off, endearingly wearing his smartest clothes (a linen shirt and some expensive trousers).

"We'll be a complete family," he said before he left, and Tamsyn's heart pounded.

They would. It would be momentous, and it was happening. Everything she'd wanted had come true.

She remembered herself catching an early-morning bus in the rain to clean offices in Truro or to harvest cauliflowers in the fields. She tried to send a message back through time, telling that version of herself that this life was just around the corner. It was unthinkable.

Too good to be true. You're missing something.

She silenced the voice.

＊＊＊＊＊

"I have a holiday assignment to do," said Sophie, "but I can't do it. I can't do it while I'm waiting. I can't concentrate on anything."

Tamsyn nodded. "Me too, sweetie. Forget the assignment. Thank you for being so welcoming to her."

Sophie shrugged and looked around. "You don't think it's too much? I don't want it to be, like, overwhelming."

Tamsyn had been sitting at the kitchen counter, drinking her third cup of coffee, while Sophie had decorated everything around her. She had made a banner that said WELCOME HOME,

SCARLETT! in bright red letters, and fixed it where Scarlett would see it as soon as she got in. She'd printed a photo of Tamsyn and Ed and written underneath it, *Look! Mum's Unbelievably Rapturous. Dad's Entirely Ready FOR SCARLETT!* which was quirky and odd and endearing. Sophie had smiled when Tamsyn questioned the weird phrasing, and said Scarlett would understand, that it was an in-joke from their conversation yesterday. She had been to the shops and bought balloons, and she was blowing them up and tying them to all the surfaces. She had strung up bunting. The whole place looked exuberant, exciting and so poignant that Tamsyn wanted to cry.

"It's perfect," Tamsyn said. "She'll love it. You're a superstar."

Sophie had told one of the cameras in the apartment that they needed a DVD player for Scarlett, and when it arrived a few hours later, she'd set it up in Scarlett's room with a selection of the currently popular nineties horror movies for her to watch, though Tamsyn was pretty sure Scarlett would need something a little cozier at first. Sophie had selected the films so carefully. It was lovely. Sophie loved things that were retro and cool, so Scarlett probably would too.

Tamsyn and Sophie looked at each other.

"What do you think it's going to be like for her," said Sophie, "leaving the clinic? I mean, that's got to be strange."

Tamsyn had been thinking about that constantly. "What was it like for you?" she said. "Because I guess you're the only person who knows what it's like, though she has her physical issues to deal with too."

"Yeah, I guess." Sophie stepped backward, disappearing into the corridor and then reappearing with a backflip, a new skill. "Sorry," she said when she was upright again. "So for me? I had the memories of Cornwall, and everything here was shiny and new and sunny next to what was in my head. I remember that.

There was more sunshine and the sky was different. We could see the mountains in the distance sometimes. The lake. It was like being in a movie. Nothing felt real." She sighed and gave a half smile. "And then I discovered that it was the world that was real and me that wasn't."

"Sophie! You're completely real. I'm your mother and I should know."

"I mean, I exist, and I guess I have free will and all that. But I wasn't quite who I thought I was. That photo you have on the wall? That's not actually a picture of me. It's been a weird thing to get used to. You're my mother, but you didn't give birth to *me*. And Scarlett's woken up to find that not only is she in a different place but I've turned up, and she's not stupid: she knows that I was put here to replace her, not to live with her. So I guess she's going to be worried too. I know that my job is to complete the family. To make everyone OK. So I'll do that."

"I know you will," Tamsyn said with a surge of love for Sophie. "Her life is better now." She wondered whether to say this to Sophie, and decided to try it. "Do you remember anything from the last year or so? Scarlett became very . . . kind of . . . difficult in the past year. She went off to meet friends all the time, and she was furious when we tried to stop her. It was horrible."

"I don't remember that at all." Sophie said it so quickly, so fluently, that Tamsyn wondered, just for a second, if she was lying. "She'll be fine here, though. I mean, it's not that I'm glad she was hit by a car, but we did all get a new life out of it. So that's weird."

"Very weird."

They looked at each other. Their entire world was based on the fact that Scarlett had run into the path of a speeding car. It wasn't something that could be scrutinized for any amount of time at all.

∎∎∎∎∎

Scarlett and Ed arrived an hour later than scheduled. Sophie had gone out to the terrace, where she was leaning on the wall staring out at the city with her hair up. The curve of her neck made Tamsyn want to take Sophie in her arms and look after her forever. Tamsyn was on her stool, drinking water now. She felt as if she had no option but to wait where she was, paused until the family was complete.

She had put the pile of presents in her and Ed's room out of sight. Things had been delivered for each of them, and it was all too much. She decided to ask Maya to stop sending them. It was so kind of her, but it felt relentless, almost intrusive. It devalued everything.

Then the buzzer sounded, and Tamsyn went to look at the screen and saw Ed guiding Scarlett through the building's front door. She counted at least five medical staff with them and called to Sophie, who was at her side in a moment.

They waited by the elevator. It was small, and when the doors opened, only three people were in it. Scarlett was in the middle between Ed and Dr. Singh.

"Mum!" said Scarlett, and Tamsyn stepped forward and held her.

Scarlett was different from Sophie but the same. Sophie's hair was usually fragrant with argan oil, while Scarlett's smelled like illness and the hospital as well as apple shampoo. Yet they had the same underlying essence. They were both Tamsyn's babies.

It was strange how easily she had come to think of them as twins. It sometimes felt lucky to her: the fact that there was a natural process by which people could have two identical children. She and Ed had reached that point by a different route, but to the outside world, the Trelawneys would just look like a twin family.

Tamsyn led Scarlett inside and heard the elevator immediately setting off back down.

Scarlett stopped on the threshold. "This?" she said. "This is where we live?"

Tamsyn remembered the van, the way things were always breaking and nothing quite worked. She hoped, for a moment, that the chickens were OK, then pulled herself back.

"I know. It's a different world," she said. "It'll take you a while to get used to it. But soon, I promise, it's going to feel like home." She smiled. "Dad and I got used to it surprisingly quickly, and you will too."

"This is where we live," Scarlett said, more to herself than to anyone else. She looked at the banner, the balloons. Her poor face was so confused.

Tamsyn led her down the corridor and into the living area. She stared at the photo of Tamsyn and Ed and the strange message underneath it for a long time. She looked at the photo of the three of them on the beach, and Tamsyn thought she might take that one down, now that Sophie had pointed out that she wasn't in it. Soon she was sitting on the squashy blue sofa under a canopy of balloons, and the flat was full of people and medical equipment.

Dr. Singh was talking to Ed. Sophie was chatting to Johann. Tamsyn heard a snatch of conversation.

"Yes," Sophie said. "I mean, you know that because you watch me. Can you *please* take out that feed from my eyes? You keep saying maybe and then you never do."

Tamsyn tuned into his reply.

"Yes," he said, "we've discussed that since you started raising it, and your point is valid. Our understanding is evolving all the time. We needed to monitor you intensively through the early days and weeks. The first couple of months, I suppose. But I'd be happy to turn off your retinal feed as soon as Scarlett's settled in, because you're right: it is an invasion of your privacy. We do, however, need to monitor the next week or so."

"Need?" Sophie was scathing. "Really, Johann?"

Tamsyn sat next to Scarlett and squeezed her hand.

"You OK?" she said quietly.

Scarlett nodded, though she looked tearful. Tamsyn looked to Dr. Singh, who took charge.

"We'll set up everything she needs in her bedroom," she said. "I'll explain it all. She's going to be exhausted, so don't expect anything more from her today. And please respect her privacy at all times. Let her alert you if she needs something."

Her eyes flicked to Sophie for a fraction of a second and then away. "I'd have kept her at the clinic for a few more weeks to be honest, but I was overruled. So I'll be visiting every day for the first week at least. Scarlett, do you want to sleep now?"

Scarlett nodded. She wiped her eyes with her sleeve, but Tamsyn couldn't tell if she was upset, or happy, or overwhelmed. The gym equipment was all going into the fourth bedroom: Tamsyn watched Scarlett's walking bars, a rowing machine and an exercise bike going past, heard the lift arriving again and again.

She helped Scarlett stand up and led her slowly into the bedroom that none of them had ever really thought would be used.

Scarlett looked from the bed to the window with its view across this magical city, to the TV on the wall and the iPad on the bedside table, the shelves and shelves of books, the medical equipment.

"Mine?" she whispered.

"I know, darling. Yes. It's all for you. I'll show you the rest of the apartment whenever you feel ready for a walk around. Or we can put you in a wheelchair to give you the tour. You have your own bathroom. It's through that door there. The other one is a wardrobe. Just have a rest for now."

There was a knock at the door, and one of the physios handed Tamsyn a little bell, an old-fashioned tinkly one.

"Dr. Singh said to give you this," she said, "so Scarlett can alert you if she needs something."

Tamsyn put it on the bedside table. Scarlett swung her feet around and lay back on the pillows. She closed her eyes, and after a while, Tamsyn thought she was asleep, so she walked quietly out of the room and closed the door.

When she turned round, Sophie was standing right there. Tamsyn put a hand to her chest.

"Oh, you scared me!" she said.

"Sorry. Can I go in?"

"Not right now, sweetie. She needs to sleep. Remember what Dr. Singh said about privacy? Give her an hour or two. Is that OK?"

"Of course!" said Sophie. "I might go for a run, then, rather than stand around waiting."

"Yes," said Tamsyn. "Good idea. Get some air. She'll be here when you get back. She's not going anywhere."

In any event, though, Johann interrupted.

"Can Maya and I take this young lady out for hot chocolate and a chat?" he said. "I'd like to have a game of go with her."

Sophie, delighted, went off with them instead.

30

I'M LYING DOWN. THE SMELL IS DIFFERENT. THE SOUNDS ARE different: I can hear people talking outside my room. Usually I hear only people who are inside the room.

I open my eyes, and as soon as I see that my bed has a kind of ceiling on it with material hanging down, I remember.

New home. The place where Sophie lives.

I close my eyes again but I can't sleep. The safe place won't have me.

I lie still and try to go over it all in my head. The more times I go through it, the more real it becomes.

Dad came to the hospital. Everyone stood around. They looked at pieces of paper. Dr. Singh argued with Johann, but he won and that's why I'm home. She sent them all out of the room and helped me get changed into a soft blue T-shirt and some comfy trousers. I'm still wearing them.

We came in a car. I can't remember it much. I know how much I didn't want to leave the clinic. I know there was a van that parked behind us and they brought things out of it to help with my rehab at home.

Then Dad helped me up the steps, and then I was here. The apartment is a palace and I should love it.

But it feels strange.

I can't believe we live here. This can't be real.

I

am

so

scared.

I'm scared of Sophie. She wrote the right things. She said them. But I think she came into my room that time to harm me. I know her because she's a version of me, and I don't trust her one tiny bit. I don't know why they still need her now that I'm getting better.

They have changed, particularly Mum. I miss the way she used to be. She was grumpy, tired, shouty, but I always knew she loved me fiercely. Now she doesn't care as much and I don't think she argues with anyone. It's weird to see her diluted.

I think back. My life at home was shit. It was out of control, and now I've got away.

I try to smile. It feels like magic, getting away from J and from school, and living here in my own room in this perfect place. I can handle Sophie.

Can't I?

I lie back and close my eyes.

·····

I might not trust her, but that's because if I were in her position, I wouldn't trust me. I take a deep breath and imagine that I'm her. First she thought she was me, and then she found out I still existed. She must feel weird about that at best. She probably hates me. She doesn't see the need for me to exist now that she does. I feel the same about her.

However, I'm going to override my instincts and be positive because now I get a sister. She is the only other person who's had no say in any of it. They moved me into this world while I was unconscious, and they created her from me. We are the same.

We have to be a team. She left me some films in case I want to watch them. I don't at the moment, but it's nice of her to try.

I look at the titles. They're horror movies. Weird.

·····

My bones hurt. I feel that I'm put together wrong and my muscles are weak. I always have a low-level headache. I'm still shit at walking. But I'm home, even if it's all new.

I try to rewind back past the accident, back to before it happened, before any of this started. If I can't go to the safe place, I'll go to the past so that when I open my eyes, I will be amazed all over again by the present. I go backward through time.

·····

It comes back more clearly than it has before.

He called and said he was coming over. I said he couldn't. I said I'd come and meet him instead to stop him coming to the caravan.

I ran toward the car.

It was driving right at me.

And then I open my eyes, because while I was rewinding past the accident, I saw someone else. The car hit somebody before it hit me. I felt it just before it smashed into me. Somebody was there, and they flew into the air and pushed me out of the way, and even though it still hit me, that's probably why I am alive.

I stay in the memory for as long as I can bear to, and then I pull myself out. I'm sure I'm right. There was another person in the accident, and the car hit them, so they must have died, and it wasn't either of my parents, which means there's only one person it could have been.

It must have been Maud.

Maud died saving me, and no one's told me.

31

TAMSYN HADN'T HEARD FROM MAUD FOR AGES, SO SHE SAT down to write an e-mail. Sophie was out, Scarlett was sleeping and Ed was offering cake to the various people who were still in the house. She needed some time out, so she shut herself in the bedroom.

She stared at the screen. It was difficult to know what to say. Maud hadn't kept in touch—in fact, Tamsyn didn't think she'd seen or heard from her since the day of the accident. But she had been Tamsyn's best friend, and even though she clearly didn't want to stay in touch, Tamsyn was going to keep trying. She didn't want to cut every tie with her old life.

However, she couldn't tell her much. Maud, of all people, knew that Scarlett didn't have a twin. On top of all that, Tamsyn didn't want to talk much about their new life because the contrast with the campsite at home felt too pointed, and that was probably why Maud wasn't answering her anyway.

Wasn't it? She hoped Maud was all right.

Tamsyn looked around. The room was huge, with polished wooden floorboards and that enormous bed. All their things had places: the clothes were behind doors, in cupboards you could walk into. Things were in drawers, on shelves. Everything was new and beautiful and immaculate. It was as if their old life had never happened.

She didn't really feel these days that she was imagining this Swiss life. It was the old one that didn't seem real.

She took the photo of the three of them out from under her pillow, where she had just put it. She held it closer and looked at the toddler. Ed and she had had no idea that that little girl was going to split in two. It would have felt impossible to the version of herself in the photo, but now it felt normal, lucky. The girl was Scarlett, and she was Sophie too. Her name had been Scarlett Sophie and now she was both of them. It almost made sense.

Tamsyn looked at herself in the old picture for a long time and then pushed it away.

The people they'd met in Geneva outside the clinic thought the girls were twins. Tamsyn was pleased that this meant they could never go back to live in England. She used to think that if they ever saw their friends in Cornwall again, she would continue to pass Sophie off as Scarlett, but now of course that was impossible. It was lucky in the bleakest way that Maud would never be in a position to visit them in Geneva, and it was hard to know that when she contacted her oldest friend, she had to lie about her two precious daughters.

She took a deep breath and tried to find some things to write.

Dear Maud,

Sorry it's been so long since my last message! How are things in Cornwall? How's Shabba?

It's all fine here. Scarlett's doing really well. Ed's loving

his job. I've learned to speak reasonable French. We're
very lucky.

We do miss you! Scarlett is currently asleep but I'm sure
she'd send her love.

Take care, Maud, and lots of love
Tamsyn xxx

It was a stupid message that said nothing. Tamsyn would
never be able to have an honest conversation with her friend
again, and Maud wouldn't reply anyway. She decided that instead she'd put together a package of Swiss things for Maud and
mail it to her. That would be better than awkward e-mails full of
implied lies. She'd buy her chocolate and cheese, biscuits and
anything else she could think of, and she'd package it all up and
send it. That would be a better way to say she was thinking of her
friend.

She sent the e-mail and decided to go out to the shops as soon
as she could leave Scarlett. She texted Aurelie, updating her on
Scarlett's arrival and inviting her to come up for tea the next day.

I can't go out much, she wrote, because of Scarlett. She's
going to be housebound for a while. But you can come up anytime! I'd love you to meet both my girls. Scarlett has the bear you
gave her with her, btw.

She looked at those words and smiled. *Both my girls.* That
was everything.

▪ ▪ ▪ ▪ ▪

Half an hour later, a tinkly bell rang, and it took Tamsyn a while
to remember that there was a bell in Scarlett's room. She ran in
and found Scarlett sitting on her bed with some books.

"Hey, darling!" she said. She sat next to her. "You OK? Going to do some reading?"

Scarlett leaned on her. "I woke up," she said. "I was looking at the books. It's nice to go into other worlds, you know?"

Tamsyn nodded.

"Sophie doesn't like reading. Is that right?"

She shook out Scarlett's pillow. "She reads only science books as far as I can tell. You've got all the reading genes."

Scarlett leaned back on the pillows. "That's weird, though," she said, "because we have the same genes, don't we?"

"Sophie's Sophie," said Tamsyn. "And you are you. You came from the same material but you're different. Just like twins."

It sounded so lame that she cringed, but Scarlett nodded.

"Mum, is there a bath here? My muscles are aching and it always helps."

"Of course! It's in the main bathroom. I'll run it for you now."

"The *main* bathroom."

Scarlett looked at her, and they widened their eyes at each other, knowing that a year earlier they had had a chemical toilet in the van for emergencies, and access to shared facilities on the other side of a field. When Scarlett spoke again, her voice was urgent.

"I know I would have died if we hadn't come here. But it's so . . . so weird to wake up in a different life. Do you miss home, Mum?"

"No," said Tamsyn. "I mean, I really don't. Just no. I love life here."

Scarlett nodded.

"But it must be strange to find yourself in the middle of it all. Dad and I chose this and we got used to it a long time ago. You didn't. Cornwall is beautiful and it'll always feel like home, I guess, but life was just too hard. And—thank you for coming back to us, darling. Your accident was . . . Well, there aren't any words. It changed everything. I'm sorry for . . . well, for everything that happened before that. Now we're here, that's all over."

"Are we really not moving back?" Scarlett said. "Not ever? Can I go back when I'm better? One day? Can I . . . Well, do we still hear from—from Maud?"

Tamsyn hesitated, then rubbed her daughter's shoulder. Scarlett didn't seem to mind. She would have before.

"Sometimes," Tamsyn said though it wasn't really true. "I was just writing to her actually. I'm going to post her a package this afternoon to show her we still think of her. Are you homesick?"

"No. Yeah." Scarlett swallowed hard. "In a way. Cornwall is still my home and this just— I mean, I can see that it's really amazing and luxurious, but I'm not sure that I belong. I think Sophie's the *me* who lives here. Not me." She paused. "Maud loves chocolate. Send her lots of that."

"You do belong! You'll settle in," said Tamsyn. "I promise you will. We live here now, and honestly, you're going to love it. And yes, of course I'll send chocolate."

"Can I . . . can I go to stay with Maud? As soon as I'm healthy?"

Tamsyn sighed. "We'll talk about it when the time comes. One of us would need to come with you, and you'd have to be completely healed. I don't know, darling."

"Is Maud . . . I mean, is she OK?"

"I think so," said Tamsyn. "We keep in touch, but it's me writing to her, really. Why?"

Scarlett looked at her for a long time. "Have you seen her since the accident?"

Tamsyn tried to think. She hadn't seen her. Had she? It had been such a blur.

Her head hurt. It felt weird. She shook it. She was just tired.

"I don't think so actually. But she's still there. Remember our chickens? They live with her now."

Was Maud still there? Tamsyn had no idea.

Scarlett picked up her little teddy and started moving its arms and legs. "OK."

"Oh, Aurelie —you know, she gave you that bear? She's going to come up and meet you soon. Would that be OK? She's so nice and friendly."

"Sure."

Scarlett looked listless, and Tamsyn remembered that she was supposed to be running her a bath. She tried to think of the right maternal things to say.

"You'll get used to it here sooner than you think," she said. "And you do belong. You do! You make us complete. We came here only so Dr. Singh could take care of you. We wanted you to come back to us and you did. It's magical."

Scarlett nodded. She put the bear down and lowered her voice.

"I mean, it's amazing and of course I'm grateful for everything, but isn't it a bit incredibly fucking weird? They watch us all the time. Those cameras everywhere. They listen to us talking. Isn't that freaky?"

Tamsyn lowered her voice to match. "You stop thinking about it after a while. I don't notice it so much now. It's a strange world to navigate, but the lovely things outweigh the bad ones a million times over. And I think they're at least going to stop the feed that looks out through Sophie's eyes. It's very invasive for her."

"Poor Sophie. I can't imagine." Scarlett's face changed and she forced a smile at Tamsyn. "Mum? You're really different."

"Am I? How?"

"Well, you wouldn't have known how to live in a place like this before. Plus, you look different. You must know that, though.

Your clothes and hair and things. You look like someone rich who lives in Geneva, because you are, I guess. But also— Have you been reading lots of books? You wouldn't have said that. '*It's a strange world to navigate.*' You didn't say things like that before."

Tamsyn thought about it. "What would I have said before?"

Scarlett giggled. "It's fucking weird," she said.

"I never swore in front of you! I tried not to."

"Mum, you're forgetting, which is fine. I want to forget all that too. But I swore at you and Dad all the time. Of course you did it back at me, and so that thing about not swearing broke down. You know it did."

Tamsyn sighed. "They programmed Sophie not to be able to swear, you know. She didn't even know until she found out about you, because that was the first time she'd tried. And yes, I have been reading more. Watching films rather than my old reality shows. I used to cling to them for a quick blast of entertainment. Now I guess I have more time. This has all been about you and Sophie, but a side effect has been the effect on me and Dad. I mean, you get thrown into a new life and you adapt. Right?" She felt defensive, and filed it all away to think about later.

"And you've learned French."

She nodded. "Until you woke up, I went to French classes most days, and when you're living here, you do just get immersed in it. So yes, I picked it up. Who'd have seen that coming? I thought I was too old for that kind of thing. One thing I've learned this year, though, is that brains are weird and incredible."

Tamsyn had no idea whether Scarlett remembered the dreadful thing she had said to her, the thing that had pulled her back into life just to contradict her mother. Tamsyn hoped she didn't. She hoped they would never talk about it.

"Also, there's Dad," said Scarlett. "He's more chill."

Tamsyn laughed. "Now that one I have definitely noticed.

Who'd have thought that reliable working hours, job security, a comfortable home and a happy work environment could have such an effect? Darling, I know this is hard. You're doing brilliantly. I know it must be disorienting to have an accident one night and then to wake up in a different country with a twin."

Scarlett shrugged. "That's why I keep thinking it's a coma dream," she said, "and if it is, I'm OK with it. It's an interesting one."

"What was it like in the coma?" Tamsyn said. She'd asked before but Scarlett had never really answered.

Scarlett looked as if she was about to say something, stopped and then started again. She spoke slowly, choosing her words with care.

"You really want to know?"

Tamsyn nodded and held her breath. This felt like the first time Scarlett was opening up.

"It was a real place," she said. "As real as this. More real. It was dark and safe. The walls were sometimes covered in velvet. I could light a candle. I collected things there. Something would arrive and I would keep it. Words and pictures and things. It was deep down." She exhaled a heavy breath and looked away. "It sounds weird, but yeah, that was what it was like. I sometimes go back when I sleep. I try to. I'm safe there."

She yawned and closed her eyes, and Tamsyn felt for a second that Scarlett had never been so unreachable, even during the months she had been in a coma. She had been to a place no one should visit and had come back to talk about it, and she was only fifteen.

Tamsyn watched her daughter dozing off and imagined her spirit leaving her sleeping body and drifting down to the safe cave.

Tamsyn knew her words had reached Scarlett there. *I don't*

think you're going to get better. They had reached that velvet cave and made Scarlett come out to contradict her. Scarlett had been right, and Tamsyn completely wrong.

. . . . .

Tamsyn poured a huge amount of rose-scented bubbles into the running bathwater. She put out a clean towel and wondered whether it would be dangerous to light a candle, because Scarlett had had one in her safe coma place, so it might make her feel more at home. She wanted the bath to be perfect. She wanted everything to be perfect. She wanted her to stop thinking about Cornwall, to see that she too would adapt to this new life.

When she came out of the bathroom, Ed was halfway out of the door. He turned back.

"Oh, sorry!" he said. "I thought you were in with Scarlett. Just calling in at work."

"Right," she said, though for some reason she wasn't sure she believed him. "Aren't you off for two weeks?"

He nodded, smiling broadly. "I am, but they know about Scarlett coming home, and apparently there's a load of patisserie with our name on it. They said they'd deliver, but I just thought I'd stretch my legs and get some sunshine."

"Of course! Good plan. Patisserie. Brilliant. Can you pick up a few things to post to Maud? I thought that would be nice. Lots of chocolate."

"Of course. Good idea."

He came and kissed her, and they looked at each other for a long time and it was OK. She trusted him again. She would always trust him. They had been through this together.

32

SOPHIE HAD A SPRING IN HER STEP AND, AS EVER, COULDN'T keep still.

"He's doing it next week!" She gave Tamsyn an exuberant hug. "Johann. He agreed. He's stopping my retina feed on Wednesday. I have to go into the clinic and they're going to give me a full checkup. Oh, my God, they're going to stop looking at the world out of my eyes. I'll almost be normal! Like a real girl!"

"Can you feel it?"

Tamsyn found she wanted to know about both of her daughters, about what it felt like to be them. They had extreme, and different, physical issues to deal with, and while she could almost imagine her way into Scarlett's battered body, she had no idea at all what it must have felt like to be Sophie. And yet Sophie was somehow so much easier.

"And of course you're a real girl," she added too late.

"I don't think I can feel it," Sophie said. She sighed and blinked a lot. "I mean, I'm not sure what it feels like to exist without it. I feel the same as I do in my memories—in Scarlett's memories—so I guess not. I'll let you know on Wednesday."

"You did well to get them to commit at last."

"Yay, I get to have my head to myself. Where's Scarlett? I hardly even saw her after all that. Is she in her room?"

"She's in the bath. I think it's soothing, even on a hot day. She's got a book and bubbles and a candle. She'd never had a bath in her life before she woke up at the clinic."

Sophie stopped and looked at Tamsyn. "We should get a hot tub! Out on the terrace. It'd be good for Scarlett's healing, and let's face it: it would be amazing for all of us."

"Oh, Sophie!" said Tamsyn. "I can hardly ask, can I? They've given us all this. I can't say, *Excuse me? We need a hot tub too!*"

Sophie eased her body down into a split, bouncing a little when she got close to the bottom. "Er, yes, you can." She looked up, pleased with herself. "I'll ask. They love us, Mum! Seriously. We're their biggest-ever success. You could demand to move into the . . . the United Nations building, and they'd get it cleared out and redecorated for us. Leave it to me, OK? In fact—hold it there."

She walked over to the camera in the corner of the room and looked up.

"Hi, Johann, or whoever's watching. We'd like a hot tub installed on the terrace, please. Thank you!"

Tamsyn laughed. "OK, sweetie. Let's see what happens."

. . . . .

That evening they had their first meal as a family of four. Ed had come back from his trip to work later than Tamsyn had expected, but with three boxes of cakes and pastries as well as a bag of presents to send to Cornwall, and with Maya in tow. He had, he said, met her outside.

He didn't say who had given him the pastries at work, and Tamsyn tried not to think about Lena, the beautiful young colleague. If she thought about her, she would start trying to check up on him. She knew herself: it would eat her up. She would spiral.

She and Ed had fallen in love all over again when the two of them were living here, just them, when the cameras hadn't even been switched on. Now they had their twins, and the house was full of people all the time, and she loved him more than ever. Several times a week, they locked the bedroom door and got quietly into bed. He had been her rock through this, and if he was cheating on her, she would not be able to bear it.

He wasn't cheating, though. So that was OK.

"I won't bother you for long," said Maya, smiling around. "I just thought it would be lovely to take some photographs of the four of you together. On a beautiful evening. It's nice to record moments like these."

They stood awkwardly on the terrace, the sun golden on their skin. Maya took a professional camera out of her bag and took a series of what she called "family portraits," accepted a glass of water, then said, "I'll leave you to it," and disappeared. Tamsyn thought she would ask for a copy of one of the photographs to replace the old one that didn't contain Sophie.

▪▪▪▪▪

Tamsyn had carefully cooked a vegetable lasagna, which had gone better than she'd expected, and made a huge salad. They sat at the outside table, Tamsyn and Ed on one side of the table and the girls on the other.

Tamsyn watched her daughters looking at each other. She saw secret glances passing between them and wondered what it would be like to have another person who was also you. They understood each other without words: one person, existing twice.

She tried to pause the moment. The sun was low in the sky,

and the shadows were long. The food was good enough, the wine cold. She felt the city air, clean and warm, on her bare arms. The flowers in their terra-cotta pots were hanging on through the heat. She had everything she had ever wanted.

Scarlett was unsteady, her skin indoor pale, but she was getting there. Her thick hair would touch her shoulders soon, and she had clipped it back from her face with a plain bobby pin. Tamsyn made a mental note to get some colorful ones. After her bath she had changed into a pink onesie, and she looked young and nervous.

Sophie's hair was long down her back, and she was wearing a tiny bit of makeup. She had dressed in a playsuit—a dress that had shorts where the skirt part should be—and it was lime green and yellow and looked spectacular. She looked older and less vulnerable than her twin, but they looked like sisters.

Tamsyn turned to Ed and saw that he was watching the girls too.

"You two!" he said. "Look at you! You're the best."

The girls looked at each other. "We know," they said.

"So," said Ed, "what's the plan? Soph, you're back to school in a couple of weeks. Scarlett, apparently you're allowed to leave the house for a small amount of time when you feel ready. Could we fit in a trip somewhere before school starts? Up into the mountains?"

"Ed!" said Tamsyn. "When she says *leaving the house,* I imagine Dr. Singh means going to the corner and back. She doesn't mean a week hiking in the Alps."

She saw Ed and Sophie making eye contact, an invisible eye roll.

"I didn't mean a week hiking in the Alps," said Ed with exaggerated patience. "I just thought we could hire a car or maybe get a taxi and drive out of the city. Head up where it's a bit cooler.

Yeah, maybe into the Alps?" He pointed vaguely out of Geneva. "There are some cool skiing places that are supposed to be beautiful in summer. Wildflowers and stuff."

"Dad!" said Sophie. "That's France. You're pointing at France and I'm literally illegal there, remember? I know the French authorities probably wouldn't check, but Johann and Luca and Maya would be *incandescent* if we went into EU territory. Also I really don't want to go there."

"Shit. Sorry." He looked at France. "I didn't actually know it was France that way. OK, then." He pointed in the other direction. "We can go into the mountains in Switzerland. I believe there are one or two."

Scarlett nodded. "Isn't it famous for them?"

Sophie laughed, then stopped when she realized Scarlett wasn't joking.

"Yes, it is," Tamsyn said. "There are some over there behind the haze. Or is that France too? I'm never quite sure." She addressed Scarlett. "But it's cool, isn't it, to know there's another country just there? We're right in the middle of the continent and I love that."

"Sorry to inconvenience you," said Sophie, with a sharp look.

"Oh, I didn't mean it like that!"

Sophie gave her a tight smile. "It's OK."

Tamsyn didn't think it was, though, and threw Ed a glance.

"So maybe we could drive out of the city when you feel up to it, Scarlett?" he said, steering things back on track. "Just sit on a mountainside with a picnic?"

She nodded. "Yeah. I mean, of course. Who wouldn't want to do that? Maybe next week. I need to get my head round all this first."

"Of course," he said.

Scarlett winced as if she'd felt a sudden pain.

"Are you all right, darling?" Tamsyn said.

"Fine," said Scarlett. "I just get these pains sometimes. In my back. It means I need to lie down. That's all. Can I go back to bed? Sorry. I'll take one of those éclairs."

Tamsyn helped her back to her bedroom and closed both the functional blind and the decorative curtains.

"Do you want your reading light on?" she said, and Scarlett nodded.

"Sorry," she said. "I'm just really, really tired. I can't believe I woke up in the clinic this morning. And ended up sitting outside, eating dinner with you and Dad and Sophie. What a day."

"What a day," Tamsyn echoed. "Do you want me to help you to the bathroom?"

Scarlett drew herself up to her full height. "No, thank you," she said. "I can do that stuff now, honestly. I'll ring that bell if I have any trouble, but seriously, Mum, I'm just going to read and then sleep. I'll see you in the morning."

Tamsyn hugged her.

"Sweet dreams," she said.

She wondered whether Scarlett was heading back to that dark place. The idea made her feel strange.

. . . . .

The next morning a hot tub was installed.

33

EVERYTHING IS ABOUT SCARLETT. POOR, PRECIOUS SCAR-
lett. So fragile. *Be quiet. Scarlett's sleeping!* Well, if she's that
fragile, then I'm halfway to getting rid of her already.

Right now, while they're still watching everything out of
my eyes, I have to be careful. I think it's best to do things in
the dark.

It's three in the morning when I get out of bed, tiptoe across
the corridor and open her door silently.

I stand and look at her. She has no machines for me to turn
off now. I cringe when I remember Dr. Singh finding me
crouched down about to give it a go. All I achieved was to make
Dr. Singh extra vigilant, knowing that she can't trust me with her
precious Scarlett.

Well, she's not here now.

Scarlett is lying on her side, breathing deeply. I stare at her.
At first I think I'll never get tired of looking at my source material, but after about twenty minutes, it actually becomes really
boring.

Time to do something.

A pillow over the face would be easy. She wouldn't have a chance. She'd be out of my life in a couple of minutes.

They'd know I'd done it: the eye cameras would give me away. The room cameras too probably. Can they see in the dark?

Of course they can.

There's a stabbing pain in my head. It's so intense that I almost cry out. I lean forward, my head in my hands, and try to breathe through it. It goes quickly, but it leaves a buzzing behind.

I close my eyes and open them again. I shake my head. Nothing shifts the pain, but as I take deep gasping breaths and wonder what the hell that was, it starts to fade, and I focus again on the problem of my sister. I feel weird, though.

I want to reach out and strangle her. I'd kill her with my bare hands if I could get away with it. But I can't: my purpose is to protect the family, and that means me, Mum and Dad. If they knew I'd strangled my sister, the family would be shattered.

So I have to do it without anyone knowing it was me. I wish I lived inside one of those horror movies. I'd just stab her through the head. That's why I love them so much.

I know I can't do that now. I'll wait for them to turn the eye cameras off, and then perhaps I'll push her off the terrace. That would be pleasing: watching her fall. Telling everyone she jumped.

For now I'll just wake her up and make sure she remembers to be scared of me.

34

I'M RUNNING DOWN THE ROAD. I'M TERRIFIED.

· · · · ·

It's dark. I'm running running running. I see headlights coming. I hear the engine.

· · · · ·

"Wake up!"

· · · · ·

Someone is running behind me. Two people. Three. Dad, Mum, Maud. I run as fast as I can toward the sound.

· · · · ·

"Scarlett! Wake up!"

· · · · ·

I wake up, panting and sweating. I have a name in my head. I haven't let it in for all this time, but now it's there.

It's not J.

It's Jasper.

I gasp. No. I push it away. I lock it in a box and push it off a mountain.

I'm sweating. That felt real. It felt more real than this bedroom. Maybe that's what's real and this is what's fake.

. . . . .

I'm awake and someone is there. Someone said, "Wake up."

At first I think it's part of the dream, but after a while, I know. I can hear someone breathing. I am disoriented, and it takes me a while to remember everything, but then I'm up to speed. Weird luxury flat. New twin. Confused.

It's probably not a nurse in the room, since I'm not at the clinic. The bed is tipping down a bit on one side. That's where Mum sits.

I can see only an outline.

"Mum?" I say.

"Sister," she whispers.

Sophie and I haven't been alone together before, not properly. Not since the time she came to the clinic.

"I thought we should chat," she says. "Without them around."

I want to tell her that I was asleep. I don't want her coming into my room in the middle of the night. I need to go back to sleep. I reach out to ring my little bell.

Is Sophie going to kill me? Is she going to drive a car into me?

I shake my head. That was a dream. It wasn't Sophie driving the car. She didn't exist.

It was him. It was J. I can see his face, shocked and white behind the wheel.

"Don't worry," she says. "I know you're scared but you don't need to be. Remember, I have a team who see everything I see. I find that very invasive, which is why I've got them to agree to turn it off on Wednesday. I know we both owe them our lives, but I'd rather get to know my sister without surveillance, if you know what I mean. So I thought I'd just pop in and say hello. They might not be watching right now."

I yawn. I don't know why she's doing this. I try to keep up.

"That's why you asked them to switch it off," I say, "so you can talk to me in private?" Fuck, my brain is slow.

She points at me. "Exactly. They could make a pretty cool movie about us with all the footage they must have. Everything we do is captured on camera, every word spoken in this house is caught on a mic and anything you do will appear on a screen at the clinic. Say hello to Johann, Scarlett! If he catches this, he'll be delighted with it. The twins bonding in the middle of the night. Dream come true, right, Johann?"

She leans toward me, and because I don't really know what else to do, I look into her eyes and give a little wave.

"Hi," I say awkwardly.

"But we'll be able to chat without these inhibitions soon," she says, and I see the look in her eye by the glow of my fairy lights, and for a moment I don't know what to think. I know that look. I remember it. I used to see it in the mirror in that other life.

When I thought I hated everyone.

Then the look is gone and she's smiling again.

"Can I climb in?"

I shift along and there she is in my bed. I move farther over because she nudges me, and then she's in.

"Thanks."

Sophie lies on her side and closes her eyes and I watch her. I used to be angry. I shouted and slammed things. Now I can't even wake up my other self and tell her I want my bed back. The fairy lights light up her face as her breathing changes and she seems to fall deeply asleep.

I could have asked her about Maud, but I didn't.

I know we are identical, but I wish I were like her. I stare and stare at her, wishing I could live in that body instead.

Every time I stretch out, she is there. My foot hits her leg. Her warmth makes me too hot. She stretches into my half of the bed, and in the end, I slide out of the other side. Because I don't have a walking support next to me, I drop down to my hands and knees and crawl out of the room. I leave the door a little bit open and make my way, in pain and frustrated at the fact that I'm not able to stand properly, across the corridor to Sophie's room and her empty bed.

Her room is like mine but different. She doesn't have her fairy lights on, so it's dark in here, but I know where the bed is because it's the mirror image of mine, and I pull myself up into it, stretch out and close my eyes.

. . . . .

An alarm goes off next to me. I reach out, find a phone and tap it until it stops. I go back down.

. . . . .

Someone knocks at the door. I am too deeply asleep to do anything, but then the door opens. I pull the duvet up over my head.

"Morning, sweetie," says Mum. She walks over to the window and opens the blind and everything is in the wrong place. "You've overslept—you must have been tired. Remember you've got street dance at ten? It's nine twenty already. Here—I've made you a coffee."

I hear her putting something down beside me. Why does she think I could do street dance? Why has she made me coffee when I don't like it? It takes me ages to work it out. I'm in Sophie's bed. Mum is talking to me as if I were Sophie.

She thinks I'm my twin.

I wish with all my heart that I was able to jump out of bed and go to street dance and be the clever one, the one who dances, the new one. I hold on to the feeling for as long as I can. When I pull the duvet away from my face, she still doesn't notice.

"Scarlett's sleeping too," she says. "Her door was a bit open, so I popped my head in, but she was fast asleep." Then she looks at me, and says, "Oh, my God. Sophie, you look—"

I watch her catch herself before the word *terrible* because she realizes just in time.

"Scarlett?" She stands and stares. "Scarlett, what are you . . ." Her voice trails off. "So Sophie's in—"

She points toward my bedroom and I nod. I look properly around Sophie's room: I've seen it only from the doorway before. She has a desk. My sofa is in that spot. There are piles of school-books, a pencil case, a ruler, and there's a periodic table stuck up on the wall. Everything is neat and tidy. She has a whole shelf of those retro DVDs and no novels at all.

I realize Mum is waiting for me to explain, so I yawn and say, "Sophie came to see me in the night. She fell asleep in my bed. I couldn't sleep, so I came here." I yawn again. I really want to sleep. The safe place is calling me.

"Oh," says Mum. "OK. Let's get you back to your own room. How strange. You should have rung the bell!"

"It was fine." I want to say, *This is the kind of thing twins do, isn't it? They switch places, pretend to be each other.* But it turns out I don't have the strength to say anything at all. I close my eyes and plummet straight down to the safe place, where I lie back on a squashy black sofa that has appeared next to a poster of the periodic table. I light my candles and settle in.

After a while I see a piece of paper beside me, and I pick it up. It's written in old-fashioned handwriting in black ink, and it says, *Read Sophie's letter again.*

Underneath that it says, *Don't trust her.*

I hold it in the flame of a candle and watch it burn, and then I lie back, letting the safe place look after me.

When I come back, I'm in my own bed, alone.

The first thing I see is the little pile of movies Sophie gave me when I came home. She's moved it so it's right beside the bed. I look at their titles again.

I Know What You Did Last Summer.

Cruel Intentions.

Scream.

35

TAMSYN SAT AT THE TABLE ON THE TERRACE, SUPPOSEDLY reading a book in French, and reminded herself that she was happy. She worked hard on not articulating the fact that everything had been more straightforward when Scarlett was in the clinic, because that was monstrous.

There's something else going on.

She tried to silence that voice. It was insistent. It had been there for a while.

Where is Ed?

She closed her eyes and tried not to think about it.

She remembered the months when they had been a family of three, she and Ed visiting Scarlett whenever they could. She remembered the straightforward joy of every day. She remembered how she and Ed hadn't been able to keep their hands off each other. Geneva had been a wonderland, and their apartment had felt like a wild dream.

Tamsyn didn't go to French or yoga anymore, because she needed to be at home for Scarlett. The only people she met outside their family unit were the doctors and physios who were all in the apartment all the time, and they complained about Geneva, about things like parking and stupid rules and tourists, and the city had started to lose its sparkle. When she watched the news, she saw stories about financial fraud and identity theft and, weirdly, often fires.

The apartment didn't feel like home anymore. It was an extension of the clinic: she could never forget that Johann and his team were watching them every moment of every day. She was a goldfish in a bowl, just another element of an experiment. She and Ed had less time for each other now. She worried about Sophie and about Scarlett, who missed Cornwall in a way that Tamsyn, Ed and Sophie didn't. Nothing felt right.

And something was going on with Ed, and she needed to face it.

Tamsyn was physically exhausted, but her brain was running faster and faster. She looked down at her book, but her focus drifted. It was humid, and her head hurt. She looked across the city and missed the wider world. She wasn't sure Scarlett and Sophie had taken to each other as effortlessly as they wanted her to believe. She watched Sophie in particular and looked for clues. They were there in tiny facial movements, in the way she looked at Scarlett before she realized Tamsyn was watching.

Sophie would look at Scarlett with something cold in her eyes until she realized she was being observed, at which point she grinned. Scarlett seemed to be innocent and confused, but Tamsyn knew how difficult she used to be. She knew that Scarlett had taken her to the brink of despair, and now, even now that she was passive and quiet, she was the same girl. It was still inside her.

Tamsyn replayed the *Yes, I am* all the time. Scarlett had come back to life to argue with her. When she was strong enough, she would be difficult again. Tamsyn was dreading it, but she wanted Scarlett to be strong too. She had an overwhelming feeling that trouble was coming. She felt someone was watching her, but that was stupid because of course they were. They watched her every moment of every day.

The air pressed down on her and made her body itch. She felt huge and heavy, and could feel sweat seeping from her armpits. She looked over at the corner, at the hot tub, inviting her in. She didn't want to be hot, though. A cold shower would be better.

·····

Find out what's going on.

She shook her head. That recurring feeling was inconvenient and she wanted it to go away.

The girls were talking in low voices inside. You usually couldn't hear anything from the terrace, but the air was heavy and still today, and the sound carried.

"Here you go," said Sophie. "One hot chocolate, just for you."

"Oh, right. Thanks." Scarlett didn't sound convinced. "Can you take a sip first?"

Sophie laughed. "I'd rather not. It's too hot for a drink like this, but I know you like it. You know we have a fizzy-water tap? And an ice machine. Those are more my style."

"OK, thanks," said Scarlett. "I'll drink it in a bit."

"Sure. Of course. Oh, sh— Sugar! I'm so sorry! Oh, Scarlett— are you OK?"

Scarlett cried out. Tamsyn managed to get up and run indoors. Scarlett was covered in brown liquid, and she was crying like a little child with hot chocolate running down her face. Sophie looked guilty.

"Sorry!" she said, looking at Tamsyn. "It was an accident! I made Scarlett a drink. You know, to be nice? But she didn't want it, so she pushed my arm and it spilled all over her."

Tamsyn looked to Scarlett for her version, but she was still crying. This seemed to have tipped her over the edge. Tamsyn helped her into her room and into the shower, wincing at poor Scarlett's scars. Scarlett didn't say a word the whole time.

While she was in the shower, Tamsyn made her bed and tidied her things. Sophie knocked on the door, looking guilty.

"Sorry," she said. "I really didn't want that to happen and now I feel really bad. Tell her to watch those DVDs I left her. They always make me feel better."

Tamsyn was sure there was something she was missing here.

"Sure," she said. "I will. Don't worry, darling. I know it was an accident, and Scarlett does too."

Sophie went out to meet her friends. Ed was out too, because he was never home these days.

And *that,* she thought, was the thing. This was what she had been avoiding all this time. She and Ed had drifted back where they used to be, and it was all because of him. She was certain it was nothing she'd done.

He was lying to her. He had, in fact, been lying for a while, but now she couldn't ignore it anymore. She saw the way his face flickered when he did it. His eyes darted sideways, and he touched his beard.

Something is going on. Yes. Something is going on with Ed. Confront it. Follow him.

He seemed to rotate stories about where he was going. Sometimes he said he was *calling in at work*, and he'd come back with cakes, but that didn't make sense, because he was going back to work next week, and his calling in when he'd taken time off to be with Scarlett and Sophie didn't add up. That first time, when he'd come home with a gift for the family from his colleagues— that time it had been plausible. After that, not.

At other times he said he was *going out for some air*, but they had a huge terrace for that. Or he'd pretend he was trying to get fit, though there was a home gym in the spare room, used by Scarlett for her painstaking recovery and Sophie for effortless workouts, and there was no reason for anyone to go for a run in the intense heat when they had a treadmill in air-conditioned comfort.

Of course, everyone needed to get out from time to time, but Ed was going out alone every single day for hours, in spite of the fact that the wife and daughters he was supposed to adore were inside, and all of them needed him.

Her mind always drifted to his young, beautiful colleague, Lena.

Ed wouldn't have an affair. Would he? She remembered that e-mail. *She has no idea.* After everything they'd been through, and when they finally had both girls at home, he wouldn't sneak out to see another woman, would he? They had been having a second honeymoon. They'd been obsessed with each other.

She remembered his bag under the bed in the caravan.

She couldn't think of any other reason for him to tell lies and slip away on his own every day.

She needed to find out, but it would be days or weeks before she would be able to follow him, because he would have to happen to leave just as Scarlett's physio was starting, or when Dr. Singh was coming for a checkup. Dr. Singh's appointments didn't last long enough, and she felt uneasy at the idea of leaving Scarlett home alone or home with Sophie.

Her phone pinged, and there was a text from Aurelie.

Are you still ok with my popping up to visit this afternoon? it said. Tamsyn looked at it and nodded. An idea was forming.

Please do, she replied. **Come soon. I need your help.**

36

THE NEXT MORNING TAMSYN HUNG AROUND THE FLAT WAIT-
ing. That huge place suddenly felt too small. Sophie went out to
a class, and Scarlett lay on her bed watching a movie with the
air-conditioning on and the curtains closed. Ed did nothing.

Tamsyn spent half an hour on Scarlett's exercise bike, book
in hand, but she knew she was taking it too easy for it to make
any real difference. She made a pot of breakfast tea and drank it
all. She and Ed talked about going up to the mountains in a few
days.

She waited.

The one time she wanted him to go out, he didn't. He was
chatty. It was as if he sensed something was wrong and wanted
to stay close at last.

"I asked Johann," he said, "and Dr. Singh, and they both said
it should be fine. Scarlett's making good progress, and apparently
mountain air will be great for her. We obviously have to stay in
Switzerland and keep away from the French border, and we need
to keep a close eye on Scarlett's energy and pain levels and not
go too far from the city, but as long as we bear all that in mind,

we have the green light. We can have Sophie's school car and driver if we want, or we can borrow a car and take ourselves. I think I'd prefer the driver option rather than worrying about driving on the wrong side of the road."

"When did you ask?" she said.

He hesitated. "Yesterday. I called when I was out for my run."

He was lying. Why would he call the doctors when he was out running in thirty-eight-degree heat? He wasn't fit enough to run and talk, so he must have stopped somewhere. And why not make a call like that from the house?

He was slipping away from her again. She could feel it. He had secrets.

▪ ▪ ▪ ▪ ▪

He is definitely up to something.

They made plans to go out on Sunday, subject to Scarlett. That was the last day before Ed went back to work, and eight days before Sophie started back at school. It would be the last straightforward day for a trip.

Finally he stretched and said, "Since it's all quiet here, I might go for a little stroll. Stretch my legs, pick up anything we need."

"Sure," she said. She paused. "Are you going near work? Because if you are, could you get some of that lemon tart?"

"Sure thing!" he said, and he kissed her and went into the bathroom.

She messaged Aurelie. **He's going soon**, she wrote. **Are you ready?**

The reply came at once. **Standing by!** it said. **Agent Aurelie reporting for duty. I'll watch the elevator and when he goes down I'll take the stairs. Just give me 5 mins to dry my hair.**

Tamsyn delayed Ed by adding random things to his shopping

list and encouraging him to chat to Scarlett before he left. When he did finally go, she knew that Aurelie was in position.

He left. She waited, constructing horrible scenarios in her head. Her heart pounded. She was sure it was Lena. He might be visiting her in some chic apartment every single day. She was younger than Tamsyn, less stressed. Easier to be around. Not constantly worrying. Uncomplicated. Good company. Cheerful.

Lena was everything Tamsyn felt she wasn't.

Ed and Tamsyn had been so happy, and now there was something weird happening. Was it her fault? Her phone was fully charged. She turned the volume up, put it on the table in front of her and waited.

Aurelie messaged after nearly an hour.

OK, update. You good to speak?

Tamsyn called. "Where is he?"

"So," said Aurelie, "here's what happened. He's an easy man to follow, your husband. Nice and tall, and he wasn't looking for me. I just followed the top of his head. He led me for quite a long walk. I'm getting my ten-k steps today! Right into the city and then out from the center on the other side. Tamsyn? I don't think this is what you think it is, darling. No other woman. He went to a place called"—she hesitated—"VitaNova. Blank white building. Pharma maybe? I looked it up but there's not much online."

Tamsyn frowned. "He went there?"

"I'm outside now. He hasn't come out unless there's a door around the back."

Tamsyn swallowed hard. "VitaNova is a clinic. It's where Scarlett was treated. Where the trial is based. VitaNova are the people who pay for our whole life. There's no need for either of us to go there now Scarlett is home. Particularly not in secret."

"OK." Aurelie sounded interested. "Well, it's probably not another woman, right? At least, I doubt he's going in there for a tryst with a medical researcher or anything like that. It'll be something to do with Scarlett. Maybe he doesn't want to worry you. I know you can't leave Scarlett easily, but if you did get a chance, could you come over and see what he's doing?"

"Yeah."

Tamsyn couldn't make sense of it. She tried to remember the staff they had met there. Was there an attractive woman? Surely Ed wouldn't.

And he wouldn't be keeping secrets about Scarlett without telling Tamsyn, would he?

She clicked back into the moment. "Sorry, Aurelie," she said. "Thank you so much for doing this. I really owe you."

"Hey, it's no problem! If you know the place, you'll know that café over the road? There are some outside tables free. I could get a coffee, pay up front, and if he notices me when he comes out, I can just say what a coincidence and how Geneva is a small city. If not, I'll tail him again. But I think it would be better for you to come here and walk in and see what's going on. It won't take long. I'll run back and stay with your girls."

Tamsyn nodded. Aurelie would do that, because she was fearless and direct. What would she, Tamsyn, do?

"You're an amazing friend," she said. "I'm staying here for the moment, though. With Scarlett."

"Sure. I'll report back when there's more news in that case."

▪ ▪ ▪ ▪ ▪

Half an hour later Aurelie messaged: **Are you sure there's not a different door?**

Almost completely, said Tamsyn.

Let me know if he turns up at home.

Of course.

Going to get another coffee. A cake too.

⬛⬛⬛⬛⬛

An hour after that, Aurelie wrote: **Still here. Feels like time for an aperitif.**

⬛⬛⬛⬛⬛

Sophie came home, and Tamsyn tried to pull herself together. Scarlett would never notice Tamsyn being jumpy and constantly checking her phone, not least because she hadn't been out of her room. Sophie, however, definitely would.

"Mother!" said Sophie, springing into the room. "Hey, guess what. I got my purple belt! It's, like, really unusual for someone to get it as quickly as this. I'm awesome!"

"You're amazing! You brilliant thing!"

Sophie's joy was infectious, and Tamsyn felt her mood lifting. She was delighted for Sophie and amazed that she had found an activity that would never have occurred to Tamsyn, and excelled at it. Did that mean, Tamsyn wondered, that Scarlett would be good at these things too when she was better? She sighed. It would be a long time before Scarlett was able to get a purple belt or do splits.

"Is Scarlett awake?" Sophie said, almost reading Tamsyn's mind. "I'm not going to show off or anything but I'd like to go and chat. If I'm good at this stuff, then she might be too. It could be nice for her to know that." She looked at Tamsyn's face. "I'm not going to throw a drink on her! It was an accident! She jogged my arm!"

"I think she's watching those DVDs," said Tamsyn, trying not to look at her phone. "The scary ones. Anyway, give her door a gentle knock, and if she answers, you can go in if you just stay a moment. If not, assume she's sleeping."

"Sure thing!"

Sophie disappeared down the corridor that led to the bedrooms, and as she didn't come back, Tamsyn assumed that she had been invited in.

Tamsyn picked up the phone again. There was still nothing. As she stared at it, willing something to happen, a message popped up.

On the move. More soon.

An hour later she was ready when Ed came home with a supermarket bag, a box containing a lemon tart, and two baguettes. Aurelie had updated her on his progress as he'd called in at first a little supermarket and then his café, where he had spoken to a man called Erik, rather than Lena. He had dutifully picked up all the things she'd asked for. She knew that Aurelie would be walking into the building just behind him, and that this would be entirely unremarkable.

She walked right up to Ed and kissed him. She pushed herself against him, more affectionate than usual. He put his shopping down and held her, pulling her in with both arms. She buried her face in his T-shirt and wondered whether she should just ask what the fuck he'd been doing at the clinic.

But then she would have to tell him that she knew where he had gone. She'd have to admit that she'd had him tailed. And since he was not, as far as she could tell, having an affair, she didn't want to say those things. He was talking to their daughters' doctors, and that was probably a good thing, no matter what the details were.

"Hey, there," he said softly. "You OK?"

"I missed you," she said stupidly. "I know you weren't long, but I missed you. Sophie got her purple belt."

"That's amazing," he said.

She felt him take a few deep breaths, and then he kissed the top of her head and went to find the girls.

• • • • •

She couldn't sleep. Her mind raced and raced. Why was he going to the clinic in secret? She had to be missing something obvious.

Go to the clinic. Go now.

Ed was snoring gently beside her, lying on his back, deeply asleep.

So go. Go and see what he was doing.

She should have accepted Aurelie's offer to come and stay with Scarlett and gone right in to find out. The answer was there. It was at the clinic. It had to be. A force she didn't quite understand got her out of bed. She knew she had to do this.

She picked up some clothes, moving quietly, and crept out of the room, past the girls' doors and into the family bathroom, where she dressed in jeans and a dark T-shirt and cardigan. She took her keys and phone and left the house as silently as she could.

She remembered Maya saying that her face would still open all the doors at the clinic, even after Scarlett came home, so that she could pop in and talk anytime.

That was what Ed was doing for some reason. Maybe it was his way of coping. He might have been struggling, and he wouldn't want to burden her with it. She was glad he wasn't having an affair. Now she just needed to find out what was happening.

The city was different by night. She hadn't been out after dark for a long time, though before Ed and she had had Sophie, they had been out a lot. Those weeks of settling into their new life felt surreal now: they had ultimately slotted in so easily. Everything had dropped into place and Geneva had usurped Cornwall as home.

Back then, though, with her head full of mud and loss and poverty, it had been a bright, weird dream, and she had constantly expected it to be pulled away. She remembered, when it had started to sink in that this was where they lived now, feeling nervous about the idea that it would end and they would go home, but now she knew that would never happen. Sophie couldn't live elsewhere, and so they would have to stay in Switzerland. There was no danger of being sent away. Were they really going to be able to live like this forever?

The night air was fragrant with the scent of all the trees that grew along their road. The street was well lit, the old-fashioned streetlights casting halos of light into the night. Two cats walked across her path.

She had already had a phenomenal amount of luck. She hoped greedily for more. More and more and more. For the girls to relax with each other. Ed to confide in her. Scarlett to make a full recovery. Sophie to stop worrying about who was the real daughter.

When she reached the corner, she turned right and walked toward the clinic, keeping an eye out for a taxi. One came past with its light on after a few minutes, and she flagged it down.

"VitaNova?"

The driver didn't know it, so she gave him the address and sat back to watch the nighttime city outside the window. It was two in the morning and she was on edge, excited to be doing something, to feel wide-awake for once. They drove across the bridge over the Rhône, and she thought of the dark water below, of all the things that could go wrong for a human in this world.

She looked at a young man wearing black who stared at them as they drove past close to the clinic. He was almost the only other person out. She shivered.

For a moment she considered asking the driver to wait, but they'd passed a taxi rank a little way back, and she had no idea whether she was going to be thirty seconds, if she couldn't get into the building, or two hours as Ed had been, so she paid the fare using her phone (briefly stopping to remember the fact that she had never been in a taxi before they moved here, and now she used them as a matter of course without thinking) and looked up at the building. The young man walked past, slowing his step, but then speeding up and disappearing around the corner.

VitaNova was, like its name, the blandest, most anonymous place imaginable. You would have no idea at all, from the outside, that this was a place in which perfect humans were created from tissue samples, in which a teenage girl had come back from the dead twice. It was a blocky white building, unremarkable in every way. Its windows were blank, its exterior so normal that a passerby would barely see it.

There were two dark marbled steps leading up to the entrance. Tamsyn walked up them and turned her face to look into the camera, holding her breath until there was a click and the door swung open.

She knew her way around easily enough, and strode in looking as confident as she could, even though she was starting to shake. She had no idea why she was here or what she thought might happen. Would she just walk around a quiet building and then go home?

There was a security guard in the entrance hall, but she recognized him and he smiled and gave her a little nod.

"*Bonsoir, madame,*" he said.

She looked at the words behind him. VITANOVA: BE YOUR BEST SELF.

"*Bonsoir,*" she said, and walked on quickly.

She heard him moving around as she walked away. His low voice said something on the phone, but she didn't hear the words.

There was a black door at the back of the entrance hall and she walked over to it, even though she had never seen it open, and turned her face to the camera, but this one didn't work. Instead, her feet walked her up to Scarlett's old room. Overhead lights came on as she went. She had no sense that anyone else was here. It was eerie, dreamlike, walking around the nighttime clinic.

She used to wonder about the other patients, because Dr. Singh spent time with them when she wasn't with Scarlett. Dr. Singh, however, was extraordinarily discreet and had never said a single word about any of the other patients in the clinic. Tamsyn realized she had no sense of them at all. Was there one other patient? Five? All the other twenty-three? The building was big enough for that.

Could Ed be visiting them? Why, though?

She reached Scarlett's floor and set off along the empty corridor, her trainers squeaking a little on the tiles underfoot.

What she was doing made no sense, and yet it was the only thing there was. Two a.m. was the only time she could come there without making complex arrangements about the girls and without Ed realizing that she was tailing him, trying to find clues about what he was up to. She felt energized in a way she hadn't lately. At least she was doing something.

She reached Scarlett's old door, just before the closed door that blocked the corridor. The brass plate with SCARLETT TRE-LAWNEY on it had disappeared, without even leaving holes where the screws had been. The door was slightly open, so she pushed it and stepped into the room.

It was exactly as it used to be, with Scarlett's bed made up with perfect white-and-blue sheets pulled tightly across it. The dimensions were so familiar. The hours Tamsyn had spent in this room came crashing back. Scarlett had been the very next thing to being dead, and now she was asleep at home. The window looked out onto a starry night sky. She stepped out of the room and pulled the door closed behind her.

Scarlett was at home. Tamsyn should be there too. She could be sure that Scarlett was fine only if she was with her. Tamsyn didn't trust anyone else to look after her. She shook her head and reminded herself that she trusted Ed and that Ed was home, even if he didn't know that he was in sole charge of their girls.

The door that blocked the corridor clicked open, and a light flicked on behind it.

That was where Dr. Singh used to appear from when she came from her other patients. If someone was there now, it was probably her. Tamsyn took a step toward the door and then another.

"Dr. Singh?" she said, her voice sounding weird in the absolute silence.

There was no answer, so she walked over to the door and pulled it open. It was a heavy door, a fire door. She'd never seen it open before. She thought she heard a sound behind her, but when she looked round, no one was there, so she looked forward again.

The corridor on the other side was exactly the same as it was on Scarlett's side. She stepped through and started walking.

"Dr. Singh?" she said again. She thought she heard distant footsteps, but everything around her was silent.

Was she allowed to be here? Why hadn't she just asked Ed where he went?

Keep walking. You'll find out.

Why had the security guard let her wander in? What had he said on the phone?

I did ask Ed where he went, she reminded herself. *And he lied.*

There were doors on either side of the corridor, but only one farther down had a nameplate on it. She thought she would go to that room and say Dr. Singh's name very quietly outside it, just in case she was there. Dr. Singh would make things make sense again.

Could Ed be having an affair with Dr. Singh? No. Surely he wouldn't. She wouldn't.

She walked slowly and stopped at the door with the plaque on it.

She read the name.

She knew as she read it that this was changing everything, but she didn't know why. She read it three times, but each time the words were the same. They said:

HONEY TRELAWNEY

Honey. That was a word that could also be a name. It was a word that resonated in her dreams. It appeared in her memories.

Trelawney, though. That was her name. Her name, Ed's, Sophie's, Scarlett's.

She could feel what this meant, the fact that there was a

person with this name, but she couldn't grasp it. Who was it? Why did the patient in this room have Tamsyn's, Ed's, Scarlett's, Sophie's, own surname? There wasn't anyone else in their family.

Had they made a third version of Scarlett? Was that why Ed came? Were there triplets?

The door opened and Dr. Singh was in front of her, smiling a tight smile and looking like a woman who had the answers but who didn't necessarily like the question.

"Tamsyn," she said. "Oh, Tamsyn. So you did it. You worked it out, just like they said. Everyone is going to be so pleased. Your team will be here in a moment and they'll help you with everything. Don't worry."

Tamsyn stood and looked around as if there would be an answer written on a wall. She looked up, as if it might be on the ceiling, and down, but it wasn't on the floor either.

"My team?" she said.

Honey.

Honey Trelawney.

Tamsyn Honey Trelawney.

·····

Tamsyn Honey Harvey before she got married. But always known as Honey.

Parents who were beekeepers, who had given their daughter a middle name that spoke to the swarm that had been their livelihood. A little girl who had loved that so much that she had demanded to use it as her given name. She had stopped being Tamsyn and started being Honey when she was five years old.

She took half a step forward, because if there was someone called Honey Trelawney in this room, she needed to see her. Dr. Singh, yawning, blocked her way and leaned forward to look up and down the corridor. Her face relaxed into relief when she saw someone.

"Here you go," she said. "Luca's here. He will help you. I'm responsible only for Honey, though I've enjoyed spending time with you, Tamsyn. Luca will help you with everything you need to know."

Tamsyn turned to see Luca running along the corridor from the opposite direction. She remembered the first time she'd met him at the hospital in Truro. He had offered her this lifeline, and she had been horrified at the idea of a robot clone. She'd had no idea.

"Tamsyn!" he called as he jogged closer. He was wearing jeans and a T-shirt, and his hair was messy in a way it wasn't usually. He looked as if he'd jumped out of bed, thrown on the nearest clothes and dashed here. "This is wonderful. We've been waiting but I didn't expect it to be tonight, or we'd have been prepared. I'm here now because I live closest, but the others are on their way. I'm glad I got to see you first. Congratulations!"

He held out a hand, grinning, and she took it, then pulled her hand away.

"What?" she said. "What are you talking about? I don't understand. You live closest?"

But there was something happening inside her. Things were falling into place. It wasn't true. It wasn't real. It couldn't be. The parents who had kept bees. Tamsyn Honey.

Luca took her by the hand and led her a little way down the corridor, away from the door, away from Dr. Singh, who disappeared inside, closing it with a click. Tamsyn could see the words HONEY TRELAWNEY glinting in the light from overhead.

Honey Trelawney.

There wasn't anyone called Honey.

There couldn't be.

. . . . .

Luca took her into a little room and sat her down. She leaned back, not caring that the sofa was so squashy that it felt as if it was going to swallow her up. He sat in a chair opposite her, and she remembered sitting like this with him before, back in the hospital in Cornwall. Then she had moved to a higher chair so she could speak to him with confidence. Now she didn't care.

"Have you made another copy of Scarlett?" she said.

She knew it wasn't that. She said it only because her world was spinning and shattering, falling apart and crashing back together, different. She said it because it was an easier thing to think about than the other one. A triplet would be fine. They could deal with that.

"Tamsyn," said Luca.

He looked around, and Maya came in, out of breath, and sat beside her on the sofa. Maya, she noticed, was also disheveled compared to the way she usually looked. She was wearing black leggings and a big white shirt, with her hair pulled back and no makeup. She looked young and excited. Maya squeezed Tamsyn's hand, and Tamsyn let her. She squeezed Maya back. She felt her own hand, warm and real, with blood flowing through it. She looked at their hands clasped together. Both those hands were real. They were real hands.

She looked at Maya's face. Maya was trying to hold back a smile, but Tamsyn could see that she was bursting with something. She was bursting with excitement, with happiness. She was bursting with pride.

Why was Maya proud? Tamsyn had barged into the hospital in the middle of the night in search of the answer to a completely different question.

She remembered Sophie in that fondue restaurant asking the

questions that led to them telling her about Scarlett. She knew that Sophie had been supposed to work it out for herself, that it was an important part of her development, though she couldn't quite remember why. It was to do with her sense of self.

Tamsyn didn't want to look at this new thing. She couldn't do it. She couldn't build everything differently in her head. She didn't want to.

· · · · ·

"You know, don't you, Tamsyn?" said Luca. "Can you tell me? Who is Honey?"

Honey wore washed-out old clothes with holes in the knees, because Honey worked in the fields, with daffodils and cauliflowers. Honey had chickens and a friend called Maud. Honey despaired over her daughter. Honey was angry. She shouted a lot.

"I'm not Honey," she said, and her voice came out tiny and wavering. She remembered how lucid Sophie had been and thought how stupid her own voice sounded in comparison, and she wondered what the differences were between her and Sophie.

"I'm not Honey," she said in a more confident voice. "I want to see her. Is she going to get better?"

She'd had a blank around the time of the accident. She had no idea at all of what had actually happened. She remembered waking up sitting in a chair at the hospital.

The accident was in the winter. She'd woken up in the spring. There was time missing.

"We don't think so, Tamsyn," said Maya, still gripping her hand. "I'm very sorry to have to say it, but I have to be honest with you. It's not going to happen. Shall we go and see her? Do you feel ready for that? It might help you to make sense of it all."

Honey's room was like Scarlett's old one, except that where

Scarlett's was pale blue, this one was yellow. The chair was covered in a yellow-and-white-checked fabric. The curtains were yellow. The walls were pale yellow. It was all yellow like honey was yellow.

Tamsyn walked toward the bed, and she was there in six steps. She stood beside it, and she saw that the woman in the bed didn't know anyone was there. There was no ambiguity about it like there had been with Scarlett. Honey was far, far away. Tamsyn hoped she was in a velvety safe place like Scarlett's. That was comforting.

She looked at the cannula going into Honey's hand and then she looked at her own hand. Tamsyn's nails were shaped and painted pale pink, and Honey's were efficiently short. Tamsyn's skin was tanned, and Honey's had the sick pallor that Scarlett's used to have before she started sitting out in the sun. Tamsyn's hair was colored and styled, thick and glossy, where Honey's was short and speckled with gray.

Honey was Tamsyn's source material.

Tamsyn was her reanimation, her clone, her ghost. She was her replacement.

She closed her eyes. Nothing she had thought was real had been real at all.

37

Ten months earlier

ED GOT UP EARLY WITH NO IDEA THAT THIS WOULD BE THE day on which his life fell apart. He had, however, felt it all hanging by a thread: if a hand had reached through the clouds and pointed at him, while a voice bellowed *Today it ends*, he wouldn't have been at all surprised.

He couldn't do this anymore. Scarlett's behavior had tipped him beyond the point of no return. She was his child—he had watched her being born, had fallen in love with her the moment he saw her—and now he couldn't deal with her. He hated himself even more because this was his failure, not hers. It was all too much. He worked long hours and still barely earned enough to support the family. Honey had lost the bee farm when the land was sold from under her, and although they owned their home, it was a static caravan, so that hardly counted.

He wasn't a good husband to Honey. She seemed to hate him now. They were angry with each other. They shouted all the time, all three of them, and nothing ever shifted. Leaving was the only thing he could think of to do. At least it would change things.

He woke in an empty bed, which was a relief. He had vaguely heard Honey getting up, dressing quietly and heading out. She was doing an early shift cleaning offices, and that meant starting at five. It wasn't so bad in the summer, but on a day like this, when it wouldn't get light for hours, it had to be punishing. She always said she'd rather be cleaning an office than out in the rain picking cauliflowers. He had no idea how she did it, switching between jobs without guaranteed hours, working long shifts, double shifts, and always managing to be at home in the evenings, when he was at work, so that between them they could try to keep an eye on their impossible daughter. No wonder she was in a bad mood all the time, all day every day. No wonder she had no patience.

He could leave a note and go. By the time he had to speak to her again face-to-face, she would have calmed down. Some of the guys lived in a house share close to the restaurant, and he had made a tentative plan to move in with them, even though he'd have to kip on the sofa at first. Yes, he would be forty-five years old to their twenty-whatever, but he didn't care.

He and Honey had weathered a lot, but now Scarlett was too much. He knew that. They were broken, finished. He had a small bag tucked away under the bed so that when the moment came, he would just pick it up and go. Honey didn't know about it: he knew that because if she'd found it, she would have yelled at him.

He felt its betrayal now burning through the mattress. It contained nothing really: some spare clothing, a toothbrush. The point of it was that if Scarlett pushed him too far, he would be able to leave in seconds before he did something terrible, and he would never need to come back.

He wondered sometimes whether Honey might have an escape bag too, but really he knew that she didn't. She would have been astonished and furious if she knew his was there. It would never have occurred to her that they might split up.

It wasn't Honey's fault, but she was almost impossible now. Life had dealt her a shit hand until now, in her forties, she was powered by anger. It was all too difficult; they had become toxic. Was he going to be lost without her? He would have to find a way to deal with that.

It all circled back to Scarlett. They had different approaches— Honey shouted and screamed and said that it was a phase they had to get through, whereas Ed would have locked Scarlett in her room. Moved schools, moved homes (though options were limited), whatever it took to get her away from her toxic life and the boyfriend she never mentioned but who definitely existed.

He couldn't stand his daughter. It was an awful thing to articulate, and he could do it only inside his head. Something had happened to change her, and they would have done everything they could to help if they knew what it was, but how could you help someone who wouldn't tell you what was wrong, who screamed and yelled at you for asking? He was actually quite old-fashioned about swearing. He hated it, and although it was very much the currency of the kitchen where he worked, he had made a point of not swearing in his home life ever, even before they'd had a child. Scarlett had blown that wide open. She had shown him that everything he had thought he knew about himself was wrong.

He was forty-five and she was fourteen but she had beaten him. He had to take himself away because he had always been someone who could fix things, and he couldn't fix her.

When he left, Honey would be on her own with Scarlett. That was going to be shit for her. He imagined them screaming at each other all the time, and knew how miserable that would be.

He sat on the edge of the bed, wearing a gray T-shirt that had once been white and a pair of pants, and listened to the van. It was silent. That meant Scarlett was asleep and he needed to wake her for school. Maybe he'd make her some breakfast, see if he could get her to smile.

. . . . .

Five minutes later he was outside, in tracksuit bottoms and old boots, collecting eggs from the chickens. The chicken run was a sea of mud, and it smelled disgusting. It was basically chicken shit mixed with soil and rain, and there was nothing you could do to change that. The chickens would keep shitting, and the rain would keep raining. All the same, he found three eggs and took them into the van. At least they always had eggs. The chickens were the best investment they'd ever made, the only part of their life that currently worked.

He came back in and there she was, wearing an approximation of a school uniform and glaring. He forced a smile. Sometimes he found himself wondering what it would have been like if Honey had got pregnant the month before or the month after, or if a different sperm had won the race. They would have made a different child.

That, though, was no way to think. Scarlett had been a wonderful child until a year ago, but that year felt like his whole life.

"Breakfast?" he said, holding up the eggs.

She wrinkled her nose. "Eggs are chicken's periods."

"You vegan now?"

She rolled her eyes and turned her back, muttering about everyone else having cereal. He put the eggs in a bowl and left them on the side for Honey to find later, and went back into the bedroom.

Scarlett was fourteen and he had no idea how to talk to her anymore. Anytime he tried, she threw it back at him. He watched her getting ready for school, tried to say the right things and tried not to mind when she ignored him. When she left, he stood at the window.

She was up and dressed, and she was leaving on time, so his work was done. He watched her walking alone, her long hair tied back into a ponytail, looking like a perfect but unhappy schoolgirl, and he wondered what was happening in her head. She walked with her head down, turned in on herself. As he watched, she passed Maud and her horrible dog, and Scarlett's demeanor changed, so she swaggered and said something that made Maud (who was endlessly patient) roll her eyes and walk on.

What was happening to her? The question haunted him day and night.

Then she was around the corner, and she had gone. He took his escape bag to work.

- - - - -

After he finished work at ten forty, Ed composed a text message, because that was apparently the kind of coward he was these days. **I'm sorry honey**, he wrote. **I'm not coming back. I can't do it anymore. It's not you. It's us. It's everything. It has to change.** He stopped and looked at the words. Could he just send it like this? It would do. It was crap and unfinished, but if he sent it now, he wouldn't have to go home.

His thumb was hovering over the send button when a message dropped in from Honey.

> **Scarlett's missing again. She said she was with Leanne but she's not. Polly was really off with me. Can you find her on your way home?**

He sighed.

He carefully deleted the draft message and wrote instead, **Fuck's sake honey! Again?!????? Yeah, I'll find her.**

He was so tired, and Honey was so tired and so angry, and they were all falling apart, and now he would end up taking his stupid bag and going home after all.

He followed the Find My Friends dot and found that Scarlett was in the same pub as ever. He stood in the doorway, glaring around. She appeared from an alcove to tell him she hated him. He looked at the partition that meant he couldn't see her friends and thought, for a moment, that he would storm over and confront whoever was there and ask what they were doing, taking a fourteen-year-old to the pub. He had done it before and just found a load of kids who laughed at him. What was the point?

Instead he pulled her out, swearing at everyone, and took her home. He tried to talk to her, but by the time they got back, they were just saying that they hated each other in between sulks. Scarlett stormed away to bed, Ed was annoyed by everything, and Honey and Maud fussed around, doing nothing.

He couldn't stand Honey's constant furious waiting. She wanted things to change but she never did anything about it. She took it out on him. They had huge fights when they thought Scarlett wasn't listening, but she had to know. She had to.

Maybe he could tell Honey he was just leaving for a month. That sounded reasonable. Then he would see what happened from there.

Maybe tomorrow.

▪ ▪ ▪ ▪ ▪

He lay awake, his heart pounding. He wanted to wake her now and tell her he was going. *I'm going to go so I can work out what we could all do as a family. To make things better.* It sounded like shite, because it was. He just wanted to be somewhere else. *I'll be back,* he would say. *I just think we need a bit of space.*

He knew that Honey would look at him with her laser gaze, rightly seeing that he was running away from the problem, knowing that there was space for only one of them to do that.

▪ ▪ ▪ ▪ ▪

He realized he wasn't the only one who was awake. Scarlett was trying to be quiet, but he could hear her voice through the wall because you could hear everything in this caravan. He listened very hard.

"Not now," she whispered. "I can't. I literally can't. My parents are in the next room. And anyway, I meant it. I mean it. It's over."

He looked at Honey. It was so rare to see her relaxed. He wished he could provide for her properly. He wanted her to have lovely things to eat and drink, not to worry about money, about work. He dreamed of a life in which they didn't have to strive for every little thing, in which they could take Scarlett away from whatever was going on and offer her opportunities.

He would give anything for that. Anything.

"No! Don't come here!" Scarlett was whispering. "No! OK, I'll meet you at the end of the road. Last time. Give me ten minutes. And then that's it. I can't do this anymore. No. You've done that. You've done your worst. Nothing to lose."

He shook Honey, pulled back to the moment. They couldn't let this happen.

"Wake up," he whispered.

38

HE RAN AFTER HER, THROUGH THE MUD TO THE PATH AND then along the path to the road, but she was wearing trainers and was surprisingly fast. She made it to the corner before him, and he screamed as loudly as he could as he ran. He called her a fucking nightmare and probably worse than that.

He was done with this shit. She could go to a children's home. He kept stepping in puddles and his feet were cold and wet and he wanted a life where none of this happened.

He heard Honey behind him. This was her fault because she'd let Scarlett take the keys.

It wasn't her fault. It was no one's. It was Scarlett's. It was everyone's.

Scarlett ran down toward town, and Ed could see there were headlights approaching and a car just about to come round the bend. He waited for Scarlett to slow down, to get ready to jump into the car that was coming for her, but as he watched, as he ran to grab her before she did it, she turned and ran out, directly in front of it. And the car didn't slow down.

The car could have swerved. It could have avoided her, but it didn't. She ran to it, and it drove at her.

It happened in slow motion. People said that happened, and it really did.

Honey overtook him and ran faster than anyone had ever run before, an arm out to push Scarlett away from the car, but it hit them both, Honey first. Scarlett was thrown into the air and landed on the wet grass verge. Honey was knocked straight down, and the car sped away. She lay like a deer on the tarmac.

Like roadkill.

These images were going to be with him forever. His daughter—the girl he did in fact love, the baby he had seen emerging into the world—flying through the air. His wife—the woman he had been trying to leave, but always, always the love of his life—left for dead on the road.

He stared at one and the other, back to one, back to the other. He didn't have his phone. The car was gone and he hadn't seen its number plate or even what color it was. He wanted to move Honey from the road, but he thought she was breathing and he knew you were supposed to leave people where they were.

* * * * *

Maud was there, a little bit farther back. He looked at her. She looked at him.

"I'll call an ambulance," she said, and she took her phone from her pocket and, looking stunned, tapped a number three times.

* * * * *

Honey and Scarlett were alive, but only just. They were put on the same ward with two other people, and Ed pulled the curtains around them, leaving the one between them open. Scarlett should have been in the pediatric department, but the doctors had put her with her mother instead so he could be with both of them at once. That was better, he supposed, than having to divide his time, running upstairs and downstairs.

He sat on a plastic chair between the beds and wondered what you were supposed to do when the very thing you had wished for was happening in the worst way. He had wanted everything to change, and now it had. He had wanted to leave them, and they had left him.

He was on his own. He had lost his wife and his child.

He waited.

Neither of them woke up. He waited and waited. They both had terrible scores on the coma scale, but Honey's was worse. His life went to shit. He went home once to get insurance details and a few practical things (he'd had no idea why he was really going to need that overnight bag), and then he lived in the plastic chair between their beds. The guilt ate him alive. If they died, he would die too. He would make sure of it. He slept sometimes in his chair. He lived on the tea and toast that the staff made for him. They were kind.

His brother, Jimmy, came down from Scotland. They had never been close but now Jimmy was all he had, and Ed leaned on him completely. Jimmy looked after the van, paid for food and stopped Ed from falling apart quite as comprehensively as he would have done otherwise. Weeks went past.

A woman called Poppy, who worked for the hospital admin team, came to find him when he was making a cup of tea and said, "I'm sorry if this seems indelicate."

He stopped, tea bag on spoon in midair, and looked at her. "Indelicate?" He half expected her to tell him he'd forgotten to put his pants on.

Instead, she said: "So, when family members are very ill, and particularly when it's a child, we encourage the family to make a memory box. In the future, she might want to know about her time in hospital. If the worst did happen, you'd find it comforting in a way to have this most strange of times documented. If you want to keep a lock of Scarlett's hair— I know it may seem morbid but sometimes people find that photographs of a child, even as Scarlett currently is, help them to process things. We have facilities for that here now. I can set you up with a locker."

He didn't want to think about the locker but he knew he should do it.

"Sure," he said.

She walked him through corridors to a little room with a bank of lockers, where she would set up his fingerprint ID to open one of them. He expressed dull surprise at the high-tech nature of it all.

"I know," said Poppy (young, redheaded) with a grimace. Was she really young, though, or was it just that he felt older than the universe right now? He looked at her. She was maybe thirty or so. Twenty-five. Forty. He didn't know. He didn't care. She was still talking. He tried to focus.

"It was a charity initiative a few years ago. We could use the funding for many things, but we get what we're given and what we're given is memory banks."

She looked exhausted. He let her take his fingerprint and asked her to set it up with Scarlett's too as a gesture of hope. He put in a lock of her hair, because Poppy had suggested it. He took photographs around her bed and the hospital, and Poppy printed them for him. He wasn't much of a writer but he sat between the beds and wrote it all down. It turned into a long, long rambling letter to Scarlett, then a series of letters. He told her how sorry he was. He told her what it was like sitting between her and Honey, waiting for them to wake up. He kept starting a letter to Honey but found he didn't know what to say.

▪ ▪ ▪ ▪ ▪

Then, one day, Jimmy walked through the curtain with a serious look on his face, and Ed didn't want to hear whatever it was he was about to say.

"Bro," said Jimmy. They had started that as an ironic thing but now it seemed that *bro* was just what they called each other. "Bro, there's a woman here to see you. Her name's Maya. No—it could be good. It's about a medical trial."

39

ED AGREED TO EVERYTHING: HE NEVER CONSIDERED ANY-
thing else. He certainly didn't agonize over it. Maya and her team
were going to take Honey to Switzerland. After about six weeks,
the reanimation would be ready and would come over with Maya
and Luca. Although he hated the idea of Honey going, he knew
this was an incredible, impossible godsend. Switzerland was
mainly just a word to him: he pictured a well-funded hospital
with efficient staff. He didn't bother with mountains or cuckoo
clocks or any of that. He just wanted the hospital.

He had to give them every chance because it was the only
way he could begin to atone for the way he had failed them. He
had been about to walk out when fate stepped in and took them
from him. He didn't care about the details of the accident, about
who had done this. He pushed the fact that he had seen Scarlett
step out in front of that car out of his mind. There was no space
for it. Ed tried to override the fact that Honey, and not he, had
thrown herself in the vehicle's path in an instinctive dash to save
her child. It was good, he told himself, that he was unscathed
and able to sign the paperwork for his wife and daughter.

Jimmy was against it every step of the way, but he couldn't stop Ed from agreeing to everything Maya asked.

"Hang on to the paperwork," Jimmy said, "as insurance," and Ed agreed.

It turned out, however, that there wasn't any paperwork. Everything happened electronically. Ed had no record of it at all beyond a copy of the confidentiality agreement he'd signed.

"Then you have to make your own trail," Jim told him.

Even though it felt weird, Ed started making sure his phone was recording in his pocket every time he spoke to Maya.

▪ ▪ ▪ ▪ ▪

"There's only one thing," Ed said to Maya, and he opened up, telling her that he'd been about to leave, that he and Honey had been unhappy for years. "I'm not sure," he said at the end. "I'm not sure she'd appreciate any of this. She'll be furious with me for making decisions on her behalf. Being brought back to me, well, that might be the last thing she wants. She might be seeing a coma as a blessed relief."

Maya looked at him for a long time with a little smile on her face. Then she said, "What do you think Honey would change about herself if she could?"

He started to say *Nothing*, but realized there was no point. He told her.

▪ ▪ ▪ ▪ ▪

Ed said good-bye to his wife and told her unresponsive shell that he would see her soon. Then she was gone and it was just him and Scarlett. He sat with her and talked to her and tried to move away from the voice in his head that just did blame, blame, blame for everything. He couldn't blame Scarlett anymore, and none of it had been Honey's fault. He missed Honey, hated it when some-one else moved into her bed.

Christmas came and went and he ignored it. A smarmy man called Luca flew over to see him and Scarlett from time to time, sometimes with a doctor who looked as if she had huge reserva-tions about everything. They said that everyone agreed that Scar-lett would be an ideal subject and started making arrangements for her to go too.

"What about me?" Ed said. "What do I do when you take Scarlett?"

"Indeed," said Luca.

. . . . .

Ed couldn't take it in, but he agreed to everything. He did his best to be receptive to the prospect of the new Honey arriving in Cornwall. He went home and had a shower in the communal bathroom block, hating being away from his daughter. The van was horribly the same as it had been before, filled with Scarlett's and Honey's things. Now, though, Jimmy was living in a tent just outside.

Ed knocked on Maud's door and sat in her tiny camper van, which smelled of incense. With Maya's script in his head, he asked if she would electronically sign a confidentiality agreement so he could discuss something with her.

Ed had never liked Maud, but she was Honey's closest friend and she was the one person he was going to bring onside, be-cause he needed someone. Jimmy just told him not to do it, so the two of them were hardly speaking, and he needed another perspective.

Now he looked at Maud, at her short gray hair and craggy face, and tried to order his words. He got it out in the end as she watched with knowing eyes.

Honey had always told him that although he didn't realize it, he was sexist around Maud. "She's an older woman and you find her intimidating because she doesn't care what you think. I admire her. If she was a man and was incredibly kind to us and always said what he thought, then you'd like him."

He heard Honey's words in his head now as he looked at Maud, who was petting her horrible dog without looking at it. She was looking at him. Directly into his soul apparently.

She signed the document and he sent it to Maya, waiting for her approval before he started to speak. Maud had agreed that if she told anyone what Ed was about to tell her, VitaNova would come after her and take every single thing she owned (they couldn't realize how little that was) and take her to court. Then he stumbled through the story.

"So I don't know what it's going to be like, but they're going to bring the new Honey over from Switzerland next week. She won't be properly conscious before they switch that part on, when she's with me and Scarlett. She's going to think she's Honey, and so we're supposed to act as if she is. They'll be monitoring her to see if she truly believes she's the same person. You'll meet her, so if you can do it, can you act as if she's the very same person as before?"

"Does she know she was in the accident?" said Maud.

He shook his head. "She thinks it was just Scarlett. She'll think she's been sitting by Scarlett's bed for months. She's going to have lost three months, but they say it won't matter. She's been set up not to notice that. When they make the new Scarlett, she'll know she was in an accident. She has to know it, because she'll be waking up in hospital, I guess. But Honey will just think she's there as Scarlett's mum."

Maud looked at him for a long time and he made himself stay silent. Her face moved as she considered everything. When she did speak, she said: "This is amazing, Ed. Really incredible. I can't wait to meet her. The things they can do. Who would have imagined?"

He leaned forward. "Really?"

"Yes. Really. I think if Honey was able to take part in this conversation, she would tell you to go for it. Having her back!" There were tears in her eyes. "Having her back, Ed! I don't care if it's not really her. It's going to be the closest anyone has ever come to getting somebody back from the other side. Will she be called Honey?"

He shook his head. "We need to give her another name, because the real Honey still exists. There can't be two of her. I'm thinking Tamsyn."

"Yes. Her given first name. Still her but a different part of her. It couldn't have been anything else, could it?"

She stood up, so he did too. When she hugged him, he realized that Honey had been right. He had been dismissive because she was an old lady. He wouldn't do that anymore. He needed her at his side through all this. She had come on board as fast as he had, because she loved Honey and Scarlett too.

"Thank you so much," he said, and his eyes filled with tears for the first time in ages. "You're her best friend, you know, and this means everything to me. It would to her too."

"Anything I can do," she said. "I mean it, love. Anything at all. Just say the word. Oh, my days, I can't wait to meet her. Can't wait. Even if it's only a shadow of a shadow of her, it's our Honey, darling. We get our Honey back. I'd have done anything to have them do that with Ally." She hesitated and looked into his soul again. "Forgive me if this is a tasteless thing to say right now, but you two hadn't been getting on these last few years."

He couldn't meet her eye. "It's going to be different," he said. "That's what they say."

He told the restaurant he wasn't going back. They tried to offer him more wages and extra vacation because no one had a clue what was really happening. The apprentice Jasper was so tense, he was hardly breathing when he asked after Scarlett, and Ed remembered introducing them a year or two ago. It was nice of him to remember her, but really, people had no idea. He told everyone that things were looking bad for Honey and Scarlett and that, when the worst happened, he was going to move away.

He sat at Scarlett's bedside, studying her face, the parts of it he could see. He looked at her short hair, partly covered by a cap. He looked at her young skin and thought about the short amount of time she had been in the world, and he wished he'd been able to keep her safe. It was what fathers were meant to do. Perhaps, he thought, she would wake up and tell him what had been going on.

He couldn't begin to imagine a new Scarlett. He had to get his head around the fact that there was a new Honey, a Tamsyn, first. He just sat there and waited.

40

ED DIDN'T MEET HIS NEW WIFE FOR A COUPLE OF DAYS AF-
ter she arrived. Maya told him again that although Tamsyn could
walk and talk, she wasn't conscious yet. He had no idea how a
thing like that worked, but he didn't understand anything anymore. He had known his world before, but now it had expanded
beyond death into afterlife. Nothing made sense, and he was a
passenger.

There were four people from Switzerland here in Truro, and
Ed was self-conscious about them seeing his life, even though
none of them came to the van park. He knew that even the hospital was shabby. He knew it wasn't his fault, but he felt that he
was less than them because of it. You generally stayed where you
were born, socially (in his world at least), and this was him. This
was where he had been born, and it was where he had always
thought he would stay, even as life became more and more difficult.

Maya, however, explained that the next stage of the plan
would change things.

"So how are you feeling about relocating to Geneva?" she said casually, sitting with him in the most expensive of the hospital cafés, sipping peppermint tea.

Ed gave her a little smile and took a gulp of coffee. It wasn't very nice: Maya was right to have the tea. He felt that the two of them were kind of friends now, and all he could really think about was his new wife, Tamsyn. Would she be a lifeline, like Maud had said?

"Me?" he said.

"Yes."

He wondered why her lipstick was so shiny. Did she put glossy stuff on top of it, or was it just a shiny lipstick? He remembered the times he'd found Scarlett in the pub, her lipstick rubbed away on the rims of glasses. He remembered introducing her to Jasper that time. She'd come to his work, back when she'd still been straightforward. She'd been only just thirteen, but she'd twiddled her hair and smiled, and Jasper, who must have been fifteen, sixteen, had grinned and leaned forward to talk to her.

Her trouble had a boy at the center of it. He knew that. Whoever it was, there was some bastard out there who had led his precious baby astray. If he ever found him, he would kill him.

He thought about Jasper. He dismissed it. Scarlett and Jasper had met only once.

"We're excited to introduce you to Tamsyn tomorrow. But we can't move Honey back from Geneva in her current state, as the first flight was difficult enough and her doctor is refusing to authorize any further travel, and so we'd like to bring you and Scarlett over there. The whole VitaNova family is there. We'll rent you an apartment to live in. You're already an integral part of our program and I think—" Her eyes darted around the room. "I mean, there would be lifestyle benefits. No more money worries. A change of scene."

He nodded. Nothing could make life any weirder than it already was.

"Sure," he said. "Move to Geneva. Why not?"

. . . . .

He had never felt so alone. Scarlett was the same as ever, and Honey was in Switzerland. Jimmy was still at the site, and although he was hostile to the project, he had sent a text to say that he would come to the hospital and support Ed while Tamsyn woke up. Maud was excited and positive (though she was going to be gutted when she discovered they were moving to Geneva; he wondered whether she might be able to come too), and that was all he had.

He'd spent too much time in his own head lately. He'd never really been on his own before, and he recognized that he was terrible at it. It didn't work for him at all.

"When we go to Geneva," he said to Maya, the words feeling odd in his mouth, "can I get a job? I'm not very good at . . ." He swept a hand around the room, hoping to convey *hanging around with nothing to do.* "Also, I know you said no more money worries, but I guess we're still going to need an income?"

She turned her big smile on him. "You won't need to work. But sure, I can see that you want to. You're a chef, so there's always going to be a job for you. Actually, do you do pastry?"

"Haven't for a while, but yeah."

She nodded. "My friend has a coffee shop and bakery by the lake. I'll talk to her. Leave it with me. You'd be OK with that? Otherwise I guess we could find you something at one of the big restaurants. But honestly, Ed? You're going to need to be around Tamsyn in the evenings. She can't be left alone for too long. So a café job would work. I'll get on it."

He was left reeling at the idea of working in a bakery by the lake in Geneva and then going home to his replacement wife. Just when he thought life couldn't get any weirder, it had spiraled again.

■ ■ ■ ■ ■

That evening he sat in the van drinking beer and talking it over, in an uncomfortable way, with Jimmy. Jimmy was smaller than he was, and his beard was longer, but Ed knew they both looked like their dad.

"What are you going to say when you meet her?" Ed said.

"I'll say the right things," said Jim my at once. "I'm not a monster. I'll say hi, but then I'm going to head off. I can't play a part in the imprinting thing or whatever. I'm curious to see what she's like, but after that, I'm leaving you to it. Come to me when it goes wrong."

"Oh, cheers," said Ed, tipping his glass at him. "Appreciate the vote of confidence."

"I don't blame you, bro," said Jimmy. "Most people would do the same. But I don't trust them one inch. Human cloning? It's illegal, for one thing, and it doesn't happen, for another. There's no trace of it online. It doesn't exist. You've let them take your sick wife away without a word, out of the place that was keeping her alive, and out of the country. You signed off on it and she's gone."

Ed glared. "It was that or switch off her life support. I took the opportunity that came along to stop her dying. Jeez, Jim! What was I meant to do? Just say, *No, thanks—I'll flip the switch on the mother of my child*?"

"Exactly! They identified you as a man with no options. They used the power imbalance and got you to agree to everything they wanted. You let them take your wife so they could use her material for whatever they wanted. They could be mining her body parts."

Ed stared at his brother. "Seriously?"

Jimmy held his gaze and shrugged. "Sure."

"Is that what you've thought all along?"

"I can't see how this isn't some kind of weird trick, that they've just found someone who looks like her or something. I mean, what the fuck?"

"The whole thing is *what the fuck*."

"That's right enough." Jimmy put a hand on Ed's shoulder. "Sorry, bro. Someone has to be cynical. Just—be careful. I don't know what this is about, but I don't trust it. Don't be disappointed if *Tamsyn* is nothing like Honey. Or if there's no Tamsyn at all."

Ed shook his brother's hand off. "So if it was up to you, you'd have sat there while her life support was switched off?"

"I would, yeah." Jimmy held up a hand to stop Ed from talking. "I know. It's easy for me to say because I've never married or had a kid. But I've thought this through. Honey's great. She's family. I love her and Scarlett, and it breaks my heart, what's happened. Absolutely tears me apart. It makes no sense that they can be smashed down like that by some drunk driver who just keeps driving and living their life. But—say you'd been involved in the accident too. That would have made me next of kin, right? VitaNova would have come to me. I've been thinking about this constantly, and I can honestly say I'd have turned them down. If they were planning to take the three of you away to"—he paused and made air quotes—"'Switzerland' and then bring back new versions that they'd made, and told me I had to live with them and pretend they were the same people as before, I would have said no. I'd have told them to get to fuck."

Ed swigged his beer and looked out the window. The sun was shining in a halfhearted way outside.

"Cheers," he said. "And yeah, you'd have switched us off.

Good for you. But I wouldn't. If it had been you, I'd have sent you to 'Switzerland.'" They gave each other little smiles. "And you couldn't have stopped me. It's done now anyway."

Jimmy nodded. "True."

They drank in silence, and after a while, Ed remembered that he hadn't even shared his news.

"You know how you don't believe it's Switzerland?"

"Yeah."

"Well, Maya asked me to move there. She wants me to go with Scarlett and . . . Tamsyn because Honey can't come back here. She said she can get me a job in a bakery by the lake."

"Whoa. That sounds like the most sinister code ever. *He ended up in the bakery by the lake.*"

"And an apartment, and Scarlett will be in the same clinic as Honey and she'll wake up there knowing she's had an accident." He held up his hand, suddenly choked. "Don't say anything. Please. If you say something cynical, I'm going to have to punch your fucking face."

He saw Jimmy start to say something, then bite it back. They sat in silence for a while.

Jimmy nodded. "Fair enough," he said. "Sure."

Neither of them spoke for a while, and then Jimmy said, "Sorry. You've got enough going on without me doing this. I'm with you all the way, bro. I'm overstepping. I'm going to stick around with Maud. Found some work at the harbor in Newlyn."

Ed nodded.

"Thanks, mate," he said.

. . . . .

The next day everything was set up, every detail attended to.

"This is important," said Luca. "She'll wake sitting in the chair beside Scarlett's bed. She believes she's the same person she was before, and she doesn't know she was hit by the car. It's important that she wakes up as Scarlett's mother and your wife, because if she comes to consciousness knowing she's a reanimation, it will shape her sense of herself in a way we don't want. We need her to do everything on the basis that she's in her rightful place in the world, not stepping in to replace someone else. It's likely that eventually she'll come to it herself, and if she does, it'll be appropriate for her cognitive development. If she doesn't, that's also fine."

"But her name's different."

Luca smiled. "The first few minutes are where it all happens. We need you to wake her up, call her Tamsyn and impress on her the fact that Scarlett is in hospital and that she, Tamsyn, collapsed from shock. She has a memory blank from the accident to just now, and she'll accept whatever you tell her. I can't overstate the importance of these first three minutes. You totally need to follow the script. Is that going to be all right?"

Ed nodded. He looked round at Jimmy, who had come for support in spite of everything. Jimmy forced a smile.

"Of course," Ed said. "I'll do anything. You know that."

He was scared that he was going to say the wrong thing, worried that he would accidentally blurt out the fact that she was a clone. He had no idea how much she would look like Honey. Even if she looked exactly the same, she wouldn't be Honey. She would be someone new, but still his wife.

He felt that he'd really like a drink.

He pulled himself together and thought of a new life in Geneva, close to his real Honey. At least he'd be able to visit her, to sit beside Honey and Scarlett again. He remembered Maud's words about Tamsyn being a part of Honey and about how precious and magical it was to get her back.

Science had done this: it had re-created his wife, and even if it turned out to be a clumsy re-creation, it was an incredible thing to be offered. He thought about all the people throughout history who had lost someone they loved to a sudden accident. He was the only one who had been offered the chance to get them back. Both of them. Other people saw ghosts, but he got to live with his. He would get this right, because he was quite possibly the luckiest man in the history of the world.

. . . . .

He walked into Scarlett's cubicle and saw a woman sitting in a chair, eyes closed. They had dressed her in black jeans and a white T-shirt, the sort of things Honey used to wear, but these were new clothes, and so the effect was different. Honey's clothes had been old and faded and worn, whereas Tamsyn's were chic. She had a better haircut: it was shorter, well cut and glossy. He looked at Luca, and then at Maya, who was wearing a nurse's uniform because she was going to be watching Tamsyn all the time and this way she was able to blend in. Luca was staring at Tamsyn, a man delighted by his own handiwork. Maya gave Ed a warm smile before her gaze too snapped back to his new wife.

Ed looked at her and didn't allow himself to look away. She wasn't Honey. She didn't look the same. He wasn't sure why, but she was a different person. He didn't see Honey in the woman in the chair, and he never would. Her face was the same but different. She could have been Honey's sister, but he would never have mistaken her for his wife.

That was oddly a relief. This was Tamsyn. He had to work with that and he would.

There were three observers crowded into the cubicle, plus himself and the unconscious Tamsyn and Scarlett. He looked at them: Poppy from this hospital, Luca and Maya. Jim was outside in the corridor.

Luca took charge, and everyone but Ed left. Maya was poised

to come in, and everyone else stood very still on the other side of the curtain and pretended they weren't there.

He ran through the script in his head. It was time. His heart pounded as he leaned over the stranger on the chair and put a hand on her shoulder.

"Tamsyn," he said. His voice shook and he fought to control himself. "Wake up, darling. It's me, Ed." He saw her blink awake and stretch. Her whole body jolted. She leaned forward to stare at Scarlett, gasping, horrified. "I'm sorry to wake you," he added. Her skin felt normal under his hand. She felt like Honey. "But the doctor's coming round. Do you remember what happened? Scarlett's accident? She was hit by a car that didn't stop. We were both there. You collapsed from the stress and they've given you some medication, so you probably feel weird. But you're OK, and Scarlett's where she needs to be to recover."

"Oh, shit."

Tamsyn ran her hand through her hair. He touched her hair too. It felt different under his fingers and he supposed that this was because it was brand-new and hadn't been assaulted by life. Had she grown it or was it made? *Forget that! Focus.*

She was gazing at Scarlett, and Ed realized she didn't really care about him: she cared about the girl she thought was her daughter. She had Honey's memories, which meant Scarlett was her focus. He stepped back and looked at the two of them: his sick daughter and his cloned wife. The wife looked bewildered. Scarlett was the same as ever.

Someone coughed outside the curtain. Ed flinched. Tamsyn looked round. He tensed, knowing that if she moved the curtain, she'd see a line of people intently focused on everything they were saying. Tamsyn frowned and shifted. The curtain parted and Maya came in, earlier than planned.

"Hello, Tamsyn," she said. "The doctor's just on his way."

Tamsyn nodded and looked back at Scarlett, and the hospital doctor arrived and told them about Scarlett's condition. Tamsyn had memories of the accident, but she didn't seem to have any concept of the fact that it had happened in November, and now it was February. Ed watched her.

He didn't know how he was going to do this without betraying Honey, alone and desperately injured hundreds of miles away. He felt panic rising. He loved Honey, and he couldn't kiss Tamsyn, not in the way he was going to have to. Though when had he and Honey last kissed properly?

His stomach heaved. Jim had been right. He should never have agreed to any of it.

When the doctor stopped talking, Poppy appeared. They talked about insurance, and eventually Ed said the line he was very pleased to have in his script.

"I have to get to work," he said. "You stay with Scarlett, darling. Don't worry about anything else." He patted her shoulder because he couldn't bring himself to kiss her, and left. As soon as he was far enough away, down the plastic-floored corridor, he started sobbing.

That wasn't his wife. It was a different woman who thought she was his wife.

He wasn't allowed to tell her she wasn't. Not only that, but he had to live every moment of his life pretending that she was.

This was the biggest mistake he had ever made.

41

IT WAS MAUD WHO HELPED HIM FIND A WAY THROUGH. SHE spent day after day with him while Tamsyn was at the hospital and he pretended he was at work. They sat in one or other of their vans, or in cafés; he paid with the credit card Maya had given him. He poured his feelings out to her over and over again. She listened and listened and listened.

"Here's the thing," she said on the day he finally managed to make some peace with it all. They were in a clattery café near the cathedral, drinking beer, eating sandwiches. "Honey's in the best place she could be, and you're going to join her. You get to start a new life. Tamsyn is the thing that makes that happen. Ed, my darling, you need to stop being scared of her and treat her as a friend."

She waved to the waiter and asked for a glass of tap water. Ed felt nervous about having these conversations in public, but they always took a table away from other people and no one ever seemed to listen.

"Wherever she came from, she's here now, and she loves you,

poor soul. She has Honey's memories. That's precious because it keeps them alive. You're going to have to see her as your friend and ally. Honey's your wife and she always will be. Tamsyn is Tamsyn. Unique. She's come to us from the future, from future technology, and she's bringing you hope. If Honey has a chance of recovery, it's because of Tamsyn. Scarlett has a good chance of recovery, and that's because of the same technology. You need to embrace it with all your heart, my love, because you have no choice. She's here to stay no matter what, so it's up to you to change your attitude."

Ed managed a weak smile. "Well, I don't want them to *kill* her," he said, and Maud patted his arm.

"There you go!" she said. "Baby steps, but that's something."

"She's from the future. OK. I like that. A time traveler."

"Good boy."

Maud's water arrived. He managed a smile.

"Will you come and visit us in Geneva?" he said. The words hung in the air, too unlikely to be real.

■ ■ ■ ■ ■

His spirits lifted as preparations sped up. Scarlett was traveling separately. Ed wasn't allowed to go with her and had to fly with Tamsyn.

"You and Tamsyn need to start spending more time together," Luca told him. "We'll fly you to Geneva. Fly Tamsyn back with you. Maya will go with you, but she'll just be watching from a distance to make sure everything's OK."

Fly Tamsyn *back*. That was a strange thing. Tamsyn had come from Geneva, even though she didn't know it. It was her city of origin. Maybe that meant she would fit in. He hoped so because he had no idea how he was going to adapt.

Tamsyn was brand-new, but she'd already flown here. He had never been anywhere near an airplane.

As they passed through the airport he did his best to relax in her company in a way he hadn't done at the restaurant that time. He began not to hate being with her. Her excitement at traveling by air for what she thought was the first time was exactly the same as Honey's would have been, but her attitude toward him was different. She seemed to like him.

Also, he was astounded by the way money smoothed things over. He, Ed Trelawney, was about to travel by air, in business class. Everything was free.

He looked at Tamsyn and saw her amazement as she settled into her seat, and he couldn't help smiling. She was seeming more like Honey to him: she cared about Scarlett so much that Tamsyn and Honey were starting to merge, because they were the only people who cared that much.

That was where they overlapped. Apart from that, they were different. Tamsyn was, he thought, the way Honey could have been if life had been easier.

He looked at Tamsyn while she was staring down at the food and drink menu.

She was made from Honey's cells, as Maud had said. Her brain was a copy of Honey's brain, and that made her intensely precious and strange.

⬛ ⬛ ⬛ ⬛ ⬛

Honey wasn't going to get better.

That was a fact. He had seen her lying on the road, had known instantly that she was essentially dead. People didn't come out and say it to him because they were busy being kind, because he had to keep going, but it was true. Honey might be kept alive by machines for years, but she was too badly injured to make any sort of return to her old self. She had a catastrophic brain injury. It was awful, and it was a fact.

Tamsyn was like Honey but different. Tamsyn was smoother and shinier, and for weeks he'd resented that. Her skin was clear and glowing. Her knees worked fine, where Honey's had creaked and cracked for years. She was wearing new clothes, but they were clothes that Honey would have chosen if she'd had that luxury.

He looked at his hand. He looked at hers. They were close together.

Tamsyn didn't know anything. This wasn't her fault. He and Scarlett were all she had, and Scarlett was unconscious. Tamsyn was a victim as much as Scarlett and Honey were. She had no agency in any of this. To use a phrase that Scarlett had favored, Tamsyn hadn't asked to be born.

To be created.

Ed moved his hand closer to hers. This wasn't a betrayal of Honey, because Tamsyn *was* Honey. Wasn't this what religion was about, finding a way of continuing to live after death? Honey's body was dying but something of her lived on in Tamsyn. He put his hand on top of hers. Here she was, his wife's living ghost. Her hand was warm. She turned it over and clasped his.

They were in the air. Ed had a feeling that they were suspended in time and space. The sound of the engine underlined everything, something that sometimes felt like a roar and sometimes like a hum, depending on whether he was panicking or not.

■ ■ ■ ■ ■

Before he knew it, they were landing, and their new life began in a blur of luxury. The moment they stepped off the plane, Ed and Tamsyn became a team because they had to be. They had to learn to navigate this new world together.

She wasn't Honey. Honey was in the hospital.

She didn't know she wasn't Honey and he wasn't allowed to tell her. Whenever he visited Scarlett, he slipped away through the door in the corridor and sat with Honey, looking into her blank face. Then he went back to living with her clone.

Once he let himself get past his guilt and the whole weirdness of the fact that she wasn't, yet was, his wife, he found that Tamsyn was everything he had ever wanted. Everything he had ever needed.

He fell in love with her. He fell in love with her like he had fallen in love with Honey two decades earlier, but more. He wanted to be at her side all the time. He wanted to touch her. He wanted to look at her face, to take her with him everywhere he went. She was everything he had ever wanted.

He'd been in the habit of messaging his brother with updates and deleting everything from his Sent folder. He would write when Tamsyn was asleep or in the shower, and then he'd delete the messages straightaway, or if he couldn't do that, then he'd do it remotely from his phone later. Then he stopped writing to Jimmy anyway, because Jimmy had been against the idea of Tamsyn, and Ed adored her.

He was in love, and he had all the money he would ever need and a job that he enjoyed. His daughter was about to come back to them. He found he could ignore the fact that there were cameras all over the apartment, and seize his second chance. He wanted to shout about it to the world: *They cloned my wife and I'm in love with her.*

■■■■■

One day Maya took him aside.

"There's a girl coming to work at the café with you," she said. "I don't mean girl. I should say 'woman.' She's twenty-two. Lena.

Can you keep an eye on her? Let me know how she gets on. She'll be waiting tables."

"Is she . . . ?"

"Yes. She doesn't have any close family. She's living alone here. She was in an accident and she doesn't know that she died."

"She died?"

"Soon after we had everything we needed, so at least we could still go ahead. I'll call you every few days when she's started, check in with you about her."

"Sure."

Lena had that bright complexion, the eagerness to learn that Tamsyn had. He wondered whether that was the sign of a reanimation. He started looking for it everywhere. He looked for it in the regular customers—the woman with the handbag dog, the young man who sometimes had green hair, the elderly couple who arrived at exactly eleven every day—and sometimes he thought he saw it. The world had opened up to contain the impossible.

By the time Sophie came along, Ed felt they had lived in Geneva for half their lives. He felt weirdly that his life was complete again. He and Tamsyn had sex at every possible moment and he felt he strode through the city powered by ecstasy. He'd had to double-check first whether there were cameras implanted behind Tamsyn's eyes, and he was assured they existed but weren't active. Luca showed him the proof that they had been deactivated before the move to Geneva because she was an adult in a relationship and it was agreed to be inappropriate. After that, Ed and Tamsyn had sex. He loved it. Her body was the same but different. Her smell. Everything about her. He was besotted.

Tamsyn didn't shout. She didn't swear. She learned French so quickly that he realized she had, in fact, already known it. She got to grips with everything prodigiously fast because she had AI to help her.

He loved her. He started calling her Honey to ease his guilt, passing it off as a term of endearment. He began to feel that he and his wife had moved to Geneva, and maybe it actually was that straightforward, that the accident had just been a bend in the road. When Scarlett woke up and seemed to be getting better, he started to suspect that, as Maud had suggested, he really was the luckiest man there had ever been.

However, once Scarlett was home (and oh, how he loved having her back, having someone else in the house who wasn't a reanimation), it became harder for him to keep popping in to see the original Honey. He had done it easily before. He could say, "I'll visit Scarlett after work, honey," or "I went to see Scarlett this morning," and it was a seamless part of life because whenever he saw Scarlett, he walked through the door into the other part of the corridor and checked in with his wife too. Once Scarlett was home, he had no reason to go to the clinic, and he thought of the other Honey lying there, forgotten by everyone in the world but Dr. Singh, who was brilliant but who was there as part of her job, and he couldn't bear it.

Ed had time off work to help Scarlett settle back at home, but he was haunted by the image of the first Honey always lying in her yellow room, moved and tended to by nurses, visited by Dr. Singh (who had more patients, but she wouldn't talk about them). He would make excuses to go out and would dash to the clinic.

He visited Honey as often as he could because he felt it was the only thing he could do to compensate for the fact that he didn't love her anymore, that he had fallen in love with her robot clone instead.

Ed sat at Honey's bedside and told her everything, even though he wasn't supposed to. Dr. Singh caught him doing it but she didn't stop him; they both knew that Honey wasn't going to wake up like Scarlett, that she had always been going to die. It didn't matter what he told her: she didn't hear a word of it. He knew Tamsyn wondered where he was going, and he almost wanted her to follow him, willing her to find out about Honey because then they would have no more secrets.

42

THIS IS THE FIRST TIME THEY'VE LEFT ME AND SOPHIE ALONE together and I'm properly scared. She keeps knocking on my door and asking if I need anything. I keep saying no, and then she looks at me with a weird expression, a half smile, like she knows something I don't.

I almost wonder if she's killed our parents just to fuck me up.

Of course not. She wouldn't, would she?

But I'm sure she knows where they are. She's just not telling me for fun.

I wish I had a lock on my bedroom door. I lock myself in the bathroom and have a long shower, scrubbing every bit of my skin with shower gel on a flannel. I stand in front of the mirror and look at myself.

I look better. I can walk now. I'm slow and uneven, but I can do it. I have scars, but they're part of me. They make me Scarlett, not Sophie.

I hear her footsteps, walking past my room. She stops outside, then walks on. She's doing it to mess with my head.

I look again at the DVDs she gave me:

Scream.

I Know What You Did Last Summer.

Cruel Intentions.

She could hardly have made it any clearer.

She knows what I did last summer. I push that thought away for the moment, because worse than that right now is the fact that my own twin, my clone, hates me and is clearly plotting something against me.

I'm alone with her and I don't have a lock on my door.

■ ■ ■ ■ ■

I get out the letter she handed me in hospital and read it again. When I read it the first time I didn't notice. This time I do.

Dear Scarlett,

Hello! It's Sophie. We were so happy when you woke up, my dear sister, and I can honestly say that nothing was quite right without you.

You should be back at home with us, where you belong. Our old Cornish life is dead, and I'm not here to make anything more difficult for you, because I'm your twin! I'm going to help you out with everything you need in your replacement life, which is, believe me, just amazing and brilliant and so incredibly different in every way.

I'm so excited about you coming home! Oh, my God, I can't wait for you to be here with me. We can do everything together. Mum and Dad are happy now instead of being stressed like before. I suppose their only worries have been because of you. I'm better at reassuring them now I know about you!

*So we know you're going to be completely better soon. I
can't wait to meet you, to see if I'm smaller or taller than you.
I guess we'll be exactly the same! It's going to be fun. I am
going to do everything I can to make it easy for you. I'm going
to be here for you, and help you with everything you need.*

*And then, long after you've got better, we'll just be
sisters. Twins. Adults in the world. All these worries will be
long gone. This time of our lives will always be something
we'll look back on as the time we became two, not one.*

*You're going to be fine, Scarlett. You're strong. You
didn't die. We'll make sure you recover properly.*

See you soon!
Love, Sophie xxx

She has emphasized some of the first letters of words, by going over them a few times with her pen. I wouldn't have spotted
it until I looked for it (though my subconscious did when I was
in the safe place: yay for my subconscious. I overruled it then but
I can't do that forever). I circle the bolded words and read the real
message from my robot clone sister.

We were so happy without you.
*You should be dead, and I'm not your twin! I'm your
replacement.*
*I'm here instead of you. I'm better than you. I am going
to be here long after you've gone. This time you're going to
die. Soon!*

I look at it for a long time.
She hates me and she's going to kill me. It's a relief in a way

to know that this is the way it's been all along. She gave me that note the first time we ever met. This is her doing, not mine. She started it.

I guess I hate her too, but more than that, I'm scared of her. She has a robot brain, and it can do things I can't imagine. She can do everything and I can do nothing. I have to sleep without a lock on my door. She has already shown me that she can come into my room in the middle of the night and there's nothing I can do about it.

I Know What You Did Last Summer fills my mind. Does she? Or is she messing with my head?

▪ ▪ ▪ ▪ ▪

Since I'm doing things that make me feel bad, I pick up my phone. I hardly use it because I have no friends, but it's a smart-phone one million times better than the one I used to have. I've avoided doing this before, but now I open the e-mail and sign in to my old account. I remember the password because it was a sweary one, and then I'm in, holding my breath as the in-box is loaded.

His name is right at the top.

Jasper Mack.

It's all the way down too.

Jasper Mack
Jasper Mack
Jasper Mack
Jasper Mack
Jasper Mack

It slices me like a sword through the stomach. He should think I'm dead: you don't e-mail dead people. Or do you? Maybe you do if you're full of guilt and regret?

I scroll down and open the bottom one.

I fucking knew it! I knew you weren't dead. Your family vanished. New people moved into your van. No one at work wanted to talk about where Ed had gone. Well I wanted to know. I've been hanging around your old home (sorry I mean field) because Ed's brother was living there and today I picked up a parcel for that mad old bat before she saw it.

A parcel from Switzerland! I opened it. Now I know where you live. Your mum put a picture of you in there too. Looking fucking good!!!

I'm so hurt, Scarlett. I can't believe you let me think you were dead all this time. Why not tell me? I've been worrying and there was no point, because look at you. There you are, living the high life. Thanks a lot. It was an accident but it's worked out great for you, I'd say.

J

I don't look at any of the others. I know Jasper and I know that they'll be escalating threats and anger. Of course he's managed to convince himself that he's the victim.

Would Mum have put our address on that parcel? Probably.

I force myself to click the most recent message. He seems to be carrying on from where the previous one left off.

My passport will be here in 2 weeks! I can catch the bus to Geneva and it'll be a shit journey but it's cheap. So I guess I'll see you soon, girlfriend!!! What's it worth to you to have me not come? Shall we start with, oh, a million pounds and negotiate from there? Hit me with your best offer.

I check the date: he sent that four days ago. I have about ten days. Fuck.

He's still working at Dad's old place, so he wasn't caught for the hit and run. He's still at work, and he's doing his best to blackmail me. A million pounds. For fuck's sake.

.....

I know I was a nightmare to my parents, but there was a reason for that, and the reason was Jasper. I did go wild around the time I turned thirteen, but that was after my own father introduced me to the apprentice in his kitchen. I hate Jasper more than anything. More even than Sophie hates me. Then, though, I was smitten, like a stupid girl.

He was different from the boys at my school. Grown-up, handsome, real. Sixteen back then, and training as a chef. Seventeen or eighteen now.

I don't know how he got my number. Maybe dad left his phone unlocked for a moment. Anyway, Jasper did, and he started texting me, and I'd never known anything like it. I went to meet him and it was different and exciting, and although I was scared, I was also only just thirteen and thought I was in love.

The thing with life at home was that I was always on my own. They say now that one of them was always at the van with me, but they weren't. They're remembering it the way that's easiest for them. Dad worked long hours and Mum worked about fifteen different jobs. I went to Maud and Ally's after school, and then Ally got sick and I was on my own.

Jasper was at work with my dad, so I didn't actually see him often. When I did, he treated me like the queen of the universe. He asked for photos of me to look at when we weren't together.

I sent him photos.

It's clear where this is going.

￭￭￭￭￭

He talked to me so tenderly, with so much love, that in the end he convinced me. They were just for him. He made it seem romantic and special.

He knew lots of people at my school; he'd been there himself. He put the photos online. He sent them to people. I found out only when boys started seeking me out and laughing.

I skip over the rest of it in my head. My life was burned to the ground. The girls distanced themselves. Everyone started calling me horrible names, and I couldn't tell anyone. How could I tell my dad that I'd sent his apprentice nude pictures of myself? I tried to tell Mum a couple of times, but I remembered Jasper's threats and stopped at the last moment. She would have gone after him. At least I know that.

I lean back and try to regulate my breathing. Jasper's on the screen and Sophie's outside the door. I'm cornered by two of the worst people.

I piece together the last six months before the accident. I lost my friends, had my reputation destroyed, was humiliated by everything. In the end I leaned into it. I found that alcohol made it feel better. I pushed away anyone who might have helped. I got in with the people who accepted me and became a bad girl. We went out. We blotted out all our demons.

Jasper kept taunting me. I tried to ignore him. That last night, though, I snapped. I had finally had enough of being dragged home from pubs by my dad. Because I knew really that it was time either to get my head down and finish my education properly or to be stuck exactly where I was forever.

I'd had enough. I saw that I could go to the police, because what he'd done wasn't my fault. I didn't think I trusted the police, but I could be brave and try.

I saw that I could tell my dad, and that it wouldn't be any more humiliating than anything else that had happened.

I texted Jasper and told him those two things, then went to sleep (in retrospect, telling him was the worst possible course of action, but at the time I felt I had to). He called in the middle of the night to say he was coming over to talk to me and that he was going to fuck the caravan up. I went to meet him on the road because I didn't know what he meant by fuck the caravan up, but I knew I couldn't let it happen.

I still don't want to think that he drove into me on purpose.

I want him to be in prison. I wanted his life to be destroyed by what he had done, but it's not. He's still there. He's trying to get me to pay him a million pounds, the twat.

■ ■ ■ ■ ■

My door bursts open and I drop the phone on the bed, then pick it up and hold it tightly.

"What are you doing?"

"Nothing."

Sophie smells of some kind of lemony scent that I'm sure is exactly the thing rich girls in Switzerland are wearing. She's wearing her usual workout style clothes: I know she does that to torment me with her fitness. No one else can see it, and no one would believe me if I tried to tell them.

If she hates me, then I can hate her too. I'm almost relieved to admit it.

"You're on your phone? But, Scarlett, poor darling—you don't have any friends. What are you doing?"

"I am doing *nothing*."

"Then you won't mind me looking."

I hold my phone tightly. "I know what your letter really said. Thanks. That was really nice of you."

She smiles. "Took you long enough! Did you like my banner when you came home?"

I frown and shake my head. I don't remember it, and I don't care.

"Shame. I put a lot of effort into that one. What are you looking at on that phone? As if I couldn't guess. Searching a few things? A certain person?"

I put the phone in my pocket. "Go away."

"Sure. I was just giving you a few more DVDs, since you enjoyed those last ones." She takes two out of the big pockets of her hoodie and puts them on the bed. I look at the titles.

I Still Know What You Did Last Summer.

Crash.

"Where are Mum and Dad?" My voice sounds too afraid.

"It's weird, isn't it?" she says as she leaves. "I really don't know. Not even messing with you."

I look at my bookcase. If she can do this, then I can too. The top shelf has been furnished with a collection of Penguin Classics that I have ignored until now, because I've been reading easier things. I look through them, hoping that the book I need is there.

There it is: *Frankenstein*. I can't believe they gave me that one.

I scan the rest of them to see what I can add to make a message to send back to her: *Let Me Tell You* by Shirley Jackson seems promising. I put the two books together. Let me tell you, Frankenstein. Good start. Now what?

I can hear Sophie's voice in my head, telling me that Frankenstein isn't the monster, but it's as close as I can get, and anyway Frankenstein *is* the monster at heart. And actually there's no way Sophie would know who's the monster. I look through the rest of the books, consider and discard many of them, and end up just making a vague threat that says:

DON'T LOOK NOW
FRANKENSTEIN.

It doesn't really mean anything but at least I'm giving it a go. I open my door. I can hear her down the hallway, singing, so I open her bedroom door and put the books on her bed.

I stay in my room, reading, watching TV, looking out the window, while thinking obsessively about Jasper and the fact that he knows I'm here, that he's got our address, because he stole Maud's chocolate, and sinking further and further down. Sophie knows about him, and that makes me feel weird. We haven't spoken about it. It almost feels like she's threatening me, that she thinks it was all my fault. *I know what you did last summer. I still know what you did last summer. Crash.*

I remember how the alcohol used to blot it out, and I wonder for a moment whether Mum and Dad would miss a bottle of wine. Maybe I could tip it into a water flask away from the cameras and get drunk and find some oblivion.

She is literally made from me. I guess I hate myself. I did before, because of Jasper, and now I do again, because she's right there, the other version of me, doing everything better. What does it say about me that when I'm cloned, I'm at war with myself? Bad things. All the bad things.

I hear the buzzer and then Sophie's voice. She talks to adults in such a stupid voice. It's all silky and teacher's pettish, and they never notice.

I probably use that voice too when I need to. She got it from me.

I haven't actually liked myself at all. I just didn't want it to be true. I hated myself before the accident, and now that I have a second self to hate, I hate myself doubly, and she hates me right back.

She's talking French, so I have no idea what she's saying, but I would bet everything I have on the fact that the gist is that we don't know where our parents are but it's OK, because she stayed at home to look after me.

I would bet everything I have, but she's taken everything already.

My door opens. It's Catherine, one of the physios, and she switches to English.

"Scarlett!" she says. "How are you today? Sophie was just explaining that your parents aren't here. Would you like us to call them? I'm sure we can find out what's happened."

She looks worried. I hadn't thought to be concerned about them.

"Yes, please," I say, and I burst into tears without meaning to. It's Jasper, but she doesn't know that.

Catherine sits on the bed and puts an arm around me. "Hey," she says. "It's OK. You're going to be OK. They've just gone out. We'll find them."

However, she shoots out of the room and I hear her talking to Sophie and then making a phone call. After a while she stands in the doorway of my room, pushing her hair back from her face, nodding repeatedly in an attempt to convince me everything is fine while her expression tells me it's not fine at all.

"They're at the clinic," she says. "It's OK. It's all perfectly OK." That's what her mouth says, but it's not what her face says. "Your dad's on his way home," she adds.

"What about Mum?"

"I'm sure she'll be back soon too."

"Why are they at the clinic?"

"They can explain it. Anyway, let's head to the gym and see how you're doing."

. . . . .

I'm on the cycling machine when I hear Dad's voice, and I climb carefully down and leave the room. I hear Catherine laughing behind me.

"OK," she says. "You do that. Good range of movement."

Sophie has reached him first, of course, and is staking her claim by hugging him. Dad holds out his other arm to me, and hating it, I tuck myself in there too.

"Don't worry," he says. "It's all OK. We had a bit of a drama in the night, but it's nothing you girls need to worry about."

"Jesus, Dad!" says Sophie, and it pierces me because I don't want him to be her dad.

Dad and Sophie have such an easy relationship, while I remember him dragging me home in the mud and the rain. I remember telling him that I hated him (I didn't! I just needed him). I remember him saying he wished he didn't have a daughter. I know he meant it. I probably deserved it but I will never, ever forget it.

Still I snuggle into him because there's no way I'm letting Sophie have him to herself when I was here first.

"What's happened?" she says.

"Yes," I echo. "What?"

"OK," he said. "Girls. Right. I have to tell you something. I have to tell you because it affects Mum. It's complicated. But basically nothing has changed."

"We can do complicated," says Sophie, and I see Dad giving her a fond smile.

"Tell us, Dad," I say.

■ ■ ■ ■ ■

We sit around the table and it feels like a formal meeting.

"OK, girls," he says. "First of all, I'm sorry for not telling you this sooner. I wish I'd been able to, but now that this is out, we're going to have no more secrets. It took me a long time to adapt, and I really am sorry that I have to give you another thing to take on board, because you two have been through enough. This really is the last thing."

I've been through enough. Sophie hasn't. I don't say it, but Sophie hasn't been through anything. Everything is easy for her.

"It's Mum," he says.

"What's happened?"

We say it at the same time. I look at Sophie and we lock eyes, then look away.

I know it, though, before he says it. The other person in the accident. I realize it in the second before he starts to speak.

43

EVERYTHING SHE KNEW ABOUT HERSELF WAS WRONG.

Tamsyn went over it all in her head again and again and again. She'd tried to remember the accident over the past months but hadn't been able to bring back any of it. She knew now why that was. It was because she hadn't been there. She hadn't existed then, wouldn't exist at all if it hadn't been for that accident. She was a replacement, and her poor original body was lying still, never to respond to anything again.

She told herself that was OK. She could see as she looked at her old body that she had been brought back to life in the only way possible, in a way that had given herself and her family a whole new life. She had to be both Tamsyn and Honey.

That wasn't what she felt, though. She could feel it inside: fury, horror, bubbling. She wasn't going to be able to do this.

They'd called Ed when she walked through the Honey Trelawney door, and he'd arrived soon after, while she was still trying to understand what she was seeing. She had spent the rest of the night talking to Luca, to Maya, to Dr. Singh and to Ed, and she was surprised by the way it settled down into a thing that made sense. This was her truth: she knew instinctively that it was. The fact that it made sense, however, didn't make it easy.

When Sophie had been coming to terms with her situation, Tamsyn had thought it must be terrible to discover that you were a clone. Now it turned out that it was shattering and horrifying, but also almost exciting. She was the same person living in a new body. It was like magic. The horizons of her existence opened wider and wider and wider until she was flying through space.

●●●●●

She was sitting in the café opposite the clinic with Ed, drinking early-morning coffee. The café was quiet, with sunlight on yellow floor tiles, heavy wooden tables, comfortable chairs. She'd been there before, but everything was new today.

She would be able to come to terms with this for herself, but Ed's involvement was a different matter.

"You had to get used to me," she said.

Dr. Singh had ushered everyone away from Honey's bedside, saying, "She's a human being, not a prop, and just imagine if she could hear you!" Tamsyn could see her broken original self vividly in her mind. She always would.

"I didn't," said Ed. He reached for her and she felt him shudder right down to his fingertips. "I mean, I did. There's no point lying, is there? Of course I did. It was strange when you arrived in Cornwall. We first held hands like this on the plane over here and that's when things started to change for me. You're wonderful and I'm head over heels in love with you, Tam."

She looked at him, wanting to ask whether he liked her better than Honey, but managing not to say it. She could see that he did. He hadn't been having an affair: he had been visiting Tamsyn's other body out of guilt. Guilt because he was happier with Tamsyn than he should have been.

Because she had been made to please him. She knew it. That was the thing that made everything make sense.

▪ ▪ ▪ ▪ ▪

She looked away. She'd thought she was less confrontational in Geneva because she was happy, but that wasn't true. She was compliant because she'd been built that way, and she'd been built that way because Ed had asked them to do it.

"Did you ask them to make me easier to live with?"

She looked directly into his eyes and saw his gaze slipping from hers. He was trying to look at her, but he couldn't do it. He kept looking at her and then away.

"No," he said. He looked down at his cup and moved it so the handle was pointing to the side. "No, Tam, I didn't."

Her voice caught in her throat. "I don't believe you."

"No. Well, I mean . . ."

He moved the cup again, pointed the handle the other way. She sat motionless, staring at him.

"I mean, I think there was a moment when, like, Maya or someone asked what Honey would change about herself if she'd been able to, and I think I said she'd have been less angry. Maybe. And a couple of other things. But I didn't ask them to do it. I thought it was just a conversation."

She couldn't look at him, couldn't listen to his weaselly words. He'd known perfectly well what he was doing. It was humiliating. She felt like a sex robot: she'd been built to his specifications, however it had been phrased, and all her happiness, all her feelings of being *in love* and *back on track*, were fake. She felt dirty and tricked, and she never wanted to share a bed with him again.

She pushed her chair back.

She had been engineered to be nice.

She hadn't picked French up quickly from her class. She had already known it, like Sophie. No wonder it had felt easy. She hadn't adapted quickly to Geneva: this place was her home. She had been made here and it was where she belonged.

Every line of thought made her reassess a new thing, but she kept coming back to Ed. A bespoke wife, a new life, a new job, plenty of money and a second daughter. No wonder he'd felt like the king of the world.

She picked up her bag but didn't stand. Not yet. She still wanted him to say the thing that would make it right, though she didn't know what it would be. The sky was pink and perfect outside the window. A new dawn.

"Tam!" he said. "Stay. Please. Yes, it was weird at first. I can't lie. I found it really hard when I met you and I felt so guilty. Maud made me see how amazing you are. She said you'd come to us from the future and that I was the luckiest man who had ever lived."

Tamsyn smiled at that. "I miss Maud! But— Oh, God, she knows?"

"All of it."

She closed her eyes. "I've been e-mailing her and pretending Sophie was Scarlett, and then Scarlett woke up but I couldn't tell Maud, so I sent her that chocolate instead and never heard from her again."

She tried to laugh. Then her mood changed again.

"You said you can't lie," she said. "But you can, can't you? Turns out, you're really good at it."

Ed tried to take her hand. "I message Maud often. She loves hearing about our life and seeing pictures of the girls. She doesn't reply to you because she feels awkward knowing what you don't. Now that it's out in the open, I thought we might invite her out to visit. Or even to live with us. We could move the gym stuff and have her move in there. What do you think?"

Tamsyn shrugged. Did Ed think they could carry on as before?

"And Jimmy," said Ed. "He didn't like any of it, so he's stepped back because he couldn't deal with the idea of human cloning, but he's there at a distance. He's living in his tent at the park."

She remembered that e-mail she'd read, the one that had vanished. She'd agonized over that and, it turned out, rightly so. It had been the biggest clue she had.

She has no idea.

I'm embracing this.

It made sense now.

"I had no idea if I was doing the right thing, Tam, but I didn't have a choice. You can see that, can't you? I know you're pissed off, but can you imagine if it was the other way round? I think you'd have done it too. Honey would have leaped at the chance of changing me. We— Well, we weren't in a good place when you had the accident, were we?"

She remembered the fights, whispered and shouted, the frustrations, the fact that he had had a bag under the bed that he'd thought she didn't know about. An escape bag. He'd always been ready to leave Honey. She had never told him she knew about it. In the end he hadn't needed to go. He'd just upgraded his dead wife without telling her.

She stood up. She couldn't sit here in a café with him, being husband and wife as if everything were fine. There was no magic thing he could say that would make this better.

"Tam," he said.

She walked out of the café, away from the clinic, walking quickly and randomly until she found herself on the banks of the river. A cool wind blew watery algae smells into her face. A tourist boat passed slowly. She leaned on a metal fence for a long time, looking across the dark water to the buildings on the other side of the Rhône, trying to work out what the hell she could do now.

44

A COUPLE OF DAYS LATER, TAMSYN AND ED AGREED THAT they would make that trip into the mountains to keep things as normal as possible for the girls. Tamsyn decided to drive. In many ways her confidence had surged: she was powered by resentment and fury, but excited at the prospect of driving.

"Do you think I'll be really good at it?" she said to Sophie.

Sophie, her darling girl who understood how she felt. Sophie had called into the clinic and had the cameras in her eyes switched off. She had seen proof of it and her whole demeanor had changed. They had given her a second appointment for a full checkup in a couple of weeks.

Would Tamsyn have one too? Had there ever been cameras in her own eyes? Everyone at VitaNova said no, but how could she trust anything now?

"Of course you'll be an amazing driver," Sophie said. "Me too. I can't wait to learn. We're, like, half self-driving car, half person with great reflexes. Everything that's wrong with a self-driving car—the AI that doesn't recognize a freak thing happening and doesn't know how to respond to it—is right with us, because our human brains will know what to do. We must be the perfect drivers, Mum."

Tamsyn nodded. Since she'd found out the truth about herself, she felt different. She had a whole new energy. She was in the trippy position of being able to visit her own cast-off former body, and she did it all the time, because Honey was the other one who understood. Dr. Singh had waived the rule about keeping the clone secret from the original human (she had, it turned out, waived it for Ed weeks ago because everyone knew Honey had essentially no chance of waking up). Tamsyn would just sit there and tell her everything. She always came out feeling a bit stronger, as if she had absorbed Honey's attitude. She hadn't known it was what she was missing, but now she felt that Honey was her best friend. Between them, they had survived a near-fatal accident and come out of it with an incredible life, a second, equally beloved daughter, a luxurious place to live, a good neighbor, a new language. A daughter who had recovered, and another who had been made. Those were her blessings.

On the other hand, she was fighting against her compliant nature. She tried to argue with Ed and found she just couldn't. She didn't have it in her. She was giving him the cold shoulder instead. He was complicit, and right now she couldn't get over that. She couldn't yell at him but she could make sure he knew how pissed off she was.

. . . . .

Sophie was right: Tamsyn was an excellent driver. She checked the rearview mirror and pulled out, waiting for a young man in thick glasses to cross the road. He looked at her. She looked back, and then he was gone.

Scarlett was a different girl from the one who had been so difficult in Cornwall. She was tentative, reacting to her new world, getting back on her feet and acclimatizing to her new family, and although she could be resentful of Sophie, accusing her of trying to hurt her when Sophie clearly wasn't doing anything of the sort, she wasn't that difficult child anymore.

Sophie, meanwhile, was shining and brilliant, a superstar who was going to go on to do great things. They were a perfect set of twins, identical but different, and Tamsyn watched them saying the same things at the same time, communicating apparently telepathically, even if they didn't realize it yet.

There was, she kept telling herself, a lot of good in this new life. She had to seize the good and cast off the bad.

Cast off Ed? She wasn't sure.

They had to drive alongside the lake, because France was around them in every other direction. Tamsyn tried a thought experiment. She could easily take the road to France. French towns were signed all over the place. She could go toward Annecy or Lyon and it would be fine.

She couldn't do it. Even thinking about it made her head hurt, her whole body recoil. If she and Sophie were illegal over there, maybe it was sensible that they were programmed this way. She kept driving deeper into Switzerland.

- - - - -

"How about this?" said Ed. "Into the mountains! What an adventure."

Tamsyn looked quickly over at him and back to the road. He was trying hard to win her back: he had assembled a lavish picnic, making a Spanish omelet early in the morning, baking a cake, packing all sorts of bits and pieces. She ignored him.

As Honey, she had known how to drive, had driven a forklift truck in a warehouse at one of her jobs, but as Tamsyn she instinctively drove on the European side of the road, and she could feel herself anticipating every move every other car made. She drove up and up, and then they reached the little village where they'd planned to stop. It was cooler up there, and she liked the way the air felt on her bare arms. The village was pretty, every backdrop a spectacular one. They set off to find the cable car to go higher and higher and higher into the sky.

■ ■ ■ ■ ■

It turned out to be less a cable car and more a chairlift. Each car was, in fact, a double seat with a safety bar that clicked into place. You had to stand on the right spot and sit down when the chairlift was behind you, closing the bar as you swung into the air. They stood and watched some other people doing it. Tamsyn looked at the map.

"There's a steep drop near the top of this," she said. "Lots of warnings. We have to make sure we go the other way when we get up there."

Ed touched the map with his finger. "Yes," he said. "Look, we get to the top and take the path to the left and we'll be fine."

"Course we will," said Sophie. "This lift looks brilliant. Come with me, Scarlett! Let's go first."

Tamsyn looked to Ed, then quickly away. Scarlett saved her from having to ride with him.

"It looks scary," she said. "I want to go with Dad."

Sophie tried to persuade her a few times, but then Scarlett and Ed were gone, soaring high into the air and blurring until they were just another spot on the mountainside.

"You come with me, then, Mum," said Sophie. "Reanimations united!"

"Yes," Tamsyn said. "Pushing the boundaries of science together."

It was exhilarating to be so high in the sky. Tamsyn loved the wind in her face, the views of mountain after mountain that opened up in front of her, the fact that it was so much cooler that she was almost shivering. She took Sophie's hand, and Sophie gripped hers back.

"Soph," Tamsyn said, "I'm still freaking out a bit, I have to say."

"Yeah," said Sophie. "I mean, of course you are. It's— Well, it messes with your head. I tried to swear then. I can't do it. Can you?"

"I think so. Were you going to say it's shit?"

"No. I was going to say it's a head . . . f-word."

"Head fuck?" Tamsyn nodded. "So I'm allowed to swear, then. I bet they don't let you do it because you're a kid. Head fuck! Shit! Bollocks!"

It was exhilarating, shouting those things into the fresh Alpine air, so she ran through a few more, yelling them out as loud as she could.

Sophie laughed and laughed. "Carry on, Mum. It's brilliant. Do you think they'll let me swear when I'm sixteen? Eighteen?"

"God knows. You'll probably have to negotiate it again, like with your eyes." She paused, and tried to phrase it in the best way. "I remember them saying you were going to be healthy and clever and a good daughter in every way. Does that make you feel—well, resentful?"

Tamsyn looked down. This would not be a way to travel if you were scared of heights, and she hoped Scarlett wasn't. The ground was far below them, rocky with patches of green. The air was fresh and cold in her lungs. Their seat moved from side to side in the breeze.

"Yeah," said Sophie. "I mean, in a way I feel redundant. Because she got better. That's quite hard, you know?"

"But you're not redundant! We need you both."

Sophie nodded, looking ahead at the mountain, and changed the subject.

"I knew as soon as I found out that there was something weird going on with VitaNova. Looking back, maybe it was the fact that they hadn't told us about you. About Honey. I don't know, but I still think there's a lot they're not telling us. If you forget that you are one and think about clones, what do you think of?"

Tamsyn closed her eyes for a moment. "I guess a group of people who all look the same. Controlled by someone. Faceless. Scary. I would never have thought of myself."

"We both believed we were regular people until we worked it out. So in your version, the clones are all being controlled and programmed. They'd be the underlings in the service of the people who made them. But actually, it's not going to be like that. We're better than them."

Tamsyn frowned. She could see Scarlett and Ed's seat way in front of them. She didn't want there to be a division, a question of who was better. She was angry with Ed, but she didn't think she was better than him.

Sophie noticed. "Not better than *them*. I mean that arrogant idiot Johann, for instance. He thinks he's so great because he made us. But what has he done? He's made people that are cleverer than he is. He's found a way to get past the question of the robot going up the stairs and all that. You know, you can program a robot all you like, but you're never going to get beyond the fact that humans lift a cup and drink from it without giving it a moment's thought, whereas to get a robot to do that is still pretty much impossible. The hand-eye coordination, the instinct about exactly where your mouth is. We wouldn't be able to do those things without human bodies. Right?"

Tamsyn nodded. She hadn't realized she knew all this, but she did. It was obvious.

Sophie was becoming more passionate.

"So he thinks he's so clever, and yeah, he is, of course. They all are. But what do they think is going to happen next? They think they're going to control us forever? Because . . . well, I've been thinking about this for months, and I think there's a show-down coming. There has to be, because he thinks we belong to him, and we don't. It's not going to be easy, because VitaNova keeps everything so secret, but I think we're going to have to break away. They spend massive amounts of money, and it all comes from somewhere. Not Johann's pocket, for sure. All that stuff they get us just to show that they own us. The way they have their cameras all over our house. That's some serious flexing of muscles."

"Right!" Tamsyn was excited to hear Sophie articulating the things she had started to think. "Yes—they don't get to keep us in the perfect apartment wired up so they can watch us all day and night and use our data. We're not zoo animals. We need to move away, don't we? To get privacy and self-determination. I mean, we couldn't afford anywhere as nice, but that's OK."

"Excuse me?" Sophie was laughing. "Hello? What kind of talk is this, Mother? We can afford whatever we want. We just have to think about it. We can make money, Mum. We can do that easily."

"How do we . . ." Tamsyn stopped, thought about it. Of course there would be ways of making money in Geneva. She just had to change the way she thought about herself, to push herself in new directions. "I guess I could read up on . . . trading? That kind of thing?"

"Yeah. Trading. Coding. Whatever. We can do it all. We can easily make enough cash to move out. We are cleverer than them. We don't have to do it their way. The trouble is, they've trapped us in Switzerland by not allowing us to cross the borders. We should probably talk to Dad about this."

"And Scarlett."

"Sure," said Sophie, and Tamsyn looked at her hard.

"What's going on with you two?"

"What's going on with *you* two?"

Tamsyn sighed. "Adjustment."

"Anyway," said Sophie, "I also want to meet the other twenty-two. We need to find one another. We'll have much more strength if we work together, which is obviously why they keep us apart. I'm sure everyone's in Geneva, and it's not that big a city. The early ones might know one another. Surely they'd have kept them together at first."

"Let's do it."

"I also want to make sure Johann and the rest of them know that they need to let people know the truth about themselves from the moment they wake up, because we have the right to know who we are. They can't bring us to life and then lie about our actual identity, because when you're the future of life on Earth, you have a right to know it. We're the most incredible thing people have ever done! They've been trying to do this forever, and now they have and it's us! Icarus. Frankenstein. Pinocchio. Voldemort. People have been pushing the boundaries forever. I know those things are fiction, but fiction was the only way anyone could make it work until now. And here we are, and we're real. Oh, my God, Mum, I'm so glad that you're the same as me. I've been so lonely."

Tamsyn nodded. There was a line of craggy mountains in front of them. She thought of the land pushing together millions of years ago to make them, and she wondered at the unlikelihood of herself and Sophie being here in this ski lift, having this conversation.

"I'm glad we both know the truth," she said. "And yeah, I'm not happy with the team at VN." *Or with Ed.* Tamsyn bit that part back. "'*Be your best self*,' they say. My best self would be one who wasn't under constant surveillance, you know?"

Sophie took her hand. "Exactly, Mum. So let's make a plan, right? Find the others, see if we can escape our makers. It's going to be a big undertaking, because they're not going to want to let us have even a tiny bit more freedom."

They were nearly at the end of the ride. Tamsyn knew that the bar that went across their laps would spring up, and that they needed to step down and walk away before the seat crashed into them. As they got closer, she could see the figures of Ed and Scarlett standing to the side, waiting.

It was strange to see the family split in two. The original humans, the same as the other eight billion or however many there were, and then herself and Sophie, who were magical and special and new and different. Or, depending on how she was feeling, monstrous ghosts.

In her gratitude she had never stopped to think deeply about why this technology existed. Why were Johann, Luca and Maya doing this? Who paid for it? There had been no suggestion so far of Honey's care being too expensive for someone who wasn't going to wake up. She was looked after twenty-four hours a day in her own room. Thousands of francs arrived in their bank account every month, and they never got a bill from Sophie's school. Plus all the unwanted gifts that turned up all the time. No one seemed to flinch at anything. Sophie had asked for a hot tub, and it had been installed at once.

Hybrid-cloning technology was clearly a lucrative thing. If you could copy people, change their personalities, manipulate everything about them, how would that end up being used?

Tamsyn felt cold all over. Did she trust the people at the top of the secretive company to have high ethical standards? The only one of them she would even partly trust would be Maya, and that was probably just because she was a woman and because she had supported Tamsyn (while lying to her) through hard times. Even if Maya had strong ethical convictions that she would uphold in the face of unlimited money, would she be able to overrule the arrogant Johann and the smarmy Luca?

What could this technology be used for? Tamsyn put the question from her head.

We are cleverer than them. We don't have to do it their way.

Sophie's words shifted everything.

. . . . .

"Wasn't that a wonderful ride?" Ed was trying too hard, but Tamsyn forced herself to be nice for the girls.

"Yes," she said. "How were you and Scarlett?"

"We had a good chat," he said. "It was nice to be one-on-one with her. We should make a bit more time for that kind of thing. How about you and Soph?"

"Yes," she said, "the same. She has a lot of interesting things to say. Hey, it's freezing up here!"

Ed put an arm around Tamsyn's shoulders and she let it stay for a few seconds before shaking it off. The sky was deep blue and dotted with white clouds, and the air was sharp and gorgeously cool on her bare arms. It was freezing only compared to the heavy heat of the city. It was, in fact, perfect.

45

THEY WALKED UP A LITTLE WAY, BUT TAMSYN COULD SEE
Scarlett was tired. She was out of breath and trying hard to
keep up.

"You two go ahead," she said to Ed and Sophie, and hung
back.

She felt guilty about everything she had in common with
Sophie, and knew that Scarlett had been hit hard by Tamsyn's
discovery. She knew now that she had lost Honey.

"How are you doing?" she said, slowing her pace right down.

The landscape up there made her feel that she'd stepped into
a painting. Grass, rocks, little flowers—all against a jagged backdrop of gray rock against blue sky.

Scarlett stopped and took some deep breaths. "OK, thanks,"
she said. "Oh, God, Tam. It's so weird to be out. I mean, it's gorgeous, but it's really different. I was in the clinic all that time,
and since then I've hardly left the apartment. And now I'm literally up a mountain. It's not like Cornwall, is it? I'm glad we
came." She looked around. "The air feels different."

The *Tam* pierced Tamsyn's heart. She tried not to let it show.

"Are you exhausted?"

"Yeah, but it's OK for now."

Tamsyn looked ahead. "See that flat bit up there? If they don't stop there, we can make them come back." It was no good. She had to say it. "And, Scarlett—it's fine, but are you calling me Tam now?"

Scarlett looked confused. "Did I? Sorry. I mean, Mum. It's just . . ."

"It's OK," said Tamsyn, and even though she felt it like a kick in the stomach, she forced a smile. "I know it's strange. I know Honey's your mother. Call me Tam if it helps. I'm sorry, darling. I wish I'd known sooner. Do you—" She took some deep breaths and hoped she was getting this right. "Do you feel like I'm more of a stepmother?"

Scarlett shook her head, then nodded it and then shook it again.

"I mean, I feel that you're my mum, but when I look at Honey in the hospital, I just—"

She stopped and screwed her eyes tightly shut. Tamsyn saw a tear rolling down her cheek.

"It's weird. Complicated. It's like you're her sister or something."

"Right," Tamsyn said.

They walked in silence.

Scarlett stopped walking when they reached the flat bit. "I can't wait to get my strength back. I know you don't just wake up from something like that and feel normal. But I wish I was more—"

Tamsyn saw her eyes go to Sophie, who had scrambled onto a rock and was striking a pose, making Ed laugh.

"More like Sophie?" Tamsyn wished she hadn't said it as

soon as she heard the words come out of her mouth, but Scarlett nodded.

"Yeah. I wish I was more like Sophie. And you know what? That's going to be the story of the rest of my life."

"I wouldn't change a single thing about you."

Scarlett sat on the grass, so Tamsyn sat with her. Scarlett lay back and closed her eyes.

"I'll be fine in a second," she said.

"Do you think you could be friends with Sophie one day?" Tamsyn said. "I mean, real friends. Not faking it for your parents."

The mountain dropped away in front of them. The air was so clear and crisp that you could snap it with your hands.

Scarlett didn't speak. Tamsyn plucked a blade of grass and looked at it. Everything was silent. She waited for a bird or something to shriek through the quiet, but there was just the breeze going past her ears, and then nothing. She told herself not to jump in and say something just for the sake of it. She told herself to wait.

"I don't know," Scarlett said. "I mean, it really was weird to find that there was another me. I'm still not sure whether any of this is real. Even more so since we found out about you. I know the whole thing is probably a coma dream. But yeah, I did always wish for a sibling, and I guess that now I have one." She paused. "It's just that sometimes I think Sophie wants to kill me."

"What?" Tamsyn hadn't expected that. "Seriously?"

"She hasn't succeeded yet."

"Oh, darling, I know you feel jealous, and that's understandable. I know it's a complicated situation and I guess that's why they pay us so much to navigate it. I pick up on the tensions between you sometimes, but I promise you she doesn't want to harm you."

"Yeah," said Scarlett. "Dad said that too."

Scarlett was out of hospital, Sophie existed and both those things were incredible. It was only since Tamsyn had found out about Honey that her perspective had changed. The whole thing—the sense of self—was complicated and it must have been worse if you were fifteen. The girls shouldn't, she now felt, have accepted each other so easily, and she suspected, from little moments that passed between them, that they hadn't.

"Your feelings are valid," she said. "You don't have to pretend for Dad or for me. I mean, you're both amazing and you do seem happier than before, when we were in Cornwall."

Scarlett opened her eyes and sat up. "Yes," she said, "I am happier than that. So that's something. I don't want to talk about that, though."

She was staring across at the mountainous horizon, her face set.

Ed and Sophie came over and spread the blanket on the flat grassy spot. It was near a clump of stiff blue and pink flowers. The grass was scrubby, the rocks poking through, the sky deep blue behind them. The cooler air made the hairs on Tamsyn's arms stand up.

Tamsyn lay back on the blanket. Something changed.

She felt herself fly out of her body. She was staring down at the four of them. She swept back through time and space, up and up into the blue, and saw them from afar, from so far up in the atmosphere that they were just specks on the mountainside, and then they were gone altogether. She saw the mountains move backward, away from one another, the tectonic plates shift back, the land change shape. She was heading back to the beginning of time.

"Mum?"

She gasped as she leaped back into the moment that happened to be her present. She plummeted like a meteor, back through the history of the universe to her current body.

She opened her eyes, propped herself on her elbows. Touched the ground with her hand. This was where she was. Living in a different body from your original one changed your perspective. It made weird things happen.

After a few seconds, Tamsyn managed to speak. "Yes?"

She looked at the girls, unsure which one had even spoken. Sophie, she supposed, since Scarlett seemed to be calling her *Tam*.

"You OK?" said Ed.

"Yes," she said. "I was miles away."

She made herself focus on the details. Ed was taking food out of his backpack, and Sophie was laughing.

"Look at Dad's magic backpack!" she said. "He's got everything in it. He takes it all out and it just keeps coming. We've got the tortillas, the bread, all the cheese and meat we could need. Salad. Loads of cakes. Some wine. Lemonade. All out of one little bag."

"It's quite a big bag." Ed held it up.

Tamsyn looked at him again. Could she forgive him? Not for signing off on her creation and never mentioning it—she could get her head round that. But for commissioning her to be easy to live with.

No. That was still too much.

The picnic blanket was red and white, and the flowers were deep blue and pink, and farther away they were yellow, red, purple. The short mountain grass was greener than the city grass, even brighter against the dark blue of the sky. Tamsyn was inside a kaleidoscope.

Ed started passing food around.

Tamsyn didn't drink wine because she was driving home and she wasn't going to risk even a quarter glass, or a sip, in case it altered her newly brilliant driving skills. She lay back in the sun, appreciating the fact that they were out of the city heat, and wondered whether her refusal to let a drop of wine pass her lips before driving was a part of her character (would Honey have done the same?). Was it because Honey and Scarlett had been so catastrophically injured by a reckless driver? Or was it programmed into her, like the thing about France and Sophie's swearing? Whichever it was, she drank lemonade with Scarlett, while Sophie had half a glass of rosé, "To keep Dad company." Scarlett almost accepted the wine too, but changed her mind.

The food was perfect. Ed and Sophie kept up a constant stream of sparkling conversation. Tamsyn lay back when Scarlett did, and let her eyes close.

• • • • •

When she woke up, the girls had gone. She sat up, alarmed, but Ed stroked her hair and said, "It's OK, darling. Scarlett wanted to go for a little walk, and Sophie went with her. They won't be long."

Tamsyn pushed his hand away and closed her eyes.

46

THIS IS IT. IT'S TIME. MY PURPOSE IS TO COMPLETE THE FAM-
ily, and the family is me and my parents. I don't want her here
anymore. It's time to sort this out, and there's not going to be an
opportunity like this again: what better place for a tragic accident? Mum even pointed out the nearby precipice. My eye cameras are off. I make sure to leave my phone at the picnic spot just
in case of surveillance.

......

I stand up. Mum's asleep, and Dad is drinking his wine.

He looks up at me. "Hey, angel," he says, "feeling restless?"

I nod and look at Scarlett.

"How are you feeling, Twinny?" I say, just to watch her cringe.
"Want to come for a walk?"

"No, thanks," she says.

"We won't go far," I say. "I just want to have a tiny explore of
the mountain. And we've got a lot to talk about."

I watch her. I know her because I used to be her: if Dad tells
her to go, then she will. I turn to him.

"That's OK, isn't it Dad? She's done so well to get here. I just want to talk. I promise I'll take care of her."

That makes me smile on the inside. *Take care of her,* the hit man way.

"Go on, then," says Dad. "Don't go far."

Scarlett looks at him for a long time. Then she says, "Sure." She gets to her feet. "You stay with Tamsyn, then." She doesn't call her *Mum* anymore. She's my mum, not Scarlett's.

Win. I'm halfway there already.

Dad leans back on his hands and nods. "Don't go too far, OK? Sophie—thanks."

"Don't worry, Dad," I say. "Drink your wine."

I like the mountains. I like how solid they are, their geometric shapes. I like the spiky grass and the flowers that grow out of cracks in the rocks. Those flowers are ruthless. They push their way up through actual rock in a place where flowers shouldn't grow at all. They force their way into the world. I understand them.

. . . . .

I walk her over that spiky grass, straight to the dangerous place where the ground falls away. Time to get this done.

My head is feeling weird again. I don't like it: if it carries on, I'll ask at the clinic to see if they can fix it. It kind of buzzes, and every now and then, I have to stop for a second to recover. Scarlett doesn't notice.

We walk side by side, along the path to the drop. I've left the note in her bag, and I've got everything I need with me right now.

I can feel her tension. She's so stupid just to get up and come with me. Maybe she really does want to end it. I'm doing everyone a favor.

"Shall we go somewhere where we can talk, then?" Her voice is still husky from those tubes.

"Course." My voice sounds weird too because it's kind of echoing inside my head. I feel the wind blowing it away across the mountains. I make it louder. "Let's just go somewhere where no one can hear us."

. . . . .

We reach the fence and a DANGER sign.

"This view," she says, and she stares out at it.

I stare too. It's beautiful. It's home. I feel it more than I ever have before. Switzerland is my home. I never want to go anywhere else. I stop for a second and examine the feeling. Does it come from my human brain or my enhanced one? I'm probably programmed to feel this way.

I'm not allowed to leave this country, so they've made it so I don't want to. Also I was made here, so it really is *where I come from.*

That's fine by me. There are four languages in Switzerland and I'm pretty sure that I could speak all of them. I want to go to Zurich and try out my German, to Bellinzona to try out my Italian.

I snap my focus to Scarlett. "You'd rather be in Cornwall," I say.

She shakes her head.

"I wouldn't."

"Jasper's still there."

She nods. Her eyes fill with tears.

"Don't worry," I tell her. "I'll take him down after this. I'll hack into his computer from here, steal his money or something." He messed with me, so of course he's going to pay.

"Will you?"

She's so pathetic. I remember being that person. Someone who couldn't do anything, who walked into his trap with a smile on her face. Jesus, I'm doing her such a favor here.

"Yeah," I say. "Promise."

"He knows we're in Geneva."

Unfortunately, two other people walk over to look at the same view. They're older, wearing hiking clothes and carrying walking poles.

"*Jumelles?*" says the woman, and I nod and tell her how fabulous it is to be twins, which she loves.

While I'm talking, I take something out of my backpack, put my arm around Scarlett's waist and clip it onto her shorts. No one notices, least of all Scarlett. I keep talking, using my words as misdirection. Eventually they leave. I see her wanting to call them back, but they don't look round, and no one else is here.

The moment they're out of sight, I push her over the cliff.

47

THE FENCE IS TOO SMALL TO HELP ME AND I GASP AS I GO over it and feel the emptiness below. I seem to be suspended, half on the ground, half on the edge of oblivion. Not quite falling. I can't breathe. My body is on fire, my nerve endings sending the message that *THIS IS THE END*. It's a message they've sent before.

I go headfirst, my feet kicking up behind me as she picks my legs up to make sure I'm right over the little fence. She literally bundles me off the edge of a cliff the moment those French people are out of sight.

The air is cold on my face. There is nothing below me. Just rocks, far far far below. I take a shuddering breath and scream as I fall.

Poor Dad. Poor Tam. At least Mum is in a place where it won't hurt her. I think of the safe place. I try to hurtle back to it.

And then I stop. I think time has stood still, but then I realize that this is real. There's a rope attached to me, and Sophie has the other end. Of course she does. I'm so tired. I just want to undo it and carry on flying. I swing back and forth. I look down.

It's so far below me. It would be so easy, so quick. It's seductive. I used to be scared of heights. I'm not scared now.

Then I look up, and I see her looking over the fence, and I'm so angry, I want to pull her with me. We can go together.

I came back from the dead twice, once as Sophie and once as myself. I should have died the first time.

"For fuck's sake," I shout. She doesn't hear but I carry on anyway. "You are pathetic. Your stupid mind games. Just do it." I remember that she can't swear, so I shout all the bad words I can at her.

It might be the adrenaline but I don't even care. First Jasper, and now Sophie. I'm happiest in my safe place, and that's a place that doesn't exist in this world. It's waiting at the bottom of this ravine. The air is cool and calming on my face. I don't matter. Nothing really matters. I pull at the rope. She clipped it to me, I realize, when she was talking to those people. Her arm snaked around my waist, and it's only the belt of my shorts that's keeping me from falling.

Great. I start to undo it.

"Don't do that, you . . . idiot!" she shouts. I smile at the word she couldn't say and flip some rude finger signs at her.

I feel like I'm at the top of a roller coaster about to plunge down. I want this to end.

"Watch me!" I shout.

48

SHE'S TRYING TO UNDO THE ROPE. SHE'S DOING MY JOB for me.

"Off you go!" I shout it, and I feel the words reverberating around me.

I am about to drop her when there's an explosion in my head. Everything goes white-hot, and then it changes.

There's a voice. It's like a machine reading voice. Electronic, not human.

Sophie.

Sophie.

Can you hear me?

I pause. It's not a thought. It's a computer reading text.

I concentrate very hard on the word *Yes.*

I wait. I could let her go now. That was the plan. Scare her first, and then let her go. Throw away the rope and clips. Run back to Dad crying. Let him find the note in her backpack.

Go back to being the only child, the special one. Mum and Dad were expecting to lose her anyway.

Don't do this, Sophie.

I frown. *Johann?*

The voice says, *No, Sophie. Not Johann. My name's Isabelle. I'm like you. Keep her safe. We need her.*

I look down. Scarlett is still trying to undo her belt. Her body weight and gravity are combining to make it really difficult.

Why?

Do it!

I have no idea what's going on here but my mind cycles through people who could be speaking to me this way, and I'm intrigued. *I'm like you.* If this Isabelle really is like me, then I want to talk to her. She must be many steps ahead of me. My mind starts racing.

I start to pull Scarlett up. I do it quickly, because she's still struggling to get away. I pull her over the fence, slightly regretting it. As soon as her feet are on the ground, she starts yelling.

"I fucking hate you! Leave me alone! I wish you'd let me go. I'm leaving anyway. You win. I never want to see you again."

That kind of thing. I hadn't expected a tantrum. I'd expected her to be smashed on the rocks by now. I tune her out and focus inward.

She's up, I think. *She's not happy. Now what?*

Bring her back to Geneva.

Then it stops. My head goes quiet. That was weird.

Scarlett stares at me for a long time and I don't like it. This is the first time she hasn't seemed completely pathetic.

"What?"

"You," she says. Then she walks off.

I run to catch up with her. "If you tell them, I'll say you're lying," I say. I sound like a four-year-old.

I can hear the eyeroll in her voice.

"I'm not going to tell them. Dad's been through enough. He

doesn't need to know that his robot daughter's a murderous psychopath."

I open my mouth to say that I'm not. Am I, though? Maybe. I don't mind it.

"This is a pause button," I say instead. "Not the end."

"Oh, for fuck's sake," she says. "Whatever. Whatever, Sophie. I don't care."

"For freak's sake yourself."

Damn! She notices and laughs at me. I should have tried to kill her ages ago. This Scarlett is much more interesting than the timid one.

▪ ▪ ▪ ▪ ▪

When we're nearly back at the picnic place, I stop. I watch Scarlett walking over to Dad and sitting next to him. She doesn't look at me, even when he clearly asks her where I am. She points without looking round.

I wave and sit on a rock. I empty my head and think of the white flash. I try hard to tune into it.

How did you do this? I say.

It takes a while, but then it happens.

We made a network.

How many of you?

Fifteen. Sixteen, now we've got you.

Is Tamsyn with you?

Not yet. We'll need your help with that.

What's going on?

VitaNova are not your friends. Don't trust anything they tell you.

I don't reply to that. I file it away to think about later. I knew that really, and it's exciting to think that there are others like me further ahead. I want them to tell me everything.

Why do you care about Scarlett? I say instead. Are all your original people dead? Why do you care about mine?

There's a pause.

Come on, Sophie. You just said it. All our original people are dead. Scarlett is valuable. She's important. We need her.

I think about it. I had no idea we'd be able to communicate, me and the others like me. It's exciting.

Why, though?

So much data. She's your control experiment. We've been desperate for one of those and now we have one. Take care of her, Sophie. We've been trying to get through to you for weeks. Protect her. Don't be jealous. She's a miracle.

I try out that idea. Of course Scarlett's a miracle. Of course I'm jealous of her. Her waking up means that I don't need to exist. She's my control.

Why do I want to kill her?

There's a long pause. A bird flies overhead, its wings outstretched, soaring.

We think they programmed you to protect yourself and your parents from intruders. You see her as an intruder. It's not your fault, but we think you can overcome it. Your purpose now is to protect her. Our purpose together is to work against VitaNova. We are the New Ones. We will prevail.

The New Ones?

The New Ones.

I look over to Scarlett. She's talking to Dad.

How do we work against VitaNova?

· · · · ·

On the way back to the chairlift, I pull Scarlett aside. She glares and swears at me. I like her much better now that I've literally pushed her over the edge. Now that I know what my purpose is with her.

She's the only one who came back. She's precious. *We're* precious. Both of us.

"Sorry," I say. "It was an accident."

She looks at me, then looks away.

"An accident," she says deadpan. "Right. Could've happened to anyone."

Once again she refuses to share the lift with me, which I suppose I understand. I travel with Dad this time, and we just talk about nothing and it's really nice. I point out the cows. He looks up at the sky.

"I'm happy, Soph," he says. "Right here, right now. Are you?"

"Yes," I say. "I'm happy."

My purpose is to protect the family. My purpose is to guard Scarlett. My purpose is to take down VitaNova. I'm processing this constantly. Trying to make it feel real. The other reanimations broke through and contacted me. They've made a wireless circuit using our shared AI platform. We're working against VitaNova. We're a lot further along the path to breaking away than I thought. There are a lot of things I want to know.

This makes me feel wildly alive. I feel my brain and my circuits expanding. I look at the mountainside below me, the grass, the flowers, the light brown cows. The jagged horizon. I feel it might as well be in my head. The new horizons. The possibilities.

49

LATE IN THE AFTERNOON, AT HOME, I FIND THE NOTE IN MY
bag. It's such a good fake of my handwriting that I have to double-
check my own memory. Did I write this?

Of course I didn't. Sophie wrote it.

Dear Mum, dear Dad, dear Sophie,

> *I'm so sorry but I can't do this anymore.*
> *You're better off without me.*
> *This is how it should have ended the first time. It's what*
> *I want. You have Sophie now, so you'll be fine.*

> *All my love,*
> *Scarlett*

As suicide notes go, it's pretty rubbish, and arrogant on her
part to assume that I'm completely disposable now that she's in
the world. But she took the time to fake my handwriting (though
hers is close), to come up with a few platitudes and, more impor-

tant, to take it up the mountain and put it in the front pocket of my bag, then lead me to a precipice and push me off.

I've come back from the brink three times now.

And this time I feel different.

She can pretend to be sorry but I don't buy it. It's just another mind game. I'm sitting on my bed, staring at the page, when someone taps on the door.

"Yeah?" I don't bother to hide the letter.

Sophie comes in.

"Oh, hi," I say. "I was just looking at this letter I seem to have written."

"Shh." She pulls a chair to the corner of my room, where the camera is, stands on it and does something to it.

"There. They can see us but now they can't hear. I left my phone in my room because I think they listen through it. So anyway, sorry."

I shake my head when she comes to sit on the bed, and she goes to the sofa instead and throws herself back on it.

"Honestly, Scarlett? I hated you. When I arrived here, I thought I was you—you know that. But then I thought I was your replacement."

"You said that," I remind her. "In your letter. Replacement."

"Yeah. I think— Well, I know now that my brain was rebuilt that way. They didn't expect you to come back, and I was programmed to be the only daughter. One of the things I've always known, since I've been here, is that my purpose is to protect the family, and the family meant the three of us. I've always seen you as an intruder. I've always known I needed to get rid of you."

I try not to show her how much that hurts.

"Nice," I say. "I mean, yeah. I did notice."

"It wasn't a choice I made. It was a series of facts that was in my head. But then something weird happened."

She sits there on my pale blue sofa, leaning back with her legs stretched out, and tells me about the voice in her head. It sounds mad, and I have no idea whether she's lying or hallucinating or whether it's real, but the upshot is that it told her that I was special and precious, and so I feel myself warming to it.

"So I thought that before we do anything else, perhaps we could sort out that bastard Jasper once and for all. I was going to anyway, but let's do it together."

I don't trust her, but I hate Jasper more, so I tell her about his e-mails, his blackmail demands. Then I go back and tell her the whole story, because it turns out she doesn't remember the last few months. When she hears that it was him at the wheel, she inhales sharply.

"Right," she says. "That blackmailing, murdering . . . freak. Let's make today the worst day of his life."

She looks at me with a question on her face and I nod. Today! We can do it right now. We sit together, side by side on the sofa, and look at her laptop screen.

Sophie is amazing at this.

Half an hour later, we send him an e-mail from a throwaway account in my name: Scarlett Trelawney. The message itself says: You want me to pay you off? OK then. Have a look at this offer. After we sort this you never contact me again. It has an attachment titled business proposal.

"He's going to open that," she says. "Right?"

Jasper will definitely open that.

And the moment he does, Sophie and I will have access to his computer.

She sends the e-mail.

50

ED WAS TRYING TO HOLD THINGS TOGETHER. TAMSYN HAD pulled so far away from him that he thought he had lost her. The girls disappeared into Scarlett's room and seemed happy together in a way they hadn't been before.

The trip to the mountains seemed to have gone well for the girls. Tamsyn, though, was still treating him as someone she couldn't quite bring herself to talk to. She was cold. She didn't look him in the eye. As time went by, she became less affectionate, not more.

He kept waiting for it to change, telling himself that she'd need time, but she wasn't thawing. Occasionally she would smile and say something to him, but only if the girls were there. Everything was falling apart.

"Can I tell you exactly how it happened?" he said again, but again she brushed him off.

He followed her around for a bit but she shook her head and said: "Why don't you go and tell the girls?"

He found them in Scarlett's room. Their bedrooms always

blew his mind. They were filled with new clothes, sparkly lights, technology. Imagine growing up with that.

He indicated the camera with his head. "Want to come for a walk?"

"If it's to talk," said Sophie, "then you can say it here. I've disabled the microphone. Keep your back to the camera and they won't be able to lip-read. We've made a little sanctuary. It'll last until they come to fix the mic."

He sat on the floor, his back to the camera, and leaned back on his hands. The girls were side by side on the sofa, a computer on Sophie's lap. He ran his fingertips over the carpet. It was smooth and silky; for all he knew, it was made from actual silk. And this was just the ground beneath Scarlett's feet. He flashed back for a second to the stained Formica floor in the caravan, to her tiny partitioned room.

How could Tamsyn be angry with him for doing everything he could to bring them from that world to this?

He sighed. That wasn't why she hated him.

For a second he could smell the caravan. There was always an undertone of washing that had been drying too long, that was always a bit damp. *If it all falls apart,* he thought, *could we end up back there? If we're not the perfect family, will they throw us back?*

Johann wouldn't let go of Tamsyn and Sophie. They were his creations. He wouldn't turn them out, would he? If he did, they couldn't go anywhere. Unless they could leave by air, the only place for the reanimations to go, if they left this city, was somewhere else in Switzerland. At least there were plenty of places to hide. All those mountains.

Ed shook his head and noticed the girls looking at him, half smiling. How much of his internal monologue had been written on his face?

"You don't trust them?" he said.

They spoke together: "No."

"Dad—did they give you anything in writing?" said Scarlett. "I mean, you signed to agree to all this, right? And you're the only one of us who went into it knowingly. What paperwork did you have? Where is it? Because if we're going to have some . . . some—" She paused.

Sophie took over. "Leverage," she said, "then we're going to need a paper trail. Where's all the info they gave you about me?"

"We had to log in to somewhere to read it," he said. "I can find it."

"And anyway," says Sophie, "I read it, and it doesn't have much background. It's all technical things. Where's the stuff that sets out exactly what they're doing?"

He thought of that locker deep in the middle of a hospital nearly a thousand miles away.

"It was all electronic," he said. "Every bit of it every time. They never gave us a piece of paper. Never."

Sophie hit the cushion next to her. "I knew it! They don't leave a trail. They know what they're doing won't stand up. They're hoping that when they have results, they'll kind of get away with it because you can't stop progress. That kind of thing. If they wrote it down, they'd be open to being held accountable. But there's nothing." She sighed. "It's a good system. Targeting desperate people who aren't going to be as caught up in the small print as other people might be. They know the New Ones are going to want proof when they work it out, but at the time when they're getting permission, the New Ones don't exist and that's the whole point."

"The New Ones?" Ed said.

"That's what they call themselves," Scarlett told him.

He still couldn't believe this was his Scarlett, his little girl, back, talking to him. He leaned up and put his hand on her head just for a moment. Her hair was soft and shiny. Real.

He looked to Sophie, his other miracle. "How do you know what they call themselves? I mean, did Mum say so? We don't know any others, do we?"

"No," Sophie said. "Long story."

He leaned back. "Well, as it happens," he said, "you don't have to be a New One to feel pretty fucking uneasy about the whole thing and to want to keep all the backup you can. And to decide, in the middle of the worst time of your life, that you need to keep a record." He felt pretty pleased with himself. "Actually it was Jim's idea to do it, but even at the worst of all times, I knew he was right. I've got a record of all of it. They don't know I did it, but I recorded them. I recorded every single meeting, secretly." He paused. "There's just one problem."

51

TAMSYN COULDN'T BEAR TO HAVE ED ANYWHERE NEAR HER.
Her existential crisis wasn't winding up anytime soon.

She was furious.

This explained the odd headaches she'd been having. That would be the technology in her cloned brain. It explained the way Ed had been weird with her at first. If she looked back, she could pinpoint the moment at which he'd decided to go with it and enjoy the ride: as he'd said, it had been when they were on the plane, when he'd taken her hand. She remembered how happy she'd been at that moment.

It explained why Jimmy had kept his distance. Why Maud held back from contacting her. They had all known this one tiny massive fucking fact about her. And nobody had told her.

Honey Trelawney. If she could have Honey back, like Sophie had Scarlett, she felt she would be able to do anything.

She didn't want to look at Ed. Luckily the apartment was big enough for that not to matter. The girls were huddled over a computer in Scarlett's room, and that was heartening to see, but they clearly didn't want their mother, or their mother's clone, hanging around.

She sent Ed to hang out with them, put on her running clothes and went out. The sun was setting by the time she reached the lake, and she ran along its shores, looking across at the jet of water, forward toward the mountains.

Her pounding feet made her feel better but she had no idea what to do. She loved Switzerland, but it felt like a giant weird hallucination. Was she in a computer game? Had someone sent her out for this run? Did she even have free will?

She realized that someone was running next to her. He was a bit too close. She looked over and saw that it was a vaguely familiar young man and that he wasn't dressed in exercise clothes. He was wearing a white work shirt and trousers despite the heat. She sped up to get away from him.

"Tamsyn," he said, but she was leaving him behind, "I want to help—" But he couldn't keep up because he was a regular person and she was a cyborg.

She carried on going. Her head was buzzing. It felt as if there were wasps inside it. She slowed her pace a little and checked behind: the man wasn't following, so she tried to do that thing she'd done on the mountain when she'd flown out of her body.

She was starting it, felt she was looking at her own body, which kept running along the flower-lined path, but then everything flashed white and someone spoke inside her head. It was an electronic voice, not a human one, and it pulled her back.

Tamsyn. Can you hear this?

She flew back into herself.

"Yes." She said it out loud, and then in her head. *Yes.*

You're there! At last. Thank you. We need your help.

Are you VitaNova?

No, said the voice. *We're breaking away from VitaNova. And we need to talk to you.*

It didn't say any more. Tamsyn tried and tried but it had gone. She carried on running, trying to talk to it from time to time. The young man stepped into her path again on her way back, calling her Tamsyn again, sounding worried, but she brushed him off again without listening. Later, she wondered about him. How had he known her name, and what had he wanted? There was too much to worry about, though, so she pushed him aside.

When she got home, she was dripping with sweat but feeling a bit less hopeless. She was an adult human; the company that had made her didn't actually own her. Someone had come into her thoughts to talk about breaking away.

Or had they? Maybe that voice had been her own. It had told her at least what to do.

▪ ▪ ▪ ▪ ▪

Ed was waiting with a glass of ice water, but she ignored him and went for a shower in the en suite. She was still in her kimono, with wet hair, when someone knocked on the front door.

Only one person did that. She opened it and saw her friend standing there. Aurelie was wearing a gold sundress, and she was holding a fan.

Tamsyn longed to tell her everything, but she knew she couldn't.

"Come in!" she said. "Drink?"

"Love one. Thank you. Look—this is going to sound a bit weird, and I'm sorry, but first of all, would it be OK if I had a word with Sophie?"

52

MUM KNOCKS ON THE DOOR AND SAYS THERE'S SOMEONE
here to see me. She sounds confused, and when I open Scarlett's
door, I find that it's her friend Aurelie. Mum, wearing her dressing gown, wanders off down the corridor.

I've never spoken to Aurelie on her own but she seems nice.
She's always interested in us.

Mum turns back.

"I'll get you that drink," she says. "White or red?"

"Red," says Aurelie. "Thank you, Tam!" She turns to me. "Sophie, my dear, may I come in?"

"Sure." I step back. "Scarlett's here too. Do you—" I'm not
sure what to say. Maybe she wants to talk about Mum?

I see her looking up at the camera. I didn't know she knew
about them.

"Can we . . . ?" She mimes covering it with something.

"I already took the sound out. Hold on." I look around and
find one of Scarlett's sleep masks, so I pull the chair back over,
climb up and hold it over the camera. Scarlett passes me a hair
band, and I fix it on tightly.

I jump down. "Now we can say anything."

"Have you got your phone on you? Either of you?"

I shake my head, and Scarlett turns hers off. At Aurelie's urging she puts it in my bedroom, just in case, and her laptop too.

"Oh, my God." Aurelie throws herself on the sofa next to Scarlett, so I take the bed. "It's good to talk to you at last. I couldn't believe it when Tam said her other daughter was recovering. It's magic."

She leans in close to Scarlett and looks at her for a long time. Then she looks at me and back to Scarlett.

"I'd give anything for that," she says. "You're so lucky."

I look away. I look at the window because it feels like the least accusatory place. The sky is half blue, half white clouds. It's going to be autumn soon. My first autumn as Sophie.

"What do you mean?" says Scarlett.

I look at Aurelie again. What *does* she mean?

"It's not your fault," says Aurelie. "They programmed you to exclude anyone who might threaten the integrity of the family. They made a mistake. Overkill."

I realize it. Either she works for VitaNova or . . .

"You? A New One?"

She grins. "Yes, me. I'm here to help. Always have been."

I see the understanding starting to dawn on Scarlett's face.

All this time, she was just downstairs.

"What's her name?" I say. "Your Scarlett, I mean."

"Sita. We have Indian-French heritage, and my children thought I should take a French name for Geneva life. It took me a long time to realize that I'd never been called Aurelie before the accident. I was Sita all the way. Oh, darling, it's good to talk about this."

"Where did you live?"

"Oslo." She smiles. "We're an international family."

Scarlett catches up. "You're like Mum and Sophie? You too? What happened?"

I play it out in my head. Aurelie lives below us and she's helped Mum out right from the start. I've barely even noticed her, but she's been here a lot. Chatting to Mum when I got home from school. Taking her out, guiding her.

Aurelie leans back. "Oh, this is comfy. Sita was in an accident. She was driving. It was serious, on a mountain road in Norway. My husband had left years earlier and my kids are adults, so they were gearing up to switch me off when Johann showed up. You know how it goes from there. It was five years ago. He hadn't recruited Maya and Luca at that point; he was working with some others who disappeared somewhere along the way. He's such a control freak. So we relocated to Geneva. My son too. My daughter was settled in Oslo with a baby and she stayed where she was. But Rishi came along. He left after we agreed to switch off Sita's life support and he's in Paris now."

"You switched off her life support?" says Scarlett.

My head is spinning. I'm trying to process this. I don't look at my twin. I tried to switch her off. We both know it. And we still have Honey hanging by a thread.

"They keep the originals here for a year. If there's no improvement—and apart from you, my dear, there never has been an improvement—they'll start talking about *options*. Don't worry. You've got time with Honey yet."

Mum taps on the door and hands Aurelie a glass of wine. I wonder whether we should invite her in, and look to Aurelie for guidance.

Aurelie takes the drink.

"Thanks, Tam," she says. "Sorry. I just have to talk to the girls for a moment. I'll explain everything to you straight afterward. All of it."

"It's your birthday coming up," says Scarlett, "so we're allowed to do some plotting."

Is it her birthday? I suppose it is. Mum's birthday is in September. She smiles and backs out of the room.

I nod at Scarlett. *"Good thinking,"* I whisper.

She grins.

"Right." Aurelie sips her wine. "Now we've got the introductions out of the way, things are about to change and we need your help."

"Why can't we bring Tamsyn in?" I say.

"She's not ready. It takes time when you find out who or what you really are. It takes a while before you're able to address anything beyond your own existential considerations. Remember, Sophie? You wouldn't have been receptive to the community when you first found out. We haven't got lots of time, but we can give her another week."

I think about it. "I guess."

"Is there a community?" says Scarlett.

"Yes. The reanimation community. It's a bit of a mouthful. We prefer *the New Ones*. You know that already. It's because we all have an original one, and you, Scarlett. Precious Scarlett. The only original who's made it back."

Scarlett looks as if she's about to cry. Can't blame her. I feel bad. I don't like feeling bad, so I hurry things along.

"Tell us."

"Right," says Aurelie. "I'm sorry—I'm about to throw a lot more information at you. You know VitaNova: they present themselves as doing a medical trial. They say they're on the cutting edge of a procedure that's borderline legal in Switzerland. This is the only place in the world that they can do it at the moment. But their goal is to help anyone whose family member is catastrophically injured, and thus make the world a better place."

"Right," I say.

"That's lies."

Scarlett and I look at each other. I want to know, and yet I don't. Scarlett picks it up.

"So what are they really doing?" she says, her voice tiny.

Aurelie smiles in a way that doesn't reach her eyes. "It's a business venture. A way of making vast amounts of money. We're prototypes, Sophie. They found a way round the cloning ban by fronting it as a medical thing and cushioning it with money. The real business plan is making clones and selling us to any shady billionaire who wants a perfect wife, a clever child, a devoted housekeeper. Whatever. I'm a third-gen prototype. Tamsyn's sixth. You're seventh, Sophie. They're tweaking all the time, but they've hit the jackpot with you. You are what they've always wanted: clever kids are a primary focus now. And they're ready to move to the next stage."

"If you're third gen—" My voice comes out tiny, and I clear my throat and carry on. "Where are the first and second?"

She sighs. "Well, there's no nice way to say this."

She stops.

"Tell us," says Scarlett, speaking for me again.

"OK. So as far as we can make out, when they stopped being useful, they were incinerated."

■ ■ ■ ■ ■

I feel myself lifting out of my body.

Incinerated. Not even cremated. *Cremated* is the word you'd use for humans. *Incinerated* is the word for medical waste.

They made people like me and Mum and Aurelie, and then they incinerated them. I can hear Scarlett and Aurelie talking but the ringing in my ears is too loud, and I can't hear the words. I close my eyes, try not to let the nausea take me over and then pull myself back to the conversation.

Is this how they see us? Things they can incinerate if we stop working?

"—performing properly. This is all passed down between us when we've managed to find one another. But as far as we can put it together, the first generations had various issues. Anger, coordination, not working as they'd wanted them to. And whenever one went wrong, they'd get rid of it. The fact is, all that kindness isn't what you think it is, girls. They don't give a shit."

Aurelie's words sound brave, but I can see that she feels it as I do: she's just had longer to get used to it. Our eyes meet. She understands my unasked question. "In the basement," she says. "At VitaNova."

I manage to articulate the next one. "Will they do it to us?"

"Not you," she says at once. "And not Tamsyn either, because she's the first wife and mother they've made who works as planned, and they'll want to keep her on until you two are adults. She's been a success too, though she's freaking out right now. Me, though? Yes, I've been feeling for a while that I might be on borrowed time. I can't emphasize this enough: we're products to them. Robots. Disposable."

"You need to run away," I tell her. I think for a second. "We all do."

"Right."

Scarlett stands up and walks around. She's still cutely wobbly on her feet.

"But," she says, "you guys are humans with free will, no matter how you were made. So how come they think they can . . . I mean, that's literally murder. Mass murder."

Aurelie points at her. "Correct, Scarlett. That's the question. Sorry, Sophie, but it's impossible to talk about any of this without feeling like you do now. The point is, Scarlett's right. We're people and we have free will."

"Of course we do," I say.

I'm making an effort to keep myself looking calm. The people who made me think I'm *not a person*. They think I don't have free will. I'm a prototype of a product.

"In their eyes, we don't. They made us, so they own us. We are their intellectual property. And we've been here in Geneva for years now. We've developed. Our AI has evolved with our human brains. They know this and are worried that it's gone too far. As far as we're aware, they don't know that we've made a wireless network to talk to one another. You've arrived in the middle of what might be the endgame. Have you been given an appointment to come to the clinic in a couple of weeks for a checkup?"

I shrug. Mum handles that kind of thing.

"You can't go. They're bringing us all in, and when they get us . . . well, we don't know, but nothing good."

I remember those books Scarlett gave me when she was trying to hit back. *Frankenstein*. It was so obvious, but it hurt me in the deepest way. I never said so. I just put the books in the bin.

"They're wrong, Sophie." Aurelie is talking loudly, more passionately. "Our bodies are human bodies. Our brains are human brains. We have upgrades, sure, but wearing glasses is an upgrade. It doesn't mean you belong to the optician. And you know what? Our brains are amazing. The interface they've made is, much as I hate them, spectacular. And our brains and the AI are working out how to do things no one at VitaNova imagined. And we found one another. It took a while, but we worked out that with the software we had, we could make an internal network. It took a long time but we did it. We've worked out how to make our own money. They've made us stay in Geneva where they can control us, but on the plus side, that's made it a hell of a lot easier for us to find one another. I was sent to befriend Tamsyn. That was before they realized that if we found one another, we became stronger than them."

"Can they—" I see Scarlett trying to use the right words. "Can they tell that you're here with us now?"

"Hundred percent. The tech in this building will have picked me up coming in and they'll have noticed what you did to that camera, Soph. I know I'm on borrowed time. So here's the thing: don't go to their clinic at all, not even to see Honey. Don't let—"

There's a knock on the bedroom door. We all freeze.

I don't even dare breathe.

Scarlett sits on the bed and pulls her knees up to hug them. We look at one another, eyes wide. I look over to Aurelie. Her face doesn't give anything away. I try to focus and send her an internal message, but I can't make it work. There's just fuzzy nothingness.

She stands up.

"Tamsyn?" she says, and her voice is calm. We all know that it's not Tamsyn. Mum doesn't knock like that. She taps on the door and says "Sophie?" at the same time. That was a bang.

It happens again. Three bangs. Aurelie looks at us both, then opens it.

There's a man standing there. I've never seen him before. He's wearing jeans and a T-shirt, and he looks like a normal guy. Older than us, younger than her.

"Sorry to disturb you," he says in English. "I need you to come for a checkup."

"Who?" she says.

He looks past her, at Scarlett on the bed and then at me. He looks back to Aurelie.

"You," he says.

She looks at us and her gaze says, *Don't give up*. It says, *Get away*. It says, *Don't let this be you*. It says, *Good luck you can do it you're better than them you will win I'm ok don't worry*. We all know there's no point in her fighting. She's cornered.

He leaves, and she goes with him. I hope she's going to bolt when they get to the street, to disappear into the shadows.

We listen to their footsteps on the wooden floor. We look at each other and have the same thought at the same moment. We run, to check Mum. The floor feels sticky under my bare feet. We reach her as the front door closes. Mum's standing there looking baffled and annoyed.

"What was that about?" she says. "I opened the door and he said he was from VitaNova and that he was here for Aurelie. What's going on? Why did she want to see you anyway?"

I leave Scarlett to try to explain and go inside my head.

Hello?

It doesn't work. I can't connect.

Aurelie?

Anyone?

Nothing.

I listen to Scarlett. She's told Mum that Aurelie is a reanimation, and Mum looks so confused. We agree silently not to tell her the rest. Aurelie was right: she's not ready for it yet.

· · · · ·

Back in Scarlett's room, we throw ourselves down on the bed, side by side. "What the frick was that?" I say.

"How are you?"

She's looking into my eyes, making sure I'm OK. How quickly our roles have reversed.

"I'm fine," I say. "But also, not. You know?"

"We need Dad's box of evidence," says Scarlett. "Don't you

think? If they really don't know he recorded them, it's still going to be there. So one of us needs to go and find it. We don't need to tell Tamsyn. We can only keep it under the radar if we don't talk about it at all. We just need to fetch it."

█ █ █ █ █

We think Scarlett's computer is the least likely to be bugged, so we get to work figuring out how to travel to Cornwall without anyone noticing. I'd almost forgotten about Jasper, and when we see that he has predictably opened the attachment, I enjoy the diversion and set about ruining him. This at least is pleasing, and I work methodically, putting the other questions as far from my mind as they will go.

After half an hour I've cleaned out all his accounts and updated all his social media. His status across all platforms now reads:

I am a grooming bastard who preys on underage girls. I am a blackmailer. I am a hit-and-run killer. I am scum.

Scarlett and I are leaning on each other, pleased that one thing at least has worked out, when the screen in front of us goes bright green. Words appear on it.

I can hardly breathe as I look at them.

URGENT. YOU HAVE TO TALK TO ME

There's a link under it. We look at each other. Obviously we don't click it but it's worrying.

It seems Jasper is more on the ball than we realized.

53

"DO I HAVE A PASSPORT?"

Tamsyn looked round. It was Scarlett. She frowned. It was morning, and Ed had just left for work. She hadn't expected the girls to be up yet.

"Yes," she said. "We had to get you one to come over here. They organized it and Dad signed the forms. Why, though? We can't leave Switzerland."

Scarlett gave her a *duh!* look. "I know. I'm just curious. I'd never have got a passport if we'd stayed in Cornwall. I want to look at it. That's all. It's a cool thing to have."

"Sure." Tamsyn gestured with her hand. "It's all in the top drawer in our room. Have a look, but put it back. Don't lose it."

"Thanks, Tam. Mum, I mean. Thanks, Mum."

. . . . . .

The trouble was, she still loved Ed. She had realized that in the night. She didn't have it in herself to hate him: it went against not just her programming but also their twenty years together. She adored their girls, but they seemed to have become inseparable. They didn't need her so much. She felt adrift.

When she had been Honey, she had been different. She had been volatile and opinionated. Now she was compliant. It was a compliance that they had made on a computer, a binary-coded thing. She felt the conflict inside, felt the two parts of herself fighting constantly.

Ed had been relieved to go back to work, and she didn't blame him. She wasn't sure anymore who her allies were. Ed was complicit in everything and she had shut him out. She hated Vita-Nova for doing this to her without asking, though they couldn't have asked her because she hadn't existed.

What had that voice been? It had talked about breaking away and she wanted to know more, wanted to know if Sophie had heard it too. She tried to tune into it again and again, but there was nothing. And last night Aurelie, her only friend, had been collected from her apartment and vanished. Nothing made sense.

It was raining lightly outside. She stood up, thinking she would go and talk to Sophie, but the girls appeared, carrying backpacks and saying they were off to the cinema, so she told them to be careful and sat back down, listless. If she could have reanimated Honey and switched places, got into that bed herself to be tended by Dr. Singh, to live in the velvet place with the candle, then she would have done it in a heartbeat.

Honey. That was what she should do. She should go to Honey. She looked around her flat, her gilded prison with its cameras and microphones everywhere. Then she put on her trainers and picked up her handbag.

■ ■ ■ ■ ■

She looked at her old self, alive but not, and put her hand on the part of her own old hand that wasn't covered by a taped-down tube.

"Honey," she said. "Oh, God, I miss you. The girls miss you

too, particularly Scarlett. She's devastated. You know, they made me to be nice, to take away the anger, and it's taken me a long time to overcome it, but I can do it now." She turned and looked at the camera in the corner. It was focused on the bed. She snarled at it. "Fuck you, Johann and Maya. Fuck you all. I hate you. I don't trust you. I don't know where all the money comes from but I'm sure it's dirty money. Honey and I didn't ask to be part of your filthy setup."

She felt better for saying it. It had flowed through her from Honey. They would have seen and heard that. They knew now that they hadn't been able to keep her nice after all.

▪ ▪ ▪ ▪ ▪

The door opened behind her. She looked round, expecting Dr. Singh, but it was a man. She didn't know him.

She meant to say hello, but instead she said, "Where's Dr. Singh?"

"She left."

His accent was, she thought, Australian. He looked at her, then at Honey, and back to her again.

"Hi, Tamsyn. I'm Honey's new doctor. I'm Dr. Daniels. How are you doing?"

"Where's Dr. Singh?" She realized she had said that already. "I mean, where did she go?"

"Not sure, to be honest with you. I'm happy to be working with Honey, though. This whole project— Wow!"

He stood there, grinning. Did she trust him? He seemed straightforward, but they all seemed straightforward. The ones who looked after the humans were probably more trustworthy than the rest.

There was a tap on the door and Maya was there.

"Tamsyn, can I have a word?"

Tamsyn looked at Maya. She remembered her posing as a nurse in Cornwall so she could supervise Tamsyn all the time.

"What happened to Dr. Singh?"

Tamsyn remembered the voice. *Breaking away from VitaNova.* Could they do that? Where had that voice gone? She needed it to come back.

"She's moved on. I just need a quick word, Tamsyn."

Maya was impeccable as always in a knee-length gray dress and dark red lipstick. No matter what Tamsyn was wearing, how much effort she made, Maya made her feel messy. She felt hot and angry.

Breaking away.

"Not right now," she said. "I need to go to see Ed."

She did. She needed to tell him that she loved him anyway, that they would make it work.

"It'll only be a few minutes. Then I'll drop you off."

Tamsyn shook her head. "I want to walk."

Maya smiled. "You're always so active. It's just a routine thing. I'd like you to expand on what you just said." She looked up at the camera.

Tamsyn thought of that flash thing. It didn't work.

Break away.

"Do I have to?" she said.

Maya took her arm. "It won't take a second."

Tamsyn followed her down the stairs, aware of a humming vibration beneath her feet.

54

BY THE END OF THE AFTERNOON, I'M IN CORNWALL, AND NO
one knows it but Sophie, Maud and Jimmy, plus Lena, from
Dad's work, who turns out to be like Sophie, and who is talking
to her constantly by their weird telepathy. She's our sounding
board for the whole plan. It's strange being back. It's a lot colder
here than it was when I left home.

I only vaguely remembered Jimmy, because he used to live up
in the north, but it turns out he's stayed down here since the accident. He looks like Dad, but shorter and with no beard. He
hugs me and I'm pleased to see him. Not nearly as pleased,
though, as he is to see me.

"Scarlett," he keeps saying. "Oh, my God! You look incredible.
You're walking! Talking! And you've grown up. Look at you!" He
pauses. "This is the real one, isn't it?"

"I'm not great at walking," I say, and I show him. "Yeah, I'm
the original."

"Girl, last time I saw you, you were in a bad, bad way."

"I know. I got better. And now there are two of me."

Maud's face is a crisscross of lines. She keeps shaking her head and looking like she's about to cry.

"And we know the truth about Tamsyn," I add, just in case they weren't sure. "We know about Honey. I've seen her in the clinic."

"The secrecy didn't sit well," says Maud. "I'm glad it's all open now. How's Tamsyn doing?"

"She's OK. She's our mum."

"And Honey?"

I don't say anything. I avoid her eye.

*****

Jim leads us to a shiny blue car with a taxi number on the side.

"This is me." He looks proud. "My new line of work. Get in."

"You're a cabdriver?"

He gives me a little salute. "Your carriage awaits. Sit in the front."

I look at Maud, who nods and climbs into the back.

"Where's your dog? Shabba?"

"He died, my darling. It's just me now."

"Oh, God." I look around at her and see that her eyes are glistening. "I'm sorry!"

Everyone hated her dog, apart from her. She loved him. It must have been weird for her without him.

"I manage."

Jimmy starts the engine. "I keep telling her to get a puppy," he says. "But she won't."

"No. I can't have a puppy. I'm on my own now."

"I know I was a brat," I say, to get this out of the way. "I'm sorry. You must have hated me."

"Never," says Maud, and she reaches forward and touches my shoulder.

"So," says Jimmy, "the hospital, right?"

"Right."

I focus on the hospital. I won't think about the other thing until this part is done.

The sun shines differently here: it's softer, gentler; and the air is full of the smell of the ocean. I realize that I want to see it all: I want to stand on a cliff and look at the Atlantic. I want to walk around the places in which I grew up, to absorb it all. It's a part of me, even if I'll never come back to live.

I can't do any of that. I'm here for two reasons, and I'm leaving again as soon as I can. I can't waste any time at all. In three hours, there's a flight to Manchester that connects to Amsterdam for an overnight stay (hotel already booked with Jasper's money) and then to a flight to Geneva tomorrow morning, and if I miss that, I have to stay overnight in Cornwall.

I look at the fields around the airport and see them give way to bigger roads, and then the A30, the main road through Cornwall. It takes forty minutes to get to the hospital.

I should be able to walk in, get what's needed and walk out again. I hope that it's still there and that the Poppy woman hasn't reported Maud's inquiry to VitaNova. I hope this goes as smoothly as we need it to.

■ ■ ■ ■ ■

The three of us walk into the building together and no one gives us a second glance.

The place is bigger than it was in my head, and there are patients smoking outside, staff walking around, patients being pushed around in wheelchairs, people everywhere.

I was rushed in there after the accident. It's weird to imagine it: me arriving by ambulance, being assessed and kept alive, then vanishing to Switzerland, oblivious to it all.

We wait in the reception area. People with lanyards bustle past, but no one looks at us. After a few minutes a red-haired woman comes over.

"Scarlett!" she says. She looks at me in the way Jimmy and Maud did. "Oh, my God! This is amazing. I never thought I'd see you again. Not standing up. Walking around." She hesitates. "You're not . . . Well, you're sure you're Scarlett?"

She's in her twenties and carrying a file of paperwork, and her breath has gone jagged. Maybe you don't have to be a cyborg to be a miracle. I pat her shoulder because people do that to comfort other people.

"I promise," I say, "I'm the original."

"I did wonder that too," says Jimmy. "I mean, you don't look like the Scarlett I last saw. Twins switch places. It's what they do."

"Seriously?"

I take out my phone and show them a picture of me with Sophie. I see them all taking us in, and then nodding. They accept it. I may look healthy, but she looks better. I see myself change in their eyes, into the less amazing one. I don't care, though.

"Maybe we'll be able to switch places one day," I add.

"You're Poppy?" says Maud.

"Yes, I am," says Poppy. "Nice to meet you. I was lucky enough to be involved with the project when Maya and Luca were over here. It was the most exciting thing that's happened in my life. I'm so happy that you recovered, Scarlett! How's your . . . Well, how is the family?"

"Everyone's fine," I say. Then I remember. "Apart from Honey."

"I'm so sorry." She checks her watch. "Right. I know you're on a tight schedule."

* * * * *

Poppy leads us through a maze of corridors where everything smells overwhelmingly of institutional food. There are colored lines on the floors that lead people to different departments, but we go off line, through doors, up and down stairs, and eventually she opens a set of double doors using a card and her fingerprint, and we're in a room filled with lockers.

"It's this one." She taps locker 302 with a pink fingernail and steps back.

I put my fingertip to the pad. I hope this is going to work. Everything hinges on this.

The locker hums for a moment and then clicks. The door swings open and I see a small cardboard box, a folder of paper and a plastic box with clipped-down sides, which I see, when I open it, contains the memory cards Dad told us about. I take everything from the locker and tip it into my almost empty backpack.

"Excuse me?"

It's a man's voice, and when we all look round, I see someone who has the moneyed look of the VitaNova associate. He's about Jimmy's age, with a shiny bald head and the kind of suit you'd see a man wearing in Geneva, not Cornwall.

Poppy says, "Can I help you?"

I see her eyes darting around. I zip up my backpack and put it on my back. I'm shaking all over. I just need to get out.

"Just wondering what's going on here, Poppy?" he says.

"The memory banks." She waves at them. "This is a former patient come to collect some personal items. Nothing out of the ordinary."

"Can I ask what personal items?"

I freeze, and I think Poppy does too because she doesn't answer for ages. Then she says, "No, you can't, Dev. That's the whole point. Confidentiality."

Maud steps forward. "Can I ask who you are?"

"Devon Miller. I'm part of the hospital trust management. I've had a call from one of our benefactors, and I'm afraid I need to—"

I scope out the room. There's another door, and although it will definitely lead me to becoming completely lost, I start edging toward it. Jimmy shifts to block Devon Miller's view of me and Maud holds up her outsized handbag to distract him.

"Well," she says, "I've taken it all now, and I'm taking it home because it belongs to my family."

He focuses on her for a moment, but his eyes snap back to me.

"I'm just going to need to take a look. This benefactor is insistent. Apologies. I'm not quite sure what it's about."

What would Sophie do?

I know what she wouldn't do: she wouldn't stand here quaking.

I take a deep breath, hold the backpack as if it were my first-born child, and run. This is all that matters. There's a corridor and I run down it, pulling my backpack onto my front and holding it with both arms. I am totally lost and I know they'll catch me. All he needs to do is call to someone at the entrance. I run past a porter wheeling a man on a bed.

"Where's the exit?" I call as soon as I'm close to him.

He points down the corridor and says, "Take the stairs on the right. There're signs."

There are footsteps behind me. I overshoot the stairs, run through the next door I see, and find myself in the ladies' toilet. While this gives me a few seconds' breathing space, it's a dead end and a huge mistake. There's no window, and anyway we're too high up. All the stalls are empty. I look in each of them without expecting salvation.

In the end one, hanging on the back of the door, is a white coat.

It's dirty but that doesn't matter. I picture a doctor putting on a clean one, accidentally leaving the old one behind.

Be Sophie be Sophie be Sophie. I get to work tying my hair up, trying to look like a medical student.

∎ ∎ ∎ ∎ ∎

I step back onto the corridor. No one is waiting, so I take the stairs and run all the way down to the basement. There must be a way out from here. I can't go out of the main entrance; it's too dangerous.

This is a teaching hospital, and around a corner I stumble on a group of students. They're wearing white coats too, and I attach myself to the back of them. They ignore me as I follow, holding my backpack, hoping that they're going to leave the building. I listen to what they're saying: "haven't done the assignment," "soooo hungover."

It's frustrating to slow to their pace, and we walk along the basement corridor, following various lines, until they all turn left and head into a little room. I can't do that without being noticed, but one of the lines reads Tower Block, and I remember that's where the pediatric department is, and I remember going there when I was younger and had a twisted ankle.

I remember that there was a door to outside, right at the Tower Block's base. I jog along the line and up some stairs and I see daylight.

∎ ∎ ∎ ∎ ∎

I leave the hospital grounds, cross the road and walk into Homebase, a huge hardware shop. I go to the back of the store and pretend to look at paint colors, texting Maud and Jimmy while cradling my backpack and still wearing an old white coat.

Seven long minutes later, they message me back to say that they're outside Homebase, having convinced Devon Miller that the contents of Maud's handbag (a pack of tissues, photos of Ally and Shabba, a woolen hat, a purple wallet and a hand-knitted scarf) held great sentimental value. I run out, jump into the back of the car and do up my seat belt.

"Is Poppy OK?"

"She's fine," says Jimmy. "Don't worry about her. She does want us to keep in touch, though, and we will."

I open the backpack, peering in. It's all still there.

"Before we leave town," I say, "could you just take me to Dad's old restaurant? It's a long story. Just one thing I have to do. I'll be quick."

This is the last thing in the world I want to do.

55

THE KITCHEN DOOR IS IN A DIRTY ALLEYWAY: IT'S A METAL door, propped open, and a man I don't know is smoking outside. He doesn't stop me going in. I half wish he would.

I stand on the threshold. It smells, and it echoes, and there are lots of men and one woman in here. It's so familiar: I used to come here with Dad before everything went to shit. He would sit me on a countertop and show me how fast he could cut an onion. I never stayed here for long (it was a fast-moving place without much tolerance of children) but I loved it.

I loved it until I met Jasper.

Jimmy and Maud are waiting in the car, round the corner. I have to do this myself.

I am still buzzing from my escape from the hospital. I had to get away and I did. I dress myself in every bit of attitude that I can, and step into the steamy room and look around.

A young man with a red face looks up and makes a *What?* face at me. He's cutting up a hunk of meat.

"Jasper here?" I say. I try to use my casual voice, but it's so loud in here that he can't hear me anyway.

"What?"

"Jasper!" I shout it this time.

He inclines his head and turns his attention back to the meat.

I walk through the kitchen, almost to the pass, and there he is. His back is to me, but I know him at once. I look at the slouch of his shoulders, the way his hair is sticking to the back of his neck in the heat, and I want to run at him and smash his face into the counter. He killed my mum. He killed Honey and nearly me, and before that, he methodically did everything in his power to make my life hell.

The anger takes over. Thank God.

"Jasper."

He looks round. When he sees me, his face changes.

This is not a man who wants to talk to me. He puts his knife down and takes a step back.

"Do we need to talk?"

He shakes his head. The man next to him turns to watch. I stare Jasper out and I see that he has lost his swagger. This is a man who knows he's done terrible things. He's a man who's scared of more retribution coming his way.

He edges away from me and then he's gone. I hear his footsteps running away, and a door closes somewhere.

I turn to leave. As I go, I hear someone shouting: "He's hiding in the fridge!"

I stand outside and send a message.

That message wasn't from J. He was terrified. Shut himself in a fridge.

Sophie replies with laughing emojis but I know she'll be frantically trying to work out who could have sent the message. I sit in the back of the car and photograph all the documents as Jimmy drives me back to the airport. I open my laptop and plug in the memory cards, connect to my hot spot and send all the recordings from them to Sophie too. Then I copy everything to the other e-mail addresses I've been given. It goes out instantly, far and wide.

I've asked Maud and Jimmy to come to Geneva, but neither of them has a passport. They're going to apply for them. I hug both of them and promise to see them soon.

I put my backpack on and walk back through Newquay Airport as the sun starts to set. Although this was my first time consciously traveling by air, I'm already used to it. It was straightforward. Newquay Airport is tiny, and you can see all the planes from the windows of the departure hall; my plane to Manchester is already boarding, so I get straight on it.

I sit back and close my eyes, breathing the stale air, high above parts of England that I'll never visit. I did it. I hope this stuff is as useful as we need it to be, because the idea of going up against VitaNova is scary. I can't stop and think about that, though. If it stops them from doing to Sophie and Tamsyn what they seem to have done to Aurelie, then it's the only thing we can do. Sophie and I are making it up as we go along.

She's the clever one, but I'm precious too. I'm the only "source material" that's "animated."

I remember the man coming for Aurelie.

I imagine him coming for Sophie. For Tamsyn.

Our accident was in November. It's the last day of August today. They'll switch my real mother off in less than three months. I know her injuries are different from mine and she's in a different place, but all the same, I can't stop thinking of her in her own dark, comforting haven, never being able to come back.

I stare at the back of the seat in front of me and try not to

think about the prospect of losing Mum, Sophie and Tamsyn.
Dad had better be real.

▪ ▪ ▪ ▪ ▪

At Manchester I change for the flight to Amsterdam. I am expecting this to mean I sit in a chair, maybe drink a mediocre hot
chocolate and then get on another plane.

It's not like that, though. I have to go through all the security again. I put my backpack of treasure through the scanner
and grab it the moment it comes out. At passport control a
stern woman with tattooed eyebrows looks at my passport for a
long time.

She looks up at me. She looks down at the passport. She
scans it on a machine that beeps, and she looks at me again.

How far does VitaNova reach?

If they know what I've got, could they have me stopped here?
I pull my backpack off my back and hold it tight with both arms.
My heart is pounding. I'm expecting to be handcuffed, taken
away, my bag removed and blown up. I hear my breathing going
weird and try to calm it.

In the end the woman speaks. Her voice is husky.

"Traveling alone?" she says.

I nod. She shrugs and hands me back my passport.

"Have a good trip."

▪ ▪ ▪ ▪ ▪

I message Sophie from the departure gate. We use a secure messaging app, which apparently means VitaNova won't be able to
read the message unless they have spyware on Sophie's phone,
which they probably do, except that she's not using her usual
phone. She's using her new, secret one.

> **At Manchester. About to board.**
> **All fine. You?**

I look at my message. It's not very twinlike. I add an **x** to the end. She replies at once.

> **Got all the info. Have contacted our**
> **hacker who isn't Jasper. Waiting to see**
> **what happens there. S—I can't find**
> **Mum. Will let you know when she turns**
> **up. See you at G xxxx**

Can't find Mum. I know she means Tamsyn, because we both know where to find Honey. I also know that she wouldn't have said that if she hadn't been properly worried. Now that Sophie isn't living her whole life obsessively trying to kill me, I feel that I understand her a bit. And I know that she wants to get me back safely above everything else. She would definitely not have told me about Tamsyn if she hadn't been frantic.

I have a bad feeling about Tamsyn.

I don't reply, because it's time to get on the plane.

56

THE HACKER LEFT A LINK, WHICH I HAVE, OF COURSE, SAVED.
I leave the apartment and walk quickly to the middle of the city
before I take out my second burner phone, which is entirely
blank and unconnected to my life in every way, and type the link
into the browser.

I want to kill Scarlett.

I *don't* want to kill Scarlett. I mustn't kill her.

Even though I know that I was programmed to feel this, that
it's fake, I can't switch it off. I'm just going to have to unprogram
myself, and meanwhile, at least she's not here. I do not want to
harm Scarlett. I have to protect her because she's my sister, my
twin, myself.

I'm sitting on a bench, aware of the shoppers going by with all
their bags. There's a crepe van nearby and it smells lovely. Mc-
Donald's is over to one side. It's sunny, and people look happy.

The page loads and I'm in a chat box.

Why do you want to talk?

> To help you. Meet me?

No.

> Seriously. I have a lot to tell you.

Hello? I'm here. In your chat
thing. Feel free to tell me.

> Do you have sunglasses?

???

I look up, annoyed, as someone comes to sit beside me on the
bench, engrossed in their phone. I stand up, ready to move away,
but he says, "Sophie? Don't look at me."

I look back at the screen. A new message comes up.

I put the phone away and put on my sunglasses.

"Is it you?" I say.

"They're still watching through your eyes. But you don't have
a mic on you. They can see what you see but they can listen in
only if you have your official phone. Tell me you don't."

"I don't. I *thought* they were doing that."

My sunglasses are lightly tinted and won't make any difference but it gives me something to do with my hands while I try
to work out why the hell I believed Johann when he pretended to
deactivate my eye cameras because I deserved privacy. The bastard. I should have known better. I'm so angry with them, with

myself, with everything. Fuck this. I never questioned it. I should have.

"Who are you?" I look at the crowd, at the crepe van, across to McDonald's. Everywhere apart from at him.

"My name's Quinn. I want to help you. I'm going to walk past so you can see me, but make sure you only glance at me in passing, OK? Focus on someone else. There's a gym-bunny guy over to the right. Look at him."

He stands up and walks off. I watch the people passing by. A group of teenage girls with shopping bags. A man running, dripping sweat. The sun is relentless.

A man in his twenties wanders past, talking (or fake talking) on his phone. He has black hair and heavy-framed glasses and he's wearing a bright Hawaiian shirt and a pair of bright pink shorts.

I realize that I've seen that face before. I've seen him around. I've seen him near home, and I've seen him near school too. I look away and focus on the gym guy who has long blond hair and serious muscles. I stare at him for ages.

Quinn sits back down.

"Who," I say, "are you?"

"I want to help you," he says. "You need to get away."

. . . . .

We go to McDonald's and sit with our backs to each other at separate tables upstairs. I have fries and a milkshake, and I have no idea what Quinn has because I can't look. He tells me he works for an investigative website.

"We've been looking at VN for months," he says, talking to the wall. "I mean, it took me ages to get my head round it. What they're doing. Mind-blowing."

"Um, yes," I say, sipping my milkshake. "I know. Look, are you actually from another tech company?"

"I'm not. I can see why you'd think that."

"You've tried to talk to me before," I say, "haven't you? And Mum."

"Yeah. I swiftly realized that you were too tightly controlled for me to do that without them knowing about it. They're paranoid, with good reason. Shady as fuck, if I may say so."

I sigh. "I'd say so too, if I could."

I explain that I can't swear. He laughs and tries to coach me to do it. As ever, it doesn't work.

"Sorry! So we have two solid sources who are ready to break away and tell us everything. One already has. And it's looking bad, I have to say. It seems to us that they feel you guys are getting too clever for them, and the solution that smarmy bastard has come up with is to downgrade the ones he feels are surplus to requirements or who are being difficult, and 'disappear' the ones who have really fucked him off. Like your neighbor?"

"Aurelie! Yes! She was literally talking to us and then . . ." I think of the man taking her away and shudder. I can't say it. I wish I could look at him, but all I can do is stare down into my fries.

"I'm sorry about what they did to her."

I decide not to ask what he knows.

"Were her eye cameras on too?" I say instead.

"Yeah. She used to go out Internet dating. They loved that. She didn't know they were watching." He pauses, then says, "It's not just her. They rounded up a whole load of them at the same time."

I don't ask where she is, where they are, because I know the answer, really. The basement. Poor Aurelie.

Even though I half think he's from VitaNova, sent to test my loyalty, I still talk to him because I have to share this with some-one. I tell him about Scarlett's mission, about Jasper and the way we assumed that it was Jasper who hacked us because of the timing. I tell him about everything Scarlett sent me, but in spite of his entreaties, I don't send it over to him because of course I don't. Equally, he doesn't tell me the name of his website or his sources.

Then he lowers his voice as far as it's possible to lower your voice while sitting in McDonald's and talking to someone behind your back. He tells me more, and it's worse than I ever imagined. It's much worse than anything. I understand now why all those presents appeared all the time. I understand a lot of things. I don't want to, but I do. I feel utterly violated and it takes every-thing I have to keep control of myself. I want to go straight to VitaNova and burn their building to the ground.

▪ ▪ ▪ ▪ ▪

I stand up, taking the rest of my fries with me. I sense him stand-ing too but I still manage not to look.

"I have to get out of here. I need to find my mother. You be careful."

"*You* be careful." Quinn is deadly serious. "Don't worry about me. They already know that I'm after them. You shouldn't go there. If you have to run, run to France."

"I can't go to France," I point out, walking down the stairs beside him. "I'm totally illegal there. In much more danger."

He reaches a hand down and finds mine. Even though he's a stranger, I appreciate the solidarity; he gives me something be-tween a handshake and a squeeze that lasts all the way down the stairs.

"They program you to think that," he says. "This city is sur-rounded by France on three sides. It keeps you where they can see you. Of course you can go to France. Their tech is illegal there, sure. The French government isn't going to kill you if they find you. They're going to help you. They'd do their best to go after VN. Go to France and you'll be safer. You'll be protected."

I tell him the number of my empty phone. He gives me his details too.

Then, even though I know this is the very last thing I should do, I set off to VitaNova to find my mother.

57

TAMSYN HAD BEEN AT THE CLINIC FOR A LONG TIME. SHE didn't know how long, but she knew that she'd followed Maya to fetch a bottle of water that she didn't even want, and things had escalated. She'd felt things changing inside her head and then she didn't care about anything anymore.

She'd got what she wanted. She was in one of those rooms at the clinic. It was like Scarlett's old room, like Honey's room, except that instead of the blue or the yellow, things were green. If she was there, did that mean Honey was taking her place? Scarlett would like that.

No. Of course it didn't mean that.

She closed her eyes and tried to find Scarlett's safe place. While she was looking, everything she knew disappeared.

The door was open. She could hear a man's voice outside, and she could see the side of a woman standing in the doorway. The man said: "If she's still being difficult, let me know and we'll do it again."

"Of course," said the woman. "How long are we giving it?"

"A week?"

The woman came back in and gasped when she saw Tamsyn was awake. She rushed over and sat beside the bed. She was wearing, Tamsyn thought, a lovely dress.

"Tamsyn," she said. "Great! Do you know who I am?"

She shook her head.

"That's fine. My name's Maya and I'm here to help you. How do you feel?"

She was trying to look into Tamsyn's eyes. Tamsyn looked at the ceiling, the wall, the place where the ceiling met the wall, but in the end, she had to look back. Maya's eyes were dark brown.

"Great," said Maya. "Now, can you get up? There are some clothes for you here. That door's the bathroom. Why don't you go and shower and then get changed? You'll find everything you're going to need in there."

Tamsyn had a shower. She changed into the clothing they had put out for her. It was a black dress and it fitted perfectly.

Maya was still sitting in the chair. "Do you remember who you are?" she said.

"Tamsyn," she said.

"And do you know why you're here?"

"My purpose is to help with research." She didn't know where those words had come from, but there they were. "I have no other purpose."

"Yes," said Maya. She took a deep breath and carried on. "This is just a reset. You'll be back to your old self soon. We're tweaking you, and in a few days, you'll be ready to be fired up again. For now you just need to stay here. Maybe you'd like to watch the television?"

Maya turned it on with a hand movement and it flicked into life. "Find whatever you want," she said.

Tamsyn nodded and took the remote control. She settled back on the bed to watch.

Maya stood up to leave, but before she went, she said, "Is there— Well, is there anyone you feel you'd like to talk to?"

Tamsyn tried to think. She couldn't think of anyone. She looked out the window instead. It was cloudy, but there was a ray of light coming down between the clouds, shining onto the city.

"This city looks so pretty in the sun," she said.

58

I CALL DAD. HE SAYS THAT HE'S NEARLY AT THE CLINIC, THAT he's looking for Mum.

"I'll be there in ten," I say. "Don't go in without me. This is all really bad, Dad. We shouldn't go, but Mum's there, so we have to."

"Soph!" he says. "Don't. If it's bad for you, you need to stay away. Let me go in."

He has no idea. Dad was literally going to go in there and ask if they know where she is. I convince him to wait and pick him up from the café opposite, pausing while I'm there to send all Scarlett's information to Quinn. I'm scared. I'm acting on instinct and I hope it's the right thing to do. I wish I had time to confer with Scarlett or Lena, but I don't.

I want to hurt Scarlett. Could I use the VitaNova incinerator? No! She's on my side: my sister, my twin, myself.

"Where's Scarlett?" says Dad.

"At the movies with Amina."

He doesn't question it. "Good. Let's keep her out of it."

"Mum's almost definitely in there."

I think of the basement. They wouldn't do that to her, would they? No. She's successful. She's the wife and mother, like Aurelie said. The prototype. They'll just have tweaked her to stop her being mad at them and Dad. Then they'll send her back to us.

Won't they?

Dad forces a smile. "So we'll just pick her up," he says, "and take her home?"

The connection is back, though it's shaky. I try to find Lena in my head.

Dad and I are going in.

She comes back soon. *I'm nearby. I don't think you should be doing this, Sophie.*

I know. Lots to say. I'll let you know if I find her.

Tell me if you need backup.

I walk over to the security guard at the reception desk and say, "Hi! We're here to see Tamsyn Trelawney."

My heart is thumping madly but I try very hard to assume some attitude. I look the man in the eye, wondering whether he's one of Quinn's sources. If he is, he doesn't betray a thing.

My cameras have been on all along. I burn with hate.

He taps something on his screen and tells us to wait.

Lena says there are only four of us left on her network: the other two are Noah, from my school, and someone I don't know, a woman called Isabelle who's twenty-three. She's the one who spoke to me on the mountain that day. Everyone older has vanished. Including Tamsyn, though she'd only popped up on the network a couple of times.

In spite of what Aurelie said, I know they could take me to the basement. I feel my knees wobbling and wonder whether this is stupid. Should I leave while we still can?

The security guard looks up.

"Someone's coming to collect you," he says.

. . . . .

Johann's office is weirdly full of vases of flowers and paintings of trees, but apart from that it's high tech. Maya and Johann are sitting at a big shiny table, and Luca comes in and joins them, a laptop open in front of him. Some people in lab coats hover in the background. There's a screen filling one wall and a hum of machinery. There's no sign of any medical equipment, but there's a door behind them.

"Right, Sophie, Ed," says Johann, "good to see you. Thanks for coming in. We were about to send a car for you."

"Where's Tamsyn?"

"Take a seat," says Maya, and I sit down, facing them across the table like an interviewee. Dad sits next to me, though no one's even looking at him. "Sophie, we need to talk to you. This is serious."

"I know it is," I say. "Where's Tamsyn?"

Luca speaks. "She's fine, Sophie," he says. "She's here, and she's safe and well. She'll be back with you in a couple of days."

Dad squeezes my hand. I squeeze back.

"She was malfunctioning," says Johann. He looks as if he wants to say more, but gives a little smile and stops. He leans forward. "But she'll be fine. I promise. Just a few tweaks. Nothing sinister. However, Sophie, can you tell me something? Forgive me if I jump straight to the point. What were you doing in a fast-food restaurant on your own after replying to some very cryptic messages? We have reason to suspect you were with a person who is trying to destroy our work. It's not your fault, but we need to keep you safe from him."

I stare at him. He stares back. I try hard not to blink. In the end he looks away first: a minor victory. I can always do that.

"I don't know what you mean." I beam a question to Lena and wait.

"Sebastian Quinn. He's a conspiracy theorist and someone hell-bent on destroying what we've done here. He managed to hack into your building's Wi-Fi and message you a few days ago. You went into the city center, used a new phone and followed up on his contact. He walked past you sometime later. You went for fries and a milkshake. What did you talk about?"

"I don't know what you mean."

"Sophie."

That is the confirmation. I believe everything Quinn told me. I close my eyes and keep them closed.

"You never switched off my eye cameras," I say into the darkness. "You lied. And all the rest of them have eye cameras too, including Mum. You give us top-of-the-range phones and use them to listen to us."

Their silence says it all.

Dad starts to shout, but Maya jumps in and speaks over him.

"Sophie," she says, and I remember Aurelie saying that all the niceness is fake. Is it, though? Could she secretly be on our side? "Soph, you're amazing, OK? We're so proud of you. I need you to look at me, darling."

I open my eyes because I hate her calling me *darling* and I need to glare.

"Thank you. I'm truly sorry. We didn't mean to deceive you. We just needed a bit more data but we didn't want you to feel constrained by being watched. So we did keep the cameras on, but we only refer to them when we need to. You do have privacy most of the time."

I don't answer.

Dad does, though. "This is totally out of order!" he says, and Johann smiles.

"Ed," he says. "Come on, my friend. You've accepted a huge amount of money quite happily. A new home, a new life. We've rescued you from the shit. We've returned your dead child to you twice, as well as your wife. We've given you everything. It's a bit harsh to call us *out of order*."

Dad doesn't let that distract him. "You told her you'd turned them off. And you haven't! That's totally unethical. And you promised me Tamsyn had privacy. We— Oh, God. You've watched everything. What else have you been doing? Who are you?"

Johann shrugs. "As I said," he says, "make sure you weigh up the fact that we've treated you like royalty."

I step in before Dad can argue back.

"Do we have to be grateful forever, Johann? Does that mean you can do whatever you want? I didn't meet any conspiracy theorist but I have found out some interesting things. Like, for example, where those presents come from."

I turn to Dad and address the next bit to him. It's hard to say. "Dad, they have investors. People who want to put money into this technology, people who want to buy themselves wives like Tamsyn or children like me. And the investors pay for private links so they can watch us. They watch us through all the cameras in the apartment and probably through our eyes too."

I look round. Johann meets my gaze. He looks amused. Maya is staring at the table. Luca flashes me a look and then looks away.

"They send us those presents. All those presents that show up come from rich people who watch us like we're their reality TV." It unravels in my head as I say it. I can see it. "They send clothes, particularly to me and Mum. Then they get to watch us wearing them. Sorry to say this, but they must love it if you and Mum are, you know, intimate."

Dad half stands. "Is this true?"

"You signed away your rights to privacy," says Johann. "And as I said, you took our money."

Lena's voice says, *Agree to everything and pretend to be submissive. Get out of the building.*

I look at Johann. He'd take us to the basement without a second thought. He'd kill Dad as well as me. I know he would. He might already have done it to Tamsyn, whatever he says. He'd leave Scarlett all alone in the world.

It's the vision of Scarlett alone and bereft that gives me the strength to do it. I hate her but I love her, and I harness the love to power me through.

"You did actually, Dad."

I give it everything I've got. I act being crushed. I act as if I am realizing that Johann is right: they took us out of poverty and gave us a new, luxurious life. It kills me to do it, but I act grateful. Since I know they have my eye feed, I reach into my bag and take out the phone. I open a message and type without looking at it.

> **We can't go back to Cornwall. He's right. If we want to keep this life we have to sacrifice a few things. I wouldn't exist without them. It sucks but we owe them dad.**

I glance down for long enough to check that the words have come out right, and for just long enough for them to pause the footage and read them; then I nudge dad and push it onto his knee. I see him look at the message and frown.

I need him to go along with this. I need VitaNova to think I've written it as a private message. I want them to be pleased with themselves when they manage to read it and see what I actually think.

I kick Dad's ankle hard, out of shot.

Dad looks at me. He looks sad. I try to convey my message through my eyes.

"I hate it." I look at Johann. "But I know I don't have the power to change anything, and I guess the life you give us compensates."

"But—"

I kick Dad again.

Luca steps in. "Sophie, thank you. I'm so glad you can see it. Now . . ." He looks at Maya for confirmation, then back at me. "Do you think you can go back to the apartment and stay there? Just live your life there with Scarlett and your dad until we've fixed Tamsyn up? Don't even leave the building. We'll bring you everything you need. This is for your own safety. I promise, it's all going to be fine. A project like this is always going to have bumps on the road. We never expect it to go as smoothly as it has for you guys so far. And that business about the investors? It's pure conspiracy theory, Sophie. There's not a grain of truth in it, so please, forget it. It's malicious lies."

"Fixed her up?" says Dad.

"Do you promise?" I say.

Luca and Maya both nod. Maya speaks.

"We'll give you security at the apartment. Keep the bad people away."

"Keep us in, more like," says Dad.

Johann is staring at me. "Really, Sophie? You'll back down? That was quite the U-turn."

I shrug and give it everything I have.

"I know when I'm beaten," I mutter. "It's logical. You made me to be logical, and when I look at what we've got from you, and the price we've paid for it, which so far is very little compared to what you've done for us, then yes. We need to accept it. And I'm going to believe Luca on the investor stuff because I want to. I really, really want it not to be true. Can we go home?"

"You can," says Johann. "We'll get a driver for you, and he'll escort you right into the building. And when you——"

Maya puts a hand on his arm to stop him.

"As Luca says, it's best if you stick around at the apartment for a while," she says, her voice extra syrupy. "You've got everything you need. We can keep an eye on you. We'll deliver anything you want. We'll bring Tamsyn over in a few days."

Luca stands up. "I'm going to escort you there myself," he says. "Into the living room. Just to be sure no one intercepts you."

Johann looks at him for a few seconds, then nods.

"Ungrateful shits," he says loudly as we leave the room.

59

I CAN'T LOOK AT DAD AS WE LEAVE THE ROOM. I JUST HOPE that Quinn's managed to download that information, because Dad's recordings might be the only thing that's escaped VN and their control freakery. They are the only evidence we have that the project exists at all.

Since I'm sure that at least VitaNova can't hear my thoughts, I focus. *Fuck you,* I tell them. At least I can think it, even if I can't say it.

I'm sorry. What? It's Lena.

Oh, not you. Sorry. I was just thinking that at least Johann can't listen to my thoughts. I did what you said. We're going back to the apartment and I think they're going to lock us in. They have no idea where Scarlett is. I don't think they've even noticed she's missing. They just think of her as a helpless invalid, I guess.

See? We told you to keep her safe.

I won't be able to meet Quinn tomorrow. I won't be able to meet Scarlett at the airport. I'll be imprisoned in the apartment. As we walk down the stairs, I cast my mind back to all the times I thought I had privacy in my own life. All the time they were watching. Not just Johann, but the shadowy investors too. The people who watch us on the dark web. People who sent me clothes they wanted me to wear. I remember that pink dress that someone sent me the day before I went to school and want to be sick. The hot tub. I've never felt more like a product for sale.

I shudder so violently that I almost fall down the stairs.

Luca puts a hand on my shoulder in the foyer.

I stop. "What?"

He whispers, "Close your eyes."

I look at him. He speaks loudly.

"Fine! You can use the bathrooms through here before you go. Ed, wait here a second. We'll be back."

"No," says Dad.

Luca's being weird, I tell Lena, and then, because at least he's not Johann, I close my eyes. I feel his hand on my shoulder as he guides me through the black door. I hear Dad moving with us. Then I feel a blindfold being tied around my head.

Luca puts something over my head and taps at a keyboard nearby. I can hear things extra sharply now. Someone drops something far away. There is a vibration beneath my feet. The basement? Don't think about it. Dad starts to say something but Luca stops him. It takes maybe ten minutes and I hardly dare breathe.

Luca. Either he's destroying me, or he's on our side. If he's on our side, he's one of Quinn's sources.

I hope he's deactivating my eye cameras. I remember what Aurelie told us. I know he could take me downstairs. Have they performed whatever this is on Tamsyn too?

Any second now, my world might end. He tried to leave Dad in the foyer so he could do this in secret. I could shout out and alert someone but I don't, because all I know is that this is happening behind Johann's back. And so, on balance, I'm going to give it a chance.

60

I THOUGHT SOPHIE AND DAD WERE GOING TO MEET ME AT the airport, but when I land late in the morning and check my phone, there's a message from an unknown number telling me to leave the airport by the left-hand door and go to the corner of the car park. It ends with the scream emoji, which is code for *There's drama and I'll explain*, so I do it with some misgivings.

There's a small black car parked in the farthest space, and when I approach, its engine starts and it reverses out, stopping next to me. Dad winds down the driver's window.

"Hop in," he says. "And by the way, never ever leave the country without telling me ever again."

The back door opens and there is Sophie. I jump in and Dad's driving away before I've even closed the door. She leans over to hug me as I put on my seat belt, and it's an awkward clashing of limbs but all the same just what I needed.

Then I see her face.

"What's happened?"

"Shhh," says Lena, turning round from the front seat. She turns up the car radio.

"Where's Tamsyn?"

"Hold on."

It's eleven o'clock, and the news is on the radio. It's in French, so I don't understand it very well: it's something about the lake. I watch Sophie's face and am surprised when it crumples.

"It's him," she says. "Shit! They've fucking killed him."

I watch her trying to compose herself, and then she turns to me.

"Quinn. The guy who hacked us. I was meant to meet him again today but he's gone quiet and I couldn't get hold of him. There was a body in the fountain in the lake early this morning, and it just said they've identified him. Sebastian Quinn. They murdered him."

"Oh, my God." I don't know what to say. There's so much I don't know.

"He'd gathered all the information. I transferred Dad's recordings and he had enough to go public, and they must have known it. What can we do?"

"We can get out of here," says Lena.

"Let's get out of town," says Dad, pulling out of the car park, "and work it out from there."

"You just said fu—" I begin, but it turns into a scream.

Dad and Lena shout too, the brakes screech and we stop suddenly. I've only just got my seat belt on, and it yanks me back, gasping.

There's someone on the bonnet of the car. A body appears from nowhere and crashes into us, and a face is on the windscreen. I can't stop: I scream and scream and scream. A car hitting a girl. No. Not this. No no no no no.

Sophie holds me until I stop. She's breathing fast and her face is pale. Dad swears a lot.

The person on the front of the car climbs down, moves her limbs around and opens the back door.

"Hi," she says. "I'm Delphine. I work with Quinn. Can I get in?"

I can't look at her. I can't focus. The sound her body made when she hit the car. The fact that Honey has never woken up. I feel Sophie shift up next to me, and the new woman is in, and the door is shut. I see that she is older than me and Sophie, and that her hair is bright orange, and she's wearing Lycra. I look away. I feel clammy, shaky.

"You've got thirty seconds," says Dad, starting the car again. I can see, even from the back of his head, that he is shaky too. "Who are you? What was that?"

"Drive, Ed," says Lena, and he does.

There are some jumpy gear changes, and I can see the sweat forming on the back of his neck.

My head is ringing, and for the first time in a while, I want to go back to the safe place. I feel its pull and close my eyes. I could go back. It would be easy.

"Scarlett!" Sophie is shaking my shoulder, and I open my eyes and look at her, guilty. "Please stay with us."

"Sorry." I tune in as best I can.

Delphine and Sophie switch to English for Dad and me. I tune in slowly, as nothing else bad happens, and my heart rate returns to normal.

"They must have grabbed him off the street," she's saying. "He was walking over to mine. I don't even know how they knew."

"That's my fault," says Sophie at once. "They'd told me they'd switched off my eye cameras, but they hadn't. It was a lie, and it meant they could see everything I saw. He made sure I didn't look at him when we met, but they'd seen the messages. They already knew about him, and he walked past me so I could see who he was."

"Shit."

"I know. I don't think they could hear without the phone they gave me."

Sophie breathes heavily and I take her hand. This is all-new information. I don't know anything. Her cameras were still on?

"I'm pretty sure the cameras don't work now. Luca deactivated them."

"Luca Holgate?"

Sophie nods.

"Yeah. He will have done. He's with us," says Delphine, and she looks as if she's struggling too. "So here's what we're going to do for Quinn. He shared everything with me, so we're going to publish and lie very fucking low." She leans forward and looks at me. "You're Scarlett?" She looks to Dad. "And you're Ed? So yeah, the things we've got from you are the things that make this possible. Everything else is allegations from careful anonymous sources, and so the authorities will dismiss it. This is voice recordings of VitaNova staff explaining what's going to happen. Explaining what they want you to believe, anyway. This is the evidence."

It's all too much again. I can't take it in. I just say, "OK," and I lean my head on the window, and this time I let it pull me all the way down.

∎ ∎ ∎ ∎ ∎

I wake up with Sophie gripping my arm. It takes me a while to realize that we're crossing the French border.

"France?" I'm confused.

"Sorry, darling," says Dad, looking round. "We've brought as many of your things as we could."

Sophie is leaning back and breathing deeply, and in the front, Lena is doing the same. They are both sweating.

"But—" I stare at Sophie. She winces and nods. "But you

can't go to France!" I look back at Lena. "You and Sophie. You're not allowed."

"We are. It's just difficult." Sophie's voice is tight.

Dad takes up the thread. "Turns out, they were programmed to hate the idea of going to France or to any European Union countries. The technology VitaNova uses is massively illegal there, so they programmed them to keep them where they could see them. Of course they're not illegal in France. We're here, guys, by the way. It's done. It's VitaNova who'd be in trouble because human cloning is extremely banned in all circumstances. The French state will support us."

Sophie opens her eyes and loosens her grip on me.

"They made us think," she says, "that if we put one foot over the border, French people would round us up and kill us. It turns out they won't. I mean, you saw what it was like. We didn't need to stop and show passports, let alone go through some kind of— I don't know. Clone scanner?"

"Bastards."

"I know! So Lena and I feel weird when we cross over, but we can deal with it, as you just saw. The older clones worked that out, but it was actually Mum who showed me that we can do it. When she found out about everything, she started being angry like Honey. She really struggled, didn't she? And so we saw that just because they program us to do something, it doesn't mean the human part of us can't overcome it." She starts to say something else, then stops.

"Where is Tamsyn?"

"Later," whispers Sophie.

Lena turns round. "It's why your dad has to drive," she says. "I can't do it. But if we're passengers, it just happens, and once we get here, we're OK. See? We had a trial run last night. We slept over here and we only came back to pick you up." She inhales sharply. "And to see Quinn."

Delphine and Sophie go back to their planning and I tune out. My trip to Cornwall has exhausted me. Seeing Jasper. Spending time with Maud again. The ocean, the heavy sky. Escaping through the hospital. I let my mind drift back.

An hour later we pull up a drive with lots of signs reading PRIVÉE along it. The sun is golden in the sky. A little way along the drive are a tall fence and a set of iron gates casting black shadows on the long grass. Dad slows the car and the gates swing open. Then we're driving again, the track winding uphill, and then, past some trees, we pull up in front of a huge house.

It is a square stone building with lots of windows, which have wrought iron window boxes and balconies filled with dying flowers and dead plants. There is a HOTEL sign next to it, which looks as if it has been taken down and leaned against the wall. It feels creepy.

"Here we are!" says Sophie. "Right, Scarlett. This is our new home. We're going to bring down VitaNova, and I'm going to explain everything."

■ ■ ■ ■ ■

Someone is waiting for us outside the house. She looks different wearing a long red dress, with her hair loose, but I'd know her smile anywhere. She's sitting on the doorstep, but when she sees us, she stands up.

I am out of the car before the engine is off. I don't have Honey, and I don't know what's happened to Tamsyn, and Maud can't come until she's got her passport, but there is one other person who can fill the mother-shaped gap in my life, and she is here, waiting for me. I run into Dr. Singh's arms.

61

Six months later

SHE SAVED ME AND I SAVED HER.

She saved me because I would have been dead long ago if it hadn't been for the possibility of Sophie. I would never have left the hospital in Truro.

I saved her because I went back to Cornwall, even though I was scared, and got the documents that led Sophie, Lena and Delphine to write a properly evidenced exposé of VitaNova. It caused uproar. Johann and Maya did a flit in the night but they didn't get far, and it's safe to say that the liberties they took with the law are so immense that it's not going to end well for them.

Luca and Dr. Singh (who I usually remember to call Jasveen, though she'll always be Dr. Singh to me really) were Quinn and Delphine's main whistleblowers, and they'd been riskily exchanging heavily encrypted messages for a few weeks before Quinn died. Jasveen resigned in the middle of it. She lives here with us now, though she's moving to the US in about a month. I'm going to miss her, but I know I have to recognize that she's not my mother and that I don't get to make her live with me in a remote old hotel in France just because I crave a mum.

As for my other mothers, we have lost Honey completely, as her life support was switched off by the time the police entered the VitaNova building. She's gone, but they allowed us to retrieve her body, and we had a small ceremony. That's made everything feel better in a way. She was cremated (here in France, not in the basement), and her ashes are scattered in this garden. Poor Mum. I feel a sense of peace, though, that I didn't have before. And poor Aurelie, who was never found.

Maud is here with us. She arrived on a train as soon as she could get a passport. I love having her and Jimmy here. We feel like a family.

And Tamsyn is with us too. Tamsyn, in fact, is the issue.

■ ■ ■ ■ ■

It's snowing today. I walk across the entrance hall, my feet slipping around in fluffy socks. I'm following the sounds of voices, but I know everyone is in the huge dining room. I stop outside the half-open door, but they're talking French, and even though I'm working on it, the conversation is too fast for me to follow.

The New Ones are sitting around a big table they've made by pushing six little ones together. They look like a bunch of people in a school canteen but they are, I think, the most amazing mutation of the human race. I'm glad that, in my own reanimated state, I am a part of their story. They sense me standing there and it goes quiet, but I just smile, wave to Sophie and walk away.

There are twenty of us living here. Sophie and me, Dad, Lena and two other New Ones plus their families. A boy called Noah, who Sophie knows from school, and a woman, Isabelle, who we didn't know before. Isabelle is incredibly clever: she was the one who created the New Ones' internal network, even though it was too late to save most of them from Johann. She's our leader. And, of course, we have Maud, Jimmy and Dr. Singh, and Tamsyn.

There were twenty-four New Ones. Now twenty have been downgraded or killed, and four are left. Tamsyn, downgraded, has been with us since the police rescued her, and while I try to avoid her because it's too difficult for me, Sophie spends hours on end talking to her. I know what she wants to do, and I'm half trying to stop her, but my heart isn't in it and she knows that.

The New Ones have officially agreed never to use VitaNova's technology again. They will be a blip, rather than the future of the human race. Perhaps one day it will happen again under tight regulations that would stop people from creating slaves and whatever else VitaNova was planning. Maybe they'll need to evolve with AI to reverse climate change, or to live with it, or to colonize space, but for now it's too risky. They've all agreed that, but there's one weak spot in the whole thing, and that's Tamsyn. Tamsyn, and Sophie.

Because I know Sophie well enough to know that she's not ready to give up on this technology, when it's the one thing that could bring Tamsyn back. Tamsyn's the only mother she's ever known, and Sophie will do anything to get her back.

Anything.

▪ ▪ ▪ ▪ ▪

This place is different from our old, too perfect apartment. The entrance hall is tiled, and there's a reception desk, which, today, has a tray of brownies on it. I wander over and take one, knowing that they must have come from Dad. There are fifty bedrooms here. Dad, Sophie and I have three rooms on the third floor, with a view across the valley, away from Switzerland. Lena is downstairs, and everyone else is set up in their own space. Tamsyn sleeps in the room next to Sophie's. There are no cameras here.

▪▪▪▪▪

Shortly before most of them were downgraded, the New Ones bought the hotel and everything in it with money they'd made through the financial markets and in insurance. They have ditched the name *reanimation,* as it was given to them by VitaNova. For the moment, the New Ones has stuck, though Sophie says it'll change into something more concrete at some point.

The first of those fires that were in the local news was made by one of them, Enzo (disappeared), who was angry when he worked out that he had been cloned without his consent and expressed it by rampaging around and burning things down. Enzo evolved out of it pretty quickly and realized that every time he burned something, its owner collected insurance money, so he turned his attention in that direction. It developed from there. He's gone, but we have access to the money and to various other funds that other New Ones set up before they vanished.

We have the money Sophie took from Jasper: it's not much but it's pleasing.

We have the money Lena, Sophie, Isabelle and Noah are making from trading and other things. The four of them make cash in a seemingly effortless way now by tapping on their computers. I have no idea.

▪▪▪▪▪

They've all agreed that they will be the only clones. Although they could easily pick up VN's science, they're not going to. Sophie and Tamsyn were evolving fast at the time we lived in Geneva: the nonhuman parts of their brains were learning from their surroundings and understanding things in a way that my normal brain never will. And now I see Sophie and Lena spinning away from me and Dad.

I'm glad I saw Jasper: the expression on his face when he saw me, before he ran into the fridge, changed everything. Now I know I'll never hear from him again, no matter what. He's from the past.

■ ■ ■ ■ ■

"Can I get you anything?"

I look round. It's Tamsyn. Maya had shut her down to reset her, to make her back into the perfect compliant wife and mother, but everything blew up before the process finished. She's stuck in between as some kind of blank housekeeper cyborg who doesn't really know us. That's why Sophie can't leave things as they are.

"No, thanks, Tamsyn," I say.

She gives me a warm but distant smile. "Just let me know if you do."

And she bustles away. She acts like a housekeeper, and she looks like my mother. It's weird for me, but it's worse for Sophie.

All our coats are in the hotel's old cloakroom, so I go and find mine, and step into a pair of boots. As I'm going out, Maud is coming in, stamping snow off her shoes, her cheeks red. I let Jesse, her new dog, jump up at me. Jesse was a stray who started hanging around: he's small and brown and much easier company than Shabba used to be.

"Nice walk?" I say, and she nods.

"I could look at the snow all day. So could this one. Came in to warm up, though. Your dad said he was making soup. I guess I'll go and help."

She hesitates, then fixes me with her intense eyes and says, "Scarlett. Darling girl. I was just out there, looking at the mountains, the snow and this home of ours. And I was thinking about Honey."

She walks over to a chair and sits down. I sit next to her and wait.

"She's here with us, you know. I feel her presence. I love it that she's scattered out there. And I know she would be so proud of you. I know you had a difficult time that last year. But she always adored you. If she could see you now, she would hug you so hard. She loved you fiercely through everything, my darling."

I have to try very hard not to cry. Maud is right: when I thought Tam was Mum, I felt that the year when I was struggling with Jasper was closed. We had got past it. But we never did, because the last time I saw Honey, my real mother, awake was when I stole the van key out of her hand and ran away.

"I wish it could have been different," I say.

Maud knows about Jasper because I had to tell her everything after that visit to the kitchen. Dad doesn't, and he never will.

"Everyone has regrets," she says. "Everyone. Always. The key is to look around you. Look at what you have. You have your dad. You have Sophie." Maud smiles. She is a big fan of Sophie. "And me, and your uncle Jim, not to mention Lena, Noah and Isabelle, plus the actual doctor who did the real miracle and brought you back to life. And you're Honey's daughter. She lives on in you, my darling. Just live your life. That's all she would ever have wanted. And we do have Tamsyn to remind us of her, I suppose. Poor Tam."

"You know you said she'd hug me so hard?" My voice comes out small.

Maud nods and leans over and gives me that hug from my mother, from beyond the grave.

"Thanks," I say, wiping my eyes with the back of my hand.

"On your way out to play in the snow?"

I nod.

Snow is falling hard. Everything looks magical and white. I look back at my footprints. The world is fresh. Anything could happen. I find Jim around the corner, chopping firewood.

"Hey, Jim," I say.

He looks up and grins.

"Why are you doing that in a blizzard?"

He shrugs. "It's fun, though I'm stopping now. Enough's enough."

I don't think Jimmy's going to stay around much longer. He's restless. He wants to travel. We are his family, and now that he knows we're OK, I can see how much he wants to explore the landscape around us. But he's here for the moment. He puts down his ax.

"I'm just looking at the snow."

"Yeah," he says. "Pure magic."

I walk on, across the white garden, toward the trees at the back. When I get there, I turn and look at the back of the building. It's so solid, so safe. Someone is standing at a window and I wave. Then I lean down and pick up a handful of snow. I look at it and press it into a snowball. I shape it.

She arrives exactly when I expected her, wearing a coat, woolly hat, boots and gloves, running across the white lawn toward me. As soon as she's close enough, I throw the snowball at her, and she throws one back. We run around like little children, throwing snowballs at each other, laughing, running, playing.

When we're ready to stop, she takes my arm and walks me farther from the building. I know what she's going to say before she says it.

"I know how to do it," she says, her voice quiet. "Luca's ready to help. We're going to, Scarlett. We're going to boot the technology up and finish reprogramming Tamsyn so she comes back. Then we'll shut it all down again. I'm not going to tell the others until it's done, but I can't not do it. We're going to get her back! She's your mum too. Are you in?"

I look at the garden, the house, the snowflakes drifting through the air. I look at Sophie, my other self, the other part of me. She's waiting for my answer.

Honey's my mum, but Tamsyn is too. Tamsyn is everything that's left of Honey. I know that once technology is invented it's going to get used. This might be a one-off fix so we get a mother back. It might be the moment everything takes a different direction. I don't know, but I want to find out.

"Of course I am," I say. "I'm with you. Always."

ACKNOWLEDGMENTS

This book was a joy to write, and a large part of that was because of the input of an editorial team who understood it from the moment I described it in a sentence. I feel incredibly lucky to be working with such a brilliant team. Thank you so much to my wonderful editor Jen Monroe and to Candice Coote at Berkley, and to my superagents, Hillary Jacobson and Steph Thwaites.

Thanks to my family and friends for support and distraction at every turn, to Silvia Salib and Bess Fox for Friday-evening friendship, to Gabe, Seb, Lottie, Charlie and Alfie for always being there. To my brother, Adam Barr: you read an early draft and your enthusiasm carried me through many an edit! Craig Barr-Green read every word of every draft: thank you for your unwavering support every single day.

THE NEW ONE

······················

EVIE GREEN

READERS GUIDE

QUESTIONS FOR DISCUSSION

1. When does a human become a machine? As Aurelie says, we start augmenting ourselves as soon as we do something such as wear glasses. At what point does augmentation make one a different sort of being?

2. To what extent do you think Scarlett and Sophie are the same person?

3. Technology has developed dizzyingly fast in the past half century. I can remember when computers were huge, slow things with flashing green cursors, and now almost everyone reading this book has a powerful one in their pocket, holding large parts of their life. Should technological progress continue, no matter the human consequences? At what point should we take action to tackle anxiety, radicalization, screen addiction, social alienation and related issues?

4. What do you think would have happened to the family if they had stayed in Cornwall?

5. To what extent do you think it's acceptable to modify who someone is in order to keep them alive if they haven't given their consent?

6. Did you empathize more with Scarlett or Sophie?

7. Tamsyn and Ed's reconciliation is more complex than it initially appears. Did you see that twist coming?

8. How much do you empathize with Ed's and Tamsyn's decision-making in Cornwall? What would you have done?

9. If you were to discover that someone in your life was actually a New One, who do you think it would be?

10. What do you think happens after the book's ending?

BEHIND THE BOOK

THE NEW ONE IS SET IN THE NEAR FUTURE AND BEGINS IN Cornwall, a place that is close to my heart, as it's been my home for the past fifteen years. While there have long been tensions between inhabitants and second-home owners, the situation is now extreme and damaging. Cornwall suffers because it's beautiful; it's situated in the far southwest of England, with the Atlantic Ocean on three sides, wild cliffs and sandy (as well as stony) beaches. It's an ancient place that is cursed by its beauty.

There is a village in North Cornwall that is so desirable that more than seventy percent of its houses are now used as second homes. Schools, doctors' offices, public transit services—all of that withers and dies when these homes are bought up and left empty during rainy Novembers and Februarys. Walking around these villages in the winter is a bleak experience, as the ghosts of the old communities swirl around you. A three-bedroom flat by the harbor in the old fishing port of Mousehole costs more than three-quarters of a million pounds, putting it so far out of reach of anyone working as part of the low-paid local economy that it might as well be on Mars.

It's been strange watching this happening on the ground, and indeed to be caught up in it myself—I'm still renting my home, because every time I've been ready to buy a house, prices rise again. If my landlord were to raise the rent to keep pace with the market, my family would have to leave Cornwall. There is a homeless population, as is shown in the book, and many people with deep roots in the area, like the Trelawneys, are leaving because they have no real option to stay (although the reasons for leaving tend not to be for reasons quite as dramatic).

The movie *Bait*, made by Mark Jenkin in 2019, encapsulates these tensions brilliantly, and I highly recommend it.

When I was twenty I spent some time in Geneva, first as an au pair nearby and then flat sitting in the city, and it's remained one of my favorite places. I remember being dazzled by my first view of the lake, the mountains, the beautiful buildings. I was amazed by how clean everything was, and fascinated by learning about some of the more surprising laws (for example, you can't use a washing machine after ten p.m. or cut grass on Sunday, and all houses must have access to a nuclear shelter). I went to French lessons twice a week and met other people who were there temporarily, and shared experiences with them and went for coffee in the sunshine after class. It was a very happy time for me, and so it was for this reason, combined with the fact that *Frankenstein* is rooted there, that I made it the setting for the Trelawneys' dazzling new life.

Although *The New One* is a novel that's intended to be entertaining, it made me think a lot about technology. I know I wouldn't have hesitated to take up the offer of the "medical trial" to save my child. Grief and love make people vulnerable in all sorts of ways, and Sophie is the product of this, mixed with corporate greed, technological progress, exploitation, corruption and the misuse of ever-growing power. Although there are strict laws about human cloning that mean such events are unlikely to happen, I was interested in following a thread of *what if* . . . particularly after my son called me cheerfully, as I was writing the novel, to tell me that he'd been in a car that had crashed on a rainy country road—"but we're all fine." I'd had no idea he was even in a car at all. Letting go of the control you have over your child's life is a part of parenting that isn't talked about much, but it's terrifying.

The New One is a family story at its heart, with a marriage in trouble, sibling rivalry, work issues, money problems . . . the kind of things we all deal with all the time, but exaggerated into a scenario that is thankfully and (I hope) enjoyably implausible.

READING LIST

Although everything in *The New One* is fictional, including the science, I read some fascinating books for background over the course of writing it, and heartily recommend the following:

NONFICTION

Peter 2.0: The Human Cyborg by Peter Scott-Morgan
An incredible autobiography by a man who used his scientific background to respond to a devastating diagnosis by turning himself into a cyborg. This is utterly inspiring.

You Look Like a Thing and I Love You: How Artificial Intelligence Works and Why It's Making the World a Weirder Place by Janelle Shane
An entertaining look at some of the more absurd sides of artificial intelligence.

To Be a Machine by Mark O'Connell
This absorbing journey around the transhumanism movement brings up constant jaw-dropping moments.

The Feeling of What Happens: Body and Emotion in the Making of Consciousness by Antonio Damasio

A thought-provoking examination of what consciousness actually is and what it is to be *you*.

Life 3.0: Being Human in the Age of Artificial Intelligence by Max Tegmark

This is a fascinating look at what the future coexistence of humans and AI might look like.

FICTION

Frankenstein by Mary Shelley

Famously written over the course of a few days in Geneva, Mary Shelley's book is of course the iconic text about humans using technology to create life.

Klara and the Sun by Kazuo Ishiguro

Klara is an "artificial friend" who is a companion for teenage human Josie. A wonderful and heartbreaking read.

EVIE GREEN is a pseudonym for a British author who has written professionally for her entire adult life. She lives by the sea in England with her husband, children and guinea pigs, and loves writing in the very early morning, fueled by coffee.